Liz Byrski was born and brought up in England and has lived in Western Australia since 1981. She is the author of a number of non-fiction books and has worked as a freelance journalist, a broadcaster with ABC Radio and an adviser to a minister in the WA Government.

In her late fifties, in despair at the absence of realistic and interesting representations of older women in popular culture, she began writing novels that feature older characters.

She is the author of *Gang of Four; Food, Sex and Money; Belly Dancing for Beginners* and *Trip of a Lifetime,* and lectures in professional writing at Curtin University of Technology.

www.lizbyrski.com.au

GW00634710

Also by Liz Byrski

Liz Byrski
BAD BEHAVIOUR

PAN

Pan Macmillan Australia

First published 2009 in Macmillan by Pan Macmillan Australia Pty Limited
1 Market Street, Sydney
This Pan edition published in 2010 by Pan Macmillan Australia Pty Limited

National Library of Australia
Cataloguing-in-Publication data:

Byrski, Liz.
Bad Behaviour / Liz Byrski

9780330425865 (pbk.)

A823.4

The characters in this book are fictitious and any resemblance to real persons,
living or dead, is purely coincidental.

Typeset by Post Pre-press Group
Printed by McPherson's Printing Group

Papers used by Pan Macmillan Australia Pty Ltd are natural, recyclable
products made from wood grown in sustainable forests. The manufacturing
processes conform to the environmental regulations of the country of origin.

For Graham

1999

ONE

Fremantle, Western Australia – September 1999

For Zoë the birthday tea is a sort of torture; it's particularly awful this year because there are so few of them. She picks up the knife and offers it, handle first, to Eileen.

'Would you like to cut it, Mum? It's your birthday cake, after all.'

Eileen peers at the cake and sniffs. 'Fruitcake again, I suppose?'

Zoë musters a tight, artificial smile; fruitcake is the only cake her mother will eat but whenever she makes her one, it is greeted with disdain and the trademark sniff. Jane, sitting alongside Eileen on the settee, smiles at Zoë and rolls her eyes.

'Mum makes the best cakes of anyone,' Gaby says, reaching for matches to light the candles. 'No! Don't cut it yet, Gran, we haven't sung "Happy Birthday".'

Shame is at the heart of it, Zoë knows that, her mother's shame and her own; it's been this way for decades, long before she was old enough to name it. There is disappointment too and resentment. This birthday business is easier when everyone is at home, but this weekend Archie is away on a fishing trip, Rosie is helping out at her university open day and Dan . . . well, who knows where Dan is, not that Eileen is the least bit concerned with his whereabouts. As the elder granddaughter, though, Rosie's absence has already been commented on with disapproval. Archie gets away with it because Eileen thinks the sun shines out of his bum.

3

So here they are: Eileen; her friend Betty from the retirement village; Zoë's cousin Jane; herself; and Gaby, who is struggling with a final, recalcitrant candle.

'Oh look, Aunty Eileen,' Jane says, 'isn't that lovely! God, you're good, Zoë, it's about a hundred years since I made a cake.'

'Right,' Gaby says, shaking out the match. 'Ready? One, two three *Happy Birthday to you . . .*'

Zoë, Jane and Betty join in.

'Very nice I'm sure,' Eileen says. 'A pity Archie isn't here, I like a good baritone.'

'Me too,' Betty agrees, 'but I think we did rather well without the men. Are you going to blow out the candles now, Eileen?'

Eileen makes a big production of inhaling and then deflates. The candle flames flicker. 'Only seven,' she says, looking across at Zoë. 'Why are there only seven?'

'One for each decade, Mum.'

'But seventy-seven is closer to eighty, so there should be eight candles.'

Zoë, who knows that eight candles would also have been wrong, opens her mouth and shuts it again.

'Well, you couldn't have eight, dear, could you?' Betty says. 'I mean, you might not make it to eighty.'

There is a small, icy silence.

Betty flushes. '*None* of us might make it. I'm younger than you, Eileen, and *I* might not make it. None of us might be here tomorrow, for all we know.'

Jane stares at Zoë, her mouth twitching in an attempt to suppress a laugh. 'That's a cheery thought on your birthday, Aunty Eileen; better have some cake quick before we all cark it.'

Gaby snorts with noisy laughter and rolls back on the lounge.

Eileen looks around in disapproval, before once again drawing breath and blowing out the seven candles with a single puff.

'Splendid!' Betty cries, clapping her hands. 'Well done.'

'There you go then, Gran,' Gaby says, pushing the knife towards Eileen.

It will all be over soon, Zoë tells herself. In another hour or so, Jane, who has nobly collected Eileen and Betty from the retirement village, will pack them back into her car and spirit them away, and she and Gaby will have the place to themselves. Until then, she just has to keep smiling.

By six o'clock they are gone and the house is unusually quiet; peaceful, Zoë thinks, or perhaps just lifeless. No music drifting from Rosie's room, no one banging around in the shed or the garage, no drone of sports commentary or early news. Thank god Archie will be back tomorrow; she hates it when he's away. Dan, though, could be anywhere by now, it's all hush-hush as usual. Sometimes – often – Zoë really hates the army and the SAS in particular. And when he's away in some secret location, when she has no idea when he'll be back, or whether he's lying wounded in a desert or jungle, or crushed beneath a bombed building, she feels rage that she has to live with this burden of anxiety time and time again.

Outside, the light is fading and there's a wintry chill in the air; wrapping her arms around herself, Zoë wanders out to the garden. The lantana, which defies all her efforts to contain it, needs cutting back again and there is something both irritating and admirable about its persistence. But the star jasmine, which is supposed to be climbing up the lattice along the side of the deck, seems to be struggling.

'What *is* up with you?' Zoë asks it. 'The woman in the nursery told me you would smother this lattice with lovely little white flowers.' She strokes a leaf, and crouches to feel the texture of the earth around the stem. 'Just get a move on, will you?'

Suddenly, it comes upon her again like a freak storm. Not just a hot flush but a fierce, overwhelming heat that foreshadows panic. Last time this happened she was in the supermarket, and she'd abandoned her trolley, walked blindly back to the car and sat there until she felt able to drive home. No one warns you about this, she thinks; they tell you about the hot flushes, mood swings, sleepless nights, but no one mentions panic attacks or their aftermath of despair. The panic grips her like a steel band closing around her chest, and she reminds herself it's just the hormones. The mind, though, is resistant, it nags. Sooner rather than later, they'll all be gone; Dan, Rosie, even Gaby, and then what? Archie always says that'll mean more time for themselves and each other, 'to do our own thing'. But that's what bothers Zoë. Her thing is the kids, Archie, being a family, knowing that she keeps it all afloat, even if sometimes it seems as though they don't actually see her. Some nights she dreams she's looking down on herself from a high place and she is shrinking, becoming paler, weaker, fading into the landscape. She wakes from those dreams bathed in sweat, gets up quietly so as not to wake Archie, makes chamomile tea, and sits alone in the darkness watching old black-and-white movies or women with glowing skin, impossibly perfect teeth and Californian accents promoting beauty products or exercise equipment. No one, Zoë thinks, tells you what menopause is really like. No one mentions the scale of the effort required to mask the physical challenges and roller-coaster emotions with normality.

Back inside the house she finds Gaby stretched out on the lounge, wielding the remote control.

'What's that you're watching?' Zoë asks, putting on her glasses to read the TV guide.

Gaby waves the DVD cover at her. 'A documentary – *The Decade That Changed the World*.'

'A documentary?'

'For school. We're doing the sixties. Each team has to take one year and do a presentation. I'm the team leader for our year.'

'Which is?'

'Nineteen sixty-eight. It's awesome – the year all the important things happened. The year that most changed the world.'

Zoë looks vague. 'Did it?'

Gaby looks at her in amazement. 'You should know, you were there. You must know heaps about it.'

'Not really,' Zoë says as the screen flickers with an opening montage of black-and-white images: anti-Vietnam banners; cars burning on the streets of Paris; a Viet Cong holding a gun to the head of a manacled prisoner; then a tall, pale-faced man addressing a crowd. 'Who's that?'

6

'Alexander Dubček, Prague Spring.' Gaby rolls her eyes.

'Of course, and there's Martin Luther King,' Zoë says. 'And that's a demonstration in Trafalgar Square and there's Vanessa Redgrave, I never knew she was there.'

Gaby hits the pause button. 'Don't you remember *any* of it?'

Zoë shrugs, 'Bits, I suppose.'

'How can you *not*?'

'In those days I didn't read the papers or listen to the news.'

'But you worked at the BBC.'

'Answering letters for a radio soap opera.' Zoë knows she sounds defensive.

Gaby shakes her head in disappointment. 'But you were living in *London*.'

'Look, I was nineteen, and Jane and I were living in a damp old house in Kilburn having a good time. We were more interested in pop music, clothes and boyfriends. I was only a couple of years older than you are now and I don't notice you taking much interest in current affairs.'

'There's nothing much happening that's interesting now. Not like then.'

'You don't always notice history happening around you.'

'Yeah, okay, but *this much* history? Didn't you march or protest, or *anything*?'

'I did go on a march once – a huge anti-Vietnam rally – but I wasn't thinking about the cause. I was in love and trying to make an impression.'

'That is *so* pathetic.'

'Maybe, but at the time falling in love seemed like the most important thing in the world. Well, that and all the sex, of course.'

Gaby's head shoots up. 'Sex?'

Zoë nods. 'Everybody seemed to be doing it, except me at first, and so getting a boyfriend, finding someone to do it with . . .'

Gaby holds up her hands. 'Too much information.' She presses play and the screen comes back to life.

Zoë curls back into her chair, gazing at the images, thinking how full of hope she'd been then; how, once she got to London, anything had seemed possible; how she had been both desperate for experience and terrified of acquiring it. Everything she knew about sex she had learned from whispered conversations in the school cloakroom, and it didn't correspond with Eileen's tight-lipped warnings that sex was nasty and dangerous. In Kilburn, sex was part of everyday life. There were no rules about not staying out late or bringing boys home, and virginity was a quaint and embarrassing encumbrance that everyone else had disposed of. The beds were unmade and frequently shared; linen was rarely washed; milk turned to sour, lumpy clouds in the ancient fridge; and cleaning was rare. The freedom from Eileen's close and critical surveillance was intoxicating. And then, of course, there was Richard.

'It *was* pretty amazing,' she says softly, too softly for Gaby to hear. And she closes her eyes, recalling the wet and windy afternoon on Beachy Head when she lost her virginity in the backseat of Richard's car; one arm dead from pins and needles, and the window winder digging into her back. 'It all seems so long ago,' she says, aloud this time. 'I was only nineteen, it seems like another world.'

'Duhhh!' Gaby says, rolling her eyes. 'It *was* another world. The past is a foreign country, they do things differently there.'

'That's it, exactly. I've heard that before.'

'It's in that book *The Go-Between*, the one about the boy who carried the messages.'

Zoë shakes her head. 'Haven't read it.'

'No,' Gaby says accusingly, 'you haven't. You were supposed to read it for book club and you didn't but Rosie and I did, and you got Rosie to make notes for you to take to the meeting.'

'Did I?'

'Yes, and she wrote you a whole lot to say about that "past is a foreign country" thing and then, when she'd done it, you decided not to go and she was really pissed off with you.'

'Ah yes, I do remember that. She *was* pretty upset. I wish I'd read it now. "The past is a foreign country", it's so true. The people are like foreigners when you look back. You even feel like a foreigner to yourself. I mean, I hardly knew who I was in those days. Mind you,' she adds with a laugh, 'I'm often not sure who I am *these* days.'

Gaby sighs and rolls her eyes again. 'Well, I'm always going to know exactly who I am however old I get.'

'I hope so, darling,' Zoë says, almost managing to suppress her amusement. 'For your sake, I really do.'

TWO

Rye, Sussex – September 1999

Julia has been making the last of the plums into jam, and thinking about memory and nostalgia. It is, she suspects, something that her generation, the baby boomers, are obsessed with or, at least, intrigued by tracing childhood friends and first loves, writing memoirs about miserable childhoods, buying reissued sixties pop classics, reclaiming cheesecloth and caftans, unpicking the past and wondering how they could have done it better. She finds herself doing it all the time. When she and Tom are with friends, they always seem to talk about the past – the music, the films, the politics – and it's always the sixties they talk about. Although, as Tom admits, he's too old to be a baby boomer, or even a war baby, he just feels like one.

'What do you think?' Julia asks, putting a cup of tea down beside Hilary. 'Does everybody start looking back as they get older?'

Hilary, dozing in her wheelchair by the lounge window, blinks and straightens her shoulders. 'Well, I'm old enough to be your mother, and I can't say I have much enthusiasm for unpicking *my* past.'

Julia would have liked a robust conversation about different generations, the sort of conversation they have had over more than thirty years of friendship, but for which Hilary no longer has the energy.

'My mother,' Hilary continues, 'would have said that going back over the past was pure self-indulgence. She'd have said that about therapy too.'

'So would mine.'

'She'd have recommended a dose of Epsom salts.'

'Mine would have gone for a large gin.'

'She did like a drink, didn't she?'

'Didn't she just,' Julia says with a dry laugh. 'Used to start about eleven in the morning. We had a walk-in pantry and she always had a bottle of gin hidden behind the bottled fruit; she'd be in and out of there all day topping up. I don't think Dad ever really knew the extent of it, but he was a big drinker himself.'

'Surely he must have known.'

Julia shrugs. 'Maybe, but she rarely seemed drunk. She used to get rather red in the face and glassy-eyed, though, and I do remember hearing some shouting matches between the two of them. Although we were never supposed to know about that.'

Hilary reaches out a trembling hand for the cup, and Julia resists the urge to dart across and hold it for her. She knows that Hilary hates fuss; having to have so much done for her causes her as much distress as does the cancer itself. But she is the least demanding of patients and Julia is determined to postpone the move to the hospice for as long as possible. In the seventies, when she had made up her mind to leave Paris, she and Hilary had moved back here to England, to this house, together. They had started the business from here, Hilary giving French lessons, Julia teaching English to overseas students, until they decided to make it into a proper language school with its own premises. So, it matters to her that Hilary is cared for here and that it is she who does the caring.

Julia thinks now that perhaps watching someone you love dying slowly is what focuses the mind on the past.

'Do you remember when we met?' she asks suddenly.

Hilary frowns. 'Not really,' she says after a moment's thought. 'Not the very first time. I know it was at one of those Sunday afternoon tea parties Eric and I ran. I loved those Sundays, you students and *au pairs*, all desperate to make English friends and speak English, just the opposite of what you were supposed to be doing in Paris.'

Julia nods. 'The relief of not having to struggle with the language for a whole afternoon. I was so miserable *au pairing* but Mum and Dad said I had to stay and learn French. Mum said I should go to the British Embassy church and find myself some friends. So I turned up one Sunday morning and as I was leaving, this hand descended on my shoulder and it was yours.'

'Sounds like a citizen's arrest,' Hilary laughs.

'You gave me a card and said you had these Sunday afternoons for young people alone in Paris, and maybe I'd like to come along. Honestly, Hil, at the time I thought it sounded deadly dull.'

Hilary nods. 'I never found a way to make a tea party run by the vicar's wife sound very attractive, but I did take comfort from the fact that most people who risked it once kept coming back.'

'It was wonderful,' Julia says, leaning forward. 'I so nearly threw that card away, but I was desperate to get out of the house on my day off, and it seemed better than nothing. And then, walking into your place was like being back in Tunbridge Wells.'

'Mmm. Well, that doesn't sound too exciting, but it was the familiarity, I suppose, that was what you all needed.'

'Too right. Those Sunday afternoons were little oases in the miserable desert of my week. And, of course, I met Tom there, and Simon.'

'I do remember *that*,' Hilary says. 'You lot were like bees round the honey pot. Understandable, I suppose; Simon *was* very good looking, and everyone knew the family had pots of money.'

'Well, Simon virtually ignored me that day and that's when I spotted Tom. I was taking round one of your huge plates of sandwiches and he was looking for something in Eric's big bookcase. He looked sort of different and interesting.'

She can see him standing there as if it were yesterday, dropping the book he was holding as she thrust the sandwich plate in front of him.

'Sorry,' Tom had said. 'I was in another world. Music and books; the vicar has a number of full scores. Thanks, I'd love a sandwich.'

His northern accent was a stark contrast to this roomful of cut-glass Oxford accents and was rather endearing.

'You're in the choir, aren't you?' Julia asked. 'You sang the Twenty-third Psalm solo the other week.'

He nodded, his mouth full of sandwich.

'You were awfully good. Are you a musician or something like that?'

'Nothing at all like that, I'm afraid,' he said. 'My name's Tom Hammond, I work for Barclays Bank.' The bank, he'd told her, was opening new branches in Europe and he was a specialist in aspects of international banking regulations. Julia wondered how old he was – older than her, of course; older, in fact, than most of the others in the room. 'I've known Eric and Hilary for years,' he said, as though he knew what she was thinking. 'As a teenager, I was in the choir when Eric was rector near where I lived in Liverpool, so it was terrific to meet up with them again. But what about you, what are you doing here in Paris?'

Julia had explained about being an *au pair* to the Le Bons' ghastly children, and the fading grandeur of the family's apartment in the Rue de Fleurus near the Luxembourg Gardens. Later she and Tom had walked together back to the Left Bank; a walk that Julia, all these years later, still remembers as the start of everything that has mattered to her.

'I met the three most significant people in my life at your tea party,' she says now. 'I wonder how many other people found their spouses and lifelong best friends there.'

'I wonder,' Hilary says wearily, reaching for her cardigan before it slips from the arm of her wheelchair. 'Is Tom picking Richard up from the airport?'

'Yes,' Julia says, getting up. 'They'll be back soon. I've made soup for lunch and I'm going over to the bakery to get some baguettes.'

'That'll be nice,' Hilary says, closing her eyes and disappearing swiftly and silently into one of the troughs of exhaustion that overwhelm her quite suddenly.

Julia slips out through the back door, and strolls through the churchyard and across the square to the bakery, where the tantalising smell of fresh bread wafts out onto the street. She's looking forward to seeing Richard. Their mother died years earlier, their father is locked in his own private world of Alzheimer's, and her best friend is dying. Richard and Tom are all that are left from the old days. Losing those few people who knew you well in youth is not just painful, it's strangely disturbing; as though your youthful self might cease to exist with the death of its last remaining witness.

Back in the kitchen the jam has cooled, and Julia seals the jars with cellophane discs and screws the caps into place. She is on the kitchen steps putting the jars on the top shelf of the pantry when she hears the car pull in.

'An apron?' Richard gasps in mock horror from the open doorway. 'And is that homemade jam? Amazing.' He turns to Tom, who is following him in through the door, 'Is she getting domesticated in her old age?'

'She is always the angel in the house,' Tom says with a wry grin.

'Shut up, you tossers,' Julia says affectionately, coming down the steps. 'How was the flight?'

'Tedious as ever but, thankfully, on time,' Richard says, dumping his bag on the floor. 'How are you, Jules?'

'Okay. Sad, tired, but okay.'

He hugs her. 'I'm so sorry about Hilary. Tom says she's going downhill fast.'

Julia nods. 'She's in the lounge, asleep at the moment. But she's looking forward to seeing you. How about you? You look a bit seedy.'

'Just tired,' Richard says, taking off his jacket. 'I've been all over the place in the last few weeks and the older I get, the more I dislike the travel and feel . . .'

'That you want to give it all up and settle down with a good woman,' Tom cuts in with a laugh, drawing the cork from a bottle of wine.

'I wish. But I have to say, it doesn't seem to be in my stars. You

14

know how it is, I make a dazzling first impression and within a few weeks I've managed to totally piss them off. *Plus ça change!*'

'Many men would think you have an enviable life,' Tom says. 'After all, look at me, in thrall to a compulsive jam maker.'

'Don't start,' Julia says, looking at Richard. 'You've only just got here and you two are ganging up on me already.'

'Only because we love you, darling,' Tom says, pouring the wine. 'Now, what about a nice glass of red before lunch? That bread smells bloody marvellous; do you think two baguettes are enough? I could probably eat a whole one myself. I might go and get some more.' He pours the wine and raises his glass. 'Cheers. I've been sorting through some stuff in my study, Rich, and I've made contact with a bloke in Prague who's sending me some more material.'

'More!' Julia groans. 'It's already like a library archive in there. Hasn't there been enough written about nineteen sixty-eight?'

'Not the way we're going to do it,' Richard says. 'And this will be different because it'll be specially written for the fortieth anniversary.'

'I'm not sure I'll survive another nine years of you two farting about with yellowing posters and newspapers, and all the rest of those crappy old boxes of stuff you've been hoarding,' Julia says.

'You're referring to my extensive collection of memorabilia,' says Tom, gasping in mock horror.

'I thought I might try to get a US cable channel interested in a film to go with it,' Richard says, 'it would make sense.'

'Bloody good idea,' says Tom. 'I'll need to start collecting film clips for that, probably have to start storing them in the spare bedroom.'

They clink their glasses, grinning at Julia like naughty school-boys. Tom has been toying with this idea for ages but Julia knows it's more likely to happen now that Richard is involved. Tom's tendency to procrastinate is legendary, whereas Richard gets things done, and he can also write accessibly. Tom still tends to write like a banker: passive voice; lengthy, convoluted sentences; long words that lurk on the margins of most people's vocabulary. His study is piled high with reference books, tatty newspapers and box files. Despite Julia's apparent cynicism about them, those torn posters and handbills he collected in Paris pluck the strings of memory for her.

'I'd like to go and see Dad while I'm here,' Richard says now, breaking her train of thought. 'Maybe tomorrow morning?'

'Good idea. He's more alert in the mornings than he is later in the day.'

They talk for a while before Tom, who has slipped across the square for more bread, reappears in the kitchen. The top quarter of one loaf has been torn off.

'You have no sense of restraint,' Julia says, taking it from him. 'I got mine home all in one piece.'

'That, Julia, is because you are a model of rectitude,' Tom says. 'I, on the other hand, am a terrible old reprobate who needs to seize the day.'

'And I am the one who needs to seize a second glass of wine,' says Richard, reaching for the bottle and refilling his glass. 'And then I'll go and have a chat with Hilary before we eat.'

THREE

Tunbridge Wells, Kent – September 1999

T here is something about the south of England that grips Richard's heart every time he comes back here, and on this beautiful Sunday morning, as he and Julia drive from Sussex into Kent, he feels the pull of home more strongly than ever. In the seventies, when he returned to London after several years as a war correspondent in Vietnam, he was anxious to move on, to find the action elsewhere. He found it in Washington, and later in New York. But he's always known that this part of England is home, not that he actually has a home here now. His parents sold Bramble Cottage, where he and Julia grew up, when they retired to Spain in the early seventies, and made their London flat over jointly to himself and Julia. Richard had lived in it with a friend, and stayed on there when he got married and until he went to Vietnam. These days, Julia manages the flat's letting and they share the rent.

'Everything okay at Craven Terrace?' he asks now, as they approach Tunbridge Wells. 'How are the tenants?'

'Fine. Such nice people, they've just signed up for another six months,' Julia says. 'But, unfortunately, they're going back to Canada next April. Anyway, I'll worry about that when the time comes.'

'You might not have to,' Richard says, turning in his seat to look at her as she drives. 'I was wondering about moving back there myself.'

'Really?' She swings the car into a parking bay. 'Let's go and have a coffee and you can tell me about it. I always need caffeine before I go to the nursing home.'

Crossing the worn paving stones and covered walks of the Pantiles, they find a café so close to the spa they can hear the trickling water.

'Remember when Mum used to bring us here for afternoon tea?' Richard asks, after they've ordered coffee. 'It used to be such a treat, and you were a whiney little pest.'

'Charming! And you were the perfect child, I suppose?'

'Naturally! I was older and needed to dissociate myself from this little monster who kept demanding éclairs, and getting chocolate in the most ridiculous places.'

Julia smiles. 'It seems so long ago,' she says. 'And it all looks a bit faded and dreary now, doesn't it?'

'Not to me. And it *was* a long time ago, almost half a century. I'm getting nostalgic goosebumps.' He sits back savouring the silence. There is something wonderfully reassuring about being in childhood places, he thinks; something that reminds you what really matters.

'So, what's this about coming back?' Julia asks as their coffee arrives.

'I think I may have done my dash in the States; I love New York but I sort of feel it's time to come back to London.'

'Would they transfer you back here?'

'Probably, and I'm considering reducing my work with the BBC anyway. Martin and I have a couple of film projects we'd like to do together. We're thinking of expanding the production company, so having one of us here and the other in the States would be ideal. I haven't made up my mind yet; I just wanted to mention it, see how you'd feel if I wanted to live in the flat. I'd pay you your share of the rent, of course, or buy you out, if you prefer.'

Julia shrugs. 'Sure,' she says, 'whatever you want. But I *have* just signed them up for six months.'

'That's fine; if I decide to do it, the timing would be perfect. And you don't think Tom would mind?'

'Tom would feel it was between you and me. But no, he

wouldn't mind in the least. In fact, he'd be over the moon to have you back here, and so would I.'

'Thanks,' he smiles and tastes his coffee. 'This is cold,' he says, pulling a face.

'But it *is* caffeine and it's better than they'll give us at the nursing home.'

'There is one thing that *might* make me stay in the US.'

'Carly?' Julia says, 'Of course, you wouldn't get to see much of her, I suppose.'

'I don't see much of her now. She's still in California, working on the *Oakland Tribune*, taken to journalism like a duck to water.'

'Or like father like daughter.'

He shrugs. 'Not too much like me, I hope. No, I was talking about Lily.'

'Lily? Why would she stop you?'

Richard looks away, awkward suddenly. 'I've been wondering . . . well . . . whether we might be able to get back together. Probably just wishful thinking on my part but Carly's moved out of home, Lily's on her own . . .'

'But Lily gave you your marching orders in no uncertain terms. Has she said anything to –'

'No,' he cuts in, 'nothing at all, we're friends still, always have been, but I was hoping . . . after all, we *are* still married.'

'And you've been separated for nearly *twelve* years.' Julia leans across and puts her hand on his arm. 'It'd be great if you two got back together, but do you really think it's a possibility?'

He shrugs. 'I haven't seen her for a few months but when we do meet we always get on well. And we're both pushing sixty now, it seems such a waste to be apart.' He leans forward, playing with his teaspoon. 'Look, I know I have a disastrous record with women and particularly with Lily, but surely there has to be one time in my life when I get it right. Maybe this is the time.'

'Well, if it's what you want.' She takes another sip of coffee and grimaces. 'You're right, I don't think I can drink any more of this. Maybe we should just get moving, get it over with.'

'Sounds good,' Richard says and slips money under the bill.

'You do know it's most unlikely that Dad will recognise you?'

Julia says as they walk back arm-in-arm across the Pantiles. 'He hasn't known Tom or me for months now.'

'I know,' he says. 'I'm prepared for that.' And as he says it, he really believes it. He has thought about it quite a lot, talked with friends who have been through it. But it's only at the nursing home, when his father turns dead eyes on him and looks away without any flicker of recognition, that Richard realises how totally unprepared he is.

'Why don't you wheel him around the garden?' Julia suggests, 'He likes that. I'll wait here.' And she finds herself a seat in the visitors' lounge and picks up a magazine.

Richard pushes the wheelchair along the paved path that encircles the lawn. Around him, others are pushing their own aged relatives in what looks almost like a ritual circuit; being on the move dilutes the intensity of sitting face to face with someone to whom you have become a stranger.

'Shall we stop here for a bit, Dad?' he asks, realising he's going to supply the answer himself. 'Yes, here, I think. I'll park your chair so you can see across the garden, and I'll sit on this seat.'

Ralph stares silently ahead. The irony of this is not lost on Richard, who remembers the untold number of times he has longed for his father to shut up and keep his objectionable views to himself. Now the silence is equally excruciating. How much does the old man know? Could he actually be playing some sort of game? He's a canny old bugger, and bloody minded as hell. The times when Ralph's blunt, ill-timed and loudly expressed opinions made him want the earth to open up and swallow him run through Richard's mind like an old movie, the worst being the weekend when he had taken Zoë to Bramble Cottage to introduce her to his parents. What a disaster that had been. His mother's patronising remarks about Zoë's family, the barbed quips about her strange accent, and finally the row over Sunday lunch. Richard shakes his head at the memory. He's never forgiven himself for not warning Zoë, not preparing her for the ordeal.

Looking now at his father, hunched and silent in his wheelchair, Richard wonders whether non-recognition means that he has been totally wiped from his father's memory. Are there bits of him still hidden in there somewhere; as a little boy perhaps, or as captain of the school's first eleven? Does Ralph remember anything or everything? Richard can't quite get rid of the feeling that his father is doing this to spite him.

'Do you remember me at all, Dad?' he asks now.

Ralph turns his head at the sound of his voice but says nothing.

'Do you remember me graduating? Did it mean anything to you? Do you remember threatening to thrash me when I got back from Aldermarston?'

Silence.

'Do you remember Zoë, from Australia, how you made her cry?'

Silence again. On the arm of the wheelchair Ralph's hand twitches slightly.

Richard sighs and gets to his feet, and takes the brake off the wheelchair. 'Okay then,' he says. 'Better get you back inside, it's nearly time for your lunch.'

FOUR

The nursery is unusually busy for a Friday; the beautiful spring weather and the prospect of the Queen's Birthday long weekend have brought the gardeners out in force. Justine loves it when it's like this, full of people looking for suggestions on how to fill a sunny corner or mask an ugly section of a fence. She's thankful she has good staff: a couple of old-timers who know the place inside out; a new woman in her forties who's just gone through a divorce and is throwing all her energy into the job; a new young guy who seems to be shaping up well; and lovely Kevin, from the Down Syndrome Foundation, who has been here for the last three years. Justine looks around with satisfaction; it'll be even busier tomorrow.

'You look pretty, Jus,' Kevin says. He is wheeling a barrow filled with sacks of potting compost through from the storage area to the forecourt. 'You should get a boyfriend.'

'Really, Kev? You think I need one?'

'I've got a girlfriend,' he says, putting the barrow down. 'Her name is Moira, she's come to live in the shared house. She's pretty too, but she's younger than you.'

'Well, I should hope so,' Justine says, laughing. 'You wouldn't want a girlfriend as old as me, would you?'

Kevin shakes his head. 'No way! But I do like you.'

'I like you too, Kev. And I'll tell you a secret. I *have* got a boyfriend.'

'That's good. What's his name?'

Justine puts her finger to her lips. 'That's a secret too. You have to keep it for me.'

'I will,' Kevin says, picking up the barrow handles again. 'I promise I will. I'm very good at secrets.' And he trundles the barrow away towards the entrance.

Justine smiles; sometimes she is bursting to talk about it but she also enjoys keeping her secret. Falling in love has amazed her; it wakes her every morning with a sense of life's extraordinary possibilities. It makes it hard to concentrate on work, but Justine knows that this happiness is translating into goodwill towards her customers, something that is often severely tested. Some, of course, are always pleasant and, just as she thinks that, one of her regulars, a slight, dark-haired woman, strolls towards her pushing a trolley loaded with two large purple glazed pots, a couple of Spanish lavenders and some sacks of potting compost. She smiles at Justine.

'It's really busy here today.'

'Very,' Justine says. 'Wasn't it you I talked to last time about the star jasmine? How's it going?'

'It's resisting all my efforts to make it grow,' the woman says. 'I'm hoping the warmer weather will encourage it. I want it to cover some lattice near the end of the verandah.'

'More sun will definitely help. Are you sure you're not over-watering?'

'I don't think so.'

Justine takes a small container from the shelf. 'Try some of this. But don't overdo it.'

The woman studies the label and takes out her purse but Justine waves the money away.

'That's okay, it's a gift. See how you go and let me know if it works.'

'That's very good of you, thanks,' the woman says, smiling. 'I'll let you know next time,' and she steers her loaded trolley out to the car park.

It's on days like this that Justine can really see the difference she has made to the nursery. Years ago, when Gwen's cousin Stan ran it and she came here as a teenager to earn some pocket money at weekends, it had been dark and damp, littered with unused pots, old compost sacks and overgrown plants. There were whole sections that hadn't been disturbed for years and that, for Justine, was part of the attraction. There was something mysterious about those dense, damp clumps of plants in the shade house, the pots covered in moss, the darting insects, spider webs looping between the fern fronds; a few birds had even built their nests in there. It had the mysterious promise of the jungles she'd read about at school. But the neglect that had created this magical world had almost brought the business to a halt. When Stan died, Gwen had brought in a team to clean it up, and employed a manager who reorganised the place and turned it into a going concern again. When Justine finished high school, she'd told Gwen she wanted to study horticulture. At the time she'd worried that Gwen would be disappointed because Justine had caught up on the schooling she'd missed and could have gone on to university. But Justine knew what she wanted and after finishing the course had gone travelling, working first in New Zealand, then at a vineyard in France, in the gardens of a National Trust estate in England, and, finally, at an olive grove in Italy.

'And you still want to come back here and work in the nursery?' Gwen had asked in amazement.

'I've always wanted to, from the first day I saw it,' Justine had said.

And now she not only runs it, she actually owns it. Gwen has put it in her name. The one thing she wishes now – now that she has this wonderful place, now that she has fallen in love for the first time, when she had thought it would never happen – is that Norah could be here to share it. But she knows she has been incredibly lucky, luckier than most of those who, like her, were torn from their mothers, sent to missions or convents, or dumped with families that exploited and abused them.

The memory of the convent still has the power to make Justine's skin crawl. She'd been eight when she was taken there and almost twelve when she left, and each day she had planned to run away, always believing that she would somehow be able to find her way home. She had even collected things for her escape and hidden them in an old cigar box that she buried in the sandy soil under the water tank stand. She had found the box out by the shed where the gardener kept his tools. It was old but strong and she'd tucked it in the waistband of her skirt and, because she was wearing one of the big kitchen aprons, Sister Edwina didn't notice the rectangular bulge when she smuggled it into the dormitory. That night, Justine had packed it with her running-away things: some coins she'd found in the garden; a lace-trimmed hand-kerchief one of the lady visitors had given her; a knife from the kitchen; a candle she had taken from the chapel; a box of matches; and a postcard-sized picture of Jesus that she'd found between the pages of a book. It was Jesus as the Sacred Heart, one hand raised in a blessing, the other pointing to his big red heart that had rays of light coming from it. Justine liked the heart because it seemed to be throbbing, which was how her own felt when she thought about running away. But the best thing in the box was a shark's tooth, mounted on a simple gold base and threaded onto a strip of black leather. Everything else was replaceable, this she would guard with her life. Her mother had worn it as far back as Justine could remember.

'Your dad gave it to me,' Norah had said. 'One day he's gonna come back for it, for us; you'll see.'

But he never did come back and Justine wouldn't have known him if he had. 'Prob'ly for the best,' Norah said, 'him being white, it just means trouble.' And every day she crushed up charcoal and mixed it with goanna fat to rub on Justine's face. 'Makes you look darker, safer, more like me.'

But not safe enough, because one day a car drew up outside, and Norah grasped Justine's hand and dragged her inside, into a corner and stood in front of her. Two men and a woman stood in the doorway. Norah's bottom pressed against Justine's face as she backed her further into the corner.

'Come along now,' one of the men said, 'it's for the best.'

They grabbed hold of Norah, and she struggled to break free as the woman gripped Justine's wrist and pulled her out of the corner.

'Take this, Justine,' Norah cried, struggling against the men and, forcing her hand to her neck, she tugged at the leather thong until it broke loose. 'Keep it so's I can find you . . .' and she hurled it across the floor towards her.

Justine wrenched free and ran to pick it up, before the woman grabbed her again. As she was dragged, stumbling, down the steps, she could hear Norah's frantic cries; chilling, gut-wrenching howls like the sounds of the bush at night.

There were two smaller children huddled together on the back seat of the car, their faces streaked with tears and dirt. Justine scrambled up onto her knees and peered out the back window as the car pulled away. Norah was running behind it, barefoot, arms waving frantically, her mouth distorted by that same chilling cry. Justine watched her mother sink finally to her knees between the tyre tracks, and disappear in the clouds of red dust.

Terrible times, Justine thinks now, and there had been worse to come.

༄

Zoë carries the lavender from the car through to the back of the house, and goes back with the wheelbarrow to unload the purple pots and sacks of potting compost. She wants them either side of the glass doors to the lounge room. When she was quite small she and Eileen had lived in a tiny, decaying weatherboard cottage, where Zoë had been convinced there really were fairies at the bottom of the weed-tangled garden. Eileen complained daily about the state of the roof, the inconvenience of the outside dunny and about the rent, which she could barely afford. But at six, those complaints floated over Zoë's head. To her the garden was a magical place and she was particularly entranced by the two overgrown lavender bushes that crowded across the path on either side of the front door.

'My late wife called them "peace" and "plenty",' she'd heard the landlord tell Eileen one day when she complained about them. 'She said that was what lavender brought to the place.'

'Huh! No peace and plenty of mess,' Eileen had mumbled when he'd gone.

But from that moment, Zoë adopted Peace and Plenty, sitting most mornings on the front step, talking to them and asking their advice, remaining convinced of their power to deliver on their names, despite all evidence to the contrary.

Now, as she drags the pots into place, rips open the compost and begins the process of transplanting the lavender, she wonders why she hasn't planted lavender before. Years ago in London, a gypsy stood every Friday night outside Kilburn station selling lavender and white heather from a basket.

'It's the women's flower,' the woman had said as Zoë handed over her money. 'The plant of love and protection; some say it brings you vision, but it's what you make of it that counts.'

Zoë had bought it for her wedding bouquet, together with half a dozen white roses.

'It's very modest,' Richard's sister Julia had said as she wired the flowers together, weaving fronds of dark green ivy between them. Briefly, before Julia had been dispatched to Paris, she had worked for a florist who specialised in bridal flowers. 'I don't know why you had to insist on a small bouquet. We should have gone for something a bit more lavish.'

'Small feels right,' Zoë remembers saying. 'It's lovely, just what I wanted and your making it for me makes it special, and much nicer than something I could get in a shop.'

She crouches down now alongside the new plants, rubbing the leaves between her fingers, closing her eyes and sniffing the perfume of love, protection, peace and plenty.

'Okay,' she says. 'The peace and a bit of vision, please – Lord knows I can do with it. The plenty can wait until later.'

'Talking to the plants again?' Archie says, coming in through the side gate. 'It doesn't seem to be working with the star jasmine.'

'The woman in the nursery gave me some new plant food for it,' Zoë replies. 'Maybe that'll help.'

Archie kisses the top of her head.

'These are lovely. Great pots, I like the colour. Isn't lavender supposed to bring love and protection?'

'Apparently and, I think, peace.'

He puts his arms around her and draws her to him. 'So, which do you need, Zo?'

'All of it,' she says, kissing the hollow of his throat, which is as high as she can reach without standing on tiptoe. 'Lots of it. I hate being this age, Arch. I'm becoming a neurotic, menopausal bore but I don't know how to stop it.'

He holds her tighter, rocking her back and forth.

'I was reading this book,' she continues. 'It's all about how wonderful and mystical and symbolic menopause is, how women should embrace and celebrate this important time in their lives. I felt like screaming.'

Archie's chest rumbles with gentle laughter and he hugs her tighter. 'Oh dear,' he says. 'I think the lavender is better than the book. I don't suppose anyone ever suggested that menopause was fun. I guess it's just a matter of surviving it.'

She looks up at him. 'For both of us,' she says. 'I'm sorry to be like this.'

'There's nothing to apologise for. Come on, let's go inside. I need a beer and, if you like, we could do a ritual burning of the book, that might make you feel better.'

'You're a very unusual man,' she says, standing on tiptoe to kiss him.

'I know,' he says with a grin.

⌇⌇⌇

'What exactly are you doing under the desk?' Julia asks, setting a glass of red wine down on top of a pile of old files. 'Digging an escape tunnel?'

Tom emerges from under the desk, his face flushed from the effort of rummaging in a box of books. 'I'm looking for my diary from sixty-eight,' he says, straightening up and eyeing the glass. 'Excellent – what is it?' He is still distracted by the loss of this particularly significant volume.

'It's the Bordeaux we brought back from Calais last month. It's grim. Should be called Chateau Rip Off; why didn't we buy something we know we like?'

'Because life must have its little challenges.' He raises the glass to her, sips it and grimaces. 'I see what you mean; maybe it'll grow on us.'

'I do hope not.'

'It tastes a bit like rust remover,' Richard says from the doorway.

Tom sits down in his chair and swivels from left to right in the hope of spotting his diary. 'I bow to your superior knowledge, though you'd drink anything that smelt remotely like alcohol.'

'Indeed I would,' Richard says. 'Is this what you're looking for?' He moves a thick leather-bound diary from the top of Tom's library steps and hands it to him.

Tom's face lights up. 'Ah!' he says, 'I've spent the last hour looking for this,' as he strokes the cover affectionately and begins to flick through the pages. Mislaying it had been disturbing; he has always been a meticulous keeper of diaries, not just recording appointments but writing a couple of sentences or a brief paragraph to record the significance of each day. He likes this sense of his own history; the reminder that life is built of small pleasures and sadnesses, minor successes and failures. It drives Julia mad, this obsessive chronicling, although there have been many occasions on which she's had to admit that it's been useful. Hilary has told her she should be thankful that Tom has never wanted to record everything in Proustian detail; it's something he threatens her with when she grumbles about the stacks of diaries that occupy several metres of the bookshelves.

'Oh – listen to this, Jules,' Tom says. *'June 15 1968: Took Julia to dinner at the Place du Tertre, asked her to marry me and go to bed with me, she said yes to both. This time I know I've got it right. This is the woman I'm supposed to spend the rest of my life with. Roll on Saturday.'*

'How touching!' Richard says.

'Only to someone who doesn't know what happened next,' Julia says. 'Come on, dinner's ready. I don't think I can stand another evening of nostalgia.' She leaves the room.

Richard looks at Tom and pulls a face.

'Mmmm. Bad choice to read that,' Tom says with a wry smile.

'She's not still pissed off about all that, surely?'

'Not really,' Tom says, 'but it wasn't my finest hour. Come on, let's dump the rust remover and open a bottle of something decent.' And he carefully puts the diary away in his desk drawer. 'It's surprising, how the past sounds when you read it again,' he says and, putting a hand on his heart, breaks into song *'Memories, wrack the corners of my mind . . .'*

'Barbra Streisand,' Richard says. He hums the next few bars out of tune; unlike Tom, Richard is not a singer. 'And then there's that bit about would we do it all again if we got the chance?'

'Almost certainly,' Tom says, urging him towards the kitchen. 'And if we had the chance to cock it all up again, we'd probably do that too. That, I maintain, is what makes us interesting; flawed, doomed but interesting.'

'Sometimes,' Julia says, looking up from the bench where she is spooning mashed potatoes into a dish, 'you two sound as though you've escaped from a bad adaptation of an Evelyn Waugh novel. You're anachronisms.'

'But she loves us to bits,' Tom says, winking at Richard.

And Julia throws an oven glove at him.

1968

FIVE

Kilburn, London – January 1968

'The house is freezing cold and a bit damp,' Jane said as the taxi drove away. 'It belonged to Sandy's great-aunt, who died, and the relatives are fighting over the will, so she gets to use it until it's settled. But, major advantage, the hot water works and the beds are okay.'

Zoë, standing between her suitcases on the pavement, stared up at the decaying elegance of the facade – the once cream walls mottled grey with damp, the chipped cornices and cracked plaster, and the tall bay windows with their peeling paint – and loved everything about it. Most of all, she loved the fact that it was half the world away from Fremantle and from Eileen.

'I don't care how cold and damp it is,' she said, 'I'm in London, that's all that matters.' And, turning to pick up her suitcase, she yelped in shock as a large hand whipped it away.

'Hi, I'm Harry,' the owner of the hand said. 'I'll take your bags in for you.' And he picked up the two suitcases as though they were a couple of bags of groceries and ran up the steps and then to the first floor.

'Does he *live* here?' Zoë whispered.

'Harry? Yep, him and Sandy,' Jane said. 'And there are some people on the top floor too but they're only here for a few days.'

'But . . . he's . . .' Zoë hesitated.

'Black?' Jane supplied, picking up the belt of Zoë's coat, which was dragging on the pavement.

'Well, yes. Is it okay?'

Jane straightened up and looked at her. 'Why not? He's Jamaican, he's a student.'

'He looks quite old for a student,' Zoë said.

'Oh, he's been studying for years,' Jane replied. 'He's doing a PhD. Not medicine; anthropology I think.'

'But Mum always says . . .'

'Zoë, you came here to get away from Aunty Eileen,' Jane said, urging her into the house. 'Forget it, this is London – different, exciting and fabulous.'

But Eileen's warnings about black people weren't easy for Zoë to dismiss: evil, dirty, dangerous, don't make eye contact.

'I'm quite civilised, really,' Harry said several hours later, catching her watching him nervously. 'I don't eat little white girls for breakfast.'

'Just for Sunday lunch,' Jane said, and the two of them laughed.

Zoë, flushing, attempted to laugh too.

Three weeks later on her first day as a commuter, heading to the job the temp agency had assigned her, Zoë was nearly trampled by the hurrying crowd as she stopped in amazement at the sight of snow. Fairytale flakes were drifting from a pearly grey sky, which cast a strange iridescent light over London, and seemed to soften the usual cacophony of voices and traffic noise. Outside the station, a news vendor stamped his feet against the cold.

'US B-52 crashes in the Arctic!' he yelled, waving the newspaper. 'Radiation alert! B-52 crashes!'

Zoë stared in dismay at the man's mittened hand, his fingers poking out and blue with cold. It was considerably colder, both inside and outside the house than she had ever imagined.

'Which way to Portland Place?' she asked the man.

'Down there, love. Regent Street, then left. American plane radiation alert!'

The imposing facade of Broadcasting House faced her, curving as stately as a great ship, as she turned into Portland Place. Inhaling a deep breath of cold air, she walked up the street, pausing only briefly to glance at the statue of Ariel and Prospero standing guard above the entrance. Then she joined the steady stream of people making their way into the foyer, hurrying to the stairs or to the lifts, unwinding their scarves and greeting each other, and anticipation turned to anxiety. Overcome suddenly by the seriousness and importance of the place, Zoë felt helpless and completely out of her depth.

'Are you okay? You look a bit lost,' said a man, stopping alongside her. 'Can I help?' Snow was melting in damp patches across the shoulders of his trench coat and in his fashionably long hair.

'I was just . . . well, taking it all in,' Zoë said, 'and wondering where to go.' He was disturbingly handsome – tall, with searching grey eyes – and she wondered if he was famous and if she should know who he was. 'It's my first day . . . it feels . . .' she paused, lost for words.

'Right, perhaps?' he said. 'It feels right? As though you're absolutely supposed to be here?'

The word she'd been looking for was 'terrifying', but the way he was looking at her made her weak at the knees, so she nodded.

'I felt like that on my first day here too,' he said, 'it's a good feeling. I'm Richard Linton, by the way. I actually work at the Television Centre, but I used to work in radio here. So, can I help you find out where you need to go?'

By the time he had escorted her to the audience research department he had persuaded her to meet him for lunch in the canteen. Zoë passed her first morning at the BBC in a haze of confusion and distracted by a longing for lunchtime to arrive.

⁂

When Richard spotted her in the foyer, Zoë was wearing a scarlet coat, black tights and shiny, knee-length black boots. He was captivated not just by her appearance but by the way she was standing: still, rapt, as though she were breathing in the atmosphere. Committed as he was to the BBC and all that it stood for, he thought he detected a kindred spirit. As soon as he spoke to her, he loved the strange rising inflections of her Australian accent and the fine bones and pixie-like face under the cap of short dark hair. Most uncharacteristically, Richard knew that his brain had taken a snapshot of her and burned it into his memory. He had been on his way to an appointment and the odds on their meeting in this way were remote. The randomness of it made him feel that this had somehow been meant to happen.

'I work on *Panorama*,' he explained to Zoë when they met for lunch. 'It's a current affairs program, like your *Four Corners*.'

'Really?' she said, nodding politely.

'The BBC is my natural home,' he continued, battling with the canteen's macaroni cheese. 'When I was thirteen I decided I was going to work for the BBC, and here I am. And I just got promoted.'

Zoë smiled and, abandoning her struggle with the macaroni, pushed her plate aside. 'That's wonderful,' she said, 'congratulations.'

And as she looked up at him, Richard's heart seemed to lurch and flutter in a most peculiar way and he had trouble catching his breath. He'd been smarting from the ignominy of being dumped recently by a very assertive young journalist from radio news. And the previous weekend he'd had an uncomfortable falling out with his parents over his involvement with the anti-Vietnam campaign. But when Zoë smiled at him and said 'congratulations', none of it seemed to matter anymore. As the macaroni congealed, and he reached across the table to light her cigarette, Richard had a sense of exciting possibilities. He had never believed in love at first sight, but this, he thought, must be about as close to it as things come.

❦

High on the ceiling above Richard's bed, a cobweb, thick with accumulated dust, hung in a loop between the light cord and the opal glass shade. Zoë lay gazing at it perfectly still, enjoying the way her body moulded into the bed, the looseness of her limbs and the luxury of Sunday morning. She felt something like affection for the cobweb; it spoke to her of the monumental difference between here and home, as Eileen would have whisked that cobweb away as soon as it appeared. But then, nothing here was anything like home, and Zoë relished her liberation from the narrow, timorous life her mother had created for them; one dominated by what people might think.

From the bedroom she could hear Richard clattering crockery, thumping the toaster, abusing his new electric percolator. He never did anything quietly. It was, she thought, probably because he did everything very fast, as though there were more important things demanding his attention. He even made love that way, although, with no other basis for comparison, she realised this might be the way all men did it.

'Your breakfast, madam,' Richard said, edging the tray onto the bedside table, which was already cluttered with books, small change, tissues, a packet of Rothmans and an overripe banana. 'Coffee, toast and peanut butter. Happy nineteenth birthday.' He dropped a rectangular gilt-embossed leather box into her lap. 'Here's your present. Shove over so I can get back in.'

Zoë, not sure if she was excited or embarrassed, wriggled across the bed to make room for him. She was unused to getting presents and those she did get were only ever from Eileen, and usually something essentially practical and unexciting. This looked totally different.

'It's antique,' Richard said, as she opened the lid to reveal a heart-shaped blue and white enamel pendant encased in silver. 'I hope it's okay.'

Zoë gasped. 'It's beautiful, Richard. The most beautiful present I've ever had,' she said as he took it from her.

'Oh, rubbish,' he said, putting it around her neck and fastening the catch. 'It's not hugely precious or anything. But I'm glad you like it.'

'I love it,' she said, 'and I'll wear it forever.'

Richard reached for his mug of coffee and took a sip. 'Good, it looks nice. It really suits you.' He leaned over and kissed her. 'Many happy returns. Oh lord, you're not going to cry, are you?'

Zoë swallowed hard and pressed her palms to her eyes. 'Only a little bit and only because I'm happy.'

'Oh, that's good. Look, I've promised to go to my parents for a weekend in a couple of weeks' time,' he said. 'Why don't you come with me?'

'You don't think it's a bit soon?' Zoë said, biting into the soggy toast and trying to pretend she was unaware of the significance of being introduced to parents.

Richard shook his head. 'You have to meet them sometime.'

'Well, if you really think so. Will your sister be there?'

'No. Julia's still in Paris; still moaning about hating it, hating the French and hating being an *au pair*.'

'I thought you said she hated small children.'

'That too,' Richard answered. 'She's very hard to please, as well as not being qualified to do anything except get married. But you don't need to worry about Julia; you just have to grit your teeth and survive the parents.'

Nothing had prepared Zoë for Bramble Cottage; it crept up on her from behind high hedges at the end of a narrow lane, revealing itself only as Richard made the sharp turn into the drive and crunched to a halt on the gravel. The rambling two-storey wattle and daub house, with its whitewashed walls sectioned by dark wooden beams, tightly thatched roof, and leadlight windows with diamond panes glinting in the Saturday morning sunlight, took her breath away.

'Some of the beams inside are very low,' Richard said, 'you should be okay but just remember to watch your head.'

It wasn't just the house that was surprising. Zoë had imagined Richard's mother as an older, female version of her son; tall, loose-limbed in elegant casual clothes, silk scarves, subtle jewellery, even perfectly fitting jodhpurs. But Anita, dressed from neck to knee in paisley patterned wool, resembled a sturdy, high-backed, solidly upholstered armchair. Her short, rigidly permed hair was rolled back from her forehead with two almost perfectly circular curls at each side, reminiscent of the Queen.

'How lovely to see you, darling,' Anita said, greeting them at the door. 'And you must be Chloe, from Australia, how interesting;

you must tell us all about it. A lot of kangaroos, I believe.' She crushed Zoë's hand in her own plump one, and peered fiercely at her through rather bulbous blue eyes. 'Come through to the kitchen and I'll put the kettle on.' She ushered them to the kitchen and set a large kettle to boil on top of the Aga.

As Richard chatted to his mother, Zoë shifted nervously from one foot to the other. She already had a feeling that she was not welcome here; there was something immediately intimidating and slightly hostile about Anita Linton. Noticing a group of framed photographs on the wall by the breakfast nook, she slipped away and peered at them; Richard and his sister on a beach with buckets and spades, and then, a little older, on ponies, staring gravely at the camera from beneath the velour peaks of their riding hats. Lastly, she saw one of Julia as a sturdy teenager. With her pale hair in a long bob, and wearing a twinset, pleated skirt and a single strand of pearls, she looked every inch her mother's daughter.

'Julia on her seventeenth birthday,' Richard said, coming up behind Zoë and putting his hands reassuringly on her shoulders, before turning back to his mother. 'So, she's staying on in Paris after all?'

'She certainly is,' Anita said. 'Daddy put his foot down, but she does seem to be settling in now. Ralph,' she called, leaning out through the back door, 'come along, dear. Richard and Chloe are here.'

'It's Zoë, Mum,' Richard said, picking up the tray, 'Zoë. In Greek, it means life.'

'I know that, dear,' Anita said, taking them into a chintz-upholstered sitting room. 'And are you of Greek descent, Zoë?'

Zoë shook her head. 'I'm Australian, Mrs Linton,' she said. 'But my great-great-grandfather came from London, from the East End. He was sent out to Australia as a convict and he married an Irish housemaid who worked for one of the settler families.'

'Really! A convict,' Anita said, twitching her shoulders, 'and a housemaid, you don't say.'

That night, in a narrow single bed in a tiny room beneath the sloping ceiling, Zoë wondered whether Richard would attempt to join her. Confused by the house – which seemed to have several narrow, curving staircases, different floor levels and strange storage spaces accessible only when bent double or on your knees – she had no idea where he was. Would he have to pass his parents' room to reach hers? Would he risk it? She almost hoped not, as discovery by the beady-eyed Anita was too horrible to contemplate. She was exhausted from the effort of trying to get everything right and getting most of it wrong, from talking about her convict ancestry to putting milk in her cup before the tea. Even her attempt to compliment Anita on the scones had turned to disaster when she had explained that Eileen made pumpkin scones; pumpkin was, in Anita's opinion, suitable only for feeding to farm animals. Could Richard, wherever he was in this beautiful, but strange, old house with its creaking timbers and creatures scuttling about in the thatch, possibly still love her after today's performance?

Early the following afternoon, as she stuffed clothes into her suitcase, still shaky in the aftermath of the heated argument over lunch, Zoë mused that home was, at least, free of arguments such as the one that sent the Lintons spiralling into chaos over the roast beef and Yorkshire pudding.

It began with Ralph standing at the head of the table, and, with the studious care of a surgeon, carving the joint and placing slices of dark, overcooked meat on the plates Anita handed him. He was a tall, angular man with a premature stoop; probably, Zoë thought, from years of avoiding the low ceilings in Bramble Cottage. As he stooped lower over the joint, she could see thinning grey hair stretched sparsely across his bald pate.

'Glad to see that some of those left-wing wallahs have got some sense,' Ralph said, apropos of nothing, as he sawed away at the meat.

Zoë, sitting opposite Richard, saw him stiffen and look up from the plate his mother had just put in front of him.

'What do you mean?'

'Dock workers marching in support of Enoch Powell,' Ralph looked up momentarily from the carving. 'These blacks think they can come here and take over the country, and the damn fool government panders to them. Says they're British.' He gave a short dry laugh. 'Apparently, the dockers were marching along singing "I'm Dreaming of a White Christmas".'

'It was an appalling speech,' Richard said, and Zoë saw the colour rising in his face. 'Why do you believe it's okay to deny people access to work or housing because of their race?'

Ralph, who had returned to the carving, stopped again. 'Why not? Why shouldn't a landlord be able to decide who he wants in his property?'

'So, you'd feel the same if it were the Swiss who were discriminated against, or Americans, or even the French?'

'Different thing entirely,' Ralph said, glaring at his son.

'It's the blacks that are the problem,' Anita intervened. 'You can't trust them, they're not like us.' She lowered her voice slightly and looked across at Zoë while passing her a vegetable dish. 'Cauliflower, dear?'

'That's the most appalling thing I've ever heard you say . . .' Richard began and Zoë, in an effort to help, stepped in.

'Actually,' she said, 'I share a house with someone from Jamaica. Not just him, of course, there are a few of us. But his name's Harry and he's very nice. He's a university student and he works in a kitchen.' The silence was chilling.

As Richard carried their cases to the car, Zoë was fighting off tears, her face still burning with embarrassment.

'Don't be upset,' Richard said, slinging the cases into the boot. 'It's not *you*, it's *them*. Hop in quick, let's get going.' And he unlocked the passenger door and Zoë slipped into the front seat.

'I'm so sorry,' she said as he switched on the engine. 'I didn't mean to offend them. But it was so awful, Richard, your mother's face, when she said, "You mean, you live in a house with a black man?"'

'Zoë,' Richard said, turning to her. 'Stop apologising and let's just get out of here.' He slipped the car into first gear and roared off down the lane, swerving wildly onto the verge to avoid a car

41

coming in the opposite direction. 'I can't believe it. Sometimes I feel I should walk out of there and never go back. But you can't, can you? Not when it's your parents, blood being thicker than water and all that.'

'I don't know,' Zoë said, thinking of home, of awkward, accusing silences laden with tension that hovered around for days before settling like another layer in the brickwork of resentment. 'Mum and I don't have arguments.'

Richard reached for her hand and drew it across to rest on his thigh. 'You are so lucky.'

'Not really, it just gets stored up; you never know if anything is sorted out. We don't talk about things like you did. Mum thinks women shouldn't get involved in politics, that it's men's business.'

'But you do *care* about all the stuff that's going on don't you, Zoë?' Richard asked.

Zoë glanced across at him, wondering exactly what stuff he meant. 'Oh yes,' she lied. 'Of course I do; of course I care.'

And, as Richard put his foot down, he glanced sideways and smiled. 'I knew it,' he said. 'From the start, I knew you'd understand.' And, keeping his eyes on the road, he lifted her hand to his lips and kissed her fingers.

SIX

Quartier Latin, Paris – May 1968

At twenty, Julia knew she lacked whatever it was that drew men to women – sex appeal, she supposed. She longed for a sense of style, the body that went with it, and the ease and grace that would allow her to flirt the way other girls did. She despaired about her own awkwardness and lack of curves, and the evidence of Anita's conservative and middle-aged taste that was so obvious in her clothes. She also lacked any idea of what she actually wanted to do, or what she might be good at. After being urged by her mother into a *cordon bleu* cookery course that she hated, she had then drifted into a token job with a florist friend and then to another with a friend of Ralph's who had an antiques business. But nothing really interested her and while girls from school were working as secretaries or personal assistants, landing pleasant little jobs in publishing or cooking directors' lunches, Julia's boredom and apathy seemed terminal. Even the young men who occasionally showed an interest in her proved boring, and she, in turn, bored them.

'I've had enough of this,' Ralph Linton had said six months earlier. 'I'm at my wits' end with you, Julia. You're incapable of getting a proper job, and all you do is sit around reading magazines, talking to your friends on the phone and sighing.'

The sighing that so exasperated Ralph was the outward manifestation of Julia's sense that there was nothing to look forward

43

to, and that included the prospect of being sent into exile as an *au pair* in Paris.

'At least you'll learn to speak French,' Ralph had said, and in January she was sent on her way.

But, of course, Julia spoke English at every opportunity and the only things that really moved her were her instant dislike of the Le Bon family and of the menial tasks that were part of the average *au pair's* day.

In April, when she met Tom, everything had changed. Now, as she took the children to feed the ducks in the Luxembourg Gardens, bought them pastries at the *boulangerie*, washed their clothes and devised games to occupy them, Julia longed for the moment she could put them to bed and slip out to meet Tom. Initially, with the total self-absorption that comes from first love, she was almost immune to the growing tensions of a city in which thousands of young people were preparing to pit themselves against the most ferocious riot police in Europe. But as brawls broke out and the streets of Paris seethed with anger, she could no longer ignore the tension that was reaching fever pitch.

'They're digging up the paving stones,' she cried one evening as she and Tom skirted a square where protestors were ripping up the cobbles with drills, picks and bare hands.

'*Dessus les pavés . . .*' Tom reminded her.

It was the slogan he had translated for her as they had strolled home together the evening they had met at Hilary's tea party. Heading for the Metro, they had gone only one block when they saw that the station was blocked by a noisy group carrying placards and arguing with others who were trying to force their way in.

'It's the students,' Tom had said, taking her arm. 'Another protest.'

'I don't really know what they're on about,' Julia had said. 'Vietnam, I suppose.' The wind whipped between a gap in the buildings and she stamped her feet against the cold. Tom took off his scarf and wound it around her neck.

'Well, yes, and about not being allowed a voice in the universities,' he said, pointing to a placard with a silhouette of President de Gaulle, his hand clasped across the mouth of a shorter, younger, man. 'See that? See what it says – *Sois Jeune et Tais Toi* – be young and shut up.'

Julia shrugged.

Tom had grasped the corner of a poster that was flapping in the wind, eased it almost whole from the wall, rolled it carefully and tucked it inside his coat. 'It's all part of the same thing,' he said, steering her around the edge of the crowd. 'A lot of protests all coming together. Look there.' He pointed to a line of posters plastered roughly along the wall of the station. '*Dessus les pavés le plage.*'

'Under the . . . um . . . paving?'

'Paving stones.'

'Under the paving stones, the beach? But what does it *mean*?'

He drew her arm through his, laughing. 'Oh dear,' he said. 'How long have you got? Let's walk on to the next Metro.'

Julia leaned into the warmth of his arm as they walked. Protesting students were of no interest to her except in terms of the inconvenience they created. But in the weeks that followed, she had, with Tom's help, begun to understand the drama that was unfolding in the city and to feel for the students who were fighting so passionately for their beliefs. Now, watching as a couple of women her own age scraped at the cobbles with filthy, bloodied hands, she hated the fact that her apathy, ignorance and sheer cowardice made her a mere observer. The prospect of actually joining them was too frightening for words but she felt, along with her shame, a longing for the commitment and passion that had brought them to this.

'We're watching a revolution,' Tom said, as the cobbles were piled into barricades. 'It's happening everywhere, Germany, America, Mexico; even back home in London. Our world will never be the same again.'

Julia assumed he was exaggerating. Still, his knowledge was seductive and as he kept gathering evidence of what was happening around them, she felt her senses come alive in a way she had never known before.

'Why?' she asked as he jotted notes in his leather-bound diary. 'What will you do with all this stuff? Some of it's torn and dirty.'

'But they're history,' Tom explained. 'One day they'll be valuable; more valuable because they carry the marks and imperfections of the time.'

'Do you ever feel like joining in?' she asked. 'Digging up the cobbles, breaking a few windows? Even just joining a march?'

'Often,' he said, steering her away from the action to a quieter street. 'But I'm a pragmatist, Julia. I'm at a crucial point in my career with the bank and getting involved in the host country's politics is not on.' He stopped walking and turned to face her. 'You probably think I'm a coward, but everybody faces it some time or other, the choice between heart and head. I'm not proud of it.'

Julia gripped his hands. 'Of course you can't get involved,' she said. 'I feel just the same, I'd be far too scared. And my parents would go berserk. But Richard, my brother – if he were here, he'd be in the thick of it.' And, as she said it, she had an unfamiliar desire to see Richard, to tell him what she had seen and how it made her feel.

'Daddy and I think you should come home, darling,' Anita told her over the phone a few days later. 'We're worried about all the riots. I know we said you must stay for a year but it's all looking rather dangerous now.'

But Julia was now determined to stay put. 'It's fine, Mum,' she said, 'I can look after myself. I've made some friends like you said.'

To Julia, the revolution on the streets seemed part of her love affair with Tom. It was, she thought, as though her passion for him had opened her heart and mind to an intensity of feeling that she had never known before. At night, in her small room at the back of the Le Bons' apartment, as she put together the pieces of what Tom had told her and what she herself had witnessed, she realised that she actually cared about it. It showed her something new about herself; that it was possible for her to care about things that did not directly affect her, about what happened to people outside her own circle of family and friends, people she would never meet. Without Tom, she knew, she would have gone home as soon as she got the chance, but it was not only Tom who kept her there now. He had planted a seed in her and she wanted to let it grow; for him, for herself, and for so much more that she still didn't really understand.

Within weeks, Paris was brought to its knees. The Sorbonne was enclosed by ranks of black-clad *flics* with riot shields, the nights were filled with the noise of sirens. Flames exploded from the petrol tanks of overturned cars, and smoke hung over the city as the acrid smell of tear-gas wormed its way through ill-fitting windows and doors.

'De Gaulle will have to call an election now,' Tom said, as they stood on the steps of Sacre Coeur, gazing at the lights of the city spread beneath them like glittering patchwork. 'It's an end and a beginning, and it's a beginning for us; for you and me, Julia. I love you, and I want you to marry me.'

Julia's happiness was marred only by a tinge of anxiety at the prospect of introducing him to her parents. As they strolled home, she imagined her mother wincing at Tom's provincial accent, his less than stylish clothes, and at the opinions that were so similar to Richard's.

'Look,' Tom said, stopping in a quiet square bordered by chestnut trees, 'a haven for lovers.' He pointed to a narrow, white-painted hotel, its entrance shaded by a curved blue-and-white striped awning.

Julia blushed in the darkness, looking up at the wrought-iron balconies and tall windows where dim light glowed through the shutters.

'What would you say if I asked you to sleep with me?'

Julia's stomach lurched alarmingly. Anita's vague and euphemistic attempts at sex education had left her woefully ignorant. While other girls threw themselves into the melée of the sexual revolution, she had been far too scared to experiment, and she still had only a hazy idea of what sleeping with someone actually involved. But she had just agreed to marry Tom and this, surely, was the time to find out.

'I don't . . .' she stammered, thankful for the dim light of the street lamps. 'You see, I . . .'

'You don't have to answer now,' Tom said. 'We could come here, to this little hotel. I'd look after you, take precautions, you know.'

Julia nodded, although, of course, she *didn't* really know.

In the lobby of the Le Bons' apartment building, the lift clattered to a halt and Tom drew back the wrought-iron concertina gate to usher her in.

'You're not upset, are you?'

'I'm fine,' she said, touching his cheek, 'I love you and I don't need to think about it. Let's go to the hotel.'

'If you're sure,' he said. 'Look, I've got a really long day tomorrow, but I'll book a room for Saturday night and I'll phone you on Saturday morning. We'll go out for lunch and then to the hotel, with lots of time just to be together.' The lift gate clanged back into place between them. 'I love you, Julia.'

As the ageing mechanism cranked into action, their fingers met and separated through the bars of the gate, and she watched him disappear below her as the lift carried her up to the third-floor.

On Saturday morning, in the Le Bons' black-and-white tiled bathroom that was three times the size of the bathroom at home in Bramble Cottage, Julia lay in the claw-foot bath surrounded by scented bubbles.

'Next time I have a bath,' she murmured, stretching her toes out to the brass taps to add more hot water, 'I will be different. I will be a woman.'

The Le Bons were conveniently away visiting relatives in Mulhouse, so there would be no awkward questions. Resting her head on the curved back of the bath, she contemplated the idea that she might at last have become desirable. Had she somehow acquired that longed-for sex appeal? She considered this question with considerable satisfaction as the water cooled around her

Back in her own room, she searched for something to wear. The pale blue shirtwaist that had been her favourite seemed suddenly dull and girlish; with her page boy bob it made her look like Alice in Wonderland. The white accordion-pleated skirt and navy blouse that Anita said was smart and ladylike was actually boring and elderly-looking. Impatiently, she tossed aside dresses and skirts, desperate for something that expressed her new sense of a desirable self. Eventually, she settled on a full-skirted black-and-white floral dress with a boat-shaped neckline of white pique cotton. It was the best of a bad lot. Shocked to find that it was mid-day, she quickly finished dressing and pinned up her hair. Surely, Tom should have called by now?

Restlessly she roamed the large, rather imposing apartment, fingering the ornate backs of the dining chairs, the damask uphol-stery, and the gilt frame on the mirror in the salon. Two, three o'clock, the afternoon crawled slowly on. Julia refreshed her make-up and smoothed the creases from her dress, anxiety build-ing as the minutes ticked away. At four o'clock she called Tom's apartment, but the man who answered said they hadn't seen him since he left for work on Friday morning. When she called again at five, no one answered. That evening, she went to the café where they always met and drank hot chocolate alone, watching the other customers eating, reading, smoking, holding hands, kissing and arguing. Then, hurt and lonely, she went back to the Rue de Fleurus and fell into a miserable sleep.

'It's most unlike Tom to be unreliable,' Hilary said at church the following morning. 'I'm sure there's some perfectly simple expla-nation.' She looked really concerned and Julia, only a few kind words away from tears, struggled to hold them back. 'Maybe you just misunderstood him.'

But Julia knew this was not her mistake and, as the rest of the day dragged on, she went from worry to hurt then anger and back again. Next morning she called the bank and was told that he was in a meeting, and she left a message with the receptionist in falter-ing French, asking him to call her. Just before five, when there was still no word, she set out through the maze of small side streets to the bank. It was almost fifteen more minutes before Tom emerged, briefcase in one hand, his shoulders uncharacteristically hunched, a crumpled copy of *Le Monde* under his arm. He looked tired and worried, and as though he might not have shaved that morning. His surprise at seeing her was evident.

'I waited for you all weekend, Tom,' she said when he asked her what she was doing there. 'Hour after hour, I rang your flat. I looked for you at church and I left messages for you at home and at the bank.'

'I'm sorry; really, Julia, I'm so sorry,' he said, taking her arm. 'Look, there's a bar around the corner, let's go there. We need to talk.'

The bar was long and narrow, with a bench, upholstered in red leather, running from front to back, and tables and chairs lined up in front of it. Curls of bluish smoke rose from the corner, where a group of elderly men sat smoking *Disque Bleu*, their animated conversation vying with music from the jukebox. Tom gestured towards a table in the window and Julia slipped behind it while he went to the bar. The mere thought of alcohol made her queasy.

'Drink this,' Tom said, putting two cognacs on the table. 'It's very calming.' He swallowed his in one gulp and signalled the bartender to bring him another.

The cognac burnt a track to Julia's stomach; she knew that something terrible was going to happen – had already happened. Tom tried to take her hands but she pulled them away, curling her fingers around her glass.

'When I left work on Friday, Alison was waiting for me,' he began.

It took Julia a few painful seconds to realise that he was talking about an old girlfriend.

'What? From Liverpool? But you said it was over ages ago.'

'It was; look, we split up months before I came to Paris. But in March, she turned up here one weekend. She wanted us to get back together. I didn't know what I wanted, but she stayed around and . . . look, Julia, this was before you and I met, okay? We . . . that weekend, we slept together and now . . . well, now she's pregnant.'

Julia stared at him. Her lips felt frozen as though they'd been given a numbing injection.

Tom rubbed his hands over his face. 'I'm so sorry. If I'd known . . .'

'So what are we going to do?'

He looked away and then back at her. 'I've promised to marry her. I have to – you do understand, don't you?'

'But you're going to marry me.'

Tom shook his head. 'I can't walk away from Alison now.'

'Do you *want* to marry her?'

Tom leaned back in his chair, his eyes raw with exhaustion. 'Given the situation, I don't want *not* to, if you know what I mean. I don't want to let her and the baby down. Alison's family and mine, they all got together, paid for her ticket, sent her over here to . . .' He hesitated, looking at her. 'It's what they all want. I have to . . .'

Julia struggled to breathe. 'But what do *you* want?'

'I love you. I want to marry you, but this is the right thing to do.'

'You were going to leave without telling me?'

'No,' he protested. 'No. Of course not. I was going to call you this evening. Ask you to meet me and tell you then – I wanted to explain properly, not over the phone.'

'I can't believe you're doing this,' she said. 'I thought you loved me.'

'I do; honestly, I do,' Tom protested. 'But, you must see . . .'

'No,' she said, standing up, swaying slightly, thinking she might vomit. 'I don't see. I believed in you and now . . .' she hesitated, and then squeezed herself out from behind the table. 'I never want to see you again.'

Tom got to his feet. 'You can't mean that.'

'Of course I mean it. You're getting married, having a baby.' A lump welled in her throat and she swallowed it.

'I don't have a choice,' Tom protested.

'You always have a choice. *You* told *me* that. People always have a choice, you said, between the heart and the head.'

'But this is different.'

'No it's not. You had a choice and you've chosen her.'

'Because I have to. You think it's straightforward, but it isn't. Please, Julia, don't go like this; at least let me take you home.'

She wanted to scream at him but the old men's eyes were darting back and forth, watching with fascination as her life fell apart in front of them.

'Where were you all weekend?' she asked. 'You weren't at the flat.'

'We couldn't talk there,' Tom said, 'not with the others around. I took her to that hotel in Montmartre. It was a good thing I'd booked a room.'

Julia wondered if she had ever really known him.

'I hoped you'd understand,' he said softly.

'Oh, I do.'

'But not in the way . . .'

'Not in the way you'd like me to . . . a way that would make it easy for you, so you wouldn't feel guilty. Well, hard luck Tom, it's not like that. I hope you feel so guilty it tears you apart.' And, pushing past him, she stumbled out into the street, where the lights had just come on and people were strolling home as though it were a normal evening, as though the world had not come to an end.

On a mild evening at the end of August, two months after Tom had left her, Julia went to the cinema with Simon Branston. It wasn't their first date; they had been seeing a lot of each other in recent weeks. It had surprised Julia when Simon had suddenly stopped ignoring her and asked her out; the other girls she'd seen him with were glamorous and sophisticated in ways she knew she could never match. What surprised her even more was that he *kept* asking her. Simon was good company; he knew how to have fun, which she sorely needed, and he had an old-fashioned sort of gallantry about him. Julia enjoyed the attention, which made her feel better about herself.

Relationships, she decided, were like a balance sheet; you totted up the pros and cons to determine your own best interests. Simon had a few irritating habits. In the way of those accustomed to being the centre of attention, he talked a lot and took it for granted that those to whom he spoke agreed with him. He was, however, an otherwise charming companion, being good-looking, well-dressed and generous to a fault. It was easy to imagine taking him home to Bramble Cottage; the beams would be a problem, as they always were for anyone over five-foot-four, but her parents would adore him, especially when they learned that he was the heir to the Branston hotel chain. As they walked beside the Seine in the mild evening air, a boat decked with coloured lights drifted past. On the deck, people were dancing, laughing, drinking champagne. Julia imagined herself dancing on a yacht in some exotic location, with nothing to worry about except looking glamorous and keeping her guests entertained.

'So, what do you think then, Jules?' Simon asked. 'Am I going to take you back to the Le Bons *again* or race you off to my den of sin?'

Julia stopped and looked up at him. She was under no illusion about loving him; he didn't inspire her or encourage her to learn about or care for anything outside their own world, but he represented everything she had been taught to respect, to value and to aspire to. So, with the new pragmatism that had also been something she learned from Tom, she totted up the columns. It had to happen sometime; maybe life would be simpler once this hurdle was out of the way. Passion, she had concluded, was misleading and dangerous. It seemed ridiculous now that not so long ago, despite her fear, it would have taken only a nudge from Tom for her throw herself into all that madness on the streets. And where would that have got her? Arrested, perhaps? Flung into the back of a police van? On the receiving end of one of those rubber batons? And for what? There was nothing she could do. In the end, you had to look out for yourself. You could understand other people's passions, but you didn't have to be vulnerable to them, any more than you had to be vulnerable to your own. That only led to hurt, betrayal and disappointment. In any case, her virginity was beginning to feel like an embarrassment.

A few hours later she disposed of it; not in a picturesque and romantic hotel in Montmartre, but in the luxury of a suite in the Paris Branston, just off the Rue du Faubourg Saint-Honoré.

Sleeping with Simon really did seem right at the time.

SEVEN

S ince the day in January when she had first seen Harry, Zoë's fear of him had slowly disappeared, and by the time she had mentioned him to Richard's parents over the roast beef, she had stopped seeing him as different; he had become a friend. It hadn't taken her long to discover that Harry was just like any of the other people who drifted in and out of the house, and, in fact, she liked him a lot. He was older than her and Jane – older even than Sandy – and considerably wiser than all of them. There was something wonderfully reassuring about having him around to deal with the temperamental hot water system, and to take a firm hand with travellers who were supposed to be passing through but outstayed their welcome. What's more, his part-time job in a hotel kitchen meant that he often came home with bags of leftovers that were a cut above anything prepared in the Kilburn kitchen.

'You girls only love me for my leftovers,' he would joke, handing over the bag of goodies. 'When is somebody going to love me for myself?' But he already had Agnes, who loved him entirely for himself. She was a nurse he'd met at a dance at the Jamaican club, and Harry adored her.

Early in June, Jane, who had already been in London for eighteen months, went back home to Australia, and Zoë and Harry became allies in the war that raged in the Kilburn house between those who lived there and the ever-changing mob who dossed down in the attic rooms for a few days. Sandy ruled the house, walking a thin line between adhering to her relatives' conditions and making a little extra on the side to fund her obsession with expensive Italian shoes. And Zoë, who had never really felt at ease with the shiftless nature of a mixed household, felt increasingly insecure with Jane gone.

'*You* won't leave, will you, Harry?' she asked. 'You could get Agnes to come and live here. You two could have the big room now that Jane's gone and I can move into your little one.'

'Agnes has to stay in the nurses' home,' Harry said. 'The matron watches them like a hawk. But now I've finished my thesis, I ought to be able to get a job with decent pay, and when I do, we're gonna get married, get a place of our own.'

'I'd hate it here without you,' Zoë said. 'You're the only really sane person in this house. Everyone else is either crazy or stoned or both.'

'Why don't you move in with Richard?' Harry asked. He was ironing the kitchen whites he wore to work, and Zoë hauled herself up to sit on the edge of the table.

'My mother may be thousands of miles away but she'd have a fit if she thought I was sleeping with Richard, let alone living with him. I still haven't even told Mum about him.'

'And your dad?'

Zoë shrugged. 'Who knows; gone with the wind. He was a sailor on a ship that docked in Fremantle and he disappeared before Mum even knew she was pregnant. She had no idea how to find him.'

Harry gave a low whistle. 'Hard times, eh? She raise you on her own?'

'Yes. She worked – in a laundry for years, then in the woolsheds in Fremantle; she's still there.'

'Tough dame,' Harry said, switching off the iron.

Zoë nodded. 'Tough and bitter. Her family refused to have anything to do with her when she got pregnant. Her sister, Dot, Jane's mum, is still the only one who speaks to her. She had a hard time and she gave me a hard time, too; always watching me, stopping me doing things, going on about good behaviour and not getting into trouble. Frightened I'd turn out like her, I suppose.'

'You two fight much?'

'Mum doesn't fight; she cuts you off, just like they did to her. She doesn't speak, her mouth goes like a pussy's bum. That lasts a few days and then it returns to normal, which is not much different, really.'

Zoë's temporary job in audience research had finished, but the BBC had kept her on, moving her to a permanent job in radio answering listeners' letters on *The Dales*.

'You'd love it, Mum,' Zoë had told Eileen on the phone. 'There are episodes every day, a bit like *Blue Hills*, but it's about a doctor's family. Jessie Matthews is in it, she's Mrs Dale. Remember you took me to see a film with her in?'

Zoë's proximity to her favourite film star impressed Eileen but didn't compensate for not having her daughter where she could keep an eye on her.

'So you won't be coming back just yet, then?' she asked. 'Dot says Jane's going for a job at the airport. I thought you might like that too. Aren't you lonely over there on your own?'

'I'm fine,' Zoë said, watching her own reflection in the phone box mirror and fingering the heart-shaped enamel pendant Richard had given her. She had not taken it off since he had fastened it around her neck. 'I love it here and I'm not the least bit lonely.'

'Jane told Dot you've got a boyfriend and he's much older than you.'

'Well . . . yes, a bit,' Zoë said, ambushed, wondering just what Jane had said.

'Eight years, Dot says. It's a lot at your age, Zoë. Are you sure he's not . . .'

'You'd like him, Mum,' Zoë cut in. She pictured Eileen standing tight-lipped in the narrow hallway, twisting the telephone cable around her fingers, and imagining an ageing and unscrupulous Lothario. 'Must go now, the money's running out. I'll ring next week,' and she put the phone down quickly.

The mere thought of her mother attempting to caution her over the telephone from the other side of the world made her cringe.

She was nineteen, she was in love, and she was confident she knew more about love and sex than Eileen had ever known or could even begin to imagine. Her relationship with Richard had become her reason for being, and she thought nothing of breaking arrangements in order to be with him, staying home in case he called and planning what she might wear to please him. This, she was convinced, was how it should be, although she did feel that Richard himself often paid too much attention to his other interests. Still, she knew better than to say so.

❧

But the passing of time was having a different effect on Richard. The blissful haze of love and lust was lifting and the resulting clarity disturbed him. There was much that he loved about Zoë; her vulnerability made him want to protect her and that, in turn, gave him a sense of power. And he loved those wide-set brown eyes with their strange green flecks, the almost perfect cupid's bow of her upper lip, her constant desire to please him and her enthusiasm for sex. But it was now clear that involving Zoë, or even getting her to take an interest in his overriding political passions was going to be much more difficult than he'd first thought. Some days he could convince himself that, given time, he could educate her; other days, he wasn't so sure. Time and again, he found himself going back over the day in March that Zoë had chosen to go to Shepherd's Bush market with Jane rather than to the anti-Vietnam rally with him.

At the time he had shrugged off his disappointment and gone down to Trafalgar Square with Charlie, his flatmate. It was peaceful at the start, but when they moved off and eventually came face to face with hundreds of police surrounding the US Embassy in Grosvenor Square, all hell broke loose. Stones were thrown, placards doubled as weapons, and mounted police rode into the crowd wielding truncheons. One of them caught Richard on the shoulder and he staggered and fell, hitting his head on the kerb. For several minutes he lay there stunned, blood trickling warm and sticky down the side of his face, until Charlie spotted him and dragged him to his feet.

'I could have been arrested,' he'd told Zoë later. 'Look – three stitches in my head. I wish you'd been there.'

'I'm glad I *wasn't*,' she'd said, pulling a face. 'It's only some war thousands of miles away, it's nothing to do with us. You should've come with us; the market's really cool.' She stuck out her leg. 'I bought these red tights, d'you like them?'

In that moment a warning niggle of irritation and disappointment ran down Richard's spine, but her smile and outstretched leg disarmed him. She leaned across and kissed his forehead close to the plaster.

'Poor Richard,' she said, nuzzling his ear.

And, despite the pain in his head and shoulder, Richard's lust was stirred, and he tilted his head back to kiss her.

Now, four months later, Richard knew that as important as sex was, it was not enough. He yearned for something deeper, more complex and more intellectually rewarding, and he swung back and forth between frustration at what he thought was her superficiality and the feeling that she had depths he had not yet managed to plumb. Was it all down to her youth, he wondered from the lofty heights of eight years' seniority, or was it the result of growing up with a controlling, narrow-minded mother in the most remote capital city in the world? Did he want this relationship to grow, or did he want to end it? But in July, a big break at work made him shelve his questions about Zoë and focus on his career.

Race riots were sweeping across the United States as a result of the assassinations of Martin Luther King and Bobby Kennedy, and the BBC's legendary television journalist Martin Gilbert was planning a documentary on the future of the civil rights movement. Richard had read widely on the subject and his briefs and analyses were so sound and comprehensive that Martin Gilbert offered him a chance to join the crew.

'You are *so* lucky to be going to America,' Zoë said, sitting cross-legged on his bed.

'I know,' Richard said, rolling socks and tucking them into the corner of his suitcase. 'It's a chance in a million.'

'I'll miss you terribly. Promise you won't fall in love with some groovy American girl and forget all about me?'

'Of course I won't,' Richard said, folding his favourite shirt with obsessive attention to mask the guilt of having already considered this possibility. 'And I know I won't be missing any developments in the *The Dales* while I'm away,' he said, putting the shirt in his suitcase. 'You could go away for six months and still pick up the storyline. Mrs Dale would still be saying "I'm worried about Jim . . . "'

Zoë threw a rolled-up pair of socks at him.

Richard's jaw tightened and he kept packing.

'Oh, don't be so grumpy,' Zoë said with a laugh. 'I know what you do is terribly important.' She grabbed the neck of his sweater and pulled him down onto the bed. 'Come on, I want to make a big impression on you before you go.'

And Richard, despite his own better judgment, slipped his hand up her skirt and tugged at the waistband of her knickers.

EIGHT

Kilburn, London – September 1968

On the first Saturday of Richard's absence, Zoë was, for the first time ever, entirely alone in the Kilburn house. Jane was gone, Sandy was on a package holiday in Majorca and Harry had set off early to study in the university library. Even the attic rooms were strangely empty. From her bedroom window she watched as people hurried past; couples, families, they all seemed to have someone to be with, and somewhere to go. The time stretched miserably in front of her. She pictured Richard, Martin Gilbert and the camera crew sitting in aircraft seats, at pub tables or in hotel bedrooms, talking with that intense single-mindedness and camaraderie that she'd seen at the BBC; men having conversations on anything from work to politics, football to house prices. Zoë felt a jolt of resentment that right now Richard was probably talking to other men and not thinking about her, while he was always on her mind. He was the first man ever to take notice of her; she ached for his attention and approval, fed off the smallest signs of tenderness and thrived on his desire. Sometimes she had an uncomfortable feeling that she needed all this in ways that Sandy and Jane did not. They were so much more sure of themselves, with their take-it-or-leave-it attitude to men. Even so, it seemed that waiting around for men was something that most women did a lot of.

'They only ever think about themselves,' had been Eileen's parting comment on men when Zoë left home. 'You can't trust them. Nothing but selfishness and trouble, you're better off without them.'

Zoë knew that her mother's cynicism was simply bravado; a way of dealing with her hurt, shame and loneliness, and placing herself beyond the reach of pity. But what did Eileen really feel? Zoë wondered now. Had she loved the elusive sailor? Had she believed, did she still believe, that one day he would come back? What was it that had passed between them?

Rummaging now in the cupboard for something to wear, she remembered one thing Eileen definitely did believe: that almost anything – heartache, illness, boredom or loneliness – could be solved by borrowing the latest Georgette Heyer or Catherine Cookson novel, even a Mills & Boon, from the library. This, thought Zoë, tugging at the zip of the green-and-white sundress, the only thing in the cupboard that was clean and didn't need ironing, could also be a hint of her mother's real longings. All those swashbuckling landowners, and serious-minded but ambitious men always just out of reach, turned out to be at the mercy of women they loved. *They* did not disappear out to sea under cover of darkness, never to be seen again.

And so, having fixed herself tea and toast in a kitchen bleak in its emptiness, Zoë made her escape from the uncharacteristic stillness. After buying a black T-shirt and an emerald green skirt in Dorothy Perkins, she asked the way to the library.

As the librarian made out a ticket for her, Zoë browsed the tatty mix of cards and clippings on the notice board. Under the section 'Activities For Ladies', there was a patchwork group, a knitting circle, a young wives club, a request for volunteers to join the cleaning roster at a nearby church, and a notice for another group that made no sense to her at all.

'Excuse me,' Zoë asked the librarian, who was pinning up a notice about stamp collecting. 'Could you tell me what this is, please?'

The woman shoved a drawing pin into the board and peered at her over the top of her glasses. 'Which one?'

'Here,' Zoë pointed to the card, '"Consciousness raising for women." It says newcomers are welcome. It's on today.'

The librarian's lips moved silently as she read the handwritten information. 'No idea, I'm afraid,' she said. 'You could always go and find out. West Hampstead's only ten minutes on the bus.'

Zoë read the card again. Consciousness raising; perhaps it was some kind of educational group, the stuff Richard was always on about. He often said she wasn't conscious of important things that were happening. She wrote down the address, bought a sandwich and a cup of tea in a nearby café, and strolled down to the bus stop.

Zoë had expected a hall with rows of chairs and a dais, but the meeting place turned out to be a pleasant-looking house in a quiet street of Victorian terraces. She knocked lightly on the open door.

'Come on in,' called a voice with a broad American accent, 'First door on the right.'

Zoë pushed open the door to what would once have been the front parlour. Women were sprawled across armchairs and an ancient leather settee, or sat cross-legged on the floor. They looked at her with interest.

'Another newcomer! Come in, honey, make yourself at home.' The woman who seemed to be in charge picked her way through the maze of legs, her long purple cotton dress billowing like a tent around her. A deeply fringed orange shawl was draped over her shoulders and several strands of chunky amber beads clacked against her large breasts. 'I'm Gloria, the convenor, and your name is?'

'Zoë,' she supplied, blushing.

'Welcome, Zoë. How did you hear about us?'

'Oh . . . er . . . the library,' Zoë stammered, 'there was a card . . .'

'Good girl, you must've known what you were looking for. This may well be the first consciousness raising group in London but there's plenty going on back in Boston.' She steered Zoë towards an old leather ottoman. 'Make yourself comfortable. This is Claire, she's here for the first time too.'

Claire, who looked almost as embarrassed as Zoë felt, gave her a nervous smile and moved further along the ottoman. She was a little older than Zoë and wore her pale hair plaited into a thick loose pigtail.

Gloria explained that at each meeting the topics for the following week were set so that everyone had time to think about them. 'So don't worry if you don't want to join in this week,' she said. 'You'll be jumping in real soon. Today we're talking about menstruation, how we feel about it, the messages we are given about this normal female bodily function. Let's start by sharing how we felt when we had our first period. Marilyn?'

A deep flush crept up Zoë's neck. Was this some kind of joke? The morning she'd woken to find blood on her knickers, Eileen had explained that it was natural, and took her out to buy thick and bulky sanitary pads, and an ugly elastic belt with hooks. There were, she said, other things called tampons, but they were only suitable for married women. She also gave Zoë a booklet called *My Monthly Visitor*. The booklet had made it sound as though there was to be an exciting journey to womanhood in regular monthly episodes.

Having periods was bad enough but the prospect of having to talk about them made Zoë want to curl up and disappear. Once she had nearly fainted with embarrassment when, having queued in the pharmacy to buy pads, the girl who was serving disappeared to a back room and Zoë was left facing the pharmacist, a brusque man in his sixties. Mortified, she'd asked instead for a packet of throat pastilles, and hurried back through Fremantle to the other pharmacy, where, thankfully, she was served by a woman. It was only here in London that she had discovered the reason for Eileen's ban on tampons.

Now, as the women talked, it was clear that they had all been brought up to think that menstruation was shameful, dirty, and must be kept hidden so as not to embarrass anyone, particularly men.

'Men both fear and envy women's ability to bleed without dying,' Gloria said eventually, 'and, as we all know only too well, that fear translates into hostility. We are made to feel unclean when we menstruate.' And she went on to quote from the Bible.

Zoë was deeply shocked to discover that periods were mentioned in the Bible, and that Saint Thomas and Saint Augustine had both had something to say on the matter; they were, after all, men and saints, albeit dead ones. She wished she could crawl into the dark corner behind the ottoman and hide her face, or, better still, escape into the street. But leaving would involve a precarious navigation of outstretched legs, cushions, handbags, abandoned shoes and books.

'Menstruation is a natural part of being a woman,' said Marilyn, who had started the conversation by describing her dismay when she woke one morning at the age of twelve thinking the bloodstains in the bed meant she was dying. 'We can't allow ourselves to be shamed and intimidated by the fact that men simply can't handle it.' There was a murmur of approval around the room, and, just when Zoë was thinking that she might dissolve with embarrassment, Gloria announced that it was time to move on.

Moving on, unfortunately, did not present an opportunity to slip away. It simply meant moving on to the next topic.

'Alice,' Gloria said. 'You wanted to discuss the power issues inherent in the concept of "the nice girl". Take it away, honey.'

Alice wriggled forward in her chair, stood up and cleared her throat. She was a pale, dumpy young woman, possibly, Zoë thought, in her late twenties, with excessively large breasts, which, clearly unsupported by a bra, swayed as though they had a life of their own. Zoë was transfixed.

'Er . . . well, yes, thank you, Gloria,' Alice said in a breathless little-girl voice. 'The concept of the nice girl is the subject of my work on the psychology of women.' And, as she turned to include her audience, the bouncing breasts almost blinded the woman sitting beside her, who moved her chair slightly to avoid a repeat attack. 'Niceness is, as we know, synonymous with femininity, which is in itself grounded in deference to the male.'

Embarrassment was, it seemed, to be succeeded by boredom, which, for Zoë, was a definite improvement. She sat straighter in her chair and tried to pay attention to Alice, the monotony of whose voice seemed to have extinguished the previous discussion's fire.

'Deference is often produced at profound cost to women, both at home and at work, and if it is withheld, the apparent niceness is diminished and interpreted by others as a loss of femininity . . .'

After almost ten minutes of this, Zoë, who was watching the minutes tick away on the rather elegant grandfather clock in the corner, was surprised to feel the gentle nudge of an elbow in her ribs. Beside her, Claire sighed deeply and rolled her eyes, and Zoë did her best to suppress a giggle.

'Alice, dear,' Marilyn cut through the diatribe with a pleasant smile, leaning forward in her chair, 'this isn't a tutorial, it's a sharing of our experience as women. Could you be a little more . . .'

'Just what I was thinking,' piped up a rather fierce-looking grey-haired woman perched on a chair near the table, 'and you know what? This takes us back to our earlier discussion, and to the deference we show to men who are too squeamish to face the reality of women's biology. Our niceness in deferring to the male terror of menstrual blood means that we are trapped in the need for approval from . . .'

Zoë's heart sank as the conversation fired up once more.

'You see, biology *is* destiny,' one woman called.

'No, no, I blame the church,' said another and, once again, Claire and Zoë exchanged a conspiratorial smile.

'Now, before I put the kettle on, and we tuck into Sally's chocolate chip cookies,' Gloria said, when she had finally steered the discussion to a close, 'perhaps one of our new members would like to suggest a topic for next week?' She looked encouragingly at Claire and Zoë.

Zoë looked away immediately, but Claire, in a voice so soft that even Zoë, sitting alongside her, had to strain to hear said, 'Well, actually I'd quite like to talk about housework, if that's all right; you may have talked about this before.'

The women nodded. 'Heaps of times, actually,' one said, beaming at her, 'but there's always more to say on the subject.'

'Indeed there is,' Gloria agreed. 'And Zoë? Would you like to add anything?'

Zoë's mouth went dry. 'I think I'd rather just listen at the moment, thanks.'

'Housework it is, then,' Gloria said, getting up. 'The tyranny of domesticity, the way we're judged by our houses, and why we spend so much time doing for men and children what they could do for themselves. Now, tea, everyone?'

The women moved and stretched, and Zoë picked her way across the room and followed Gloria to the door, horrified as she did so to see a pair of women on the sofa snuggling closer to each other like lovers, one sliding her hand along her partner's thigh.

'I'm afraid I'll have to go,' she said as they reached the hall.

'You're not stopping for tea then, honey?'

'Thanks but I need to get home. It's been very . . .' Words failed her but Gloria seemed unperturbed.

'Challenging? It is at first, we've all been through it. Anyway, it was real nice that you came. Come next week, bring a girlfriend.'

'Yes, yes, of course,' Zoë lied, 'I'll see you soon then, and . . . er . . . thanks very much.' And she let herself out the front door, and walked down the path into the street as fast as she could without breaking into a run.

It was almost five by the time she got home, and Harry was in the kitchen, pouring himself a mug of tea.

'Hi, doll. What you bin up to?' he asked, waving the pot at her. 'Tea?'

'Please,' Zoë said, flopping into a chair. 'I went shopping.' As she said it, she realised she'd left the Dorothy Perkins bag in Gloria's room and that there was no way she was going back to get it. 'But then I lost it.'

Harry handed her a mug of tea and she gulped it down gratefully.

'I wish Richard was here,' she said, 'I really miss him.'

∽≈∽

Justine waited on a rickety chair in the corridor outside Mother Superior's office, wondering what she'd done wrong. She'd been pushing pillowcases through the mangle when Sister Edwina had appeared at the laundry door.

'You're to go to Mother's office,' she'd said. 'Hurry up now, run along and wait outside until she calls you in.'

Justine's eyes were red and sore with steam from the copper. Her arms ached from lifting the waterlogged linen with the copper stick, and from turning the mangle.

'But, sister, what . . .'

'Don't stand about here talking, child, go.'

And so she went; out of the laundry room, round the back path, in through the door and up the stairs, to arrive damp and breathless here in the corridor. She knew better than to knock at the office door; when Mother Superior was ready to see her, the door would be opened.

At the far end of the corridor, Sister Muriel lumbered out through the door of Justine's dormitory, a cloth bag made of old curtains bundled under her arm. She was a small, hunched woman with an uneven gait, and the bundle made her look like one of the Seven Dwarfs. She stopped in front of Justine, and looked her up and down.

'She hasn't seen you yet, then?'

'No, sister.'

'Stand up when you talk to me, girl.'

Justine slid from the chair and stared down at the scuffed toes of her shoes. 'Sorry, sister.'

'"I'm sorry, Sister Muriel".'

'I'm sorry, Sister Muriel,' she repeated and the nun tapped on the office door and was summoned from within. A few minutes later, she emerged and stopped to look at Justine again.

'Well, I won't see you again,' Sister Muriel said, 'so remember your manners and don't forget your prayers. God bless you.'

Justine stared at her, confused; was Sister Muriel leaving? The nuns never seemed to go anywhere. The sister trundled off in the direction of the dormitories, and Justine sat down again. What would the punishment be this time? Maybe the cane? If she tried really hard, she could almost make herself not feel the cane. The worst thing was when Sister Edwina used the copper stick behind her knees; that really hurt. Once it was so bad that Justine had bitten her own hand and made it bleed. The big brass-framed clock with the white face and black hands ticked noisily in its dark wooden casing. Justine watched the long hand jerk its way through the minutes, thinking of the things that the nuns did every day that were worse than the actual punishments. Sister Mercia twisted ears so it felt as though they would drop off, and Sister Leticia pinched. She pinched so hard and so often that the girls' legs and arms were covered in small livid purple bruises. Justine stared at the crucifix above Mother Superior's door, and wondered if Jesus told the nuns to pinch or to cane the girls, or to make her stand by the copper where the boiling water bubbled up and splashed her arms and neck. Is that what he meant when he said 'Suffer the children'?

The door opened. 'Ah! Justine, come in,' Mother Superior said.

Justine slid off the chair and walked in, eyes down, as she had been taught. A lady in a pale green dress and a small white hat was sitting near Mother's desk. Justine had seen her before; it was the lady who had given her the lace handkerchief.

Mother Superior picked up the cloth bag that Sister Muriel had been carrying and pushed it into Justine's hands.

'Mrs Fitzgerald's come to collect you; here, take your things.'

'You're coming home with me, Justine,' Mrs Fitzgerald said, getting up. 'We're going in my car. Have you been in a car before?'

Justine nodded, remembering the last time.

'Mrs Fitzgerald wants you to help her,' Mother said.

She understood then that she must be going to help with the cleaning; it must be dusters and polishers in the bag and maybe a scrubbing brush. Justine's heart slowed to a normal rate – cleaning was a lot better than having her knees caned. She risked a small smile in Mrs Fitzgerald's direction.

The two women shook hands and Mother Superior put a hand on Justine's head. 'God bless you, my child,' she said, 'you mind you're a good girl now.'

As Mother Superior opened the front door, Justine stopped abruptly. The car parked in the sunlight was similar to the one that brought her here years ago. Her stomach lurched.

'You pop into the front seat, Justine,' Mrs Fitzgerald said, putting a warm hand firmly on the small of her back.

Justine took a deep breath, opened the passenger door and climbed in, feeling the scorching heat of the leather through her thin cotton dress. The car smelled of polish just like the floors in the chapel. Mrs Fitzgerald settled herself in the driver's seat and switched on the engine. From the front steps, Mother Superior lifted a hand in a brief wave then turned back to the building.

As the car swept down the drive, Justine glanced across the garden to the water tank. It felt good knowing her box was there. Tomorrow, she told herself, tomorrow I'll get my box and go. And she leaned back in the seat and considered whether it was best to leave straight after lights out, or very early in the morning.

NINE

London – September 1968

'**B**ut they're not *like* your parents,' Julia said as she and Simon queued to go through customs at Heathrow. 'And they're not expecting me back for another month, so turning up on the doorstep and announcing I'm engaged might not be the best way to do it.'

Simon checked the duty-free bags to make sure that their allowances of whisky and cigarettes were intact. 'You mean, I won't be able to turn on my fatal charm?'

'Oh, you'll be able to turn it on, but it might not work.'

'It's always worked in the past.'

'How many times have you got engaged and turned up to surprise the parents?'

'Well, never, obviously. But you know what I mean.'

'Yes I do. But *you* don't know my parents. They'll love you, and they'll be thrilled about your family – it's just the surprise I'm not sure about.'

'Parents are parents,' Simon said, rolling his eyes. 'And if you know your Jane Austen, you'll know that parents of daughters love handsome, well-connected, wealthy fiancés – and I'm all three.'

'And modest too.'

'But I'm right, aren't I? And I *can* actually do modesty very nicely when I need to, and I promise to do it with your parents.

Don't worry, sweetness, it's going to be absolutely fine. Look how thrilled *my* parents were. They love you, just like I said they would.'

Julia watched as a customs officer asked the man in front of them to open his suitcase. Simon was probably right, she was worrying unnecessarily. And his parents *had* been lovely to her, but they were different, much more modern and sophisticated than her own parents. Lewis Branston was a Londoner, a self-made millionaire; his wife, Marina, was a New York heiress whose inheritance had been sunk into the hotel chain.

Julia was confident that Simon exceeded everything her parents could hope for in a son-in-law, even if he was sometimes a little too confident. A sliver of humility would certainly go down well, but humility was not one of Simon's qualities. Sometimes, Julia admitted to herself that even she found him a little over the top, but in the couple of months they had been together, the balance sheet had shaped up strongly in his favour. She liked him a lot, and occasionally considered that she might really love him; it was all so different from the way things had been with Tom. Mostly, she found it easiest not to think about that too much. She was still amazed to find herself the recipient of two proposals of marriage within a few months; it had done wonders for her self-esteem.

The customs officer ticked their suitcases with chalk, and they made their way out of the terminal to where a car was waiting to take them straight to the Belgravia Branston, in which the family had its own luxurious apartment. And that was the other thing, Julia thought, as she climbed into the back of the car, wealth made everything so much easier.

'And you're sure this is the right thing for you, darling?' Anita asked the following day. She turned, glass in hand, away from the lounge window from which they had been watching Simon and Ralph talking earnestly as they walked side-by-side across the garden. 'You're sure he's the right one?'

'Mummy, I *am* old enough to make up my own mind.'

Anita patted her daughter's arm. 'Of course you are, and if you're happy . . .'

'I told you. I'm ecstatic. I know it's all very sudden. We thought . . . well, Simon thought it would be a lovely surprise.'

Anita glanced out of the window again. 'It's certainly a surprise; you hardly mentioned him in your letters and now you show up engaged.' She turned back quickly, looking Julia straight in the eye. 'I have to ask you this, Julia . . . you're not . . . you're not pregnant, are you?'

For a moment Julia stared at her mother in disbelief. 'Oh, I see! No, of course I'm not pregnant, definitely not.'

'Well, that's a relief.'

'You do like him, don't you?'

'He seems very nice.'

Julia leaned back against the windowsill. 'He was dying to meet you and he really wanted us to surprise you.'

Leaning back on the window seat, Anita stuck her feet out in front of her and circled her constantly swollen ankles. 'Mmmm. I'm sure he did, but a little forewarning might have been nice. After all, we weren't expecting you for another month and suddenly there you are at the door engaged to a complete stranger. Anyway, what's done is done, I suppose. And you say you want a winter wedding?'

'New Year would be lovely – it might snow.'

'Wouldn't you rather wait for spring – think of the flowers and we could have the reception here in the garden.'

'The Branstons have offered to have it in their Belgravia Hotel. We thought we'd have the service in town.'

Anita drew in her chin, creating several other chins. 'London? But we've always gone to St John's. It's beautiful for a wedding. After all, the bride's family is supposed to do the wedding. It's rather high-handed their thinking they can take over like this. Your father and I will have to meet them and sort this out.'

'It's not that they want to take over,' Julia protested. 'They offered and I thought you'd be glad not to have to do all the organising, and surely Daddy won't mind not having to pay for it?'

'It's a matter of principle,' Anita said, her face flushed, eyes wider than ever. 'It would have been better to speak to us first, Julia. These Branston people can't just go around making all the decisions.' She replenished her drink.

Julia smiled to herself; she knew she was a very different person from the girl who had left home nine months earlier. As she watched her mother, she realised that Anita had seen that change and was struggling now to re-establish her authority. But, miraculously, that authority had passed to Simon, by virtue of his obvious desirability as a son-in-law. He had, as he predicted, taken control of the situation. All she now had to do was to walk the tightrope between her parents and Simon and his family until the wedding. By New Year, it would all be over. She would be Mrs Simon Branston and in charge of her own life.

'Look, Mummy,' Julia said. 'Simon's wonderful and his parents are really nice and very rich. And I'm going to have a wonderful life in Paris because Simon's going to run the hotel there. The Branstons are just trying to help. They're used to managing things and Simon's mother is longing to meet you. Please, Mummy, for me. Please?'

Anita patted her hand. 'I would have liked to be the first to know, but there we are; it's done now. I'm sure we'll work it all out amicably.' She stood up and straightened her skirt. 'Mind you, I feel as though everything's turning upside down these days; what with this and Richard, of course.'

Julia took a deep breath and changed tack. 'How *is* Richard?'

Since, at the age of seventeen, he had shinned down the pipes outside his bedroom window and left a note saying he was joining the CND march to Aldermarston, Richard had been in political and every other sort of conflict with his parents. At times, Julia knew, she had capitalised on that conflict. During the periods of fighting over Richard's insistence on going to the London School of Economics when he could have got in to Cambridge and arguments over demonstrations and about Ralph's views on the opening of the universities to what he called 'oiks from the north', Julia had acted out the role of ideal daughter. She had done well at school, displayed perfect manners to visitors and generally courted approval. That had all changed, however, when she left school and drifted aimlessly from one day to the next, herself becoming the focus of parental disappointment. Now she realised she was really looking forward to seeing Richard again.

'He's been in America,' Anita said, rolling her eyes, 'making some television program about all those negroes causing trouble.'

'Is he still with that Australian girl?'

'I assume so. He brought her here once, back in the spring.'

'What's she like?'

'Australian; I ask you! It says it all, really. Strange girl, dreadful accent and clueless about the most basic things. She lives in a house in Kilburn with a black man. Daddy and I are hoping this time away might bring Richard to his senses; people often come back feeling restless, wanting something different.'

'They do,' Julia agreed, thinking of the difference it had made to her, and musing on how much easier it had been for Richard to leave home, get a life, break free. But now she had Simon, things would be different.

∞∞∞

Late on the afternoon of the day Richard was due home, Zoë called the Television Centre from her office, to find out what time the flight got in.

'They're staying a bit longer,' a production assistant told her. 'Back next Wednesday evening.'

'But he said tonight.'

'Something came up,' the man said. 'We got a call yesterday.'

Zoë put down the phone, feeling crushed. The least he could have done, she thought, was to let her know. She felt abandoned, as though she had been pouring all her love into a black hole. There had been times when she was with Richard that she felt he didn't actually see her. Now, he seemed to have forgotten her completely. Miserably, she pulled on her coat and walked through the fine rain to the Underground. The past two weeks had seemed interminable.

'You'd have been no good in the war,' Harry said when she arrived home. 'It's only another week. How d'you think those dames managed when their men were gone for months or years – not knowing if they were dead or alive, or in a prison camp?'

'I'd have been useless,' she said, sniffing miserably. 'But this isn't the war. If I hadn't rung his office, I wouldn't have known what was happening.'

'I've got something that'll cheer you up,' Harry said, and he raced upstairs to his room, returned with a new bottle of Baileys and poured two large measures. 'C'mon,' he said. 'Let's see what's on the telly.'

The lounge was draughty even in summer and Zoë curled up on the sofa, pulling a rug around her.

'You gotta get a life of your own, kiddo, ' Harry said. 'No good depending on Richard for everything.'

'But I love Richard, and he loves me,' Zoë said. 'I need him.'

Harry shook his head. 'Loving's good, needing's not. You've gotta learn the difference or the need kills the love.'

'What do you mean?'

'Being needed is a killer, it's suffocating. *You* need your *own* life; friends, hobbies, work, all that.'

'But that would mean spending less time together,' she said. 'We should be together more, not less; that's how it's supposed to be.'

Harry shrugged, 'Is that what Richard wants?'

'Of course he does. Why wouldn't he?' She held up her glass, 'More, please.'

Harry raised his eyebrows and topped up her glass.

Later, when she tried to go back over what happened, Zoë realised that she had drunk an awful lot of Baileys very quickly and on an empty stomach. It was so deliciously smooth and creamy, the sweetness so comforting.

'Are you sure?' he asked at one point when she held out her glass. 'It's quite strong.'

But she nodded, and later surreptitiously poured herself another extra large one when he went to the kitchen to look for something to eat.

'You should eat something too,' Harry said, coming back into the room with a tin of digestive biscuits and an elderly-looking packet of Kraft cheese slices.

75

Zoë sat up straight and took the biscuits from him.

'Cheer up, babe,' he said, crouching down beside her. 'The time'll soon pass,' and he put his hand up to her cheek.

And that was when she did it. Impulsively, she put her hand over his and held it, turning her head to kiss the palm of his hand. For a moment, neither of them moved. Then Harry leaned forward, kissed her forehead, and went to move away.

'Don't,' she whispered, wrapping her arms around his neck, 'don't go.'

He looked at her again, his eyes searching hers; then, very gently he kissed her, sliding his hands into her hair, drawing her closer. It was so entirely different from kissing Richard – longer, deeper, so much more intense. Zoë let her weight sink against him, and he slipped his arms around her and kissed her again.

'Are you quite sure about this, Zoë?' he asked a little later in her bedroom, where the light of the street lamps cast patches of soft golden light through the window.

'I'm sure,' she whispered, pressing her face to his chest, inhaling his unfamiliar smell and tasting the saltiness of his skin. 'Absolutely sure.'

Slowly, and with infinite care, Harry removed her clothes, seeming to pay intense attention to every tiny movement, to be marvelling over the discovery of her body. She slid her hands inside his shirt, pushing it off his shoulders and unbuttoning his belt. For a moment he moved away, standing up to take off his shoes and trousers, and she waited for him to come back to her, impatient in her desire but relishing every moment, every second, every small detail of what was happening. His body was like fire beside her and she shuddered with pleasure as he slipped one arm under her shoulders and gently drew her leg over the curve of his hip.

TEN

London – September 1968

Richard flew home high on the adrenaline of the trip and burning with an ambition that had previously only simmered. Martin Gilbert had proved a wise and generous mentor.

'It doesn't matter,' he'd said, when Richard expressed concern about his own lack of journalistic experience. 'You're smart, you've got the instinct and the sort of single-minded ambition that it takes. But if you want to get to the top, it'll fuck up the rest of your life. You'll have to sacrifice other things but it's worth it.'

The following day he had checked Richard's briefing for interviews with members of the Black Panthers, and then handed them back to him. 'Off you go, then,' Martin had said, and laughed when Richard stared at him. 'Go on, you want to do this job; here's your chance. Do the interviews yourself. Get going, man – this is what you wanted, isn't it?'

It was an extraordinary opportunity, one for which Richard knew he might otherwise have had to wait years.

The flight into Heathrow was almost two hours late and when he finally got back to the flat, he found a message from Charlie to say that Julia had called and wanted him to phone her at the Branston Hotel in Belgravia, even if it was late.

'Got yourself a job in a posh hotel?' he asked when he was put through to her.

'Not a job, a fiancé.'

'A fiancé? Congratulations, is it someone I know?'

'No, but you might know his name. It's Simon Branston.'

Richard gave a low whistle. 'Son of . . .'

'Exactly. Aren't you impressed?'

'I'll reserve judgment until I've met him. But you sound very happy.'

'I am and I wanted to be first to tell you. We're getting married on New Year's Day. You have to come and bring your strange Australian girlfriend with the dreadful accent with you.'

Richard, who had been feeling ambivalent about his relationship with Zoë, now bristled defensively. 'I see you've been talking to Mum.'

'Naturally. Don't be so prickly, I'm only joking. I want to meet her, and I want you and Simon to meet each other. I thought the four of us could have a drink.'

Drinking with Julia and Simon Branston didn't appeal to Richard. He was pleased to hear her so different, so happy, but would have preferred it if she could have been happy at a distance.

'I'll organise it with Zoë tomorrow,' he said. 'So, I suppose the parents are pretty pleased with you landing a rich and influential fish?'

'You *could* say that,' Julia said, hesitating, 'but Mum seems to think it's some sort of contest to see if she can get her own way over Simon and his parents. Dad's a bit better, but it's all a tad thin ice-ish. You don't know how lucky you are, escaping like you have; it's so much easier for men.'

Richard grunted, remembering the many bitter arguments with his parents, not least on his last visit home, with Zoë. 'Don't kid yourself,' he said, tucking the receiver under his chin and flicking through the small pile of mail, 'it's not easier, just different.' He hung up, loosened his tie, walked through to his bedroom, switched on the light and almost jumped out of his skin.

'It's me,' Zoë cried, startled from sleep by the bright light. 'It's only me. Charlie let me in. It was meant to be a surprise, but you're so late I must've fallen asleep.' She swung her legs out of bed and ran to him. 'I missed you so much. It feels as though you've been gone for months. Did you miss me? Tell me you did.'

'Of course I missed you,' Richard lied. He bent to kiss her, breathing in the lemony scent of her hair, sliding his hands down her body, to grasp the swell of her buttocks and press her against him. Zoë stood on one foot, wrapping a leg around one of his. Lust overwhelmed him and he picked her up and, in a single stride, crossed to the bed and dumped her on it. Fumbling with his zip, he kneed her legs apart and grasped her thighs, spreading them wider to thrust himself into her, ignoring the voice in his head that warned him not to be drawn back into the doom-laden cycle of desire and disenchantment from which his temporary absence had freed him. And yet, he went on, lemming-like, aware that he was using her and that she was unknowingly colluding in something destined to crash and burn.

༺ঽৄৄঌ

For days, Zoë had been haunted by the irrational fear that somehow Richard would know she had betrayed him with Harry, and that her only salvation lay in reminding him how great they were together. So, when the following morning, she pushed down the sheet and studied the purple smudges on her inner thighs, she was confident that being there when he got home had been an excellent move. Sometimes, when Richard was cold and silent, as he had often been before he went away, Zoë felt quite scared of him, and it was worse when he'd had a lot to drink and turned his sarcasm on her. These visible signs of his desire, though, were surely proof of how much he loved her and had missed her. Nothing had changed; they could start again, the two of them together. And it wasn't as though she'd planned to betray him. But there was something about the way Harry had looked at her, the way he touched her, the way it seemed that his mind as well as his body was totally focused on her, that had eclipsed everything else and left her reeling with desire.

'It was like that for me too, babe,' Harry had said the next morning as they sat staring guiltily at each other across the kitchen table. 'And it was real special, Zoë, I mean . . .'

'I know,' she said, 'for me too, *really* special. But I feel so bad about Richard, and about Agnes.'

'Agnes,' he said looking down into his coffee, shaking his head. 'Man, she'd kill me if she found out.'

'She won't. Neither of them will ever find out. You're not going to confess and nor am I.'

'I feel so bad that it's like they know already.'

Zoë nodded. 'But it's just us feeling guilty that makes it seem that way.'

'You're special, Zoë,' Harry said, reaching for her hand across the table. 'I don't want to make trouble for you either.'

'A pact then,' she'd said, gripping his outstretched fingers. 'No owning up just because we feel guilty. It's best that way. I know it's not honest but it *is* the best way.'

'Right,' he'd agreed, squeezing her hand. 'You're right, we don't tell anyone, not a soul, not ever.'

'Not ever.'

Zoë slipped out of bed and went to the kitchen to make tea. The danger had passed, and her guilt would eventually fade. She certainly wouldn't be taking any more risks, but even as she tried to expunge it, the memory of Harry's mouth on her breasts, his fingers slipping expertly inside her, flooded her body with heat. Waiting for the kettle to boil, she closed her eyes remembering how it felt to be in his arms; how vulnerable but safe she had felt melting into him, as though the slow, decisive tenderness of his caresses, the rhythmic way he moved inside her, had made her a part of him. Her mouth went dry as she remembered the thrill of abandoning herself to him. The kettle clicked off, jerking her back into reality, and she made the tea, and carried two mugs back to the bedroom.

'My sister's home,' Richard said, hauling himself up into a sitting position and taking the proffered mug. 'She's engaged, getting married at New Year. They want us to meet for a drink.'

Zoë sat up straighter. 'Really? What's he like?'

'Rich. His family owns the Branston Hotels.'

Zoë sucked in her breath. 'Crikey, he must be a millionaire.'

'He's probably the most awful chinless wonder but I suppose I have to go.'

'Just because he's rich, doesn't mean he's not a nice person.'

'No, but I suspect my sister would happily marry the Hunch-back of Notre Dame to get away from home. Anyway, d'you want to come along?'

'Of course I do.'

'Okay, I'll fix it later.'

'I'm dying to meet Julia,' Zoë said, sipping her tea. 'I hope she'll like me. She's not scary like your parents, is she? It would be great if we could be friends. What sort –'

'Yeah, yeah,' Richard cut it. 'Can we give all that girlie stuff a miss?'

'Why are you so grumpy?'

'I'm not grumpy,' he snapped, 'just tired, and it feels odd being back.'

Zoë took his mug from him and put it on the side table. Wind-ing her arms around his neck, she slid down in the bed. 'Come on,' she said, 'I'll make you feel at home.'

But he tugged her arms away with both hands and swung his legs out of the bed. 'You seem to think that sex is the answer to everything,' he said. 'I'll be late for work and so will you.'

Zoë's face crumpled. 'I'm not going to work. I took a day of my holiday leave so we could be together.'

Richard shrugged. 'I'm meeting Martin at nine. You can stay here if you want, but I won't be back until late.' He strode out of the bedroom and Zoë heard the bathroom door slam behind him.

⌀

Julia rested her head against the brocade of a high-backed arm-chair in the cocktail bar of the Branston. Simon had suggested a small club in Baker Street, and Richard a pub just off the Edge-ware Road, but she had wanted it here and somehow she had prevailed. Richard had always been one up on her – world-lier, more sophisticated, free to pick and choose – now it was her turn. She pictured herself as a younger version of Marina Branston, graciously receiving her guests, ordering champagne cocktails on the house and generally behaving like a society host-ess; but when Richard appeared, her desire to have the upper hand evaporated. The moment she saw him, she remembered the day he rescued her with dock leaves when her bike had skidded into a clump of stinging nettles, and the time he taught her to fly a kite. In a most un-Marina like manner, she almost ran to meet him, hugging him and bending spontaneously to kiss Zoë on the cheek.

'So, are you actually *living here*?' Zoë asked while Richard and Simon were at the bar.

Julia shook her head. 'No, I wouldn't dare. Mum and Dad would go berserk. I'm just up here for a few days.'

'I don't think your parents liked me,' Zoë said, as though seeking news that they had recently changed their minds.

'They wouldn't,' Julia said bluntly, 'you don't fit the bill at all. Oh, sorry, I didn't mean that like it sounded. I'm sympathising – really, I am. It's just that they always hoped Richard would get together with a daughter of people they know from the golf club, or one of Daddy's Masonic friends. But Richard's never gone out with girls like that.'

'So, what sort of girls did he go out with?'

Julia shrugged. 'Just ones that were . . . well . . . different. Don't worry about it, they'll come round eventually, if you intend sticking around yourself.'

Zoë's eyes sought Richard out. 'I hope so,' she said. 'It's just . . . since he got back from America, he's been different.'

'He's always been moody,' Julia said. 'What are you doing tomorrow? D'you want to go shopping?'

'That'd be great,' Zoë replied. 'I need to get some shoes, and a present for my cousin's birthday. She's back in Australia.'

Julia, who had taken to Zoë immediately, responded at once to this openness and to what seemed like vulnerability. She bore no resemblance whatsoever to the bossy, self-opinionated journalist who had been Richard's last love interest, and who had made Julia feel ignorant, dowdy and provincial. And as the conversation developed, Zoë increasingly appeared to think that Julia was some sort of authority on London, and possibly all sorts of other things, and, most of all, on Richard. As Zoë regaled her with the details of the grim weekend at Bramble Cottage, Julia, newly confident, saw an opportunity to be, at last, the elder sister; the source of knowledge, a mentor almost, for this apparently open and obviously nervous younger sibling.

'I like her,' Julia said later while Simon was showing Zoë the framed history of the hotels that hung in the foyer. 'I think I'll probably like her a lot, but she'll never go down well with the parents.'

'Probably not.'

'So is it serious?'

Richard lit a cigarette and sighed. 'I thought it was but now I don't know.'

'*She's* serious, *very* serious, about you.'

'I know.'

'So if you're not sure, you should be careful.'

'Landing a millionaire makes you the expert, does it?'

'You are such a bastard,' Julia retorted, reminded now of his unattractive cynicism and sharp tongue.

Richard raised his eyebrows. 'Paris has changed you, you never used that sort of language before. Or is it the influence of the heir to a fortune?'

'What's got into you? We haven't seen each other for months, you could try to be a bit nicer.'

'Mmmm. Sorry,' Richard said, staring at the glowing end of his cigarette. 'Guilt, I suppose.'

'Guilt?'

'What you just said, about Zoë. I probably ought to end it.'

'What's stopping you?'

'I do sort of love her, but she hasn't a clue.'

'About what?'

'About the things that matter, or about the fact that I actually *have* cooled off. I don't think she has any idea what a real relationship involves.'

'Oh! And you do, I suppose?' Julia said, lowering her voice. 'You have to tell her. It'll be worse if you leave it.'

'And you?' Richard asked, nodding towards Simon. 'Do *you* love *him*?'

Julia blushed. 'I'm marrying him, aren't I?'

'That's hardly an answer.'

'Don't spoil this for me, Rich. Simon's kind, he's generous and he loves me; that's enough.'

'Is it?' Richard asked, raising one eyebrow in a way that had always irritated her.

'So you don't like him?'

'On the contrary,' Richard leaned back, locking his fingers behind his head. 'He seems very pleasant, but I suppose I'm wondering why you –'

Julia wanted to slap him. 'Just because I said . . .'she cut in.

Richard shook his head. 'Nothing to do with that, you were right about Zoë; I should end it.' He flicked the ash from his cigarette. 'Are you sure you're doing the right thing?'

'Of course I'm sure.'

Simon and Zoë were heading back towards them.

Richard leaned in closer, lowering his voice. 'If you want to talk about it, give me a ring at work. We can meet up somewhere, have a chat.'

'I don't want to talk about it,' Julia said, standing up and brushing down her skirt.

'What don't you want to talk about?' Simon asked, slipping his arm around her waist.

'Nothing, just my brother being stupid,' Julia said, turning to Zoë. 'Do you like Russian food, Zoë? Eddie, the concierge, tells me there's a great little place just off Great Portland Street where they make marvellous borscht. What do you think? Shall we give it a go?' She linked her arm through Zoë's, glancing back over her shoulder at her brother; the memory of the nettle patch and the kite flying replaced now by the time he locked her in their father's shed and went out to play cricket, and the day he threw her doll into a blackberry bush.

'But I've booked a table at that place we went the other night,' Simon protested.

Julia shook her head. 'Russian bistro,' she said, 'candles in bottles and a little man who plays a balalaika. What do you say, Zoë?'

Zoë hesitated, confused by the undercurrents flowing between Richard and Julia. 'Probably Russian would be nice,' she began, sensing an ally in Julia. 'That is, if everyone's okay about . . .'

'Everyone is okay about it,' Julia said, and, with the air of a woman who has been taking control of events all her life, signalled to the doorman to get them a taxi.

'Christ,' Richard said. 'What's got into *her*?'

Simon smiled indulgently at his fiancée. 'Bloody women,' he said, with obvious pride. 'Give 'em an inch – you know how it is.'

And they followed the women out of the foyer and into the waiting taxi.

ELEVEN

The Wheatbelt, Western Australia – October 1968

Justine sat on the steps watching the setting sun that was poised just above the horizon flooding the sky with crimson. It was more than two weeks since Mrs Fitzgerald had brought her here and with each passing day Justine had been worrying more and more about the safety of her box, and the sort of trouble that might be awaiting her at the convent if Sister Edwina thought she had been gone too long.

On that first morning Mrs Fitzgerald had led her into the kitchen and introduced her to Gladys, the cook, a huge woman whose fat seemed to hang off her in folds. Gladys poured tea into cups made of china so thin you could almost see through it. It tasted much better than the tea the nuns made and Justine gulped it down so quickly that it burned her mouth. In the centre of the table was a tray of scroll-shaped iced buns.

'I'd like you to sweep and wash the kitchen floor first, Justine,' Mrs Fitzgerald said 'and then the bathroom. After that, you can do the front steps, the treads are very dirty and need a good scrubbing; you'll need to change the water several times.'

Justine nodded. She had scrubbed more steps than she could remember but right now her attention was fixed on the buns, their whorls coated with soft white icing and dotted with sultanas.

Mrs Fitzgerald pushed the plate towards her. 'Help yourself.'

The bun tasted wonderful: light, rich and sweet like creamy

clouds, the sultanas plump and juicy. She closed her eyes and ate the rest of the bun very slowly, savouring every mouthful while Mrs Fitzgerald talked to her. Gladys would look after her, she said, she was the person to ask if she needed anything. Gladys, as silent as she was large, nodded, unsmiling.

At six o'clock some men had appeared in the kitchen, and Gladys dished up a big meaty stew with carrots and potatoes and gave some to Justine.

'C'mon and sit here by me,' she'd said, as the men settled themselves at the table. They were noisy, and smelled of sweat and animals, and they smoked while they ate their stew. The smoke and the smell made Justine feel sick. They were stockmen, Gladys told her afterwards, in the whisper that seemed to be her usual way of speaking, and she said that she thanked the Lord Almighty that the Fitzgeralds had only a small farm, or she'd be cooking for an army of men.

'You've worked very well today, Justine,' Mrs Fitzgerald said, appearing alongside her. 'I think we're going to get along nicely. Do you like it here?'

Justin nodded. 'It's very nice,' she said. 'But I've lost that bag Mother Superior gave me. I'd better take it back or I'll get in trouble.'

'Gladys has put the bag in your room,' Mrs Fitzgerald said. 'She's going to take you there now. It's in that little building at the back of the house, near her room. It's very small but you'll have it all to yourself. Tomorrow we'll go through the bag and sort out your things, see what else you need.'

'Am I staying the night, then?' Justine asked.

'Well, of course you are.' Mrs Fitzgerald sounded surprised.

Staring out now from the steps, to where the bees jostled for space on the scarlet fronds of the bottlebrush, Justine decided that she liked helping Mrs Fitzgerald. She didn't pinch or twist your ears, or scowl with disapproval when she looked at what you'd done. And Gladys was nowhere near as terrifying as she had at first appeared.

Justine turned at the sound of footsteps. Mrs Fitzgerald was standing in the doorway, she smiled at Justine and joined her on the steps. 'The sunset's beautiful, isn't it?' she said. 'I love this time of the day.'

Justine nodded, nervous about asking but desperately needing to know the answer to her question. 'Will I be going back soon, Mrs Fitzgerald?'

'Back? To the convent?'

Justine nodded. 'Yes, it's a long time, Sister Edwina will . . .'

'But you're not going back, Justine,' Mrs Fitzgerald said. 'You live here now, with us. Didn't you know that? Didn't the nuns tell you?'

Justine opened her mouth but no words came out. 'But I'm going back,' she said eventually. 'I have to go back, for my things . . . my . . . my box.'

'The sisters packed all your things into the bag, Justine. But I'm sorry they didn't explain things to you. This is your home now. You won't need to go back there at all, ever again. I hope you'll be happy here with us.'

⌒⌒⌒

Zoë leaned against the sink waiting for the kettle to boil. She was watching Harry, who was icing a cake for Agnes's birthday.

'I learned something useful working in the kitchen,' he said, fitting the nozzle into an icing bag. 'If I don't get a job I can always earn my living as a short order cook or a cake decorator.' He was reeling from having been knocked back for the first half-dozen jobs he'd applied for.

'I don't really know what anthropologists do,' Zoë admitted, pouring water on the tea.

'Hmm. Well, it seems that people don't believe *I* know what they do either, or perhaps they just don't want to know,' Harry said. 'But who wants a black anthropologist – a black anything, anyway.'

'D'you mean that? You really think . . .'

'I don't just think it, I *know* it.'

'It seems so unfair.'

Harry filled the bag with pink icing and began to pipe Agnes's name on top of the cake.

Zoë watched, mesmerised by the smoothness of his dark hands

against the whiteness of the bag; her body ached with the memory of those hands on her breasts, on her thighs. She looked up to see him watching her and blushed.

'What's up, Zoë?'

She shook her head and turned away to get the milk from the fridge. 'Nothing,' she said, but even with her back turned she felt his eyes on her. 'So, how *is* Agnes?' she asked, taking the foil cap off the milk.

Harry paused, still looking at her and then returned his gaze to the cake. 'She's very well, very happy about her birthday,' he said, piping a row of pink kisses onto the cake. 'She doesn't know anything.'

'That wasn't what I meant,' Zoë said, 'I was just wondering, you know, how she was, generally.'

'Yeah. She's okay. What about Richard?'

Zoë sighed. 'I don't know. He's different since he got back but his sister says he's just really involved with the program he's making.'

'Okay, is she? His sister?'

'She's great, I really like her. We went shopping together and to the movies, and I'm meeting her again tomorrow.'

Harry piped his last kiss and put down the bag. 'That's good,' he said, looking straight at her as he licked the icing from his fingers, just as he had licked them when he drew them, damp and glistening, from inside her.

The milk bottle slipped from Zoë's hand and crashed onto the tiles.

⁓

The air in the editing suite was thick with cigarette smoke, and Richard, his feet propped on the desk, sat watching the cut outs from his Oakland interviews with the Black Panthers. After Martin had selected the clips they needed for the program, Richard had asked Andy, the cameraman, to splice together the discarded sections and put them on a separate reel. They had filmed early in the morning, before the fog lifted, and the streets of West Oakland looked particularly depressing and other-worldly through the swirling mist. There was a long sequence of Panthers seeing children safely across the street to school at a junction where several young black children had been killed or injured. Through the mist, and in their leather jackets and black berets with guns slung over their shoulders, they could have been warriors from another planet. Richard watched intently; the program was to go to air the following week and he was impatient for the reactions and reviews, to see his footprint on his chosen path.

The door opened, and Andy came in clutching a mug of coffee and a sausage roll in a greasy brown paper bag.

'Where's the stuff we shot in the kitchens?' Richard asked.

Andy peered at the images on the screen. 'Coming up any minute. Reckon you'll need any more of this?'

'I never throw anything away.' But there was more to it than that. He was looking for something; someone. They had filmed in the Panthers' kitchen while the volunteers, who turned out every day at dawn, were cooking for the hundreds of children who ate breakfast there.

'That was a good day,' Andy said, through a mouthful of sausage roll. 'Remember those bloody great bacon butties they made us?'

The camera panned around the kitchen and there she was at the stove, a slim black woman stirring a huge pan of baked beans. Richard's heart seemed to miss a beat. She was wearing a short black skirt and a white T-shirt with a panther on it, and the apron around her waist was splattered with tomato sauce. Richard watched as she braced herself to lift the heavy pan from the stove to the table; he sighed and tried to mask it with a cough.

'That's her,' Andy said, 'the one who made the sandwiches – bit of all right. What's her name again?'

'Lily,' Richard said, clearing his throat. 'Lily Roscoe.'

'Lily,' Andy repeated, shaking open the *Daily Express* he'd brought in with him. 'Took a bit of a shine to you.'

'Really? I never noticed.'

'Bullshit! You could hardly take your eyes off her.' He glanced across at Richard. 'Still can't.'

Richard stood up and pulled on his jacket. 'Don't dump that footage, Andy,' he said, walking to the door. 'Just stick my name on the can and hold it for me, will you?' And, letting the door swing closed behind him, he walked along the passage, out through the foyer and up the street to a snack bar where he was unlikely to bump into any of his colleagues. He waited while the blowsy woman behind the counter poured tea into a thick white mug and slapped butter and cheese onto doorsteps of white bread. Then he carried his lunch to an empty table, measured two teaspoons of sugar into his tea and added a dash of whisky from the hip flask that had been a birthday present from his father. He was restless after watching the Oakland footage and more discontented than ever with his personal life.

For the last couple of weeks he had vowed every day to end it with Zoë, and every day something stopped him. It wasn't just his courage that failed him, it was that he did still care about her. Sometimes, usually when he *wasn't* with her, he felt he still loved her. But he also wondered whether this was a Svengali-like attraction; whether what he loved was what he imagined he could make of her, because when they were together, almost everything she said or did irritated him. He felt, as he had so often felt before he left for America, that she wanted to drag him into her own narrow field of vision, to draw his attention and energy away from the things that mattered so much to him, and he felt smothered by it. His only weapons were surliness and sarcasm, but the more cutting his sarcasm and the surlier his moods, the more desperately Zoë hung on. Why didn't she just tell him to piss off out of her life? She was like a loyal but irritating dog that followed him everywhere and whined outside the bedroom door. Zoë seemed to know instinctively when he was about to cut her off and each time she hooked him right back in, always with sex. Richard wasn't proud of the fact that he always succumbed.

He unfolded his newspaper, read a story about the police coverage that was being planned for Sunday's anti-Vietnam march, and got out his notebook to jot down the names of people he needed to call. And then, sipping the remains of his tea, he drew peace signs in the margin of the paper and then an 'L', which he traced over again, finally adding an 'i', an 'l' and then a 'y'. Lily. He wrote it again and stared at it until someone bumped against the table and splashed tea on the paper. He pushed back his chair, dumped the paper in the bin and went back to work.

❧

'You must be mad!' Julia said, running her hand along the smooth edge of the cosmetics counter. 'Why on earth do you want to do that? You'll hate it, and anyway, you might get hurt or arrested or something.'

Zoë picked up a perfume tester, sprayed *Je Reviens* onto her wrist and sniffed it. 'I just thought it might make things better if I went. You know, show Richard I'm interested in that stuff.'

'But you're not! That's the point.'

'I know, but I could *try* to be. I think I should have tried before, when we first met.' She pressed up against the counter, jostled by the crowd of shoppers. 'I hate shopping when it's crowded like this.'

Julia grabbed her arm and drew her into a space near the fire hydrant by the lifts. 'You think *this* is crowded? Just wait until you see the crowds at that rally; there'll be thousands of people, pushing and shoving, and fighting each other. Honestly, Zoë, you have no idea. I saw those protests in Paris; they were digging up the streets, setting fire to cars, smashing windows. And the police! You wouldn't believe it, bashing people with truncheons. You shouldn't go; if Richard wants to, that's up to him, but you don't have to.' She gave Zoë a little push. 'Come on, let's go up to bridal. I'm going to try on that white velvet dress from the magazine. My mother is being a complete pain. She wants me to have something made by her dressmaker and it's bound to be hideous, so I'm just going to go and order what *I* want.'

They squeezed into the lift as the doors were closing and emerged seconds later into the comparative calm of the bridal department. Waving her magazine imperiously, Julia summoned a sales assistant, who then hurried off to find the dress and led them to a fitting room. Julia had already acquired the Branston style.

'It's gorgeous,' Zoë said, fingering the velvet. 'But what would you wear on your head?'

'That's the problem,' Julia replied, struggling out of her skirt, 'what do you put with velvet?'

'I'll find you some headdresses to try, madam,' the saleswoman said and disappeared through the curtains.

'Julia,' Zoë whispered, peeping out between the curtains to make sure there was no one else in earshot. 'There's something I want to ask you. Do you and Simon . . .' she stopped.

'Do we what?' Julia prompted, hitching up her tights, and putting her head inside the muslin bag to protect the dress from makeup.

'Do you . . . do you do it a lot?'

Julia stared at her through the muslin. 'Do what? Oh, you mean sex.' She took the dress from its hanger. 'Quite a lot, I suppose. But it's not like we're living together. When Simon comes home with me, we only get to do it in the car. It's okay when I come up here and stay at the Branston because he can sneak into my room. Then we do it quite a lot. You and Richard are so lucky having two places to go to.'

Zoë guided the folds of the dress and its silky lining down over Julia's head and shoulders. 'Like every day, twice a day – more?'

Julia took the bag off her head. 'Most days, when we get the chance.'

'And Simon, he . . . does he always . . . does he start it?'

'Oh yes, men are insatiable really, aren't they? They'd do it any-where, anytime.' Julia liked the way she sounded; sophisticated she thought, and experienced.

'And do you . . . do you ever . . . you know . . .'

'What? Start it, you mean?'

Zoë nodded, blushing.

'No. Why?' She wriggled, adjusting the tight-fitting bodice.

'Oh, nothing. It's just that Richard was like that. I mean, he wanted to do it all the time, but now . . .'

'He hasn't gone off it, surely?' Julia said, turning away from the mirror to look more closely at Zoë, noticing for the first time that she was unusually pale and there were mauve shadows under her eyes.

'Not exactly,' Zoë said, 'but you know how funny he is since he came back from America? Well, he doesn't seem so keen and now it always seems to be me starting it.'

'And is he keen then?'

'Yes, usually.'

'Well, then. Are you okay? You look a bit peaky.'

Zoë shrugged. 'I was up half the night, couldn't sleep for thinking about it.' And it was clear that she was fighting back tears.

Remembering their conversation at the Branston, Julia could have shaken Richard. He'd been talking about ending it then but had let it drag on for weeks, and now it seemed to be making Zoë ill. 'You shouldn't let him get to you,' she said. 'You should tell him to get stuffed. It's not that he sets out to be unkind, but he's thoughtless and can be a bit of a bully.' She paused, took a deep breath and put her arm around Zoë's shoulders. 'Look, maybe . . . maybe Richard's not the right one for you.'

'He is,' Zoë said firmly. 'Julia, he is. I love him so much and he loves me, I know he does.'

Julia patted her shoulder and took a step back. 'If you're sure. But you mustn't let him get away with treating you badly. You have to stand up to him.'

Zoë nodded.

'And as for the other stuff, that'll sort itself out. You know what men are like.'

And, as Julia said it, she realised that she didn't have a clue what men were like, and that Zoë probably knew even less. It seemed you only got to find out by a process of trial and error, in which both the trial and the error were likely to involve a great deal of heartache.

She turned back to the mirror. 'Richard'll sort himself out eventually,' she said, examining herself side-on. 'He's probably just het up about work. But don't get dragged into going to that protest tomorrow. You'll hate it and you look as though you need a rest. Anyway, what do you think of this dress? I think I like it.'

Back at the Branston, Julia kicked off her shoes and curled up on the couch with another bridal magazine. She wasn't at all sure that the flowers were right; she favoured all white, with plenty of green foliage, but Anita kept talking about apricot roses. She stretched out her legs, flexed her toes, and considered a long and luxurious bath with some of the deliciously scented oil Marina had brought her from Rome. Simon was out at a meeting that he'd been moaning about at breakfast. Lewis Branston had insisted that his son spend three months working alongside the general manager of the London hotel, before taking over in Paris in the New Year. Simon was insulted. The time he'd already spent in the Paris hotel had, he insisted, taught him all he needed. But Lewis was adamant; unless Simon went through this additional training, the deal was off. He wouldn't be going to Paris until his father was sure that he well and truly knew the ropes.

'It's demeaning; I'm a Branston, for Christ's sake,' Simon had said on the day he'd conceded defeat. 'I grew up in hotels. I've done my bit as a kitchen hand, waited tables, worked on reception, in the manager's office, oh – and in the bar too. But most of all, I've lived in bloody hotels for as long as I can remember. What else is there to *know*?'

Julia had thought it a remarkably sensible idea. Simon could be too casual about things that should be taken more seriously. He was often flippant and dismissive with the staff, and tended to think he could carry everything in his head and talk his way out of difficult situations.

'It's a people business, sweetie,' he'd said sarcastically, when she ventured that his father's plan might not be such a bad idea. 'You just need to know how to handle people and that's what I'm good at.'

'Of course you are, but it'll make your father happy, and it probably means he'll stay out of your way when we get to Paris.'

'Huh!' Simon grunted. 'Maybe, but it's a total pain in the arse just the same.'

Since her engagement to Simon, Julia had become quite interested in the business. If she'd learned anything from Tom, it was that the more you knew about something the more interesting it became. And, although she was now too involved in the wedding plans to think of much else, she did think that having some responsibilities in the Paris hotel might be nice.

'I could help you,' she'd suggested to Simon that morning. 'You could train me, and then I could be your assistant, or have some little job in the hotel.'

'Job?' Simon said. 'We can't have the general manager's wife working in the hotel. Don't be ridiculous.'

'But what will I *do* all day?' Julia asked.

'Well, you'll be my wife, so you'll be looking after me, for a start. You'll be entertaining, and all that stuff; getting your hair done; shopping for frocks, I suppose – isn't that what wives do? And there's children, when we have them. If you want something else, you can use the tennis courts, or swat up on your French; that might be useful.'

But Julia could see that the sort of 'looking after' most wives did would be done by the hotel staff. There would be no housework and very few meals to be cooked. She was quite comfortable with the idea of not picking furniture or curtains, or managing a household. But she did want something of her own, and some sort of job seemed a good idea.

Simon's words were also a warning that he was taking for granted something they had never discussed. There was no doubt in Julia's mind that she didn't want children. Looking after the Le Bon offspring had confirmed what she had always suspected – that motherhood held no attraction for her. The other thing she didn't want, though, was to go back to being the sort of person she had been, back to boredom and sighing. In Paris, she had discovered what it was to be energetic and involved and she wanted the feeling back again. Clearly, she would have to wait until she was married to do anything about it.

TWELVE

Kilburn, London – October 1968

'You look really rough,' Sandy said. 'You should see a doctor.'

'I'm okay,' Zoë replied, wandering around the kitchen in her dressing gown. 'I'm just worried about Richard. I think *he* might be sick. Do you think he could have caught something in America?'

'Like the clap,' Sandy said with a laugh. 'No, frankly, I don't. The only sick thing about Richard right now is his vile temper. I don't know how you stand it, Zoë. I mean, sometimes he's just really horrible to you. And when did he start drinking so much?'

'He doesn't drink much,' Zoë replied too quickly, defensive now that Sandy had asked the question she had been asking herself. She opened the fridge looking for butter, to avoid looking at Sandy. 'He doesn't mean to be grumpy.'

'So, what – he can't help himself?'

'No, it's not that. He's just under a lot of pressure. It's hard for him.'

'Bollocks. What exactly is so hard for him, Zoë? He's just being a rude, bad-tempered git.'

'Right on!' Harry said, coming into the kitchen. 'That is, if we're talking about Richard. Why d'you let him get away with it? Agnes would give me my marching orders if I treated her like that.'

Hot tears burned Zoë's eyes as she pulled out the butter and began to spread it on her toast. Sandy put an arm around her shoulders.

'Come on, Zoë, it's not worth making yourself ill for. Want to know what I think?'

Zoë nodded, rubbing the heels of her hands into her eyes.

'Richard wants to end it but doesn't know how, so he's trying to make you do it for him.'

'Sandy's right,' Harry said. 'Basically, Rich is a nice guy, he just doesn't know how to handle breaking up. You have to be the one to do it.'

'But I don't *want* to break up,' Zoë wailed. 'I love Richard, I really love him, and he loves me. He's said so heaps of times.'

'But people change,' Sandy said. 'Sometimes things happen to them and they can't help it.'

'Like what? What could have changed him?'

'Well, I don't know. Maybe that trip gave him itchy feet. Or . . . maybe he met someone else.'

Zoë shook her head. 'No. No, he wouldn't. I just know he wouldn't.'

Harry thrust his arms into the sleeves of his jacket. 'Sometimes things happen unintentionally, babe,' he said, turning to look straight at her. 'You know that. Sometimes people can't help themselves.'

'That's right,' Sandy said. 'You know, twenty-four hours from Tulsa and all that, these things happen.'

Zoë blew her nose and picked up the plate of half-buttered toast. 'I know what you mean,' she said, looking straight at Harry. 'But not Richard, he's too busy with what he's doing, he'd never . . .' her voice faltered. 'Anyway, I'm going to this march thing, going to surprise him. And then, later, I'll try and talk to him.'

Sandy rolled her eyes at Harry, who shrugged and headed for the door.

'You need to end it, kiddo,' he said, looking back at Zoë. 'This isn't doing you any good at all.' And then he was gone.

Zoë got off the bus at Lancaster Gate and walked on to Craven Terrace. It was twenty past eleven, so she had plenty of time; she'd heard Richard tell someone on the phone to get there in time to leave at midday. But she wished it were any other day; sleepless nights spent worrying about Richard had left her weak and exhausted, and her appetite had disappeared along with her energy. It was essential she turn up today, though. She climbed the stairs to the flat and rang the bell.

Charlie opened the door wearing just a towel around his waist. 'Zoë? What're you doing here? Richard didn't say you were coming.'

'I wanted to surprise him,' she said.

He stepped back from the door. 'Come on in, but he's not here.'

'That's okay. I'll wait for him.'

'No. I mean he's gone. He went down there early this morning. To the LSE; a big crowd of them slept there last night, and there's a meeting about tactics.'

'But I thought . . . I heard him tell someone to be here at twelve.'

'Yeah, some people are meeting here. You can come with us, if you like.'

'Thanks, Charlie, but I think I'll just go and find him now. Do you know where he'll be?'

'I think they were meeting in the Old Theatre, but you should wait for us. It'll be chaos down there. Come on in and I'll make you a cup of tea; you don't look too good.'

'I need to find Richard,' Zoë insisted, turning to leave.

Charlie grabbed her arm. 'I bet you don't even know where the LSE is. It'll be swarming with people, you'll never find him. If you want to go to the rally, you must come down to the Embankment with us. I'm not letting you go off alone.'

Reluctantly, she went inside to wait for Charlie to get dressed and the rest of the group to arrive.

The Embankment was a heaving mass of people when they got there and, looking around her, Zoë felt a mounting sense of panic about whether she would find Richard. She was furious with

Charlie, and the weariness she had felt on her way to the flat had turned to agitation that made her heart race.

'If you'd let me come earlier, I'd have found him by now. He might be up near the front. I'm going up there to find him.'

'No, stay with us, *please*, Zoë,' Charlie insisted, 'Rich'll be busy. He won't be able to look after you, and he'll be pissed off if you get in the way.'

'Richard wants me to get involved,' she persisted. 'He wants me to be here. I know he does.'

Charlie grabbed her by the shoulders. 'Like hell he does! Don't you understand, Zoë? If you get in the way, he'll never forgive you. He's already walking all over you; do you want him to start kicking you as well?'

With a sudden burst of energy, Zoë twisted free of his grasp. 'He's not,' she shouted above the noise of the crowd. 'You don't understand, Charlie. I shouldn't have listened to you in the first place; you just wanted to stop me seeing him. Leave me alone.' And she pushed past him and began to jostle her way forward, trampling blindly over people's feet and grasping at the arms of strangers to steady herself.

The marchers moved on, away from the Embankment into Fleet Street, and then towards Charing Cross and Trafalgar Square. Deaf to the protests of those around her, Zoë pushed her way through the mass of marchers. Her head was buzzing with the noise; people were merging into blurred, multicoloured shapes, swaying chaotically before her eyes. Lurching sideways, she bumped into a man who staggered to regain his balance, and the placard he was carrying slipped and hit her sharply on the side of the head, but on she went. Staying upright and putting one foot in front of the other seemed to be getting more difficult. Her chest was tight with tension; her breath coming in short nervous gasps. And then just ahead of her, she saw him. He was so close she reached out to touch him only to find her fingers entangled in a stranger's hair. She dragged her hand away.

'Richard!' she called. 'Richard, wait for me!'

Her legs were shaking now; buildings and people swirled

chaotically around her and she staggered sideways. The last thing she saw was a stone bollard as it reared up towards her face.

∽∾∿

'They'd better not start playing silly buggers around here,' Simon said irritably, coming in from the balcony, where he'd been staring along the street in the direction from which the marchers were expected.

'Or what?' Julia asked.

'Or I'll be calling the police. There was a lot of trouble with this mob back in March, apparently; people throwing stones, hitting other people with placards. They had to bring in the mounted police. We don't want another Paris happening here.'

Julia tossed her magazine aside and stood up. 'Richard'll be there,' she said, 'and Zoë said she might go too.'

'Bloody fools. They should stay out of it.'

'Mmmm. But maybe, well; you know, sometimes I think it's good to have something important to believe in.'

'Huh!' Simon said, turning to her. 'You're not going to get all bolshie like your brother, are you?'

She grinned. 'And what if I do?'

He grabbed her from behind, grasping at her breasts. 'Cheeky! Getting all assertive now, are you?' And he nibbled at her neck.

'Don't give me love bites,' she cried, twisting away. 'My mother will have a fit.'

'That would be a sight worth seeing,' Simon said, turning her to face him. 'When we're married, I'll smother you in love bites.'

Julia leaned away from him, laughing. 'You're all talk, Simon,' she said. 'Really, you're just a pushover.'

Simon gave a playful growl and pulled up her skirt. 'Mmmm,' he said, 'nice.' He moved black slightly, undoing his fly, and, taking her hand, put it on his penis.

'You're just a show off,' she taunted. 'A big show off.'

'Very big, as you can see,' he said, pushing her down onto the sofa. 'Now, I know a much nicer way of spending a Sunday afternoon than poncing around the streets protesting.'

Julia, weak with laughter, pulled him down on top of her, lost her balance, and they rolled onto the floor.

'The floor is very nice, actually,' Simon said, easing himself on top of her. 'It offers greater resistance.'

'I'm not resisting.'

'So I notice. What would your mother say about this, I wonder?'

Without bothering to answer, Julia lifted her hips so he could pull off her knickers. But, outside, the singing voices grew suddenly louder.

'Dammit,' Simon said, getting to his feet and pulling up his trousers, 'ruined my concentration.' He reached down to Julia, helping her up. 'Let's go and have a look.'

From the fourth-floor balcony, they watched as the head of the march turned into the street. At the front there was a small group carrying a stretcher draped in black, on it a figure shrouded in white like a corpse and scattered with yellow flowers. Simon snorted in disgust. But Julia felt a sudden surge of emotion; there was something noble and beautiful about the sight of this great orderly mass of ordinary people, walking together with a single purpose. She felt a twinge of nostalgia for Paris; for the excitement, the fear, the nights when smoke hung in the air and the skyline was tinted orange with fire. Where was Tom now? Was he down there, part of the marching crowd, or was he still on the sidelines? For a moment, she thought she saw him there; that he looked up and saw her, that their eyes meet. She gasped, gripped the balcony rail, and looked down again straining her eyes to find Tom.

'What is it?' Simon asked, slipping his arm around her waist. 'What happened?'

'There,' she said, pointing, but the man had gone. 'I must be seeing things. I thought it was . . . oh, never mind, I must have imagined it.' She paused, peering down into the moving sea of people, and then turned back to Simon. 'Do you ever feel like protesting about anything at all?'

'Frequently,' he said, drawing her back into the room and pulling the curtain across. 'The price of champagne, my father's quaint ideas, and the fact that I can never get enough sex.' He slipped his hand up her skirt again. 'You strumpet, you have no knickers on.'

'You're a sex maniac.'

'I am, indeed.' He pulled her down onto the sofa, more gently this time. 'That's why I've got you, for instant gratification. So, come here and gratify me.'

～～～

'But what were you doing there, anyway?' Richard asked Zoë, hours later.

Propped up in the hospital bed with her hair matted with blood, her face grazed and bruised and her neck in a brace, Zoë looked entirely pathetic.

'I wanted to be with you,' she mumbled through swollen lips. 'I wanted to show you I could be what you want. Be like you.'

Richard sighed with frustration. 'But it's not like that. Being there doesn't mean anything if you don't really care.'

'But I *do* care,' Zoë protested. 'I love you, Richard. You know I do.'

'It's not about *me*, Zoë. It's not about me and you. It's something much bigger than that. Can't you see?'

When Charlie had finally caught up with him and told him that Zoë had been taken away in an ambulance, Richard had been consumed with anger. He'd almost refused to go to the hospital at all but eventually his better nature won out. Now he knew her presence in his life was a burden from which he desperately wanted to free himself.

'Look, Zoë,' he began, knowing it was neither the time nor the place. 'I don't –'

'Miss Conran?' A bearded man in green overalls pulled back the curtains. 'I've come to take you to x-ray. Doctor wants some pictures of your neck.'

'What, Richard? What were you going to say?' Zoë asked as the orderly pushed the trolley alongside her bed.

A nurse appeared and nudged Richard out of the way. 'We're going to lift you onto the trolley, dear,' she said, lowering the back of Zoë's bed and nodding to the orderly. 'On three, Jacko – one, two, three.'

Zoë reached out to Richard. 'What were you going to say?'

Awkward seconds passed before he took her hand. 'Don't worry about it now. I'll come back later.' He stood watching the trolley disappear down the corridor towards the lifts, and pulled a packet of cigarettes out of his pocket.

'You can't smoke here,' the nurse said abruptly, pushing past him to straighten the bedclothes. 'There's a café on the ground floor where you can get a cup of tea. She'll be a while; there's a bit of a backlog in x-ray.'

Richard picked up his jacket and made his way down the ward. The unmistakable voice of Alvar Lidell reading the radio news drifted through the open door of the patients' lounge and he pushed open the door just as the bulletin finished. An old man in a dressing gown was stretching forward to reach some pages of the *Sunday Express* that had slipped from his lap.

Richard gathered up the paper. 'Anything on the news about the march?' he asked, folding the pages and putting them into the shaking hand.

'Huh?'

'The march,' he said, louder this time. 'The anti-war rally. Was there anything on the news?'

The old man smacked his toothless gums. 'Troublemakers,' he said, coughing violently and then regaining his breath. 'Trouble-makers, the lot of 'em. Protesting. Why aren't they at work?'

Richard stared at him. 'It's Sunday afternoon,' he said mildly.

'Eh?'

'Oh, forget it.' He strode out of the lounge and to the main entrance. Out in the street, the air seemed to hum with the energy of thousands of people gathering not far away. He paused to breathe it in and glanced at his watch. He'd told Zoë he'd be back later but he hadn't said how much later. And, casting a guilty look back at the hospital, Richard set off as fast as he could in the direction of Hyde Park.

◦◦◦◦◦

Zoë closed her eyes; watching the ceiling as the trolley rattled along the corridors had made her feel sick. The radiographer had taken x-rays of her neck from every possible angle, and now she was supposed to keep the brace on until the doctor had a chance to look at the pictures.

'Do you know where my boyfriend is?' she asked the nurse, once she was back in her bed in casualty.

'He went down to have a cup of tea and a smoke, I think,' the woman said. 'Feeling all right now? Doctor'll be along in a minute and then you can have a nice cup of tea.'

Zoë leaned back against the pile of pillows. She was desperately tired but each time she began to doze off, images of the crush of people, and of the bollard rising up to smash into her face, woke her with a start that made her heart pound. She'd just settled into a kind of half-sleep when the doctor arrived.

'You'll be glad to know the x-rays are clear,' he said, noting something down on the chart. 'No damage to your neck, so we can get rid of the brace, and it'll just be a bit sore for the next few days. But that's quite a nasty cut on your forehead. The nurse will clean up the wound and I'll be back shortly to have a look; it'll probably need a couple of stitches. And we've got the results of the blood test. You're acutely anaemic; have you been prescribed any iron?'

Zoë shook her head.

'Hmm. Well, we're going to have to keep you in for at least a couple of days, maybe more. I'll arrange for you to have iron administered intravenously tomorrow. It means you have a drip going into your arm for about six hours; all you have to do is lie back and rest.'

'Couldn't I just have some iron tablets and go home?'

'Afraid not. We have to fix the anaemia, and because of that and the fall we need to keep you here to monitor you for a few days until we're sure the baby's okay.'

Zoë's head shot up, sending pain like a hot poker through her neck. 'Baby?'

'Yes. You did know you're pregnant, didn't you? No? Oh dear. You're about twelve weeks. When was your last period?'

'I don't know. Months ago. They've never been regular. I can't be pregnant, I'm on the pill.'

'Mmm. Well, you're definitely pregnant. Could you have missed a day or two?'

'I do sometimes, it's easy to forget . . .' She paused, remembering finishing a packet, and not getting to the chemist for more until a couple of days later. 'I thought it wouldn't matter, just a few days . . .'

The doctor smiled. 'It does, I'm afraid.'

She stared up at him. 'But nobody told me . . .'

'It should be in the instructions on the packet,' he said, writing something on her chart.

'But surely . . .'

'Anyway, I'll be back shortly and stitch up that forehead and . . . congratulations. Yes, congratulations.'

THIRTEEN

London – November 1968

'Why?' Richard yelled, banging his fist on the table, 'that's what I want to know, Zoë. Why did you stop taking the pill?'

Zoë, devastated about her condition and crushed by his anger and the arguments that had been a daily event in the two weeks since she had broken the news to him, rested her head wearily on her folded arms. 'I've already *told* you, Richard, I didn't deliberately stop taking it, I ran out. It was the middle of the week and I couldn't get out of work early enough to get to the chemist before it closed. It was a couple of days, that's all. I didn't *mean* this to happen.'

'I wish I could believe that,' Richard said, pushing his chair noisily away from the table and pouring himself another large whisky. 'This really *is* what you wanted, isn't it?'

Zoë lifted her head and looked at him in disbelief. 'How can you say that?' she asked, hearing the despair in her voice. 'I love you, Richard, I want us to be together always but I didn't do this deliberately. Why are you being so horrible?'

There was a ring at the doorbell and they both jumped. Charlie had gone to Brussels for a job interview and they had the flat to themselves. It was a freedom that Zoë had often longed for but right now the place felt like a torture chamber. Richard's fury seemed to know no bounds and when he wasn't shouting and interrogating her, he sank into a morose silence. Zoë sat up straight and dried her eyes as he went to answer the door.

'I've brought some lovely cakes,' Julia said with an awkward smile, putting the box on the table. 'I thought you might both need something sweet to cheer you up.'

Richard made a harrumphing noise and disappeared into the bathroom.

'How's your face, Zoë?' Julia asked, bending down to kiss her and examine the stitches in her forehead.

'Bit better, thanks,' Zoë said, wiping her eyes again.

'And how are *you*?'

'Dreadful,' Zoë replied, the tears starting again. 'Richard hates me. He thinks I did it deliberately, to trap him, and he wants me to have an abortion.'

'He doesn't hate you,' Julia said, taking her hand. 'He hates what's happened, he doesn't know what to do and he's taking it out on you. What do *you* want to do?'

'I can't have an abortion, Julia, I just can't.'

Julia nodded. 'I know.'

'I didn't choose this but now that it's happened . . .'

'Do you want to keep it? You could have it adopted, you know.'

Zoë's distress was laden now with the burden of having to explain again. She had battled constantly over the last few days with her inability to consider an abortion and her conviction that she had to keep the baby. And she had also made several attempts to explain it all to Richard, although he seemed unable or unwilling to hear. Since she had been old enough to understand the limited options that had been available to her mother, Zoë had occasionally wondered why Eileen had made the decision she had. Abortion would, she knew, have been even more dangerous and difficult to arrange then than it was today. Still, Zoë thought, her mother had had more reason to choose that or adoption than she herself had. Eileen, after all, was completely alone, whereas she at least had Richard. But Eileen had given birth to her and kept her, and although it went against the grain for Zoë to admit to admiration for or gratitude to her mother, she did, she realised, feel a considerable measure of both. For Zoë to take either way out seemed to her a profound offence against her mother and herself.

'I haven't heard you say one good thing about your mother until now; until it suits you,' Richard said, coming back into the room as Zoë was explaining to Julia. 'This is just manipulation on your part, Zoë.'

'Shut up, Richard,' Julia said. 'Stop being such a prick. Zoë loves you, although I can't imagine why, considering the way you treat her. It was a *mistake*, I've done it myself. And it's easy for you, isn't it? We're the ones who have to remember to take the bloody pills every day and put up with the side effects, and you men are happy to let us do it. You moan about condoms, and can't wait to put the responsibility on us, so just shut up. You are so selfish! You and Zoë were just unlucky, that's what it comes down to in the end.'

'Ha! Well, that's a great help,' Richard said, kicking a chair leg.

'Julia's right,' Zoë began, considerably heartened by his sister's passionate support. 'Honestly, Rich . . .' She stopped abruptly for, as Richard slumped quite suddenly onto the window seat and sank his head into his hands, she saw that he, too, was crying.

'I thought I'd come with you to hospital,' Julia said on the phone two days later. 'I mean, I know you're perfectly capable of going alone but I thought you might not feel like it. Not that having stitches out is awful or anything, but . . .'

'Oh, yes please,' Zoë said; she had been dreading the trek to the hospital. 'But are you sure? I'll probably be hanging around in the waiting room for ages.'

'It'll give us time to talk,' Julia said. 'And then, if you feel like it, we can go and have lunch somewhere nice.'

It was the first time Zoë had been out since being released from hospital three days earlier, and it was more than a week since the fateful day of the march. Outside on the street, everything seemed shockingly bright and noisy, the traffic unusually fast and intimidating. As they turned the corner into Bayswater Road, Zoë's legs felt weak and she thought she might faint.

'You're probably still in shock,' Julia said, taking her arm and drawing her over to a low wall. 'Sit there and I'll flag down a taxi.'

'Sorry,' Zoë murmured minutes later as she sank into the cracked leather seat of a cab. 'I feel so pathetic.'

'Stop apologising,' Julia said, 'you've had a horrible accident, a nasty shock and you're pregnant. Anyway,' she went on, smiling, 'we're sisters now – well, we will be in a couple of weeks – and I want to make sure you get to that registry office in one piece.'

Zoë nodded. 'Poor Richard, it's not what he wants. You don't think he'll change his mind, do you?'

Julia shook her head. 'No, he knows he has to go through with it. Although, I must say that until he just folded up like that the other day, I wasn't sure what he'd do.'

'I've never seen him cry before.'

'Me neither, and never expected to. He can be a real pain sometimes but, you see, he knows what's right and what his responsibilities are.'

'I hope so,' Zoë said. 'I really do love him, Julia. I hate the feeling that I'm forcing him into getting married, but I don't know what else to do.'

'Look, you're both stuck with the situation. Richard has to stop thinking only about himself. He'll come to terms with it. It'll be all right, you'll see.' She slipped her hand through Zoë's arm. 'I always wanted a sister.'

'Me too,' Zoë said. 'And I don't know how I'd get through all this without you, Julia. Since I came to London I've put everything into being with Richard, and when he was so angry and upset, I felt so alone.'

'Well, you're not alone now,' Julia said squeezing her arm. 'I'll stand by you now, and I always will. Your wedding, my wedding, your baby, and whatever comes after that, we'll always be there for each other.'

Richard picked up the forms the receptionist had given him, slipped them into his inside pocket, and walked out of the registry office and down the steps into the street. So, it was done, the booking made; his fate sealed by completing a form. This time last year, he had just won the job on *Panorama* and anything had seemed possible. Now he could only see the walls closing in. In two weeks he would be married. It was a marriage he hadn't sought and didn't want, and it was his own fault because he should have ended things with Zoë months ago, before he went to America.

'I don't know how to be a husband or a father,' he'd said to Charlie, who'd got back from Brussels the night before.

'No one does, man,' Charlie had said, pouring them both a drink. 'It's not like there's a training course; we're all dumped in the deep end when it comes to marriage. I've known Polly for six years and been engaged to her for two of them, but the prospect of getting married next year is still dead scary.'

'At least you have time to *be* scared,' Richard said, 'and you do have a choice.'

'There's no angry father chasing you with a shotgun.'

'There might as well be.'

'Look, you said yourself it's your fault for not ending it sooner, but Zoë's lovely and it's not so long ago you couldn't keep your hands, or your mind, off her. I know you think it's different now but things'll settle down when all this is over. Before you know it, you'll be handing out cigars and boring us with baby pictures.'

Richard made a grudging attempt at a smile.

'Better make the best of it, Rich,' Charlie went on. 'If you walked away from this, you'd never forgive yourself. Life goes on, and that means your life too.'

Now, standing outside the registry office as it started to rain, Richard turned up the collar of his coat and wondered if Charlie really was right. He was right about it being his, Richard's, responsibility, but was he right that he would never forgive himself if he walked away? In that moment, Richard felt he could have happily walked away without ever turning back, if only he had somewhere and *someone* else to go to. And, as he headed off in the direction of the Underground to go back to work, he thought again of a slim, dark girl, her apron splashed with tomato sauce, lifting an enormous pan of baked beans off a stove, and he cursed himself for his own procrastination.

∽∾∿

Julia sat in the front row of seats in the registry office between Charlie and Simon. It was a small, awkward gathering: herself, Simon and Charlie on Richard's side; Sandy and Harry on Zoë's, all of them uncomfortable and embarrassed, each one nervous about saying the wrong thing. The irony of the situation was not lost on Julia. Only a few months earlier she had railed at Tom for agreeing to marry Alison and, now, in the last couple of weeks, she had been urging her brother to do the right thing by Zoë. It seemed that she had lived such a bland life until she met Tom; since then, things had changed completely. Sitting there in the silence, waiting for the registrar, Julia remembered the hurt and despair she had felt in that smoky Paris café and in the days that followed; emotions so intense that she'd felt they would devour her. Besides the hurt there was shame for having been naive enough to believe in Tom and there was a real hatred of the woman she would never meet but who had stolen her promise of happiness. But now it all seemed so different. Blame, which had seemed so obvious and appropriate then, seemed unreasonable now that she was caught between two people she cared about. Zoë's fear of what might happen to her and the baby if Richard left her seemed perfectly reasonable; as reasonable as Richard's frantic longing to escape the burden of responsibility that he feared would trap him and cripple his career.

Julia had spent the last three weeks listening to, comforting and frequently shouting at both of them. She felt as though she had been catapulted into a particularly difficult stage of adulthood for which she was totally unprepared. It made her doubly thankful that, once married, her own life would be wonderfully uncomplicated. She reached out for Simon's hand, and he took it and moved his chair a little closer.

'What have you told your mum?' she had asked Zoë that morning.

'Nothing yet,' Zoë said, straightening the white pill-box hat they had bought together two days earlier.

'Not why you're getting married?'

'Not even that I'm *getting* married.'

'But you said you would. You said you were going to tell her on the phone.'

'I meant to, I tried, but I didn't know how. She's always been terrified of me getting into some sort of trouble like this, just like she did.'

'But at least you *are* getting married, that makes it better, surely?'

'I suppose. But she sort of wanted me to make up for what happened to her by doing everything right. You know, marrying the right person, having a lovely wedding and then perfect children a few years later.'

'But –'

'You don't know her, Julia,' Zoë said sharply. 'You couldn't possibly understand what she's like.'

'But you can't just *not* tell her.'

'Richard hasn't told *your* parents,' Zoë said defensively.

'That's different. He's older than you, he's a man and he hasn't told them anything about himself for years. They'll have a fit when they find out that you're married and about . . . well, about the baby. But it's not the same. You know that.'

Zoë seemed about to cry again, and Julia had been torn between conflicting urges to slap and comfort her. She had spent much of the previous day with Richard, up close to his anger at himself and at Zoë, and to his fear of and reluctance about the marriage. Since the night at the Branston when she and Zoë had first met, they had become increasingly close. But Julia also felt closer to Richard now; seeing him broken by his circumstances had brought home to her how much she cared for him. As the registrar invited Zoë and Richard to approach him, Julia couldn't rid herself of a niggling uneasiness. She loved them both; Zoë's situation was awful and Julia was sure that it hadn't been deliberate, but was keeping the baby really just a way of holding on to Richard?

Simon squeezed her hand, and she looked up and smiled at him as the registrar began his opening address. In six weeks' time there would be another ceremony; a real one, with flowers, and church bells, guests and gifts. It was ironic, Julia thought, watching as her brother took Zoë's hand and began saying his vows, that love and sex, tied so strongly to the promise of happiness, should actually deliver such misery.

⤷⤶

For months, almost since the day they met, Zoë had dreamed of marrying Richard, of standing beside him on the steps of a church, the moment captured forever in a white brocade-covered album. She had imagined herself in a white satin dress, and a full short veil that lifted in the breeze, and Richard in a morning suit, looking lovingly down into her face as confetti and rose petals floated in front of the camera lens. The flash of Charlie's camera as they left the registry office was a reminder that there would be no album, and that this awkward moment – her with her hand tucked stiffly into the crook of Richard's arm, the cut on her forehead and the bruise beneath her left eye still visible through her makeup – would be the lifelong reminder of that dreadful march and the misery of the last three weeks. There was no white satin, just a lavender wool empire-line dress to hide her expanding waistline, and a small bunch of white roses and lavender; Richard beside her, gaunt and tense in his dark grey pinstripe suit; and around them a few joyless, but well-meaning, friends attempting to turn disaster into celebration. She wished they could go straight home, as they had first planned, but Richard, guilt stricken in the last couple of days, had decided to salvage something. He'd booked a restaurant, invited a dozen more people to join them there, and sought Simon's help in calling forth a wedding cake from the Branston kitchens. Simon had added a crate of excellent French champagne. So, it was better than it might have been but, to Zoë, it was still awful.

She doubted she would have got through any of it without Julia. Richard's sister had turned out to be an entirely different sort of person from the plump, pale-faced teenager in the photograph at Bramble Cottage, and for the first time in her life Zoë knew what it was like to have a close and trusted friend. But not even Julia could help her break the news to Eileen.

'I've decided to write to her,' she told Julia after the cake cutting was over and the waiters had distributed the neat slices. 'I just can't tell her over the phone.'

Julia nodded and lit a cigarette, 'And what about our lot?'

'Richard says he's going to tell them we got married, but not say anything about the baby. He says that by the time we see them at your wedding, it'll be obvious that I'm pregnant and too late for them to make a fuss.'

Julia rolled her eyes. 'Very subtle! Oh well; it's up to him, and to you, of course.' She looked intently at Zoë. 'Are you sure you're going to be okay?'

Zoë shrugged. 'Richard seems resigned to it now. At least he's stopped being angry with me. And Charlie's got that job in Brussels, so he'll be moving out and we'll have the place to ourselves. I don't know how your parents will feel about it; though, after all, it *is* their flat.'

'I think you can expect a mix of disapproval and condescension, but they'll do the right thing,' Julia said. 'They're not going to kick you out.'

'Let's hope so. I just hope Richard'll get used to the idea.' Zoë sipped her half a glass of champagne and watched him across the room, trying to remember what it had been like at the start; when it was simple and fun and full of promise. At heart, she thought, we're still the same people – perhaps, when all this is over, we'll be like that again.

'I've got good news,' Harry said, slipping into the seat beside her. 'I've got a job.'

'That's fantastic,' Zoë replied. 'I'm so pleased for you. What is it?'

'It's a research position at a university in Glasgow. Agnes is coming with me and we're gonna get married.'

'Glasgow? But it's so far away. I'll never see you.' She had seen very little of him in the weeks since the march, and the prospect of his leaving came as a shock.

'Course you will, babe. It's not goodbye.' He took her hand in his and kissed it. 'We're special friends, Zoë. We always will be. You know that.'

For a moment it was there again; the sexual chemistry that both thrilled and scared her. 'I know. I hope it's really wonderful for you, Harry,' she said, swallowing hard to stop her voice from breaking. 'Everything you've worked for.'

'And for you,' he said softly. 'Things're gonna settle down for you, Zoë; it'll all come good, you'll see. You're going through some rough stuff now but Richard's a great guy. It's going to work out fine for both of you.' He leaned back from her, his hands on her shoulders as he surveyed her face. 'It suits you, babe, pregnancy. You'll be a beautiful mother.' He kissed the top of her head. 'I'll always remember, Zoë, you know that, don't you? I'll always remember.'

1969

FOURTEEN

London – April 1969

As winter gave way to spring, Richard found himself in a
rather better position than even he could have hoped for.
The civil rights documentary was a critical and professional success, and had been nominated for a prestigious award.
Also, he and Martin had taken a proposal for a series of thirty-
minute programs about significant protest movements to the
head of documentaries, who approved it immediately. By February they were working together again and, while Martin was still
clearly in command, there was a subtle but significant change in
their relationship; the series had been Richard's idea and he had
done most of the work on the proposal. Rather than derailing his
career, marriage had proved to be a comfortable backdrop to it. It
seemed incomprehensible to him now that for most of the time he
and Zoë had been together, he had been terrified of being drawn
into just this sort of relationship, often fighting it with sheer nasti-
ness. But Zoë seemed not to bear any sort of grudge and she was
less needy and more serious than she had been.

They had grown closer and, in the last few weeks, Richard had
come to realise that what he had thought of as a combination of
duty and affection was, in fact, love; a love that was steadily settling and maturing. But that love was spiced with guilt. In the
four months they'd been married, she had never once referred to
the way he'd treated her when she told him about the baby. It

sickened him to remember how he had tried everything possible to avoid facing his responsibilities. Now, though, the situation felt so right, as though it were what he had always wanted.

Pregnancy suited Zoë: the extra weight had filled out her face and arms, and she was different in other ways too; calmer, more thoughtful. She had even started reading the newspaper, and talking to him about the things he was involved in. She was growing up, just as he had hoped she might. And as she did so, Richard's thoughts of Lily and how things might otherwise have been had faded.

'I do love you, Zoë,' he had said, a couple of days earlier, coming home to find her on the settee with her feet up, knitting a matinee jacket.

'You didn't when we got married,' she'd said, giving him a wry smile.

'It wasn't that I didn't *love* you,' Richard said, pouring himself a drink. 'It was just that it was the wrong time. I didn't want to be tied down.'

'And now you don't mind?'

'More than that. It's good, really good. And I'm so proud of you.' Putting his hand on her belly, he felt a ripple of movement. 'Moving!' he said. 'That's good.'

'He's been on the go all day. He kicks so hard, I think he's going to be a footballer.'

'You're still convinced it's a boy?'

'Absolutely certain.'

'A daughter would be nice, though . . .'

'Yes, but this is a boy.'

'I'm so sorry, Zoë,' he said, taking her hand. 'I was a complete arsehole about . . . well, about everything. Have you forgiven me?'

'Of course,' she said. 'I forgave you ages ago; you know that.'

Later that night, as he lay in the darkness unable to sleep, Richard realised that something quite profound had happened: the balance of power between them had changed. Zoë's neediness, which had always given him the upper hand, had gone. They were bound together by marriage and the baby, but somehow she had claimed an emotional distance that had always been his. He sat bolt upright and looked across at the dark shape of her body in the bed. Even in his worst moments of disenchantment, he had thought he might love her, just doubted that he could stay with her. Well, now he knew he could, and not just *could* but *wanted* to. But did *she* still love him?

'Zoë?' he whispered softly, leaning over and putting his hand on her shoulder. 'Are you awake?'

She gave a small soft moan, shifting slightly, and her breathing settled again.

Richard took his hand away and lay down again. She'd always loved him; now pregnancy had matured her. He turned onto his side, curled against her back and draped an arm across her. She was still the girl in the red coat and black boots, but now she had also become the woman he would spend his life with. They were growing together, that was the only thing that had changed.

◌⚯◌

At the end of April, Zoë's blood pressure rose unexpectedly and her ankles began to swell. The doctor ordered her to rest, but she was irritatingly restless and fidgety. Richard began to worry and started leaving the BBC early, bringing work home. Out of necessity, he took on the shopping and then some of the housework.

'The vacuuming is mine,' he announced one Saturday morning. 'I don't want you lifting that heavy thing out of the cupboard. And stop trying to lean over and clean the bath, I can do that. You absolutely have to rest and take care.'

'I'll have to start calling you Mr Sheen,' Zoë said. 'Do you think all this domesticity will last once the baby's born?'

'Lord knows!' Richard laughed. 'But I think I'd probably opt for vacuuming over dirty nappies any day.' As well as feeling it was essential, he found some satisfaction in taking control at home; it made him feel competent and helped to assuage his guilt.

Arriving home one evening the following week, though, he was frustrated to find Zoë making her way slowly back up the three flights of stairs to the flat with a basketful of washing she had collected from the line in the tiny yard.

'I said I'd do that when I got home,' he said sharply, taking the basket from her and following her up the stairs. 'You shouldn't be carrying it. Mrs Driscoll downstairs said she'd always get the washing in, if you ask her. I do wish you'd listen to what the doctor said. It's not long now, after all.'

'I have to move about a bit,' Zoë protested. 'I'm so sick of waiting.'

He steered her towards the sofa and, as he did so, dropped the file he was carrying and his notes scattered across the floor.

'Sorry,' she said, sinking down against the cushions, 'I'll help you.' He put his hand on her shoulder.

'I'll get them. If you must do something, just sit there and fold the washing.'

'What is it, anyway?' Zoë asked, picking up a shirt and shaking out the creases.

Richard dropped the papers into her lap. 'Stuff for the program on women's lib. I'm trying to find a women's consciousness raising group. Word is they're going to be very big, very soon; there are quite a few in the States but I can't find any here.'

'There's one in West Hampstead,' Zoë said. 'I went there once.'

Richard looked at her in amazement. '*You* went to a CR group?'

She nodded. 'While you were in California. It was an accident, really; it turned out not to be what I expected.'

'I bet it did,' he said, sitting down on the end of the sofa and lifting her feet onto his lap. 'You never told me about it.'

'You weren't very friendly at the time.'

'Fair enough. But I'm very friendly now. Tell me about it.'

Leaning back against the cushions, Zoë described Gloria in her flowing purple dress and amber beads, the two women fondling each other on the settee and the discussions about having periods. 'Mind you, after six months of antenatal visits I don't know why I was so squeamish about all that,' she said.

'I suppose you don't remember where it was?' Richard asked.

She frowned and shook her head. 'I can't remember the name of the street, but it was a Greek name, I think.' She paused. 'I got off the bus in West End Lane. I might remember, if you get the A to Z.'

One Sunday afternoon while Simon was sorting out a German pop group that had trashed an entire suite, Julia decided to call in at the Parkers' tea party. She no longer qualified as a young person alone in the city, but she didn't think Hilary would turn her away and she actually felt very much alone. She had been in Paris for just three months but was already bored with her new life; albeit, bored in luxury. She missed Zoë's company and the friendship that had bloomed during her last months in England; phone calls didn't really compensate for not being able to do things together. And Simon's aversion to Julia being anything other than his wife frustrated her. She felt trapped and resentful, and had noticed herself sighing again.

From the hall she could hear the familiar clamour of English voices, and she popped her head around the door. It all looked remarkably familiar; a roomful of young people, flirting, eating, drinking tea, wreaths of smoke rising from cigarettes. It was so familiar that it made her instantly aware how dramatically she herself had changed.

'How lovely,' Hilary said, taking her arm and drawing her into the kitchen. 'You look wonderful, Julia. We were so sorry we couldn't come to the wedding, but you know how it is . . . Anyway, we're thrilled for you both. So, Simon's running the hotel and what are you doing?'

In that moment it occurred to Julia that, although Hilary didn't have a job she was always busy: planning the catering for a church function one moment; visiting new parishioners, comforting the lonely, rushing off to meetings or organising volunteers, the next. It was so different from Julia's own mother's life. She had no idea what Anita did with her time – very little, it seemed – and what she *did* know was that she didn't want her life to be like that. Julia needed something of her own to do and if Simon was going to be difficult about her having a job, she would find something equally absorbing.

'I'm not doing anything at the moment,' she said, 'but I'd like to. I suppose you don't know of anything?'

'Maybe I do,' Hilary said, handing her a knife to butter bread for more sandwiches. 'Tom, of course, was always very interested in the protests, we wondered if you . . .'

123

Julia started buttering. 'Yes, well, that was Tom. Simon has no sympathy with all that, nor with the anti-war protests.'

'That's all very well, Julia, but if it's important to you . . .'

'It was part of being with Tom, that's all,' she said quickly. 'Do you ever hear from him?'

'From time to time,' Hilary said, without looking up. 'They lost the baby, I'm afraid. Did you know that? Stillborn. Between you and me, I don't think Tom is very happy. I'll just take this plate through into the lounge; keep buttering, please, Julia, they have voracious appetites this afternoon.'

Julia buttered on, determined not to let Hilary see her reaction to the news; determined, in fact, not to allow herself to feel her own reactions. So, Tom was sad, but he was still married, and so too was she. Examining what it might all mean was far too risky. She forced her attention to the present. Hilary was obviously much younger than Eric, at least twenty years, perhaps more. Julia wondered what had drawn her to the kindly but rather remote vicar, and, as she stacked the buttered slices, she wondered what they were like in bed together.

'There's something that *might* interest you,' Hilary said, coming back into the kitchen with a pile of empty plates. 'It's a group I belong to. I think I'm the oldest one there. A couple of them are even younger than you.'

Julia rinsed her hands under the tap and dried them on a tea towel. 'I don't know if my French is good enough for a group.'

'Oh, that's not a problem. There are other women there who don't have a lot of French, a couple of Englishwomen and some Americans, and we all manage to communicate with each other. We're working on the status of women – the group is called *Jeunes Femmes*. You could come along sometime. You might find it interesting.'

FIFTEEN

Zoë felt as though she had been pregnant for years. Getting out of the bath with ease, painting her toenails, and running up and down the stairs were distant memories. Her body, which was constantly practising for the birth by tightening up and relaxing, had become a burden over which she seemed to have very little control. But she was happier than she had ever been. It was a peaceful kind of happiness grounded in her now solid belief in Richard's love for and commitment to her. The first weeks of their marriage had not been easy, and even at the start of the New Year she had still been worried that he resented her and didn't want their baby. But by the time the first signs of spring had started to break through, she had been convinced that he had, as Julia had predicted, put the past behind him. In recent weeks, his concern for her, his efforts to help at home and the increasing tenderness with which he treated her had laid her fears to rest. And there was no doubt in her mind that his impatience for the baby to come matched her own. She was grateful, and not a day went by that she didn't think of how things might have been. But, despite her eagerness for her pregnancy to be over, she was increasingly nervous about the prospect of the actual birth.

Zoë knew nothing about babies and had never even held one; her sequestered life with Eileen hadn't included friends or neighbours who had them. The women at the antenatal classes she attended passed on tips from their mothers or sisters, but the prospect of giving birth seemed like stepping off a cliff with one's eyes shut. But she did have Richard; a different, more considerate, loving Richard, just the way she had always wanted him to be.

From time to time, she missed the dazzling light, endless horizons, searing summer heat and soft insistent winter rains of home. She missed Jane, who was now working at Perth airport and had recently got engaged to a Qantas pilot. They wrote to each other often, and Jane had promised that as soon as she and Tony were married later that year, she would come to London. But, more than anything, Zoë missed Julia, who had stood by her and given her strength in those miserable and fearful weeks before and after the wedding. Julia and Simon had left London for Paris at the end of January, around the same time as Zoë had left the BBC.

'We'll talk,' Julia had promised, 'every day; well, at least every other day. I'll call you. It'll only be a tiny blip on the Branston phone bill, and I'll get a flight over as soon as my niece is born. It's so exciting, Zoë; you do realise I'm going to spoil her rotten.'

'It's a boy,' Zoë had said with a laugh.

'Rubbish. She's a girl, I feel it in my bones. I hope you're not going to call her Eileen or, worse still, Anita.'

'Danielle,' Zoë said, 'or, if I'm right and it's a boy, Daniel.'

Their telephone conversations were like life support for Zoë. Confiding both the fears and satisfactions of pregnancy, and her growing confidence in Richard, was, Zoë realised, a way of working out her own feelings, building her confidence in her ability to cope with the prospect of motherhood and the reality of marriage. It had helped her to manage her mother and Richard's parents, all of whom were like sharp bits of grit in Zoë's shoe.

Writing to tell Eileen that she was married, and why, had been incredibly hard, as had surviving the wait to hear how her mother had taken the news. Eileen had written five pages about the sacrifices she had made to give Zoë everything she herself had lacked. She was, she said, let down and shamed by Zoë's behaviour. But on the last page, the tone changed. Richard sounded like a good man, she said; she hoped that when the baby was born, they would come to Australia so that she could meet her grandchild.

'We *will* go,' Richard had promised when he read the letter. 'Or maybe she could come here.'

'Never,' Zoë said, shaking her head. 'My mother will never get on a plane or a ship. If she's ever going to meet you and the baby, we'll have to go to Australia.'

In the letters that followed, Eileen had avoided actual recriminations but her disapproval was evident and Zoë continued to be haunted by guilt. Being the focus of her mother's constant attention had been hard enough but the burden of having failed her so miserably was harder still, and she was thankful for the thousands of miles that separated them.

Richard's parents had been equally horrified when he had called to tell them he and Zoë were married, but they had sent a generous cheque. And, on the day of Julia and Simon's wedding, totally unprepared for Zoë's pregnancy, they had managed to grit their teeth long enough to play the role of prospective grandparents. She wondered sometimes how much distress it had caused them and was grudgingly grateful that, thanks to their tight-lipped commitment to Richard, the flat was theirs for as long as they wanted. In these final months, compelled to rest, she had spent many contented hours on the window seat, reading and looking out over the rooftops of London, and, as the afternoons drew to a close, listening for the sound of Richard's footsteps on the stairs, his key in the door.

On a mild evening late in May, Richard came home, armed as usual with a bulging briefcase but this time also with a Dorothy Perkins carrier bag.

'This,' he said, holding it out to her, 'is yours.'

Zoë peeped into the bag and drew out an emerald green mini-skirt and a black T-shirt. 'Good heavens, I'd forgotten all about these.'

Richard dropped into a chair and put his feet on the coffee table. 'Maybe, but the dames in the CR group haven't forgotten you.'

'So you went there?'

'I did indeed. And you were right, the house is in Delphi Street. I met the amazing Gloria and ate an indecent amount of her pineapple upside-down cake.'

'And?'

'And they were keen as mustard to let us film them and do an interview with Gloria. And they were keener still to hear about you.'

'They? Who else did you meet?'

'A rather nice older woman called Marilyn, and Claire, fair hair in a big plait. Said she went there for the first time the same day as you. She lives there now.'

'Lives there?'

'Yep. Left her husband just after Christmas; her raised consciousness made her realise she didn't want be treated like a domestic servant. Several women live there. It's a pretty big house, three floors.'

'Wow,' Zoë said. 'I thought Claire felt as out of place as I did.'

'Obviously not. I told tales on you, I'm afraid. Told them why you went and how surprised, and then how embarrassed, you were.'

'Oh, you didn't!'

'They'd already worked it out, Zoë. They laughed, sent you their love and they're coming to see you.'

'They're not! You didn't give them the address, did you?'

'Yes. Claire's really sweet and Gloria's a hoot. Women's experience is universal,' he said, quoting Gloria and mimicking her accent. 'We all speak the same language.'

'Those women are the last thing I need,' Zoë said. 'Hopefully they'll forget about me.'

Richard took off his jacket and loosened his tie. 'I'll remind them when we go back to film,' he said, teasing her. 'I'll mention that you'd like some company.'

'No! They're not . . . they're so . . . I mean . . . I just don't think we have anything in common.' She leaned forward and went to push herself up, catching her breath at the sudden warm gush of liquid between her legs. 'Oh my god, my waters have broken!' she cried, sitting down again in shock.

Richard darted to the hall and was back in an instant with towels warm from the airing cupboard. 'What do we do now?' he asked anxiously, packing them under and around her. 'It's a couple of weeks early. Shall I ring the hospital?'

'I suppose so. I don't know. Yes, ring them, ask them what to do.'

From her damp position on the sofa, Zoë heard him dial the number. It seemed to take forever; the definitive whirr of the dial and then the slacker sound of it rotating back into place. She was awestruck by the enormity of what was about to happen, by the feeling that her life would never be the same again.

'They said to go now,' Richard said, standing in the doorway. He had gone a deathly white.

'Well, we'd better go then. I've got that bag packed in the bedroom, like they told us. I'll just put on a dry dress and then . . . then . . .'

'We'll go.'

'Yes.'

He helped her to her feet, pulling her towards him. 'I love you, Zoë,' he said, kissing her. 'And I'm terrified.'

'Me too. I mean, I love you too, and I'm terrified too. Are you still sure you want to be there?'

Richard nodded. 'Absolutely! Wouldn't miss it for the world.' And he steered her towards the bedroom.

∞

'What, *now*?' Julia exclaimed. 'You mean, she's actually in labour right now?'

'Right now. We've been here hours but it's just going on and on. She got the first contractions in the car. It's awful, Jules; she's in so much pain.'

Julia swapped the phone to her other ear and sat down on the sofa, 'Calm down. How long do they think it'll be?'

'Could be ages. They said first babies often take about twenty hours. I can't tell you how horrible it is, I can't bear seeing her like this.'

'But it's wonderful, so exciting,' Julia said. 'She is okay, isn't she? You should be in there with her now, Richard, supporting her. Get back in there and sit with her. Hold her hand or rub her back, or whatever they tell you to do.'

'I'm supposed to be in charge of the gas and air thing.'

'Well, go and do that. It's meant to make it easier, isn't it?'

'Takes the edge off the pain. I feel such a shit, Jules, she's so brave and I'm, I'm such a hopeless . . .'

'A hopeless shit,' she finished for him. 'And now you're being a wet, hopeless shit, so stop it.'

'I don't know what I'll do if anything happens to her.'

'Now you're being *really* wet,' she said, thinking she sounded like the games mistress at her old school, jollying on the girls who hated playing hockey when the ground was hard with ice. 'Nothing's going to happen to her, she's only having a baby. Women do it all the time. She'll be fine. Now, you go on back in there and give her my love. And ring me again when anything happens.'

'Trouble?' Simon asked, coming out of the bathroom wrapped in a towel.

'Zoë's in labour and Richard's panicking.'

Simon gave a little whistle through his teeth. 'I bet he is. You know Mike, my cousin? He had a terrible time when Tina was in labour. They almost had to anaesthetise him.'

'Oh, really!' Julia said. 'How pathetic. Women are the ones who have to waddle around like whales for months, go through agony having it, and you men want us to feel sorry for *you*?'

'Darling heart,' Simon said, clutching his hands to his chest in mock horror. 'You can't blame a chap for worrying about his wife at a time like this. It's only because we love you so much. We all know we'd be lost without you girls.' He put his arms around her, his hands on her buttocks. 'I'd be worried if it were you, I don't want anything to hurt you.'

'Simon! You are doing that slimy toad thing you do with difficult guests.'

'Well, maybe. But I certainly don't touch up the guests' arses at the same time. That's something I save just for you.'

Julia laughed, pushed him away from her and tugged at his towel. He stood there stark naked as they faced each other, both relishing the rising tension.

'You know what has to happen now,' Simon said softly, taking a step towards her in an attempt to look menacing. And Julia, no longer able to contain her laughter, let out a shriek and ran to the bedroom with Simon following close behind.

⤟⤟

Richard walked out onto the street wishing he could have a drink, but, in the absence of alcohol, smoked two cigarettes in rapid succession. Very soon he would be a father and the prospect was awe inspiring. For weeks now, he'd been imagining himself on a river bank teaching his son to fish; god knows why, he'd never held a fishing rod in his life. At other times, he was pushing a swing on which his daughter sailed higher and higher, squealing in delight, dark curls flying in the wind. He was about to become responsible for another human being, and the beauty and weight of it brought him once again close to tears. Grinding the remains of his cigarette onto the pavement, he went back into the hospital lobby and up the stairs to the labour ward.

'Ah! Mr Linton,' the sister said. 'Things are moving much faster now. We've transferred your wife to the delivery room. Would you like to put on a gown and come in? Remember what I told you about how the gas and air works?'

Richard washed his hands, donned the gown and followed her along the corridor, past another delivery room, from which blood-curdling screams echoed through a closed door. Zoë, by contrast, was quiet. She was propped up on pillows, her knees drawn up and her pale face beaded with sweat.

'How is it?' he asked, feeling totally useless.

'Ghastly,' she said between breaths. 'I am never having another one. Never, ever, in my whole life.'

'No, darling,' he said, grabbing her hand. 'Of course not, one's enough for . . .'

But she was panting furiously now and pointing to the cylinder by the bed. Richard grabbed the mask, put the elastic over her head and switched on the supply.

Zoë inhaled deeply and seemed to relax a little.

'Let's have a look at how we're doing,' the sister said, lifting the green cloth covering the lower half of Zoë's body. 'Oh, that's much better, Mrs Linton, you're dilating nicely now. Big breaths, that's right, lovely big breaths, you're doing really well.'

Zoë let out a low grinding howl that made Richard shiver. He put a hand on her shoulder.

'Don't touch me,' she yelled. 'Don't anybody touch me.'

He leapt back in shock, looking at the sister for help.

'Don't take it personally,' the sister said. 'Her whole body is acutely sensitive. It's quite common. She really is doing wonderfully well. I don't think it's going to be long now; after all that hanging about, she's dilating very quickly. Doctor's on his way.'

Richard tried to take deep breaths in time with Zoë; it felt like an act of solidarity, as well as helping him to calm down. Everything he had ever done seemed remote and superficial compared with this. This is what it was all about – the great unending cycle of life and death, a cycle that only love could make worthwhile. He wanted to hold Zoë and tell her how much he loved her; how desperately sorry he was for his moods, his ambition, his absences, everything he had ever done wrong. In this moment, with her face crimson and scrunched into a grimace, she was more beautiful to him than when he first saw her.

The curtains were flicked aside and a middle-aged doctor appeared. 'Nearly there, Mrs Linton? Good. Let's have a look, please, sister.' He positioned a stool between Zoë's legs and sat down.

'Is she okay?' Richard asked.

The doctor looked him up and down. 'You're the husband, presumably? Well, your wife is doing splendidly, nearly there. If you're sure you want to stay, just keep quiet and out of the way, and if you're going to throw up or faint, do it outside.'

'I'm staying,' Richard said, feeling new strength flow into his body. 'I'm definitely staying.'

'I want to push,' Zoë yelled suddenly.

'Not yet,' the sister said. 'Just pant, big breaths and then pant.'

Zoë breathed and panted, breathed and panted, groaned and growled. And Richard ground his teeth and sank his nails into the palms of his hands.

'Next contraction, you can push,' the doctor said, looking up over the top of his glasses from his seat between Zoë's legs. 'We're coming along nicely.'

As the next contraction gripped her, Zoë let out a low, animal-like roar and grabbed Richard's hand. She looked about to explode with the effort of pushing, and the strength with which she crushed his fingers startled him.

'Good, well done,' said the doctor. 'I can see the head.'

The sister beckoned to Richard. 'Want to come and see your baby's head?'

Standing behind the doctor at the end of the delivery table, Richard's skin prickled with goosebumps and a great lump swelled in his throat at the sight of the dark, slimy bulge of the baby's head. 'Oh my god, Zoë,' he said, 'I can see her, I can see her head. She's got dark hair. It's incredible.'

'Push hard now, Mrs Linton, hard as you can.'

Zoë roared again.

'Splendid, we've got the head now,' the doctor said. 'Well done. Same again next contraction and we'll have the shoulders.'

Richard caught a glimpse of the back of the tiny head, with its moist swirls of hair, cradled in the doctor's hands. He was weak with emotion.

'Right, here we go,' the sister said. 'Give us another big push now, there's a good girl.'

And, as Zoë ground her teeth, tears sprang into Richard's eyes. With a swooshing noise, the tiny body slipped out of the impossibly small gap and Zoë let out a cry of shock and relief.

'You have a son,' the doctor said. 'Congratulations.'

His view obstructed by the nurse and the doctor, Richard went to Zoë's side, took her hand and kissed her. 'You were right all the time, Zoë; we've got a son.' He knew he would always remember this moment – the most dramatic, thrilling experience of his life – and he felt incredibly grateful for being able to share it with her. He picked up the flannel that lay on the bedside table, rinsed it under the tap and began to wipe the sweat from Zoë's face. 'You were wonderful,' he said, kissing her tenderly again. 'So brave. I'm so proud of you.'

On the other side of the room, the sister had weighed the baby and was wrapping him in a small white blanket.

'Is he all right?' Zoë asked.

The doctor looked up. 'Perfectly,' he said. 'All the right bits and pieces in all the right places.'

But while the words were reassuring there was something about his tone that struck alarm in Richard.

'What is it?' he asked. 'What's wrong with him?' For the second time that night he thought he might faint and he knew absolutely that, for some reason, the extraordinary peak of joy had passed.

The sister handed the white bundle to Zoë, giving Richard a nervous sideways smile.

'What is it?' Richard demanded again, and the doctor turned away.

Behind him, Richard heard Zoë gasp. As he turned back to her, he saw the tiny perfect face, its darkness a stark contrast against white linen. And, in that moment, he knew this child had nothing at all to do with him.

SIXTEEN

The Wheatbelt, Western Australia – May 1969

'This is lovely, Justine,' Mrs Fitzgerald said, holding up the apron Justine had made with her guidance. 'I think we can move on to something a bit more interesting now. What do you think about a dress – a very simple one, of course, to begin with? Perhaps without sleeves, they're always so hard to set.'

'Would I really be able to make a dress?' Justine asked.

'Yes, you can learn to make all sorts of different clothes for yourself. You're very good with a needle; I don't think you'll find it hard.'

Praise had been a new experience for Justine, who was accustomed to the petty cruelties, punishments and constant disparagement of the convent. Life on the farm was very different and a whole lot better.

'I do miss the other children sometimes, though,' she had confided to Gladys once. 'I wonder what they're doing.'

'Well, you're a lot better off here with Miss Gwen,' Gladys said. 'So don't you go saying nothing about it. She's very fond of you.'

Justine didn't tell Mrs Fitzgerald anything about it; nor did she tell her that she also missed the regular prayers in the chapel, times that had been like little oases each day. But then, she didn't need those intervals here because although she worked hard, she wasn't bullied. The legacy of harsh treatment had not disappeared overnight, but, as the weeks turned to months, she had learned to trust Mrs Fitzgerald's kindness. Even so, she still thought daily about her box, and fell asleep at night wondering how she could get it back, and how, one day soon, she might find her way back home.

More immediate and disturbing, though, was her growing fear of Mr Fitzgerald. Sometimes the way he looked at Justine made her think he was angry with her, but there was something else about him. He made her feel ashamed. Shame was a familiar feeling, the nuns could ignite it with a word or a glance, but this was different; more intense and threatening. The maleness of life on the farm was alien to her, and Malcolm Fitzgerald and his right-hand man, Greg, terrified her.

'You stay outta his way, girl,' Gladys told her. 'He's trouble. Don't look him in the eye, and don't say nothin'.'

One morning, on her way to the kitchen, Justine heard Mr Fitzgerald's raised voice echoing out across the yard and the crash of shattering china; there were a few seconds of silence and then she saw him stride out of the kitchen, yelling something back over his shoulder. As he headed off to the barn, she darted over to the kitchen door. The floor was littered with broken crockery, and Gladys was leaning against the sink, sobbing quietly, holding the side of her face, on which a dark red mark was spreading rapidly.

'Would you make some tea, please, Justine?' Mrs Fitzgerald said, rinsing out a cloth and making it into a cold compress. 'And then clear up this mess.'

Justine did as she was told and, as she tipped the last shards of china into the bin, she noticed that Mrs Fitzgerald also had tears running down her face. She smiled weakly at Justine and thanked her, and nothing was said about what had happened.

'I don't know why she bothers with him,' Gladys muttered later when she and Justine were alone in the kitchen again. 'Miss Gwen, she's way too good for the likes of him. This is her place and he's just usin' her; he don't got nothing of his own. Her father left her the farm. He'd turn in his grave if he could see how that man treats her.'

Justine sipped her tea and resolved to stay further away from him than ever. This was to prove more difficult than she imagined.

The first time it happened was when Mrs Fitzgerald went to Perth to visit her mother. She was going to be away for a week and promised to bring back some new clothes for Justine, who had grown in the months she'd been at the farm. Autumn was cooling the air; at dawn, a white mist hovered over the fields, and the evenings were closing in. On the first night of Mrs Fitzgerald's absence, Justine heard her husband and some of the men laughing and talking. Their voices rang out across the patch of scrub that separated her room from the rest of the house. Her hands were sore from scrubbing and doing the laundry, but she was wide awake. Mrs Fitzgerald had been encouraging her to read and had given her some of the books she had read as a girl. More and more, Justine was learning to immerse herself in other worlds, in the adventures of children living lives very different from her own. Most nights, she would sit reading in bed by the light of the kerosene lamp. Tonight, lost in Canada with *Anne of Green Gables*, she was only half aware of the sound of the men leaving for the bunk house and of the approach of heavy footsteps, until her door was thrown open. Mal Fitzgerald stood in the doorway, his face flushed crimson, matted dark hair falling forward into his eyes. The look on his face made Justine's skin crawl.

'Burning my kero, I see,' he said, steadying himself against the door jamb. 'Light the lamp for me, did you?' And he stepped inside and kicked the door closed behind him.

Justine drew up her knees and dragged the blanket up to her chin, her heart pounding so hard she was sure he must be able to hear it. Was he angry about the lamp? She opened her mouth to apologise, but fear trapped the words in her throat as he lurched forward, tripped on the rug and staggered to the bed.

'Old Uncle Mal's come to see you,' he said, pushing his face so close to hers that Justine could see the big pores on his nose, smell the whisky on his stale breath.

He laughed then and slapped his hand on his knee, and in the next instant he grasped her blanket and pulled it away.

Justine clasped her arms around herself and cowered back against the wall.

'Don't be shy,' he said, leering at her, grabbing her arms.

Stripped of her protective blanket, knees drawn up to her chest, Justine froze in terror.

She was wearing the nightdress she'd had at the convent, and he grabbed at the neck; old and thin from much washing, it ripped easily in his hands. She opened her mouth to scream but he smothered it with his hand.

'Shut your mouth. This is between you and me. Our secret. Understand?'

Justine's eyes widened and she nodded, her scalp prickling with fear, as he took away his hand.

'You want it, don't you, slut,' he hissed in her face, and he then thrust his hand, rough as sandpaper, inside her nightdress, squeezing the small buds of her breasts.

Justine gasped and clawed at his hand but he laughed at her feeble effort and gripped her arms again, his fingers sinking painfully into her flesh.

'Like a fight, do you?' He shook her so violently that her head cracked painfully against the wall. 'Fight and you get hurt. Or,' he paused, running his tongue over lips cracked dry by the sun, 'we can just have a bit of fun.'

Slowly he released her arms, and Justine pressed herself back against the wall, the iron rail of the bedstead digging into her back. Breathing fast, he began to unbuckle his belt and she felt something like relief that he was going to beat her. The strap, the cane, she was used to those. But, instead of dragging the belt from its loops, he unbuttoned his trousers and fumbled with his underpants releasing a huge red and purple thing that bore no resemblance to anything Justine had ever seen on the small boys back home.

She twisted away, but he grabbed her hand and put it on the big throbbing thing, and started moving her hand up and down. He groaned and closed his eyes. She thought he was going to faint but suddenly he let go of her hand, dragged up the hem of her nightdress, and thrust his fingers between her legs so that she cried out and tried to pull away.

'Oh, no you don't,' he said, and, dragging her back, he pushed her face down into his lap. 'Now, I'm going to teach you a trick; something very useful. Something much more useful than anything you'll learn in a book.' And, with one hand gripping her neck he took the great purple thing in his other hand and forced it into her mouth.

⁓

'But you can't just leave her there in the hospital,' Julia said, handing Richard a large brandy. 'Do you really mean you haven't made any contact with her since the baby was born? That's two days; she must be feeling terrible.' They were in the Branston family's suite at the Belgravia hotel, at which Julia had arrived a couple of hours earlier.

Richard took a swing of his drink. 'I expect she is.'

'Richard, for heavens sake! Poor Zoë. When she was in labour, you were blubbing about how brave she was and how much you loved her. And what do you expect *me* to do about it?'

'Help me?' he said, and the pain of his expression made Julia shiver as though someone had walked over her grave.

'How?'

He shook his head. 'I've no idea. I just don't want to be alone.'

'But you're happy to leave Zoë alone, in a hospital where, presumably, every member of the staff and every patient disapproves of her, and knows she's been abandoned?'

Richard shrugged. 'I'm not proud of it but I'm human, for god's sake. What am I supposed to do? Pretend the baby's mine and hope no one notices that he's black?'

'Is he very black?'

'Black enough. Does it matter?'

'Well, I don't know. But you're still married to her; you have to do something to help her. They'll discharge her and you have to get her home. She must be worried sick.'

Richard downed the remains of his drink in one gulp. 'It's not my responsibility.'

'The baby isn't. But Zoë's your wife and –'

'She's only my wife *because* of the baby. I married her because she was pregnant. Remember?'

'But you *did* marry her, and said you loved her, and she certainly loves you.'

'In that case, why . . .'

Julia held up her hands. 'I don't know *why*, Richard. I don't *want* to know. It's your marriage, and you weren't the most delightful companion around that time. Whatever happened, my guess is that it was a mistake, an accident, a one-off thing.'

'That's what she said about the pill,' Richard said bitterly. 'It was an accident, a mistake.'

'Well, whatever it was, we have to do something now,' Julia said, eyeing the glass that Richard was refilling. 'I mean, I know this is dreadful for you but you can't just abandon her. Imagine how she must feel. I certainly can't abandon her.'

'Then go and see her, Jules, please. I can't go, not yet. I can't even walk into that hospital. And you're right, I can't just leave her there on her own.'

⌒⌒⌒

'You must persevere, Mrs Linton,' the nurse said disapprovingly. 'Try again and I'll be back shortly.'

Zoë stared down into her son's eyes. 'I'm sorry,' she whispered. 'I'm so sorry.'

He blinked and stared up at her, and again she attempted to push her nipple into his mouth. This time his jaws locked on and he began to suck, and she leaned back against the pillow, gritting her teeth at the pain but relieved to have succeeded at last. No one had warned her that breastfeeding would be so painful; not just the soreness of her nipples but the intense waves of pain those first few sucks caused her. The antenatal classes made it seem easy; the best nourishment for the baby, convenient, hygienic and it would help her get her figure back. There was nothing about the pain or about the fact he might not want to suck. That morning, the woman in the next bed, who had just had her third baby, had told her that it could actually get even worse.

'The nurses'll tell you it gets easier,' she'd said. 'But it doesn't, especially if your nipples crack. That's real agony.'

Zoë closed her eyes and tears, always close to the surface, squeezed between her lids. She hadn't seen or heard from Richard since he marched out of the delivery room; she hadn't heard from anyone. The telephone trolley was in great demand as it served three wards, and on the few occasions she had been able to call home from it, the phone rang out. Once she called the Television Centre and asked for Richard but someone else answered his extension.

'He's taken a few days' holiday,' the man said. 'His wife's having a baby. Give me your name and I'll leave a message on his desk.'

Zoë hung up.

She had never felt so entirely alone, or so utterly despised and disapproved of. It was bad enough knowing that the story of the white couple with the black baby had spread through the entire hospital, but she had become a sideshow. Several times a day, nurses or doctors from other wards would wander in, check her name on the chart, peer into the crib, smile awkwardly and disappear. With the exception of the woman in the next bed, the other patients in the ward had ignored her. When their visitors arrived, though, they would nod in her direction and whisper, and the visitors cast disapproving glances in her direction as they left. A couple of the ward nurses regularly demonstrated their disapproval by asking frequently and loudly, when her husband would be coming in. Sometimes they swapped the word 'husband' for 'Daddy'.

'No sign of your husband again today?' one had asked this morning. 'Got a lot on, I suppose. Expecting him this afternoon, are we?'

But no one had been to see her, or even left a message. Had Richard told anyone – Julia, his parents, their friends? Zoë was painfully aware of her own lack of friends. Sandy had taken a job with a publisher in Chicago and Jane was in Perth. Zoë's life was built around Richard; he had always been more than enough for her.

Zoë moved the baby to her other side. He took it promptly this time, sending daggers of pain deep into her breast and making her gasp for breath. She watched in fascination as his mouth worked the nipple, sucking furiously, resting, and then sucking again. Love flooded through her in great waves. Back when she thought Richard had just gone outside to get over the shock and she had waited fearfully for his return, she hadn't been able to take her eyes off the miracle of this tiny human being. Their eyes had met in a connection more profound and intimate than any she had ever known. He was so much like Harry; the broad forehead, the shape of his chin, something about his eyes. Looking into his face, tracing his full lips with her finger, stroking the whorls of dark hair, Zoë couldn't think of him as anything other than the baby she had wanted and waited for.

His lids grew heavy as he finished feeding, and she lifted him to rest against her shoulder, gently rubbing his back until he delivered a sleepy burp. Holding him against her face, she sniffed his perfect baby smell, kissed him and laid him in his crib, resting her hand on his back.

What would she do if Richard left her? That morning, the registrar had arrived to register the birth and Zoë hadn't known what to do. Should she name the baby as they had planned? Should she put Harry or Richard as the father?

'We haven't decided what to call him yet,' she'd told the registrar, and the woman promised to come back in a couple of days, before she was discharged. A couple of days; what difference would that make? Richard was gone and she didn't even know if she had a home.

A buzzer signalled the start of visiting time and the doors swished open. Zoë closed her eyes and feigned sleep as the visitors' feet squeaked and thudded across the linoleum. There was the murmur of voices, shrieks of delight, cellophane rustling around bouquets, small children grizzling. The chairs around her bed were, she was sure, the only empty ones on the ward.

A hand touched her arm, and her eyes flew open.

'Hi there, Zoë, remember us?' Gloria asked. 'The CR group from hell?'

Zoë dragged herself upright. Gloria grinned, kissed her own hand and pressed it to Zoë's cheek.

Behind her, her long fair plait over one shoulder and clutching a package wrapped in yellow tissue, was Claire.

'Yes, oh yes,' Zoë said. 'Of course I remember.' Her stomach knotted. She had longed for someone to confide in but not these weird almost-strangers.

'Don't look so horrified, hon, we're not really that bad. Look, we bought a present for the baby.'

'Yellow,' Claire said, putting the package on the bed, 'because we didn't know if you'd had a boy or a girl.'

Zoë took the package. 'A boy. This is really nice of you . . .' she began. The unexpected act of kindness unleashed a dam, and a huge sob shook her body and tears streamed down her face.

'Hey there,' Gloria said, sinking into a low chair and taking her hand. 'We've come to celebrate. Is this day three?' She looked up at Claire. 'Day three is when most people get the blues, I think.'

'How did you find me?' Zoë sobbed.

'Your neighbour,' Claire said, perching on the end of the bed. 'Mrs Driscoll. Richard gave us your address when he came to see us. So, the next day I called round but there was no one there. I met Mrs Driscoll on the stairs and she said you'd gone to hospital.'

'And then, this morning, Richard was supposed to come interview us,' Gloria continued. 'But some other guy, Mark – no – Martin, turned up instead. He said Richard took some time off because of the baby but he didn't seem to know much. So we rang two or three hospitals until we found you. Zoë, honey, what *is* the matter – you want us to go away?'

Zoë shook her head and clung to Gloria's hand, thankful now for human contact that wasn't disapproving.

'Should we phone Richard for you?' Claire asked. 'Or shall I get a nurse?'

'No. Stay; please, stay. I don't know where Richard is. He walked out two days ago, after . . . well, after the baby was born.'

'Walked out?'

'From the delivery room. Look,' she said, pointing across to the crib. 'Look at him.'

'A boy,' Claire said, walking around to the other side of the bed. 'Lucky you.' She stopped suddenly, looking down at the sleeping baby. 'Oh, oh, I see . . .'

'Jeezus!' Gloria let out a low whistle and pulled the curtains around the bed. 'Now it makes sense. Did you know?'

'No. It was only the one time . . . I was on the pill but I messed it up, missed some days.'

'He's a beautiful baby,' Claire said. 'His eyes are open. May I pick him up?'

'He's perfectly wonderful, isn't he?' Zoë asked feeling, through her tears, a joy and pride she had so far been unable to share. 'He's absolutely perfect. I love him so much.'

'He sure is the sweetest thing,' Gloria said, stroking his tiny hand. 'What's his name?'

'We were going to call him Daniel.'

'Daniel. Hello, Daniel; hello, beautiful boy.'

'Richard just left when he saw him and . . . I mean, I know it's terrible and he must be devastated, but I'm so scared and I don't know what to do.'

Gloria put a hand on Zoë's arm. 'We're here now, we can help you. Do you want us to find the baby's father?'

'No. He got married at Christmas and moved to Glasgow. I can't tell him, I just can't.'

Gloria and Claire exchanged a look. 'Well, it shouldn't be hard to find Richard,' Gloria said.

'He'll probably throw me out,' Zoë said. 'I wouldn't blame him. But I'll have nowhere to go.' She flinched at a movement in the curtains, dreading the arrival of another disapproving nurse or doctor.

'Where's the gap in the curtain? How do I get in?' someone said, and Zoë's heart leapt with joy and relief at the sound of the familiar voice.

Julia's face appeared between the curtains and she pushed them open, glancing around at the other women. 'Ah!' she said. 'It seems you've already got plenty of visitors.'

144

SEVENTEEN

Paris – October 1969

It occurred to Julia, as she crossed the Pont Neuf to the Left Bank, that this was exactly the same place she had walked with Simon the night she had abandoned caution and gone back with him to his room. Today, the river was sparkling in the brilliant sunshine, gulls swooped and circled, and *vedettes* crammed with tourists cruised back and forth. On the deck of a luxurious launch, two women, designer clad in navy and white, and wearing huge sunglasses, relaxed in deckchairs. Smaller craft ducked and weaved around the launch like mosquitoes, and Julia could see through the windows of the bridge cabin three men in *faux* naval attire, sipping champagne as one steered. She remembered the boat she'd seen that night with Simon, the colourful lights, the glamorous women, the romantic music drifting up from the deck. It had symbolised everything she had wanted for herself, everything she had been brought up to expect: money, status, glamour and the leisure to enjoy it all. The disappointing thing was that now that she had it all, it didn't seem such an attractive package.

Julia had never understood why Simon had chosen her to be his wife. She was unlike the women in the Branston circle of friends: the daughters of the aristocracy of the nouveau riche, glamorous, racy jet-setters; or the daughters of the real aristocracy, who bought their clothes at designers' private showings, flitted from one ball to another, and went hunting or sailing at weekends. They came from a gilt-edged world very different from Julia's tweedy, Home Counties snobbery. And she was acutely aware that she was not glamorous, and only appeared sophisticated alongside someone like Zoë, who had been so easily impressed by her familiarity with London and her semblance of sophistication. It had always seemed remarkably unfair that Richard was the good-looking one, while she had inherited her father's height and her mother's pale freckled skin, pear-shaped body and tendency to put on weight. What she saw, every time she looked in the mirror, was a pale woman, with fine, mousey hair, and a really big bum.

'You look rather like a Cornish pasty,' a school prefect had commented loudly and haughtily when Julia was twelve.

The name stuck, and for the rest of her schooldays she was known as 'Pasty' by her friends as well as her enemies. It had been a huge triumph for Julia that she had managed to get her wedding dress absolutely right. These days, although her clothes no longer closely resembled her mother's, they were far from high fashion, which was for women of a very different shape. Julia was not fat but neither was she small and fine-boned like Zoë, and her hips were larger than designers decreed they should be in relation to her shoulders and bust. The calm authority she had affected in the fitting room of the John Lewis bridal department was a facade. Inwardly, she had been panicking that she was going to look old fashioned and dowdy. But she had gone to her wedding looking exactly as she had hoped to look and knowing that, for once in her life, she looked her absolute best. Simon, of course, always looked good. Tall, slim and with mesmerising blue eyes, he was always immaculately and expensively dressed, and oozed style and confidence. So, Julia wondered constantly, why me?

'You're nice and normal, old girl,' he'd said once. 'And jolly pretty too, of course. You make me feel safe, very comfortable. And you're awfully good in bed.'

It wasn't the answer Julia had hoped for but it was honest and believable, and therefore rather comforting. But in those first weeks in Paris and then back in London before the wedding, when she was soaking up the excitement of it all, Julia had never anticipated that within months she would be feeling entirely unsuited to the life she had chosen. Nor could she have expected that she would be nursing this restless anger, which simmered beneath the surface and which she had to struggle so hard to control.

Glancing at her watch, she crossed the street at the fountain and hurried on, up the Boulvard St Michel, past the Sorbonne and into a narrow side street of shops, cafés and restaurants, very different from the sort of places she visited with Simon and his friends. She had grown to love Paris. It was just her life there that was out of sync; a sanitised and superficial one in which she felt like a dowdy bird kept in a luxurious cage by kindly owners.

'It's not Simon,' she'd explained recently to Hilary, with whom she had developed a close friendship, 'although he can be really irritating. Sometimes I think he's never really grown up. It's the whole hotel life thing; the entertaining, the being nice to people, making small talk and just being the wife of a Branston. I feel as though I'm acting all the time.'

'You'll find ways of coping,' Hilary had said. 'At heart I am definitely not a vicar's wife, but I've learned to do it in my own way and have a life of my own as well.'

And it was in that other life, to which Hilary had introduced her a few months earlier, that Julia too was finding satisfaction.

Reaching the end of the street, she turned into a narrow doorway and made her way up the stairs, her enthusiasm rising as the babble of voices and the smoke of Gitanes floated out of a half-open door.

The *Jeunes Femmes* met in a couple of attic rooms above a noisy restaurant, surprisingly close to the rather more elegant street in which Julia had lived with the Le Bons. The rooms were sparsely furnished, and lit by skylights and a large window, from which glimpses of the Luxembourg Gardens appeared beyond the chaotic jumble of rooftops.

'It was started by a group of Protestant women after the war,' Hilary had explained. 'It's a place where women can talk about the things that concern them: marriage, birth control and so on. It's rather like those consciousness raising groups that are starting in America, except that *Jeunes Femmes* have been doing it for a couple of decades. There are all sorts of dilemmas for women in a Catholic country if they aren't Catholics, and often even if they are.'

At the time Julia had thought it sounded pretty dull and worthy, but she had asked Hilary for suggestions about what she could do with herself, and so she had gone along. Since then, she had never looked back.

Now, months later, as she pushed open the door, the room was buzzing with the conversation of women dressed, as usual, largely in black, deep crimson or bottle green. There were clouds of cigarette smoke, and much jangling of silver bangles and long strings of beads. There were black berets worn at rakish angles, un-coiffed hair dyed a vivid red, and a mix of accents and languages.

Julia headed for one of the pots of very strong coffee on a side table, poured some into a tiny cup, lit a cigarette and looked around to see who was there. No sign of Hilary yet but, from the other side of the room, Minette, her red hair wound into an untidy knot on top of her head, was beckoning to her. Just a few months ago, Minette had taken up a lectureship in literature at the Sorbonne, much to the dismay of her parents, a count and countess still trying to live in the style of pre-war aristocracy. They had put considerable effort into identifying a suitably aristocratic husband for her, only to have their plans dismissed with disdain. They would, Julia suspected, have been even more shocked had they met Minette's lover, Therese; a fierce, feminist poet considerably older than Minette and said once to have had a fleeting affair with Simone de Beauvoir.

This was just part of what Julia loved about the *Jeunes Femmes*; this exotic mix of intelligent, often brilliant, women from varied backgrounds who cared passionately about what they were doing. Elbowing her way past an interior designer from Galleries Lafayette, several more students from the Sorbonne, a teacher from the English school, and a secretary from the US Embassy, she stopped to greet a couple of young mothers with whom she was working on a campaign for the liberalisation of abortion and contraception. Julia no longer just turned up at the fortnightly meetings, but volunteered her time in the adjacent office with such regularity that Simon was getting increasingly curious about what she was doing when he popped up from his office and found their apartment empty.

On her first visit, Julia had looked around the room and then back at Hilary in her neat turquoise suit and elegantly styled hair, and been confused by the contrast. It had seemed such a bizarre setting for the wife of an English clergyman, but since then, Julia had discovered so many other unlikely women there.

'It's not what you expected, is it?' Hilary had asked her that first day.

'Well . . . no, not really,' she had hesitated. 'Does Eric know you come here?'

'Of course he does. It was Eric who told me about *Jeunes Femmes* in the first place,' Hilary said. 'There's a political radical hiding behind that very conventional facade, you know. You'll hear it if you listen carefully to some of his sermons.'

'My father always said that the church has no place getting involved in politics,' Julia said.

Hilary smiled. 'A lot of people say that but I wonder if they really think about what they're saying.'

'What do you mean?'

'Religion is, or should be, about what we believe, what we value and how we live, so I can't really see how it can be separated from politics. The two are inextricably bound together, for better and for worse.'

It hadn't taken long for Julia to realise that on that first day she had dipped her toe into the waters of something for which she had unconsciously been searching. In addition to her pragmatic approach to love, she had learned from Tom the importance of having something to believe in. As they had watched the street battles together, as she had listened to his arguments about justice and freedom, a seed had been sown; a seed that had, since then, been struggling to grow. Now Hilary had introduced her to a group of women who had fired her own interests and passions. But the discovery also confronted her with the contradiction between what she was learning and the reality of her marriage to Simon. It had brought her face to face too, with her own part in what had happened in the dreadful days that followed the birth of Zoë's baby, a part that she now considered shameful.

'We need to get her out of the way,' Ralph had said. 'You'll have to divorce her, shouldn't be a problem in view of the bast . . . the child. But we don't want a fuss. You need to be able to get on with your work, have a new start and all that. How much do you think she'd take?'

The whole thing had smacked of the landed gentry paying off the chambermaid who had got into trouble with the eldest son. Caught between her brother and the sister-in-law who had become her friend, Julia had struggled with conflicting loyalties. She had gone to the hospital hoping to find a way to make things better, but her good intentions evaporated when she was confronted with the reality of Zoë's baby. In the days before their wedding, she had stood with and between Richard and Zoë as mediator, supporter and confidante, until they finally made it to the registry office. She could not do it again. Richard's anger and hurt had, she realised, become her own, and Zoë's betrayal felt deeply personal. Shocked and deeply embarrassed, Julia had stayed only long enough to reassure Zoë that she would return to collect her when she was discharged.

'And Richard?' Zoë had asked, once again on the verge of tears.

'He'll come and see you when you're back at the flat,' Julia said, unable to bring herself to explain that Richard's pride would not let him return to the hospital to be stared at by nurses, doctors and anyone else who had heard the story. Three days later, she had collected Zoë and Daniel, and escorted them home in a chauffeur-driven Branston car. It was a journey of tense silences punctuated by stilted conversation.

'Richard drew some cash for you from your joint account,' Julia had said, handing Zoë a bulky envelope, once they were back at the flat. 'It'll save you going to the bank. He hasn't drawn anything else and he's taken his name off the account. It's all yours now. And I did some shopping for you, there's food in the fridge and stuff for . . . for the baby.' There was a horrible silence.

'Thanks,' Zoë murmured, 'thanks for bringing me home.'

'Well, I'll leave you to it then,' Julia said, hesitating. 'I . . . er . . . I hope you get on all right. We're at the Branston, of course. Ring if you need anything. Richard'll . . . he'll be over in a couple of days.'

Two weeks later, she had returned with Richard for the terrible final conversation. Julia knew she would never forget the Zoë she saw that day. She was standing by the window, holding the baby against her shoulder, swaying rhythmically to lull him to sleep.

'I see,' she'd said eventually, looking up at them. 'So, you want to move back here, and you want a divorce?'

'Yes,' Richard said, his voice tight with emotion. 'I'll help you, though; money, I mean.'

'Is it because he's black?'

'It's because he's not mine.'

'But if he was white and not yours, would it be different?'

Richard looked around as though seeking a way out. 'I don't know. Possibly. I probably wouldn't have known. You might not have known either.'

'But say you *had* known?'

He shrugged. 'I don't know, Zoë.'

'So, it *is* a race thing.'

'It's a *recognition* thing. Daniel is so *obviously* not mine, had he been white . . . maybe . . . maybe I would have thought I could handle the reactions, maybe I could have pretended he was mine and made it work, but . . .' He shrugged and turned away.

'You're worried about what people will think when they look at you and me and then at Daniel?'

Julia saw the agony of conflicting emotions flickering across Richard's face.

'I suppose so.'

'Because he's black. So much for your . . .'

'It's because he's so obviously *not mine*,' Richard snapped. 'And because every time I look at him, I will be reminded about you and Harry and . . . I just don't think I can live with that.'

There was a silence heavy with anger and resentment.

'We can agree to a figure,' Richard said eventually. 'You'll have a lump sum and we can get a divorce. You can divorce me, if you think that's easier. Then we'll both have the freedom to start again.'

'Only you'll have more freedom than me,' Zoë said.

'For heaven's sake, Zoë,' Julia had cut in at that point. 'This is *your* responsibility, yours and Harry's. This is not about race, it's about Daniel not being Richard's baby. What do you expect?'

To Julia it seemed that Zoë swung back and forth between being a victim and an unreasonable persecutor.

Zoë stood with her back to them, gazing out the window for what seemed an eternity but was probably less than a minute.

'You're right, of course,' she said eventually. 'You have every right to feel as you do. This is my responsibility. I'll be gone by the end of the month.'

'And the divorce?' Richard asked.

'Just tell me what I have to sign.'

'We may have to go to court. Work out the grounds . . .'

'Okay.'

Tension seemed to flow visibly out of Richard's body. 'So there's just the money to arrange, then,' he said.

Zoë shook her head. 'I don't want your money; or rather, your father's money.'

Richard, embarrassed, looked away. 'But how will you manage?'

The baby was fidgeting now, sucking at his tiny fist. Zoë pressed her face against his head to comfort him and crossed the room to the door. In that moment, Julia saw that she was no longer the tearstained, clinging wreck she had been in the hospital. Ice had formed in her heart and made her unreachable.

'That's none of your business,' she said quietly. 'You've made it clear that what I do and how I care for Daniel is nothing to do with you. Could you go now, please – both of you. I need to feed my baby.'

Zoë had nothing; no income and nowhere to go, but she had Daniel, and – most surprising of all, in the circumstances – she appeared to have reclaimed her pride. Somehow, this seemed to give her the upper hand.

Since then Julia's involvement with the *Jeunes Femmes* had

helped her to analyse what had happened and to name her own feelings of distaste, and she found it impossible to justify her role in her family's efforts to get rid of Zoë. It hung heavily on her conscience.

'Ah!' Minette cried, some minutes into their conversation, gesturing towards the door. 'It is Hilary at last, so very late, and she is *distrait*? It is most unlike her, *n'est ce pas*, Julia?' In the doorway, Hilary was peering anxiously around the room. 'She is looking for you, I think.'

Julia waved and turned back to Minette. 'She does look a bit distraught. I'll go and see what's wrong.'

Relief crossed Hilary's face when she saw Julia heading towards her, and she reached for her hand and drew her into the passage away from the noise.

'Look, I shouldn't have come. It's Eric; he's not at all well but he won't let me call the doctor. He's so stubborn. Why do men have to think it's brave not to see a doctor?' She brushed a strand of hair back from her face. 'Sorry, I'm worried and cross. I was going to give the meeting a miss this afternoon but he insisted that he wanted to be left alone. And now I'm here and I really think I should be back there.'

'Would you like me to come with you?' Julia asked.

'Miss the meeting?'

'Yes, if it would help.'

Hilary hesitated. 'Well, if you really don't mind. He always loves seeing you. It might cheer him up.'

Julia steered her towards a table. 'Okay, Simon's got a business dinner this evening. My time's my own.'

'Lucky you. If I have to be nice to one more parishioner this week, I may have to kill myself or them. I know I'm supposed to be the one who's solved the problem of loving a man but hating his job, but I don't seem to be handling it particularly well at the moment.'

Julia collected her bag from the room and they made their way down the stairs.

'I feel awful dragging you away like this,' Hilary said.

'You're not dragging me away, I offered. But I think you need to calm down a bit, Hil. Let's go and get a coffee and sit quietly for a bit, and then we'll get a taxi back to your place.'

In a café further along the street, Julia ordered coffee and two cognacs. 'We need it,' she said. 'At least, you do.'

Hilary sighed. 'I have this horrible habit of catastrophising,' she said. 'Perhaps it's because Eric is so much older than me. If he's the slightest bit off colour, I think he's going to die, and, honestly, I can't imagine how I'd cope without him. It's a complete contradiction, really. All the things we talk about in the meetings, all the changes that we want for women, and here I am – an anachronism; incapable of managing if anything happened to him.'

'But you love him,' Julia said. 'I don't see how anything changes that. And you're so lucky that Eric understands what we're doing. He's not like Simon, who's totally opposed to anything that rocks his own boat.'

'Mmm. Well, love does complicate it all. It makes you a part of each other and the thought of losing the other person is very frightening. But you know all that; I'm sure you feel exactly the same about Simon, and you haven't been together long. Eric and I have been together since I was eighteen.'

'You're not going to lose him yet,' Julia said, as the waiter put their drinks on the table. 'He's probably just got some little bug that's making him feel crotchety.' She picked up her glass, swirling the cognac and holding it up to the light. 'Come on, drink up, it'll help you relax, and then we'll get a taxi back to your place. Cheers.'

Hilary nodded. 'You're right, of course. You've become a wonderful friend, Julia. It helps so much that you understand.'

Julia smiled and sipped her drink. She was very fond of Simon – they had fun together and lots of playful sex – but Hilary was talking about a profound emotional connection that she suspected she would never have with Simon. Their marriage depended on her being someone she'd outgrown, and it stretched in front of her like a life sentence. That, she thought, was a worrying way for someone who had been married less than a year to feel.

EIGHTEEN

The Wheatbelt – October 1969

It was while she was cleaning Mr Fitzgerald's office that Justine saw the map. He had left that morning on farm business and she'd been told to clean up but not to touch anything on the desk. The relief of knowing he'd be gone for a few days was huge. The worst times were when Mrs Fitzgerald herself was away, but even when she was home he still turned up in Justine's room after his wife was asleep; just as he had done last night, drunk and more brutal than ever.

'Say anything and I'll break your fucking neck,' he'd told her several times. 'You're a dirty boong and nobody will give a tinker's cuss if I kill you. This is your fault and if I don't kill you, then my missus will.'

It was hard for Justine to believe that Gwen Fitzgerald could possibly kill her but, all the same, she was terrified of discovery. And so, for months now, she had grown more and more withdrawn and could no longer look Mrs Fitzgerald in the eye. She slept only fitfully, always on edge in the dark, listening, waiting. She even stopped reading, fearing the lamplight might attract him. The lightness of life here after the convent had degenerated into a bitter darkness and now, more than ever before, she was burdened by shame and sickened by her own wickedness. At the same time, she was unable to understand how what he was doing was her fault or how she could make it stop.

'I don't know what's the matter with you these days,' Mrs Fitzgerald had said that morning. 'You hardly talk, and you walk about all hunched up.'

'Sorry,' Justine mumbled, drawing lines in the sand with the toe of her boot and not looking up.

Mrs Fitzgerald sighed. 'I had such high hopes for you. Well, just give the floor and the windows a good clean, and if you do have to move anything, make sure you put it back exactly where you found it.' She paused so long that Justine actually had to look up at her. 'Are you all right? You don't look too well.'

Justine nodded and turned away, picking up her bucket. Mrs Fitzgerald gave an irritable shake of her head and went out of the office.

Justine had finished the windows and the sills and was about to start wiping down the picture frames, when, looking up quickly, she felt slightly dizzy and had to hold on to the windowsill. Her skin was damp with sweat and there was a throbbing pain in the pit of her stomach. It was while she was standing there, waiting for the dizziness to pass, that she noticed the map pinned to a big board. For a while she just looked at it, wondering, and then, rubbing her hand across her forehead, she walked cautiously across the room to take a closer look.

The only name she recognised was Perth; she'd seen pictures of it, and of the beaches along the coast. And then, as she studied it more closely, she spotted a red dot stuck on the map about an inch to the north-east of Perth and beside it someone had written 'Fitzgerald Property'. Justine traced the line from the red dot back towards the ocean, wondering how far it was.

'What are you doing?' Mrs Fitzgerald asked and Justine nearly jumped out of her skin. 'Trying to find somewhere? You've found the farm – what are you looking for now?'

'The convent.'

Mrs Fitzgerald crossed the room and looked closely at the map, pointing to a cross close to Perth. Justine's heart beat very fast. For the first time in weeks, she looked straight at Mrs Fitzgerald.

'Where do I come from?' she asked, the question bolting from her mouth before she'd thought about it.

Mrs Fitzgerald took a step back and crossed her arms, scanning the map.

'I'm not too sure,' she said, 'but I think it's up here somewhere.' And she pointed to a place near the top. 'This whole area here is called the Pilbara. I think you may have come from somewhere here. Do you remember any names?'

'My mum's name is Norah,' Justine said.

Mrs Fitzgerald smiled, and touched her lightly on the shoulder. 'I mean, place names. The place you lived or somewhere nearby?'

Justine closed her eyes. 'It was red,' she said, 'I can see it. The earth was red, redder than here, there were rocks, but I can't remember what it was called.'

'Yes, well, I think it's up there somewhere. I'm glad you're taking an interest in something at last. When you've finished the dusting, you can start on the floor; it's very dirty just in the well of the desk because he forgets to take off his boots.' And she smiled again and went out to speak to Gladys, who was carrying a bucket of potato peelings over to the chicken pen.

Justine wiped the dust off a frame and looked again at the map. People used maps to find their way. Could she use this one to get back to the convent and then to Norah? She plunged the mop into the bucket and watched the soapy water swirl around it. She would leave before he got back. She would go at night; take food and water, a torch, some matches, a knife and one of her blankets, put them in the cloth bag she'd brought with her from the convent. And she would take the map. It would be stealing but she didn't care. She'd found it and it seemed like a sign.

Feeling hotter than ever, her head hurting as though it were banging inside, she felt something warm and sticky running down her legs. Finding it hard to breathe, she dropped the mop and grasped the door handle. The room was spinning and, as bile rose in her throat, she staggered outside and fell to her knees on the edge of the verandah. She heard Mrs Fitzgerald call out, and saw her running towards her, followed by Gladys. As she sank down into darkness, the last thing she saw was the bucket of potato peelings rolling away from Gladys's feet.

Richard was making a half-hearted attempt to clean up the kitchen when someone hammered on the front door. It was Martin, jacket undone and tie askew.

'We made it. We fucking made it. We're on the shortlist.' And, shoving a bottle of Jack Daniel's into Richard's hand, he drew a crumpled sheet of paper from his pocket and read out the names shortlisted for the Film and Television Producers Documentary Award. Richard took the paper and looked at it, needing to see the words in print. The nominees had been announced in March and the wait for the shortlist had seemed endless.

'I've watched the others; you probably have too,' Martin said. 'I think we could take this one out. Let's get plastered.'

It seemed like a good idea. It still seemed like a good idea three hours later, and even seemed to Richard to be a good idea to carry on drinking after Martin had stumbled out onto the street and hailed a taxi. It was only the next morning, when he woke lying on the window seat and thought he might be dead, that it didn't seem like such a good idea after all.

His neck and shoulders were twisted into a position from which he was frightened to move in case he fell apart. Above him, the lampshade was sliding in and out of focus. He lay there, remembering Zoë sitting on this same seat, months earlier, counting the days to the birth and knitting baby clothes. The morning sunshine flooded through the window and, as he turned his head towards its warmth, he could see her standing by this window on the day back in March when he'd told her they'd been nominated for the award.

'You're so clever, Rich, I'm so proud of you. You'll win, I know you will,' she'd said, crossing the room to kiss him.

'We have to get shortlisted before we think about winning.'

'You will. And I'm going to cheer my head off when they give you the award.'

The memory was so clear, so poignant, that Richard began to cry; big wrenching sobs that made his already aching head pound. Although her reaction had pleased him, he remembered that he'd also felt it would have been worth more if it came from someone who really understood what he was doing. Now, struck down by sudden grief, he hated himself for his intellectual snobbery. In recent months, he had bitterly regretted the precipitate and very final action he had taken when the baby was born. Why hadn't he waited, given himself time to cool down? He knew now that Zoë was the one person he wanted to share his good news with; the one person he wanted beside him at the awards if they won, and even more so if they didn't.

The last six months had been misery. When Julia returned to Paris and he moved back to the flat, he had staggered on from day to day, gritting his teeth and burying himself in his work. For the first time in his life, he was bitterly lonely. Everywhere he turned, he saw, heard or smelt Zoë, and every day he struggled to convert hurt and loneliness into an anger that would drive him and keep every other emotion at bay. But his hangover had pulled out all the stoppers.

Richard tried to make coffee, but his hands shook so violently that coffee and water splattered across the draining board. Were these really his hands? He couldn't even see straight and his eyes felt full of sand. His body must have aged at least twenty years overnight and his mouth bore more resemblance to the bottom of the chicken pen at Bramble Cottage than it did to anything human. He waited gloomily for the percolator to stop bubbling, and when he'd drunk his coffee he decided that a bath might help. Pulling off his clothes, he stood naked and shivering in the bathroom watching the water level rise and remembering Zoë calling him to help her get out of the bath.

Half an hour later, washed and dressed, he was still shivering and although the crying had stopped, he wasn't sure that it was really over. It was almost midday and he considered eating something – a greasy breakfast was supposed to be the antidote to a hangover, but the mere idea of eggs, bacon and sausages made his stomach heave.

Shame was the worst part of it. The loss of Zoë and of the child he'd initially not wanted and then grown to anticipate with fierce excitement was one thing. But his shame, his disgust at himself, was the dark underbelly of his mood.

The moment in which Richard had first seen the baby's face

was engraved on his memory; the harsh bright lights, the smell of blood and antiseptic, the tense and shadowy presence of the doctor and nurse, and the tiny round face of someone else's child. The pain still ripped into his gut whenever he thought of it. He had pulled off the gown, thrown it on the floor, punched open the door of the delivery room and strode out along the corridor, down the stairs and into the street.

Why hadn't he realised what had been going on? Had everyone else known? Sandy? Charlie? That constantly shifting mob of people in the Kilburn house? Had they all been laughing at him? Stupid bastard; too dumb, too obsessed with his work to see what was going on under his nose.

'It was only once, Richard, just one time,' Zoë had insisted when he had finally forced himself to talk to her. 'Just once. It was a stupid thing, it just happened. You were away and I was upset, I had too much to drink . . . it was stupid . . .' Her voice trailed away. 'Like I said – it just happened.'

Was it his own guilt that had made him so self-righteous? Did his own shame make him want to humiliate her, banish her? When he learned she'd registered the baby under the name they had chosen together, he had been filled with a rage so overwhelming that he had thought himself capable of physical violence.

'I picked that name,' he'd shouted, and she had stared at him, tears running down her face.

'I know, and all those months before he was born, that's how I'd thought of him, as Daniel,' she'd sobbed. 'It didn't feel right to change.'

And, by refusing to take the money for which he had had to grovel to his father, she had won the moral high ground that Richard had felt was rightfully his, leaving him floundering in the mire of his own guilty secret.

He understood now that for Zoë and Harry it could have been unpremeditated, a moment that would later have shocked them both. But *he*, Richard, had pursued Lily, spent several nights with her, lied to Martin about his whereabouts, and feasted on those memories for weeks, even months, afterwards. Zoë had certainly done wrong by him, but it was nothing to the wrong he had done her.

Richard studied the mess of the previous night. Then he collected the glasses and poured the remains of the whisky down the sink, vowing to himself that he would clean up his act and stop drinking.

When the tickets for the awards dinner arrived the following week, Richard tucked them into his pocket, walked to the station and took the tube to West Hampstead. It was five days since he'd had a drink and more than six months since he'd seen Zoë, the day he and Julia had asked her to move out. Two weeks later, the keys had turned up in the post, with a note about the electricity bill and the need to fix one of the sitting room windows. He knew she had moved to Delphi Street and as he walked from the station Richard felt his heart lifting with hope that they could forgive each other and start again. He felt confident now that he was capable of coming to terms with the child, who was the real victim of all that had happened; confident that he had it in himself to confess, forgive and accept, that he could be a good husband to Zoë and a good father to her baby, if he could only lay his meddlesome pride to rest.

The door of the house was ajar, and Richard knocked on one of the frosted glass panels and peered inside, his heart beating fast with anticipation. It wasn't going to be easy but there was a chance – a slim one – that Zoë might at least be willing to talk to him.

'Hello,' he called around the door, 'anyone there?'

'Richard?' Gloria said as she reached the door. 'Well, I sure didn't expect to see you here.'

'No,' he said, looking beyond her down the hallway. 'Sorry if it's inconvenient but I wanted to have a word with Zoë.'

'Your friend finished making that program about us yet?' Gloria asked.

'Yes. It's done, the series goes to air next month.'

Gloria nodded, looking him up and down.

'You're out of luck. She's not here. Left this morning for Glasgow.'

'Glasgow! Where Harry . . .'

'Right first time.'

They stared at each other across the threshold, each unwilling to volunteer more information. From an upstairs room came the sound of a baby crying. He raised his eyebrows.

'We have three babies here,' Gloria said with a smile. 'Not quite a cricket team.'

'I see. Has she . . . are they . . .' he faltered.

Gloria paused, looking him up and down again. It was painfully obvious that she despised him. 'You'd have to ask her about that,' she said.

His mind seethed. When would Zoë be back? Did Harry know about Daniel? Did Agnes know? If he could just tell Gloria how he felt and why he was there, would she help him?

But again his pride stopped him. 'Well, perhaps you'd tell her that I . . .'

'I'll let her know you called by,' Gloria said. 'I'm sure she has your number if she wants to call.'

Richard nodded, anticipation replaced by despair. 'Thanks, I really need to speak to her as soon as possible.' He hated his pleading tone.

Gloria put her hand on the door.

'Okay,' he said, 'please don't forget.' As he turned to walk down the path, he heard the door close firmly behind him.

NINETEEN

London – October 1969

Zoë had never been north of London and once the train was out of the suburbs, she put down her book and gazed out of the window, wondering whether the landscape would look very different. She had taken the overnight train and it was satisfying, in a masochistic sort of way, to know that she was in for a horrible time on the dusty moquette upholstery. It might help to erase a smidgen of her shame. She knew she was incredibly lucky. Living in a house with seven women, two other babies and a toddler meant that there was always someone on hand to care for Daniel. But even after five months, she still felt like an outsider, alienated from the discussions about politics and women's rights. She felt the other women were there by choice, while she was there because of the lack of it. She had found a part-time job in an estate agent's office. It was dull after the BBC, and the men there were arrogant and sleazy, but she expected nothing better.

The day that Julia had collected her from the hospital, it had been painfully clear that she was doing so from a sense of responsibility. Their friendship could not survive this. Once alone in the flat that belonged to Richard's parents, Zoë had feared she would soon be homeless. The future was blank and terrifying, and she knew that it was only the enormity of her responsibility for her child that stood between her and a fall into darkness.

By lunchtime the following day, she was even more despairing.

Daniel, unsettled by the move and missing the companionable murmurings of the other babies in the hospital nursery, had refused to settle, and cried on and off all night. Exhausted from lack of sleep, her breasts throbbing from attempts to feed, Zoë sank onto the sofa, the baby clasped against her chest. The two of them fell asleep, to be woken an hour later by a ring at the doorbell. Wearily, she dragged herself off the sofa and, with Daniel, stumbled bleary-eyed to answer it.

'We thought you might need some help,' Claire said.

'Or some company,' Gloria added, following her inside. 'And we brought Marilyn because she's a mother and knows all about this baby stuff.'

They had also brought NapiSan, a white bucket with a lid, nappy liners and some nipple-soothing cream.

'And a cake and champagne,' Gloria said, hauling the bottle from her large cloth bag. 'We're gonna have a little celebration for this gorgeous boy.' She lifted him from Zoë's arms, and he stared up at her and smacked his lips. 'See! He's a party boy, aren't you, honey?' And she swung her amber beads over her shoulder and cuddled him against her chest.

Claire with either Gloria or Marilyn, or all three of them, came every day. They shopped for her or urged her out with Daniel in the pram to shop or walk with them. And when she told them she would have to move out, they were indecently delighted that she could now join them in Delphi Street.

'You and Daniel would have to share with me,' Claire said, 'if you think you wouldn't mind that. There's six of us in the house now, not counting the children. Seven, with you.'

Despite their kindness, Zoë dreaded moving in with these women, who were entirely different from her. While they were prepared to support her in ways that went way beyond friendship, despite their brief acquaintance, she still held back, unable to make the leap of faith that would stop her feeling like an intruder. Now, six months later, she was still intimidated by her failure to understand their frequently expressed views, but, unlike her life with Eileen or with Richard, there were no tests for her to fail, no one else's aspirations for her to live up to.

The question of whether she should let Harry know that he had a son had troubled her for some time. It seemed strange that she'd heard nothing from him except for a Christmas card, since he and Agnes had moved to Glasgow, but she had made no attempt to contact them either; people, she supposed, just drifted apart. According to Gloria, Harry had no rights in the matter and Zoë had no responsibilities to him. Claire and Marilyn, on the other hand, felt that Harry had a right to know.

'I mean, it's not as if he knew and then abandoned you,' Claire said. 'And maybe Daniel will want to know about his father one day.'

'Exactly,' Marilyn said. 'How will you feel explaining to Daniel that you didn't tell his father about him?'

'I don't want to ruin things for him and Agnes,' Zoë had said. 'And I want to bring Daniel up on my own. You all keep telling me I can do that. It's not as though I want Harry for myself. We weren't in love or anything like that.' And yet, as she said it, she wondered if it were true.

Increasingly, she found herself remembering his tenderness, and the way he had made her feel that he valued her; something that she had only felt with Richard in the final months of her pregnancy. How did people know the difference between love and desire, or between love and being in love?

'You might want Harry in your life for Daniel's sake,' Marilyn insisted. 'If not now, then sometime in the future. You need to let him know.'

'So you're going to turn up on his doorstep with Daniel and say, "Hi, this is your son?"' Gloria asked when Zoë finally announced that she was going to Glasgow.

'I'm going to leave Daniel here, if that's okay with everyone. I don't know Harry's address but I know where he works. I'll go there, see him alone. I'll get the overnight train.'

'Be it on your own head, honey,' Gloria said. 'If that's what you want, that's what you gotta do.'

And, as the train raced on into the night, her nervous excitement at the prospect of seeing Harry again warned her that she had a great deal more invested in this journey than just the need to tell him about his son.

When the train pulled into Glasgow station, Zoë woke with a start and sat up. With only one other person in the carriage, she had managed to sleep curled up on the seat, her coat tucked around her, her handbag under her head. Every part of her body was stiff and sore. Yawning and rubbing her eyes, she stared out into a grey dawn. There was time to kill before she could expect to find Harry at the university. And now she was beset by doubts. What if he wasn't there? What if he was angry?

Frustrated by her own lack of forethought, she made her way along the platform to the welcoming light of the station café, where a woman in a voluminous green overall, a cigarette dangling from her lips, was dispensing very strong tea. Zoë drank the tea, and ordered a second cup and beans on toast. The woman looked at her with disapproval and said something very fast in an accent so strong that Zoë couldn't understand it. At the third attempt, she grasped that beans were off the menu, as the woman was on her own and couldn't be expected to do everything. Toast, it seemed, was manageable and so she settled for two slices with Marmite.

Two young men wandered in as she was finishing her breakfast, and she asked them for directions to the university. There was a bus, they told her, that stopped right outside the station and would take her to the university entrance. By nine o'clock, she was waiting outside the central administration office when the doors opened. Her heart beat faster as she stepped up to the reception desk.

'Could you tell me where I could find Harry Foreman, please?'

'Harry Foreman?' The woman looked at her closely. 'Are you a student?'

'I'm a friend from London.'

'A friend?'

'Yes, an old friend, from London . . .' Zoë's mouth went dry; the way the woman was looking at her made her uncomfortable. 'I haven't seen him for ages and I was in Glasgow . . .'

'If you'd like to take a seat for a moment . . .' the woman said, indicating the blue and grey tweed couch in the centre of the foyer. 'What name shall I say?'

'Zoë,' she said. 'Zoë Linton.'

'Miss Linton?'

'Mrs.'

The woman picked up the phone, and Zoë sat on the tweedy couch and stared out to the lawns and pathways crowded now with students on their way to lectures or talking in noisy groups. Maybe Harry was out there. Any minute he might emerge from the crowd, walking towards her with that familiar long stride. She had promised herself that she would ask for nothing except that he accept what she told him. It mattered that there was one other person in the world who shared Daniel, even if he never saw him.

A voice interrupted her thoughts. 'Mrs Linton? I'm Cecily MacFarlane, the university's personnel officer. I believe you're a friend of Harry Foreman?'

Zoë jumped to her feet. 'Oh, look, I didn't want to bother anyone, I just wanted to know where to find him.'

'I see. You haven't been in touch for some time?'

'No, not for ages,' Zoë said, wondering why she was being interrogated. 'It's been almost a year, but I was in Glasgow, so I thought . . .' She faltered. 'Is there something wrong? Harry does work here, doesn't he?'

'Well, he *did*,' Miss MacFarlane said. 'Very briefly, at the start of the year, until . . .' She paused. 'Look I'm sorry, Mrs Linton, there's no easy way to tell you this. Harry Foreman is dead.'

'Dead?'

'I'm afraid so. We advised his family, of course, so I'm surprised they didn't let you know.'

'But he can't be dead.'

'It was very sad,' Miss MacFarlane continued. 'It happened in January; he started with us after Christmas. He and Mrs Foreman were on their way home from the cinema with some other friends who were also from Jamaica. Unfortunately, they were attacked by a gang of drunks. Harry was quite badly beaten but got to his feet and staggered out into the road. He was hit by a passing car. There was brain damage and he was on life support for weeks but in the end . . . there was nothing that could be done for him. I'm so very sorry.'

Zoë stared at the woman's face; the eyes that matched the blue of the décor were looking sympathetically into hers. 'He can't be dead,' she said again. 'He was always so . . . so alive,' she coughed, choking on a sob. 'He can't be dead.'

'I'm so sorry. Perhaps you'd like to come through to my office. I'll get you some tea.'

'But why?'

Miss MacFarlane inhaled deeply and straightened her shoulders. 'It seems the attack was racially motivated; a handful of drunken youths. His being hit by the car was an accident, of course, the driver was devastated.'

'What about Agnes?'

'Mrs Foreman had fairly superficial injuries. She was, as you probably know, working at the Royal Infirmary, which was where they were both treated. I believe she's gone back to her family in Jamaica.'

Tea was brought for Zoë, and she was offered shortbread and accommodation if she would like to stay overnight. Eventually someone checked the train timetable and she was driven back to the station. The train moved slowly out of the station as she closed her eyes, and fell into a deep and troubled sleep.

Waking hours later, she sat numb and silent in the busy carriage until it was time to leave the train for the bus, and walk up the hill to Delphi Street. Ahead of her, she saw Marilyn standing on the step having a heated conversation with a man in black trousers and a short-sleeved white shirt and holding a Bible.

'Zoë?' Marilyn called, pushing past him to get to the gate. 'Zoë, are you all right?' She flapped her hand at the man. 'Oh, piss off and bother someone else.' She opened the gate, took Zoë's arm and led her into the house.

Trapped for weeks in the grip of a debilitating sadness that seemed unbearable, Zoë went through the motions of looking after Daniel, going to work and being a small part of life in the house. Moving, talking and smiling all involved an effort that frequently seemed impossible. She slept heavily and dragged herself through the start of each new day as though trudging uphill through mud. She clung to Daniel, and to the dual roles of motherhood and earning a living, with numb tenacity, knowing instinctively that the demands and disciplines of both were what would, in the end, hold her together.

One Saturday morning at the end of November, she woke shivering with cold. The eiderdown had slipped off in the night and a cold, frosty light seeped between the curtains. Claire had gone to visit her parents in Manchester, and Zoë and Daniel had the bedroom to themselves. Zoë picked up the eiderdown, dragged it around her shoulders and went to the window. The park across the street was white with frost, a thick crust of ice covered the pond and the leaves on the trees were a vibrant russet in the early sunshine. As she stood there, rapt in the stillness and beauty of the morning, she realised that something had changed. She felt different; stronger, perhaps, and wiser. For the first time in months, she had a sense that she had a future over which she had at least some degree of control. Hope had returned.

Daniel stirred in his cot and she turned to pick him up, tucking him inside the eiderdown and climbing back into bed. He smelt of sleep and talcum powder, and Zoë drew him closer, nuzzled his head, then held him away from her to look into his face. He was not even remotely like her. Every inch of him was Harry; her only contribution was his lighter skin tone.

'So, it's just you and me then, kiddo,' she murmured. 'I'm back now and I'll try not to let you down again.' She cuddled him closer until he began to fidget and whimper. 'Come on, then,' she said, getting up and pulling on her dressing gown. 'We've got stuff to do.'

Laying him on the changing mat, she washed and dried him and pinned a fresh nappy into place. He smiled at her, gurgling and kicking his sturdy legs as she tried to put him into a clean Babygro. 'Miles to go,' she said, grasping his feet, remembering the phrase from a poem. 'You and me together, Daniel, miles to go.' And she picked him up and carried him down to the kitchen to heat up his bottle.

2000

TWENTY

Fremantle – New Year's Day 2000

I t's a pretty ordinary January morning; oil is still pumping, there haven't been any nuclear meltdowns, computers have not triggered disasters and no aircraft have fallen from the sky. All that pre-millennium tension that cost some people millions and made fortunes for others has fizzled out overnight. It's going to be another sweltering day and the clock tells Dan that the new century is seven hours and fifteen minutes old. He lies very still, listening for sounds of life. His sisters won't wake for hours yet; he heard them come home about four this morning. They opened his bedroom door, crept in and whispered to him, but he feigned sleep and they backed out with muffled giggles. He wonders if he's getting old – a few years ago he'd have been out on the town – now staying up just long enough to see the New Year in at home seems sufficient celebration. Kitchen sounds are minimal; someone is trying to do things quietly, so it must be his mother. Archie never does things quietly – carefully, thoroughly, but not quietly.

Dan sits up, cautiously puts his foot to the floor and considers transferring some weight to it. He considers this very carefully because he is not in the mood for pain. He knows he's always been a wuss about pain. It was one of the things Archie had said to him when he was seventeen and Dan had told him he wanted to join the army.

173

'You sure about that, mate? What if you come up against a bullet or a grenade; could be a tad painful.' Archie had been joking, of course, but as he'd reminded Dan last night after several beers, he was also prescient. Something like that is more than a tad painful.

Dan grasps the bedhead, grits his teeth and heaves himself up. Pain rips like lightning up his leg to his hip and down again, swirls and circles, and then finally settles to a bearable blur. He exhales in relief, lets go of the bedhead and reaches for his crutches. The kitchen seems a long way off but he knows that the pain will decrease as his leg warms up to movement. Still in his boxers and T-shirt, he hobbles down the passage to the kitchen, the rubber ends of the crutches squeaking on the tiles.

His mother is standing by the window, waiting for the kettle to boil and watching the galahs lurching around like drunks under the lillipilli. She is wearing a grey-and-white cotton kimono that he brought back for her from a holiday in Japan years ago.

'Happy new century,' Dan says, and she jumps and turns towards him. 'The kettle still works, I'm glad to see.'

'Happy New Year, again,' Zoë says. 'Everything works, according to the seven o'clock news. So much for the millennium bug. Tea? Shouldn't you sit down?'

'Yes to both, thanks.' He lowers himself into a chair and rests his crutches against the table.

'Is it worse in the mornings?'

He nods. 'Until it loosens up. It's a bugger, actually, but without it I wouldn't be back here for New Year, so everything has a silver lining.'

She nods and pours the tea, and he notices a couple of things that he missed in the excitement of yesterday's homecoming. Her hair is greyer, and he likes it; it's softer. And he can see that without makeup, although she looks good for fifty-two or fifty-three, or whatever she is, there are a few more lines at the corners of her eyes and mouth. But there's something he *did* notice last night and sees more clearly now; it's as though a little light has been switched off inside her. He wonders if something happened while he was away.

'So,' Zoë says, putting the tea in front of him and gesturing towards his bad leg. Dan knows what's coming next. 'Maybe this'd be a good time to get out?'

He sips his tea, trying not to sigh. 'It's my job, Mum. I'm a professional soldier and sometimes soldiers get wounded.'

'Don't patronise me, Dan,' Zoë says, putting on her sharp face – the one she used when he wagged school or lied about homework. 'I love you, I worry about you. And I've never . . .'

'. . . understood why I wanted to join the army in the first place,' he finishes the sentence for her. 'I know, but I did want to and I still want to be there.'

'Presumably, you *don't* want a lump of shrapnel in your leg!' She softens her tone. 'And, as if the army itself wasn't bad enough, you get into the SAS. I mean, really, Dan, it's madness.'

Dan grins. 'I know, Mum, it's a tough job but someone's got to do it. Even a wuss like me.'

'I just wish you could have picked a nice, safe job near home.'

Her hand is worrying at the stubborn seal of a packet of biscuits. Dan leans across the table and stills it with his own. 'Well, when I'm not somewhere else, I *am* close to home. Swanbourne's only fifteen minutes from Fremantle, after all.'

'But when you're not at the barracks, we never know where you are, or what's happening,' she says. 'Sometimes we don't even have a chance to say goodbye.'

There are tears in her eyes, and Dan can see that the emotion she held back when he arrived home on crutches yesterday has taken its toll.

'I know you're incredibly tough and you're all amazing and do the hardest things, but . . . but . . .'

'But it's hard for you too,' Dan says. 'I know; honestly, I do, it's the same for all the families.'

'But *you*, Dan – you and I, in the beginning, when there was just the two of us . . . I felt so responsible. I woke up every day feeling it was up to me to keep you alive and safe.'

'And now I'm nearly thirty-one . . .'

'And it doesn't go away. Not ever.'

He grasps her hand again. 'I know, Mum. But it's my life, and I'm responsible for me now.'

She nods and pulls a tissue from the box at the end of the table. 'Sorry. I'm being pathetic. It's weird – I can't bear you being hurt but I'm almost glad you were wounded because it brought you home.' She attempts a laughs and blows her nose.

'Well, there you are,' he says, 'I'm here, so let's make the most of it.'

Zoë nods and sips her tea. 'The girls are thrilled to have you back. It was after four when they got home. Did you hear all that giggling?'

He nods. 'They're the ones you should worry about; barking mad, they are.'

'You know Rosie wants to do that youth volunteer corps thing up in Vietnam when she graduates?'

'Not my idea,' Dan says, raising his hands palms outwards. 'I didn't know anything about it until she told me last night.'

'I know. It was Rob's idea, they want to go together. He's a lovely boy but I wish he'd keep his ideas to himself.'

'And Gabs tells me her New Year's resolution is to go travelling.'

'She can get that idea *right* out of her head for a while yet,' Zoë says briskly, picking up her mug. 'She'll do the TEE and at least one year of university, if I have to nail her feet to the floor. Have you made any resolutions?'

Dan leans back in his chair. 'To be nicer to my mother,' he says with a grin.

Zoë laughs. 'About time.'

'So, what's your resolution, Mum?'

'Not sure – I'm still working on it,' she blushes slightly. 'But it's about trying to change.'

'Change?'

'Yes . . . I think I'm stuck. You know, fifty-two this year, children grown up, same old job, same old habits: walking in the mornings, book club once a month, Thursday late-night shopping, all that. Maybe I should try something else, take a risk.'

'What sort of risk?' Dan asks, the reasons why he would prefer her not to change piling up like stacks of disused tyres in his mind.

'That's the problem, I haven't worked it out yet. Not your sort of risks, of course, just doing something different. Archie says it's like the pipeline to bring water to Perth from the Kimberley; just a pipe dream.'

'Not that dreams aren't worth having,' Archie says. They hear him before they see him, because he has a deep voice and his bare feet are slapping noisily against the tiles.

'Hi, Arch. Happy two thousand,' Dan says.

Archie, wrapped in a white towelling robe, his hair still damp from the shower, grips Dan's shoulder with a large hand as he passes his chair. 'You too, mate. Let's make it a good one.' And he goes over to Zoë, who is pouring him a cup of tea, and puts his arms around her. 'Morning, lovely one.'

Dan likes seeing them together; there is something wonderfully reassuring about having them always there to come home to. He's seen enough men who lack what he has, who think that having nothing to lose makes them better soldiers. But, too often, it makes them reckless. This change thing niggles him though, consistency is one of the things he loves best about his mother. He likes her reliability, likes that he can predict her reactions, even when they irritate him. There is something unspoken between them that comes, he thinks, from what happened when he was born. He'd been twelve when Rosie was born, and when he'd walked into the maternity ward with Archie to find Zoë holding a grizzling interloper wrapped in its fluffy white shawl, a bolt of jealousy had whipped through him. What about me? he'd wanted to shout. But Zoë had reached out and patted the bed beside her, and as he scrambled onto the high hospital bed, he'd known that he was safe, that what bound them together was unchanged. He could afford to be generous to this squalling, blue-eyed baby.

Archie takes a mug of tea from Zoë and joins Dan at the table. 'Risk,' he says, winking at him. 'You'd think she'd have had enough of that being married to me, wouldn't you?'

Dan laughs. 'You are the least risky person in the world, Arch. If Mum's planning a new career as a parachutist or a caver, that's why.'

'Stop talking about me as though I'm not here,' Zoë says, pulling her chair closer to Archie's and leaning against him. 'I'll work out what my risk is without your interference, thank you.'

Archie rolls his eyes. 'So, Dan, this woman you've been keeping up your sleeve. Tell us more about her.'

Dan flushes. 'We met a couple of months before I went away, and I wasn't sure how it was going to work out.' He feels his face go hot. 'I didn't want to say too much,' he laughs, turning it into a joke to hide his vulnerability. 'You two are always trying to marry me off.'

'It seems to be the only way of getting rid of you,' Archie says. 'Finding a good woman to get you off our hands.'

Dan looks down at his tea. 'Well, I may have found her,' he says quietly.

Archie whistles through his teeth. 'May have?'

'Almost certainly have.'

'That's wonderful,' Zoë says, and he can see that she's genuinely happy for him but also anxious. He's had plenty of girlfriends but most have been passing fancies.

'So, we get to meet her this afternoon?'

Dan nods. 'You do, and you have to promise not to be weird and not to interrogate her. Just be normal. *Both* of you.'

'We *are* normal,' Archie says, putting his arm around Zoë's shoulders. 'We're very normal people, aren't we, Zo?'

'Mum?' Dan says, looking at her.

'I promise not to interrogate her, Dan,' Zoë says. 'At least, not on her first visit.'

❧

Some hours later, Zoë stands at the worktop whipping egg whites for pavlovas. It's a job she hates and she'd bought ready-made cases in Coles but, strangely, this morning she decided to make her own. Is she trying to impress Dan's girlfriend? It's hard not to want to make a good impression because he does seem serious this time. She's trying not to feel hurt that Dan's known her for almost six months and hasn't said a word about her until now.

Seated nearby at the table, Eileen is slicing strawberries and kiwi fruit. She does it slowly and methodically, watching the sharp blade and her own hands very closely, because, as she told Zoë earlier, 'I don't see so well these days, and when you're my age a cut can take a long time to heal, like when I caught my arm on that nail on the back gate.'

These days, everything Eileen does is slow, laborious and somehow attached to a convoluted story from which she emerges as a victim.

'This girl of Daniel's is coming over, then?' Eileen says now, looking up and pushing her glasses back on to the bridge of her nose, leaving a fragment of strawberry on the corner of one lens. 'What's she like?'

'I've told you, Mum, I don't know,' Zoë says, trying to hide her impatience. 'I've not met her yet.'

'He must have told you something about her.'

'No, he's being very secretive, although apparently he told Rosie that she's a bit older than him.'

'Older? Well, that's a bit odd. Men are usually older.'

'Not necessarily. Not these days.'

'These days,' Eileen sniffs, 'these days, anything goes, if you ask me.'

Zoë hates discussing Daniel with her mother. Not that Eileen ever says anything overtly critical, but she doesn't need to; it's all in her tone and the silences punctuated with sniffs of disapproval. The day Zoë and Dan arrived in Perth in seventy-four, just in time for him to start school, Jane had brought Eileen to meet them at the airport. After the first awkward embraces, while Jane went to fetch the car, Zoë, Eileen and Dan collected the bags.

'Why do you keep looking at me like that?' Eileen had demanded of Dan, who had been watching her carefully since they arrived and was still staring thoughtfully up at her. He'd looked away then, and started to jump on and off the kerb. 'I'm deciding if I like you,' he said.

'Well, really!' Eileen said, colouring in annoyance.

'He's heard a lot about you, Mum,' Zoë said. 'Now he's getting to know what you look like.' But she had known even then that this was going to be more difficult than she'd imagined. A few years earlier, her mother had told her not to come home with a black baby, but Zoë had assumed that, over time, Eileen would have softened and that she had been forgiven. But immediately she saw her mother's face at the airport and felt her body stiff as a post when she went to hug her, she knew that nothing was forgiven. Daniel was different, as different as it was possible to be in Eileen's eyes. She clearly resented her daughter for forcing this difference on her, making it part of her life.

'Let it go, Zo,' Archie had said seven years later, when Rosie was born and greeted with lavish affection and gifts from her grandmother. 'Let it go, she's never going to treat Dan like a grandson and you can only make things worse. If Dan can handle it when he's only twelve, you have to handle it too.'

Eileen adored Archie and never missed an opportunity to remind Zoë that he had made her respectable, that he had fathered two beautiful daughters, looked after them well and treated her, Eileen, as if she were his own mother. But Archie had also taken Dan into his life and treated *him* as his own, never favouring his daughters over his adopted son. Zoë thought her mother ought to have learned something from that, but Eileen had steadfastly chosen not to.

'Well, I hope she's all right,' Eileen says now, pushing aside the chopping board and knife, her task complete. 'This girl, I mean.'

'Why shouldn't she be? I'm sure she'll be lovely, and I want us all to make her feel at home.' Zoë piles the meringue mix onto the baking trays, swirls it with a fork into a perfect circles and, smoothing a small depression in the centre of each, slips the trays into the oven. She is surprisingly nervous and she constantly reminds herself that she mustn't be cross about his secrecy. It was only yesterday evening, just before the girls were heading out to their party, that Dan had mentioned a girlfriend.

'Are you doing the usual New Year barbecue thing tomorrow?' he'd asked.

'We sure are,' Archie had said. 'Jane and Tony, the neighbours, my sister and her mob. All the usual suspects.'

'And Rob,' Rosie said, winding a long strand of blonde hair around her finger.

'That's your latest conquest?'

Rosie nodded. 'Yep, he's doing architecture too; we do our assignments together.'

'Among other things,' Gaby cut in, leaning up against Dan, who had his arm around her waist.

'You'd better watch out if you want us to take you to the party,' Rosie said. 'You are, like, so close to spending New Year's Eve with Mum and Dad.'

Gaby let out a howl. 'No, Rosie, please, you promised.'

'Anyone would think you two were still in the playground,' Zoë said.

'But she's . . .' Gaby began. Archie cut her off.

'Okay, cut it out. It's the season of goodwill and that includes goodwill to sisters.'

With a big sigh, Gaby dropped sulkily into a chair and put her feet up to rest on Dan's good leg. She glared at Rosie, who totally ignored her.

'Could I invite someone tomorrow?' Dan said. 'Only if you wouldn't mind. I know it's a bit late notice but . . .'

And that was when he'd told them; the girls had pestered him for details, and he'd resisted, laughing, and managed to get away with telling them nothing. 'You'll meet her tomorrow,' he insisted. 'You'll just have to wait until then.'

Zoë washes the mixing bowl and clears the fruit debris from the table, watching from the corner of her eye as Eileen, stick in hand, makes her way out to the deck to sit in her favourite chair. Archie, who had collected her from the retirement home earlier this morning, has slipped out again to pick up some ice. Meanwhile, Dan, his leg resting on a chair, is supervising Rob priming the barbecue while the girls look on. Taking off her apron, Zoë glances around the kitchen and then wanders down to the bedroom and stands in front of the full-length mirror. Should she change into something else? The emerald green dress, perhaps; it's a bit more formal than she would usually wear but why not? It's a new century, Dan's back, there's something to celebrate. She steps into the dress and finds some white beads, wondering as she does so whether Dan's new girlfriend is doing the same thing; staring at herself in the mirror, wondering if she looks okay, worrying about meeting his family.

What has Dan told her about them while she's known about them but they haven't known about her? If he's really serious about her, things will change. Zoë doesn't like that idea much but she knows it's inevitable. And it might be fun, like having another daughter around.

As she fiddles with her hair, Zoë remembers an excruciating visit to Tunbridge Wells, when she wore a dress that was far too short, and talked about being descended from a convict and sharing a house with Harry. It all seems . . . is, actually . . . so very long ago.

'You worry too much,' Archie had said this morning. 'And you look beautiful. Just as beautiful as the day I first saw you down on the jetty, trying to teach Dan to fish. Ha! And what a disaster that was.'

'Yeah, well, that's the only reason I went out with you,' she'd said. 'So Dan could learn to fish.'

'I've always known that. But considering Dan rapidly turned out to be a natural fisherman, you've hung around a long time.'

'I'm a glutton for punishment,' she'd said, throwing a pillow at him. 'And, anyway, by the time Dan had learned to fish I'd discovered you had power tools.'

Zoë hears a car on the drive; it's Archie back with the ice, and Jane and Tony are pulling in behind his truck. Jane is still the only member of Eileen's family who has anything to do with them. Zoë runs her hands through her hair, and goes outside to greet the visitors.

Dan, who has scrambled up onto his crutches, makes his way to the deck. 'Hey there, Aunty Jane,' he says and Jane turns in surprise.

'Dan! You're home!' she cries and, turning to Zoë, 'You never said.'

'I didn't *know* until he turned up yesterday afternoon.'

'How wonderful.' She hugs him. 'But your leg . . .' She looks him up and down with concern.

'I'm fine, Jane, although it's not the best way of getting home for New Year.'

Tony puts down the esky and throws his arm around Dan's shoulders. 'Great to see you. What's up with the leg?'

'Shrapnel,' Dan says, in his usual noncommittal way, and they all know not to ask questions.

Archie hands out beers, and Rosie gives Jane a glass of champagne. 'This is Rob, Aunty Jane,' she says, drawing him forward, his blonde hair flopping over his forehead. 'He's doing architecture too.'

Gaby throws her arms around Jane's waist. 'Isn't it cool that Dan's back? But he's a boring old grump – he wouldn't come out with us last night.'

'I should think he was nursing his leg,' Jane says, smiling again at Dan and rubbing his arm affectionately. Dan has always been Jane's favourite; it matters to both of them, and to Zoë, that there is one other person in the family who knew his father.

Neighbours begin to trail in through the back gate, and bottles of wine and plates of food are handed over, and there is much hugging. As the front doorbell rings, Dan hops onto his crutches and heads into the house.

'He looks pretty good,' Jane says, turning to Zoë.

She nods. 'A lot of pain, apparently, but he's coping okay.'

Jane smiles and hugs her again. 'Poor Zoë; it must be hard. Anyway, happy new century,' she says, raising her glass. 'Aunty Eileen looks well too. Better go and say hello.' She walks over to where Eileen is surveying them all from a distance, pulls up a stool and sits down beside her.

'Here, Mum,' Rosie says, putting a glass of champagne into Zoë's hand. 'Rob is wearing his Christmas present. D'you think it looks good?'

Zoë looks at Rob's youthful neck, and the heavy silver chain that is the result of Rosie agonising in front of shop windows for hours.

'It looks absolutely perfect, darling.'

She sips her champagne and looks around her in satisfaction. This is the best time, she thinks, when people start to arrive and before anyone drinks too much and before the hassle with food; now there is just talk, laughter and goodwill. At the far end of the verandah, Archie is standing with Dan and a woman in a lemon-yellow dress, who is almost totally hidden by the lattice. Zoë's stomach gives a little lurch. She makes her way towards them, stopping briefly to greet Rob's parents, feeling almost as nervous as she had in Tunbridge Wells.

Dan's face is glowing and he gives her a smile of such delighted anticipation that Zoë's heart soars for him.

'Mum,' he says, wobbling slightly on his crutches, 'Mum, come on over, I want to introduce you.' He straightens slightly and touches the woman's arm, nodding towards Zoë. 'Sweetheart, it's my mum,' he says and the woman turns towards her. 'Mum, this is Justine.'

TWENTY-ONE

Rye – New Year's Day 2000

It's three in the morning in Sussex, and it's snowing. Julia, unable to sleep, pulls back the curtain at the front window and looks across the cobbles to the moonlit churchyard, where the grass and the sprawling bare branches of the catalpa tree are covered in a fine white blanket. She has put on her thick dressing gown and two pairs of Tom's socks, but it's cold here at the front of the house. She lets the curtain drop and goes back to the kitchen, where she has opened up the front of the Aga, and pours herself a good-sized brandy.

She is unbearably restless and rather irritable. It's ridiculous, she thinks, sipping the brandy, holding up the crystal balloon so that she can see the fire through its prisms. It's ridiculous that she's spending the first hours of the new century worrying about two men who are fast asleep upstairs.

Is this what it's come to? All that studying and writing, speaking at public meetings, letters to *The Guardian*, papers she's written on the status of women, and on nuclear weapons and the arms race, and on starting and building a business. And here she is in the kitchen, wearing Tom's socks and worrying about men. Well, not worrying *about* them exactly because they, of course, are perfectly fine. What she's worrying about is being fenced in by their needs and their wretched plans; their sixty-eight project and now Tom's mad idea of buying a place in the Algarve. Is this how it is

185

to be from now on, now that Hilary is no longer there dispensing her moderating influence? Does her future lie in cooking roast dinners, while they talk about how they'd run the country if it were up to them? Listening to Tom's analysis of Gordon Brown's pernicious plan to sell off the gold reserves, and Richard's raving about why NATO had to bomb Kosovo, and how it was a good thing that Clinton survived impeachment?

How, Julia wonders, is it that she – a woman who chained herself to the fence day after day at Greenham Common, spent a week in prison and slept for months under canvas with hundreds of other women through torrential rain, gales and sweltering heat to protest about cruise missiles – is now being dragged, once again, towards a life resembling her mother's?

'He's a dear man,' Hilary has said of Tom on so many occasions, 'the armchair politician, the intellectual activist. That's our Tom, rarely a man of action, bless him.'

'Bless him, indeed,' Julia says aloud now, 'I'll brain him if he doesn't shut up about the Algarve.'

He'd started banging on about the Algarve again at dinner; 'beautiful coastline, great restaurants, tennis, golf'. Julia loathes all games, especially those that involve equipment. In fact, she hates most physical activity, with the exception of walking. At school she frequently forged notes from Anita asking that she be excused from hockey and netball due to a heavy period or any other excuse she could think of. Crashing around on an ice-bound hockey pitch or shoving her way through a game of netball was never her idea of fun. And these days, the only one thing she would enjoy less than playing tennis or golf in Sussex is playing tennis or golf in the Algarve with a lot of ageing expats.

Julia pours herself another drink, remembering a bright September morning in 1981. She was sitting on damp grass, her bum numb and cold, while chained to the fence of the US air base at Greenham Common and longing for someone to bring her a mug of tea. Then she saw Tom walking towards her. She remembers the look of joy and amazement on his face. And she remembers his words.

'I had to come, Julia. I saw you on the nine o'clock news; you looked absolutely amazing. You *are* amazing.'

Julia's memories form a lump in her throat as she recalls him sitting beside her on the damp grass.

'I can't tell you what it means to find you again,' he'd said. 'Have you . . . could you . . . do you think you could ever forgive me?'

That Saturday he'd stayed all day at the peace camp and, later, when it was someone else's turn to be chained to the fence, they'd gone into Newbury, and there, in a small café, Tom had told her about the stillborn baby and the subsequent breakdown of his marriage to Alison. 'I doubt we'd have lasted together even if the baby had lived,' he said looking at Julia. 'I meant what I said that last day in Paris; it was you I loved, you I wanted to marry, that didn't change.' He inhaled sharply, sitting up straighter. 'Anyway,' he went on, 'what about you Julia? It seems such a weird place for you to be. From millionaire's wife to Greenham Common. I mean, what are *you* really doing at a peace camp?'

She'd given him a long, hard look. 'I'm a millionaire's ex-wife, Tom,' she'd said, 'and I'm protesting about US nuclear weapons. Remember you told me there are two sorts of people, those who watch from the sidelines and those who get involved? Well, I'm getting involved. What about you?'

He never *had* got involved in a practical way, although his interest was unquestionable and he'd always supported her in everything she did. He was generous and encouraging, but he was the analyst, who could deconstruct everything, explain the pros and cons, even predict what would happen next. His eyes would burn with enthusiasm, but he had never overcome his reluctance actually to get out there and rattle a few cages.

The odd thing, Julia realises for the first time, is that back when she and Tom first met, the difference in their ages hadn't mattered. And it hadn't mattered when they met again twelve years later and got married. But she's starting to wonder if it matters now. Although he's only sixty-eight, Tom seems to be delighting in the role of old codger, cheerful, generous, intelligent, occasionally belligerent, and he wants to take her along with him. Julia takes a big swig of her drink. Well, she isn't having it. She's only fifty-four and has important stuff of her own to do. In the months since Hilary's diagnosis and then her removal to the hospice, she, Julia, has lost her focus, but she'll get it back. She is not going to let Tom paddle her into the still waters of the elderly, and she is certainly not decamping to Portugal as her parents decamped to the Costa Blanca in the seventies, drinking cheap gin and patronising the Spaniards.

And then, as if all this isn't enough, there's Richard, ringing up a few days before Christmas and saying he thinks he'll pop home for the holidays, as it's bloody freezing in New York. She's pleased to see him, of course, as is Tom; he's delighted to have someone to open his best claret for, someone to help him put the world to rights. But since he arrived, Richard's either been shaking his metaphorical stick at anyone who disagrees with him, or getting drunk and maudlin about being single at sixty. He's still making noises about getting back with Lily but doesn't seem to have talked to her yet. What *is* it with these men as they get older, Julia wonders? Are they becoming their fathers?

Well, today there'll be some changes. They can cook their own bloody lunch; she's going to the hospice. She knows that it's Hilary's deteriorating condition that is making her short tempered with the men; there has to be someone to absorb her distress. So, when she's seen Hilary, she'll go for a long walk – it doesn't matter where, because somewhere out there, she's going to find her old self and bring it back. If she doesn't, the next thing she knows, she'll be sighing again – this time all the way to the grave.

∽◦∾

It is after nine when Richard wakes and stumbles out of bed to the bathroom, only to find Tom occupying it.

'Get a bloody move on, man,' he calls through the door. 'And isn't it time you put in a second bathroom?'

'And where exactly would I put it?' Tom replies, to the sound of running water. 'On the roof? There's always the one in the outside laundry, it still works.'

'It's fucking snowing,' Richard says, longing momentarily for his centrally heated Manhattan apartment with its two bathrooms.

'Well, come in then,' Tom says, 'you haven't got anything I haven't seen before, unless you've grown a second one.'

'I should be so lucky,' Richard says, opening the door and hurrying across to the lavatory. 'Although it wouldn't make much difference; these days, I rarely get to use this one for anything interesting.'

'Might be different with two, though,' Tom muses, studying his lather-covered face in the mirror. 'You'd be a curiosity. Women would probably pay you.'

'Bring it on!' Richard says, turning his back to him, clutching the one in question and pointing it in the right direction. 'Beats paying for it.'

'Do you?' Tom asks. 'Pay for it, I mean?'

'That's a rather personal question.'

'Yes, well, you *are* peeing in my space.'

'Okay then; for the record, no,' Richard says. 'Not these days, not for years. I did occasionally in the past, when there was a complete drought. You?'

Tom shakes his head. 'Never. I thought about it, especially when I was doing all that travelling – Amsterdam, Berlin, Geneva. Some of my colleagues used to add it to the expense account. But I'm a chronic recidivist when it comes to actually doing things. Ask your sister.'

'I don't need to,' Richard says, crossing to the basin and edging Tom aside so he can rinse his hands. 'She's always complaining about it.'

Tom holds his razor under the stream of warm water and then bends over the basin to slosh the lather from his chin. 'I know. Can't help it, I'm afraid. I'm not like you; never did have the desire to leap the barricades or fight off the truncheons.' He wipes his face on a towel, and the two of them stand side-by-side, looking at their reflections.

'Two thousand, eh?' Richard says, shaking his head. 'Another century. We made it.'

'Brothers-in-arms,' Tom says, grinning. 'Project sixty-eight: the book, the documentary, the fame and fortune.'

Richard rolls his eyes and, mimicking Julia, says, 'Whenever are you two going to grow up?'

They fall about laughing at themselves, and then Tom slaps Richard on the shoulder. 'Happy New Year, new century,' he says,

'I hope it's a good one for you.' He holds out his hand, and Richard shakes it with both of his.

'You too, Tom, all the best, all the very best.'

And they are serious for a moment, fleetingly embarrassed to find themselves half-naked in the bathroom being serious, wordlessly acknowledging how fond they are of each other.

'Er, yes . . . must get on,' Tom says, unhooking his dressing gown from the back of the door. 'I'll get started on the breakfast. Bacon sandwiches, I thought.'

'What about Julia?' Richard asks, pulling a toothbrush out of his wash bag, which is standing on the corner of the bath.

'Gone to the hospice to see Hilary; won't be back for a while, she says. I'm in the doghouse.'

'The Algarve?'

Tom nods. 'She thinks I want to cart her off to some geriatric Stepford Wives enclave. Trouble is, she won't bloody listen. All I want is to get some nice little place, somewhere warm, with a glorious view, so we can pop over from time to time and get some sun. Maybe you can make her see sense.'

Richard puts the plug in the basin and turns on the taps. 'It'd be the first time ever,' he says. 'Sounds brilliant to me. Take me instead.'

Tom laughs and walks out of the bathroom. Richard hears him singing softly in the bedroom, in French, the 'Marseillaise' of all things, word perfect, accent perfect.

He's an odd cove, Tom, Richard thinks, even though he's now not only his brother-in-law but his best friend. Hugely intelligent, socially progressive – even a lifetime in banking hasn't driven him to the right. He looks around the bathroom at all the signs of two people living an intimate life – the toothbrushes, towels, medications, perfume and aftershave – and he thinks of how he has watched their relationship grow over the years. He has seen them fight and make up, challenge and support each other, laugh and cry together, and he envies it. More than anything, he thinks, he envies the trust and the companionship. It must, Richard believes, be wonderful to know that there is at least one person in the world for whom you always come first.

Years ago he had greeted with considerable cynicism Julia's tale of how Tom had seen her on the television news coverage of the peace camp and raced out to Greenham Common to find her. But, as he watched Tom's relentless efforts to wear down her resistance until she agreed to marry him, he knew he was watching love, once lost, being rekindled until it burst into a beautiful flame. Greenham Common, he thinks now – well, Tom certainly acted then and it won him what he wanted.

Richard splashes his face with water, pats it with a towel, considers trimming his beard and decides against it. 'The thing is,' he says aloud to himself, 'that Tom thinks about everything but does nothing. While you, my friend, think about nothing and rush headlong at things and crash into walls – particularly when it comes to women.'

A few weeks earlier the prospect of spending Christmas with Martin Gilbert and his wife in Vermont, surrounded by loving couples, suddenly seemed more than he could cope with. So he'd apologised and mumbled something about needing to go home to see his father. Then he'd rung Julia and asked if he could come for Christmas as it was bloody freezing in New York.

'And I suppose you think it's gloriously tropical here,' she'd said. 'Actually, the central heating's on the blink. Tom was supposed to be getting the man in to fix it but it's taken him three days to think about making the call, so I've done it myself.'

'So, you don't mind, then?' Richard asked.

'Of course not. It'll be lovely and you can talk Tom out of his latest scheme, which involves us living in Portugal, trotting from one trattoria to the other eating tapas and patting the locals on the head.'

'Do they have trattorias in Portugal? That's Italy.'

'Whatever. Wherever it is, I'm not going. You can talk some sense into him.'

So, here I am, Richard thinks, as he pulls on the very nice navy blue cashmere sweater that Julia gave him for Christmas, commissioned by both to talk sense into the other. This triggers a feeling of emptiness and he sits on the bed and studies the pale shapes of his cold bare feet on the carpet. They play this game from time to time, Tom and Julia; this pretence of being at loggerheads when, in fact, they are devoted to each other, lucky buggers. And, as always, he is alone and, frankly, pretty bloody lonely most of the time, thanks to his ability to shoot himself in the foot when it comes to women. His mind whizzes through a series of flashbacks ending, as always, with his ruthless actions after Zoë's baby was born. If only he'd given it more time; if only he'd gone back to Delphi Street again instead of just waiting and hoping she'd call. Instead, he'd convinced himself that she'd found Harry, and that Agnes, learning about the baby, had left. He'd tortured himself with images of Zoë and Harry together; sometimes he even thought he saw them pushing a pram or carrying the baby that should have been his.

Martin had been offered a juicy contract in New York and was leaving the BBC. On the spur of the moment, Richard, needing to get away from London, had applied to join the foreign correspondents' team. A few months later, he was in Vietnam, discovering that there was nothing like a war zone to take your mind off your failures. It worked until he got too close to a land mine and was sent home to hospital in England.

'I can go back as soon as you like,' he'd told the foreign editor once he was declared fit for work.

'No way,' Mike Lennox had told him.

'But I was doing a good job . . .'

'You were wounded, Richard, quite badly wounded; largely because you refused to follow the rules and took yourself and the cameraman into a fucking minefield. Or have you forgotten that?'

'But I'm okay now. The medics said . . .'

'Look, just shut the fuck up. You're not going back; the BBC, the union, they'd castrate me. You go where you're sent, and I'm sending you to Washington.'

'Washington? I thought maybe the Middle East . . .' Richard began.

Lennox raised his eyebrows. 'I'm sure you did. But you're going to Washington because we need someone politically astute there, and because the only minefields in Washington are political ones.'

He'd wondered how he would cope, whether he was ready to have time to think about anything other than survival. But at least Washington wouldn't be dull. And then, a few days before he was due to fly out of London, he'd bumped into Claire, at the opening of a photo-journalism exhibition, and learned what Zoë had learned years earlier in Glasgow.

'Harry? Dead?' he'd said. 'I can barely believe it. I assumed that he and Zoë . . .' His heart was pounding furiously at the sudden possibility of seeing her again. 'So, is Zoë still in London?'

Claire shook her head. 'They went back to Perth last year.'

'They?'

'Zoë and Daniel.'

'Of course,' he said feeling stupid. 'And she's happy there?'

'I think so,' Claire said. 'She's got a job and Daniel's started school.'

Richard nodded, crestfallen. 'That's good news, then,' he said. 'Well, give her my best next time you write.' If only he'd gone back just one more time.

His feet are really cold now, and Richard gets up and finds some clean socks. There is a tantalising smell of bacon wafting up from the kitchen, and Tom has stopped the 'Marseillaise' and started on the nostalgia medley he's known to break into at parties: Sinatra, Perry Como, Tony Bennett. He has an excellent voice; a strong tenor that Julia professes to remember rising above the sounds of riots in Paris. As he runs down the stairs to the kitchen, Tom launches into 'Make Someone Happy', which stops him dead. He is assailed once more by the terrible emptiness that gripped him in the bedroom. He has only made any woman happy for a very brief period of time, he realises; as they grow to know him better, he makes them very miserable. Richard hesitates at the foot of the stairs, trying to control something that feels like a sob building in his chest, and then strolls into the kitchen just as Tom reaches the bit about love being the answer.

'For Chrissakes, Tom,' Richard says. 'Perry-bloody-Como on the first day of a new century?'

'Who better?' Tom says, flipping bacon onto slices of thick toast.

'Barry McGuire'd be a start.'

Tom puts a plate on the table, and obliges by changing key and launching back into song. Richard joins him now, reaching as he does so into the top cupboard and pulling out a bottle of whisky.

And together, hips and shoulders swaying, they circle the kitchen table, singing about being old enough to fight but not vote, about the world exploding in violence, until they reach the final line of the chorus and, at this point, all movement stops and they sing louder now, drumming their hands on the table in time to the music, shouting the final words '. . . *eve of destruction*'. And then they stop.

'Bloody dreadful song for a new century,' Tom says, sitting down at the table.

'Even more relevant now than it was in sixty-five.'

'So, shall we slit our wrists now or later?'

'Later, I think,' Richard says, thinking that now would be as good a time as any. He pours himself a shot of whisky and puts the glass down alongside his bacon sandwich.

'Bit early for that, isn't it?' Tom asks, biting into his sandwich.

Richard tosses off the drink and leans back in his chair. 'Never too early,' he says, 'or too late, come to that.'

TWENTY-TWO

Rye – New Year's Day 2000

'The Algarve is probably just another of those plans that never go anywhere, Julia,' Hilary says. 'Best to ignore it, I think.'

Julia nods. 'You're probably right,' she says, 'I'm overreacting.' And adds, but only to herself, I'm overreacting because I'm watching my best friend die and I don't know how I'll cope when she's gone.

'Displacement activity,' Hilary says softly. She seems particularly weak this morning.

'What do you mean?'

'All this,' she says, waving an extremely thin and pale arm around the room, and speaking even more slowly than usual. 'Me, this place; I think it's getting to you. I love seeing you but maybe you shouldn't come so often.'

'Nonsense,' Julia says, 'I want to be here, to be with you.'

'I know, dear, but it's New Year, you didn't need to come. I didn't expect it.'

'I come because *I* need to come for *me*,' Julia says. 'I know that's terribly selfish. I should be coming for *you* and part of me is, but not all of me.'

Hilary nods and closes her eyes. Sometimes Julia's pain is harder for her to bear than the pain of her illness, which is controlled, to some extent, by medication. 'I'd like to think of your doing something pleasant, restorative for yourself,' she says. 'You looked after me for so long that you must be exhausted.'

'Seeing you *is* restorative,' Julia says. 'And New Year is important; the time to think of the future, to be positive, the prospect of spring. You know.'

Hilary, knowing she will not see the spring and not much more of the winter, smiles and lets it go. They have this conversation far too often. She would prefer to reminisce and to tell Julia how much their friendship has meant to her: how she has been the daughter Hilary never had, that she doesn't know how she could have carried on after Eric's death, had it not been for her. But Julia doesn't want to have that conversation, to hear its note of finality. Tom is better at this, Hilary thinks; perhaps because he is older and therefore no stranger to the sense of time closing in. It is a relief to talk to Tom, although Hilary feels horribly disloyal thinking this.

'Tom'll be over tomorrow,' Julia says. 'He was sorting through his old photos and found some of him when he was in the choir at Eric's church, when he was about fifteen. He's bringing them to show you.'

'That'll be lovely,' Hilary says. 'He *was* a sweet boy; I was always fond of him. Things turned out all right for both of you in the end, didn't they?' Hilary closes her eyes and reaches for Julia's hand. 'I think I need to sleep now.'

Julia gets up. 'Yes, of course,' she says. 'Sorry for dumping all my problems on you.' She leans over and kisses Hilary on the cheek.

Hilary, eyes still closed, lifts her hand to touch Julia's face. 'I love you very much, Julia; you do know that, don't you? I couldn't have wished for a better friend than you've been.'

'Still am, I hope,' Julia says briskly. 'You rest now. Tom'll be over tomorrow and I'll see you in a couple of days.'

The sun is forcing its way through the clouds as Julia leaves the hospice, its narrow rays casting dazzling shafts of light onto the snow. She pauses by the car, wondering whether she really does want to go for a long walk on her own on the first day of the new century.

What she'd really like to do is go home and curl up on the couch with a book, with Tom in his usual chair with his own book, and a bottle of wine; or just listen to music, something magnificent such as Haydn's 'Mass in Time of War' or Beethoven's '4th Piano Concerto'. That is the wonderful thing about being with Tom, she thinks, he doesn't talk for the sake of it. Their conversations are long and intense but so too are their silences. But Tom and Richard together become a double act, bouncing off each other, engaging in rowdy discussions, bursting into song, or doing funny voices: Basil Fawlty, Corporal Jones and Captain Mainwaring, or the Goons. Julia sighs. She loves having the two of them in the house, but an outbreak of New Year Goonery is not what she needs today. Instead of driving back into Rye, she goes on to Camber.

It's a miserable place, of course, Camber; Tom says Mike Leigh should set one of his depressing dramas there. It does have an incredible beach though; one that can make you forget the few dreary shops packed with tourist tat, the holiday camp that looks more like a prison, and the surly youths on motorbikes, chewing gum and trying to chat up girls with bare midriffs and breasts blue with cold.

Julia parks, switches off her mobile phone, and picks a path over the dunes to the kilometres of flat sand stretching left, right and way out to the sea, which now, at low tide, is barely visible. On this beach, you can walk for ages before reaching the water's edge, and then keep walking on and on before the sea reaches your knees; it's too cold for paddling now, of course. The snow has started again, and the beach is pale and misty, eerie as a moonscape. There are just three couples, walking briskly, anoraks zipped tightly, their hoods protecting their ears from the wind. But Julia wants the wind and the snow, its excoriating bite on her face, the moaning rush in her ears. So, without a hood and only sunglasses to protect her eyes from snow and sand, she strides vigorously, inhaling huge breaths of briny air.

Hilary loves it here too – or did when she was well enough to enjoy it, which now seems a painfully long time ago. Julia knows she is not coping well with Hilary's illness, that she picks on Tom. She is aware that she is making Tom's Algarve plan into a big thing so that she doesn't have to think about the prospect that in just a matter of weeks Hilary will be gone. Despite her many interests and commitments, it is this friendship and, later, her marriage to Tom that have been the sure footholds of her life since she left Simon. It was to Hilary that she had turned when she left her first marriage, and Julia wonders whether, without her, she would have coped with building a very different life.

She stops walking now, looking out through the fine snow to the Channel, wondering about Simon, now head of the Branston empire, still living in Paris but in a spectacular house near the Bois de Boulogne. Six months ago, she and Tom had been invited to Simon's third wedding, to a Swedish model less than half his age. They'd declined, but Julia, while getting her hair cut a month or so later, had chanced across a copy of *Hello!* magazine with pictures of the wedding and of the happy couple relaxing in their beautiful Paris home. She had to admit they looked good together: Simon, hair now silver, with the same dazzling blue eyes and his usual debonair stance, his arm around the waist of the beautiful blonde. She had studied the photographs with, what she thought might be, the air of a benevolent aunt. But, despite all the evidence of Simon's satisfying and successful life since she fled the Branston coop, thoughts of him always revive her latent guilt at having married him for all the wrong reasons.

'Are you really sure about this, Julia?' Hilary had asked when she had tearfully announced that she was going to leave Simon. Hilary, who was living in the small apartment to which she had moved after Eric's death three years earlier, had drawn her inside, and sat her down with a cup of tea and a box of tissues. 'It's a very big step. You do need to be sure that there is no alternative.'

'I'm sure,' Julia had said through her tears, 'I have to, Hil, I can't go on like this. I feel as though I'm living a double life. There's so much I want to do, and the campaigns we're working on are just part of it. You know how it is; the world is changing but Simon simply doesn't get it. And the thing is that, despite what he says, he doesn't want to get it. I can't live that life any longer, I want more. But Simon wants more too. He wants children and you know how I feel about that. I can't do the whole mother thing.'

'Then, when you're ready to leave, you must come here,' Hilary had said. 'Day or night, there's a place for you here with me.' And she had pressed a spare key into Julia's hand before she left.

What had made it harder for Julia was that she still cared for Simon, but joining the *Jeunes Femmes* had changed her. As she talked with women whose lives were so very different from her own, and others, who, like her, were struggling with new ideas that placed them at odds with everything they thought they knew about themselves, Julia recognised that her days with Simon were numbered.

'You see, Julia,' Minette had said to her the next day, when she had wept in the *Jeunes Femmes* office. 'When you understand these things that are political, but are also about who you are, you cannot go back.'

'No going back,' Julia had said, wiping her eyes.

That evening at the apartment, Julia had steeled herself to break the news that she wanted a divorce.

'No!' Simon cried. 'No, Julia. Please . . . whatever I've done, I can put it right. I know I'm an arrogant prick, but I do love you and I can be different.'

But they had been through it all before, many times, albeit without the threat of her leaving, and she knew he couldn't, or wouldn't, change. Simon could not be different and she could no longer be what he wanted.

'I can't do this anymore, Simon,' she had said. 'I can't keep on trying to be what you want me to be, and not only failing, but resenting having to try.'

'I don't think I've asked very much of you,' he'd said then.

'That's the problem. You haven't asked *enough*! You haven't wanted me to try new things or take risks. You treat what I now believe in as though it's a passing fancy, but it's who I am. You wanted me to stay as I was when we got married – just happy to be an ornament . . .'

'No!' he'd protested. 'It was never that. For god's sake, you're my wife, I love you. I want us to have a family.'

'Can you understand that you're not asking enough became too much for me? I know that sounds like a crazy contradiction, but it's how it is. And the one thing you *have* asked me for is the one thing I can't do. I know you want to have children and I've told you that I don't, but you don't listen. You say we should try and just see what happens, as though if I got pregnant, I'd find I was happy about it. Well, I know I won't and I won't even risk it . . .'

'But we *have* been trying,' Simon cut in.

She was silent for a moment. 'You have, Simon, but I haven't. I've been taking the pill.'

He turned sharply to look at her, his face desolate. 'You what? How could you, Julia? How could you lie to me like that?'

She shook her head. 'I don't know. You were so insistent that we should try, and I couldn't face any more arguments about it. I'm sorry, Simon. I'm not proud of it but I didn't know what else to do.'

'What sort of woman doesn't want children?' he demanded. 'What's *wrong* with you, Julia? Real women want children, so what's wrong with *you*?'

And that was when she had collected the suitcase she had packed that afternoon and left. It was the only really hurtful thing Simon had ever said to her. Sometime later he had apologised, but she hadn't needed the apology; she knew how much she had hurt him.

A few days later, in her room in Hilary's flat, Julia woke to find shock replaced with despair. Grief and guilt seeped into her bones like damp. She despised the self she had been; the prideful, shallow girl who had weighed up the pros and cons of her relationship, and arrived at all the wrong conclusions. Her parents' aspirations for her and the hurt of Tom's abandonment had certainly been factors, but in the end she had married Simon to have an easy life; for luxury and status, and to escape her parents in the most spectacular way she could.

Later that day, she had taken the Metro to Montmartre and made the steep climb to Sacre Coeur to stand where she had stood with Tom years earlier on the night he had asked her to marry him. Marriage had proved far more complex than she had ever imagined. It was a damp and chilly day. The sky was a solid misty grey that reflected her mood, and, as she stood looking out across the city, it began to rain, a rain that felt light but that quickly soaked her clothes and hair. She turned and opened the heavy wooden door.

Inside the cathedral, light drifted in through the high arched windows and candles flickered in the wrought-iron candelabras. From the choir stalls the voices of nuns practising their chorus rose in perfect harmony. Julia slipped a handful of francs into the box, picked a candle for Simon and lit it. Was it an apology, or a wish that he would find happiness? Both, perhaps. The second candle she lit for the wisdom and integrity to be true to herself in the future.

It was Hilary who had held Julia together in the months that followed, until she finally made up her mind to come back to England and start again. And it was Hilary who had worked so hard with her to build the business, and who, years later, held the fort at home and ran the language school during the long months in which Julia felt compelled to stay at Greenham Common.

And now, Julia thinks, walking on again, feeling the snow-flakes melting on her face, their icy trickles inside her collar, now Hilary's life is ending. And she really doesn't know how she is going to cope with that.

୦ଵଈ

It's Tom who takes the call, just as he and Richard are about to go to The George for a midday pint. He writes a note telling Julia to join them at the pub if she comes in, props it up against the jug of Christmas roses on the kitchen table, and is following Richard out the door when the phone rings.

'Shortly after your wife left, I'm afraid,' the director of nursing tells him. 'I've been trying to call Mrs Hammond on the mobile but it seems to be switched off. It was all very peaceful.'

Tom puts down the phone and sinks into a nearby chair. He has known Hilary for most of his life. After his marriage to Alison, embarrassment led him to drop out of touch for several years. And then, after that extraordinary day when he had, for once in his life, abandoned caution and driven out to the peace camp, in finding Julia, he'd also rediscovered Hilary.

'Two for the price of one,' he remembers her saying to him when he'd driven down to see her the following day. 'A bargain.'

Tom rests his elbows on his knees and puts his head in his hands. Knowing it was coming doesn't make it any easier. In recent years he has grown closer to Hilary than he is to anyone except Julia, and now she's gone and he has to break the news to his wife. Tears run down Tom's cheeks. He rubs them off and fumbles for his handkerchief as sobs choke him.

'Get a move on, Tom,' Richard shouts from the front step, 'the beer's getting warm.'

Tom gulps and tries to blow his nose. He is incapable of moving.

'What the hell are you . . .' Richard pauses in the doorway. 'Oh Lord. Is it Hilary?'

Tom nods, tears coursing uncontrollably down his face. 'Just after Julia left,' he manages to say. 'Very peaceful, they said.'

Richard sits on the arm of the chair and grips Tom's shoulder. 'I'm so sorry, Tom.'

Tom nods, speechless.

'So, Jules doesn't know yet? Any idea where she might be?'

Tom shrugs. She could be anywhere, he thinks; the beach, maybe just somewhere in town having a coffee. Suddenly he feels very old. Hilary, being so much younger than Eric, had always seemed young and she was only eight years older than he is. Tom's usual sense of himself as being lodged somewhere between eighteen and thirty has evaporated. We can kid ourselves most of the time, he thinks, but at my age, every day is a bonus.

'Should we go and look for her?' Richard asks. He has collected a bottle of brandy from the kitchen, and pours some into a glass and hands it to Tom. 'Here, drink this. It'll do you good.'

Tom swallows the brandy and feels the glow. 'I don't think there's any point in driving around. She could be anywhere,' he says. 'But we could walk up to The Copper Kettle, she likes the coffee there.' He thinks he sounds in control now and that it's amazing what you can achieve with a tone of voice. Tom knows he's going to need that tone of voice a lot in the days ahead.

TWENTY-THREE

Cottesloe – New Year's Day 2000

It's almost midnight when Justine wakes. She lies very still in the darkness, listening to Dan's breathing. All the time he was away, she had feared for his safety and worried that distance might change his feelings for her. On both counts she was, by turns, confident and despairing. A few times she had wondered if, once he was away from her, Dan would dwell on the difference in their ages and decide that it was too great. He'd told her that it didn't matter, but she couldn't avoid worrying that it might. But then there would be a letter or an email or, even better, a phone call from him and the world would be restored to rights again. Then, a week ago, he had called to tell her he was on his way back to Perth. He hadn't yet told his family, he said, because he wanted to spend a few days with her before he went home. She hadn't even known he'd been injured until he arrived at the door on crutches. They'd had five blissful days together before he felt he should make an appearance at home on New Year's Eve.

Needing to touch him now, but not wanting to wake him, Justine rests her cheek lightly against his shoulder and gently strokes Dan's back, and then slips quietly out of bed. On the balcony, she lights the citronella candle and sits watching the dark surface of the ocean gleaming in the moonlight. They'd known each other only a couple of months before Dan had been posted to East Timor, and they had met in such an unlikely way that the whole thing had seemed surreal. Now, as she sits here in the mild evening air, it still has the feel of magic.

It had happened one Saturday, a day on which Justine usually worked at the nursery. A friend whom she'd met years earlier at the horticultural course was heading off to a job in New Zealand and had organised a farewell lunch in town, so Justine had taken the day off and decided to take the train rather than drive so she could have a couple of drinks. Arriving at the station just as the train drew in, she had leapt aboard as the doors were closing. She lurched thankfully into the carriage and promptly tripped over someone's feet, almost ending up in his lap.

'Whoa!' he cried, catching her arm and steering her into the adjacent seat. 'Are you okay?'

'Fine, thanks,' Justine said, looking up at him, embarrassed by her own awkwardness. 'I'm so sorry; I hope I didn't hurt you.'

'On the contrary,' he said. 'For a moment there, I thought my luck had changed very much for the better. And, anyway, I'm the one who should apologise. I had my big feet sticking out.'

There had been a brief and lighthearted argument about who was responsible, and then an exchange about the dyed green hair of a fellow passenger. Ten minutes later, as the train pulled into Perth, they were arguing over whether Cottesloe beach was as good as Leighton, or even Fremantle's South Beach.

'Watch your step now!' he'd said with a broad grin as they parted on the platform.

And Justine, laughing, strolled off through the arts precinct into Northbridge, replaying the encounter in her head. In a weird sort of way, it had felt as though they knew each other, and he was undeniably attractive; tall and well built, dark skinned but probably, she thought, like herself, of mixed race, part African or Caribbean, maybe.

A large lunch and a few glasses of wine later, back at the station, she moved close to the edge of the platform as her train pulled in.

'Would you like a hand getting on?' said a voice just behind her, and almost jumping out of her skin, she swung round to find him standing there. Perhaps it was the effect of the wine, or the huge pink teddy bear wrapped in cellophane that he was carrying under one arm, but in that moment something quite extraordinary happened.

'I felt as though we were in another dimension,' Dan had told her weeks later. 'Almost as though I'd known you from another time, and all my life until then had been leading up to that moment.'

Justine doesn't know how long they stood there, just looking at each other, but it was long enough for the train to pull out of the station.

'I hope you weren't in a hurry,' she'd said.

He shook his head, and she saw him swallow hard; embarrassed, she thought, as she was now. He shifted the teddy to the other arm. 'I have all the time in the world. And you . . .'

She shrugged. 'Me too.'

'Well then, maybe . . . I mean, could I buy you a drink?'

Justine, ever cautious and self-contained, hesitated, about to decline. But something undefinable in the way he was looking at her made her want to capture and hold onto the moment. She normally found it hard to trust strangers and yet she trusted him.

Together they walked out of the station and across Forest Place, weaving their way through the arcades, past shops that were closing and people heading out of town for the evening, down to the Barrack Street Jetty, and ran the last few steps to the South Perth ferry just as the attendant closed the gangway.

'We can go to CoCo's or one of those other places on the waterfront,' Dan said, sitting the teddy on the seat.

Justine stared at the huge pink bear, a flush burning her face as she realised what it meant. A pink teddy – he was a father, a husband. The sudden bolt of disappointment pulled her up sharply. Don't be stupid, she told herself, you're going for a drink, that's all. You met a nice guy on a train, and you're having a drink, not interviewing a life partner.

'Do you have a daughter?' she asked as the ferry ploughed away from the jetty.

'A daughter? No . . .' he said, puzzled until he saw she was looking at the teddy. 'Oh, that! No, I have a sister – two sisters, actually – and Gaby, the youngest, has a birthday next week. She reckons she's had a deprived childhood because she never had one of these monstrosities. This is the largest I could find. I'm wondering how I'll get it in the house without her seeing it. If I'd come by car I could have hidden it in the boot, but the car's being serviced.'

'I hardly ever get the train,' Justine said. 'I just didn't want to drive home after lunch.'

'We were obviously meant to meet today,' Dan said with a smile. 'Thank god for public transport.'

Later, much later, they had shared a taxi, which dropped Justine off first, in Cottesloe.

'If you take this and hide it for me, Gaby won't see it,' Dan said, thrusting the teddy at her. 'And I would have an excuse to borrow my mum's car and drive over tomorrow to pick it up, which would mean I could take you for breakfast by the beach.'

How strange that something as simple as taking a train could change your life in an instant, Justine thinks now. And how strange that one microsecond in which a person's expression changes and is rapidly corrected can strike fear in her heart. It has been a difficult day and she suspects there are more ahead.

Did Dan see what happened at his parents' place? She thinks probably not, as he would have mentioned it; he's not one to avoid difficult topics. She had been nervous about meeting his family for the first time, especially as he'd only told them about her the previous night, but Dan had convinced her that it would be fine.

'They're really excited about meeting you,' he'd told her on the phone last night. 'But they think I just got back today, and I'd rather it stayed that way.'

'I'll behave as though it's the first time I've seen you in months,' she'd said. And this morning she'd made a berry cheesecake and put on a lemon-yellow cotton dress that always gave her confidence, and set off clutching the cake and a bottle of champagne.

'Don't worry about it,' Gwen had said, just as she was about to leave. 'They'll love you; why wouldn't they?'

'You think?'

'Of course. Look, no one would think twice about it if he were older than you.'

'No, but he's not, is he? And then there's the rest of it . . .'

'Now you're just being silly,' Gwen said. 'Dan's father was black; his family is hardly going to have problems with you.'

Justine watches the distant lights of a ship, moving very slowly along the horizon towards Fremantle. Why couldn't it be easy, for once? She relives the moment when Dan's face lit up as his mother came towards them, and then the look on Zoë's face as he introduced them. She had faltered slightly, retrieved her smile and extended her hand. Justine has been on the sharp end of enough prejudice to know that for some people there is a world of difference between social acceptance and actually welcoming someone of another race into the family. And she suspected that there was a difference, too, between being an Indigenous Australian and being exotically half Jamaican. But everything Dan had told her had encouraged her to believe that his mother was a generous, open-minded woman, who would welcome her; very different, he'd said, from his grandmother.

'Jus?' she hears Dan call.

'I'm here,' she says, coming in from the balcony and climbing back onto the bed beside him. 'I was sitting out there watching the ocean.'

'What time is it?'

'Just after midnight. Are you hungry?'

'A bit. It *is* quite a long time since lunch.' He pulls her gently towards him and strokes her arm. 'Did you sleep too?'

'Yes, I only woke up about ten minutes ago. All that champagne and wild sex! Not bad for a man with a dodgy leg.'

'Mmmmm! Tell me about it. No, don't or I'll start all over again, and I'd really like something to eat first.'

'There's heaps of stuff in the fridge.'

'Hang on,' he says. 'Before we eat, I need to talk to you.'

'Talk away, then.'

'All the time I was away, I was thinking of one thing – of coming back to you. I love you so much that I can't imagine now how it would be not having you in my life,' he says, stroking her shoulder.

'I love you too, Dan . . .' she begins, but he stops her with a kiss.

'I haven't quite finished.'

'Sorry, sir,' she says laughing, 'should've asked permission to speak.'

'I'll overlook your insubordination on this occasion because I have something to ask you.'

'Ask away.'

'Okay.' He pauses and she feels him take a deep breath. 'It's about my job. You know that I can be sent somewhere on the spur of the moment, and won't be able to tell you where, or for how long. I may not even have time to say goodbye.'

Justine swallows; she has thought of this long and often during his absence. 'I know,' she says. 'You told me all that before. I just had a dose of it, anyway.'

'And?'

'And what?'

'How was it?'

'Horrible. But better than not knowing you, not loving you.'

'Really? So, will you marry me, then?'

Her throat goes dry. 'Marry you? Is that really what you want?'

'Obviously. That's why I asked you.'

She props herself on her elbow to see him better. He is looking straight at her, smiling, but she can see a sliver of fear that she might reject him. She looks deep into his eyes. 'I'm twelve years older than you.'

'So, what's your point?'

'Some people would think it matters.'

'Well, I'm not one of them.'

'Your family?'

'It won't bother them,' he says.

She pauses, her skin prickling with excitement, and leans

forward to kiss him lightly on the lips. 'Then, yes,' she says. 'Of course I'll marry you; yes, yes, yes!'

His arms are around her now, and he lets out a great whoop of delight as they roll across the bed laughing, kissing, and suddenly he is inside her again.

'There's *one* thing, though,' Justine says, as they finally get up and pull their clothes on to go to the kitchen in search of food. 'There's stuff I need to tell you.' And, as she says it, she wishes she hadn't. There is so much to explain, not just what happened with Zoë, but about the past. He knows only that she went from the convent to the farm, and that when Gwen sold the property, they came to Cottesloe to live with Gwen's mother. She will have to tell him the rest and soon, but not tonight; she needs a little more time. And that, she thinks, is perhaps what Zoë needs too.

'Then tell me,' he says. 'But not tonight, because it sounds serious and there's nothing you can tell me that will change the fact that you are the love of my life, and you have promised to marry me. You know the SAS motto – who dares wins. I've dared and I've won.'

⌒⌒⌒

'I think she's cool,' Rosie says, collecting the dirty glasses. 'And Dan's besotted with her.'

Archie stands with a bag full of rubbish in his hand. 'Yep, our Dan's a goner this time, that's pretty obvious. I liked her too, very much. Gabs?'

'Yeah,' Gaby says, picking up a stray VB can from the deck. 'She's really nice. Mum, you like Justine too, don't you? Well, you already knew her from the nursery.'

Zoë, standing in the kitchen clutching the soiled tablecloths, pretends not to hear and hurries to the laundry, where she stuffs them in the washing machine and slams the lid closed. Her face burns as she recalls attempting to mask her shock. Why did Dan spring Justine on them like this? Was it some sort of test? Well, if it was, she has failed it miserably and she's not ashamed of that.

Except, of course, that she is or she wouldn't be hiding in the laundry. She tries not to give in to tears. Justine is probably a very nice woman, but she's not the right woman for Dan. Anyway, it may not last; previous girlfriends have run a mile from his job. Justine will probably be the same: unable to tolerate the secrecy, the absences, the demands of the army.

'Where *are* you, Zo?' Archie calls from the kitchen. 'I'm making tea.'

Zoë takes a deep breath and walks out of the laundry. 'Here,' she says. 'I was putting the tablecloths in the washer.'

'You want tea?'

'Desperately!'

'Good. The girls and I were talking about Justine.'

Zoë's jaw tightens.

'We've given her the stamp of approval.'

'Yep,' Gaby says, coming in from the deck to put the unused paper napkins away in the cupboard. 'I *really* like her. She comes from the Pilbara.'

'D'you think she's one of those children who were taken away?' Rosie asks, leaning on the door jamb. 'She's not a full-blooded Aboriginal, is she?'

Archie shakes his head. 'No. I guess she might be – she's the right sort of age. What d'you think, Zo?'

'Sorry?'

'Do you think she's one of the kids who were taken from their families?'

'Stolen generation,' Rosie says. 'I might ask her next time.'

'She's really pretty,' Gaby says. 'And she's got those cool thongs, the gold ones with all the sparkly bits, like I want.'

'She's a lot older than Dan,' Zoë says.

'She's certainly older than I expected,' Archie agrees.

'She's forty-three,' Rosie says. 'But she looks much younger.'

'Forty-three!' Zoë gasps. 'How do you know that?'

'She told me,' Rosie says. 'I asked her.'

'Twelve years.' Zoë looks at Archie. 'That's a lot. Don't you think it's a lot?'

He shrugs, handing round the mugs of tea. 'It's quite a bit but it doesn't really matter, does it? I mean, we wouldn't even be talking about it if it was the other way round.'

'We might!'

'I doubt it.' He sips his tea and pauses. 'I'm nine years older than you and we never discussed that. Something wrong, love?'

Zoë shakes her head. 'Not really.'

'What does that mean?'

'Oh, I don't know,' she hesitates. 'Well, I'm a bit hurt, I suppose. They left so early. He's just gone off with her for the night and it's only twenty-four hours since he got home.'

Archie throws back his head and laughs, then tips his chair forward and strokes her hair. 'He's in love, Zo, *they're* in love, and they haven't seen each other for months. What d'you expect?'

'I think he could have stayed here, for tonight at least. We're his family, after all.' And, as she says it, Zoë can hear something horribly familiar in her voice. She sounds just like her mother.

⌒⌒

Archie doesn't wait up. Zoë's annoying him. She's doing that thing when she won't say what's really upsetting her. Her mouth goes all tight and, although you get the feeling she wants you to beg her to tell you what's wrong, her body language says to leave her alone. So he has. He believes that you treat people with respect and get the same in return, but tonight he's tired of Zoë's menopausal moods, of the effort of trying to empathise, to watch what he says in case she takes it the wrong way. It's been a good day, but now Zoë's being a pain in the arse and Archie can't be bothered.

Dan, he thinks, what a bloody brilliant bloke he's turned out to be. That serious, bright little boy – often too bright for his own good. Now look at him. Survives the toughest the army has to offer and comes out with flying colours. Archie stares up at the bedroom ceiling and locks his arms behind his head, thinking of how scared he was of Dan way back when.

'I've never had anything to do with kids,' he remembers saying to Zoë. 'I don't really know what to do with them.'

'Just be yourself,' she'd said. 'You're already his hero.'

But it's not so easy when they're not your own; when you haven't been around them from the start and you don't know what the boundaries are. What if I don't agree with the way she wants to raise him? Am I supposed to do the disciplining or should I leave that to her? Will I love him as much when I have my own kids? But Dan has become Archie's son, and now he's a man, he's a friend as well and he's got this lovely woman.

It's going to be a good year, Archie tells himself now. But he knows it has to start right. He remembers a time when Rosie was about thirteen and she'd been in trouble for something that had made him bawl her out and she had ended up in tears. Later, feeling guilty that he'd been too hard on her, he'd gone up to her room and found her sitting on her bed, reading. When she looked up there was a crushed look in her eyes that nearly broke him.

'I'm really sorry, Dad,' she'd said. And he'd hoped she wasn't going to cry again because he might find himself doing the same thing.

'It's okay, love,' he'd said, sitting down on the end of the bed. 'All over now. You were in the wrong but I overreacted. I'm sorry.' And she'd dropped her book and flung her arms around his neck.

'I love you so much,' she'd said. 'I'm really sorry.'

They'd talked for a while and when he stood to leave he picked up the book from the floor.

'*Little Women*,' he'd said, looking at the cover. 'That's an old one. Good, is it?'

'It's brilliant,' Rosie said, and she began to flick through the pages. 'And do you know what it says? That you should never let the sun go down on your anger. I like that, don't you? I mean, suppose you'd gone to bed angry with me and died, or something, or I'd died.'

The thought was so terrible that it took Archie's breath away. 'It would have been really awful,' he said, with some difficulty. 'Really, really awful, sweetheart. I'll remember that, always; I promise.' And he'd kissed her again, and left the room feeling so emotional that he'd had to take the dog out for a walk to get himself back together again.

As he recalls this now he sighs wearily, gets out of bed and pads through to the kitchen, where Zoë is, for some reason, sorting through the contents of the fridge. He goes up behind her and puts his arms around her waist; she stiffens, straightens and then relaxes against him.

'I thought you were asleep,' she says, tipping her head back onto his shoulder.

Archie kisses her neck, just below her ear. 'I missed you,' he says. 'Stop sulking and come to bed.'

'I'm not sulking.'

'Then stop whatever it is you're doing and come to bed.'

She turns and puts her arms around him, her face against his shoulder. 'Say it again,' she says.

'Say what again?'

'That thing you said when everyone was here, the New Year toast thing.'

'Ah,' Archie says, trying to recall his exact words. 'Er . . . new century, New Year, a time to break new ground . . .' He hesitates. 'Break new ground, strive to be better and love each other more than ever. Was that it?'

'Yes,' she says, 'that sounds right.'

'Then, come on, lovely one,' he says, kissing the top of her head. 'Come to bed and we'll love each other more than ever. That'll be hard, of course, because I love you so much already, even when you've got the grumps.'

Zoë looks up. 'Don't push your luck,' she says. And she kisses the line of his jaw, closes the fridge door and lets him lead her into their bedroom.

TWENTY-FOUR

Rye – Mid-January 2000

It's a glorious winter's day; the ground gleams with frost, but the snow has gone and the sun shines from an almost cloudless sky. It pours through the stained-glass windows, casting jewel-bright rays across the glowing timber of the coffin with its simple display of white lilies and green ivy.

'In the midst of life, we are in death,' says the vicar.

Tom shifts uncomfortably in the pew, Julia sighs and Richard pats the flask in his pocket.

Julia wants it to be over. She wants to be alone, or, at least, alone with Tom. They had to wait two weeks until Hilary's brother and sister-in-law could get a flight from Johannesburg, and her niece could come from Saskatchewan before having the funeral. Julia has never seen these people in the more than thirty years she has known and lived with Hilary. They have simply been names on Christmas cards or email addresses.

'Probably wondering about the will,' Tom had said this morning.

'Huh!' said Julia. 'They can wonder on.'

'Will they get anything?' Richard had asked, while warming croissants he'd bought for their breakfast.

'There's nothing to get,' Tom said. 'Only her personal things, clothes, books, ornaments. You know. There's a bit of jewellery but nothing valuable.'

'The thing is,' Julia said to Richard, dunking a croissant in her coffee, 'she and Eric didn't actually have much. The flat in Paris belonged to the church. Anglican vicars earn very little and Eric was always giving money away to good causes. When she and I came back together from Paris, she had practically nothing. That's why she started giving the French lessons. Then, when we opened the school, she had a salary, and in the end she just had her pension. Tom and I helped her out with money from time to time.' She paused, sighing. 'She did so much for us, just by . . .' she stopped, thinking she was going to cry again.

'By simply being herself,' Tom finished for her.

'Yes,' Julia said, swallowing hard. 'Just by being herself.'

The congregation launches into Hilary's favourite hymn.

'He who would valiant be 'gainst all disaster . . .'

Julia and Tom sing it as Hilary always sang it, changing the male pronoun to female. Tom's voice is as strong as ever, with perfect pitch. It is one of the things that always reminds her of Tom's finest qualities, the reasons she loves him so much still, after all this time.

'No foes shall stay her might; though she with giants fight,
She will make good her right to be a pilgrim.'

Tom reaches for Julia's hand and they stand together, tears running down their faces and splashing onto the order of service. She notices there is also a tear in Richard's eye, and she wonders if he has been drinking this morning. Across the aisle, Hilary's relatives stand dry-eyed, opening and closing their mouths but not really singing. Julia finds it difficult to think of these cold, disinterested people as having anything to do with funny, intense, passionate Hilary, who would be laughing her socks off if she knew they had travelled hundreds of miles at great expense, to check out her will. Family, Julia thinks, Hilary was much more a part of our family than she was of theirs. You don't need blood to make a family. Julia is far more devastated by the loss of her dearest friend than she was by the loss of her mother, years earlier. She thinks of friends from school, of people whom she sees from time to time and is still fond of, Simon among them, and closer, more recent, friends.

She pauses briefly, remembering a fitting room, a white velvet wedding dress, and Zoë smoothing down the fabric and asking her how often she and Simon had sex. Where is she now? Zoë and her baby, who must by now be a man, probably with kids of his own?

'I think your loyalty to Richard was totally understandable,' Hilary had said, not so long ago, when Julia had raised again the subject they had discussed many times. 'It's easy to look back with the wisdom of hindsight and say you should have done this or that. But it's done; we can only learn from these things and strive to do better.'

'Have you ever heard anything about Zoë?' Julia asks Richard much later, when they are washing up after the wake.

'Not really,' Richard says. 'Not since I met that woman years ago, the one she used to share the house with, who said she'd gone back to Perth.' He pauses.

'What?' Julia asks. 'You're stalling.'

'Well,' he says. 'I did actually look for her on that website; you know, the one where you can find your old friends.'

'Friends Reunited?'

'Yes.'

'But don't you have to trace people through their school?'

He shakes his head. 'No. Well, yes, you do, but these days you can also do it through their workplace. So, I looked to see if she'd registered on the BBC list.'

Julia turned to him. 'Was she there?'

'No. But a girl she worked with on *The Dales* was.'

'*The Dales*,' Julia says. 'My god, I'd forgotten that. So?'

'I emailed her, Jackie something or other, asked her if she knew what happened to Zoë. She sent me her email address.'

Julia swings away from the sink, soapy water flying from her arms across the quarry tiles. 'When was this?'

He shrugs. 'Oh, I dunno; a year, eighteen months ago.'

'You never told me.'

'I didn't think you'd be interested.'

'Did you email her?'

Richard shakes his head.

'Why not?'

'What could I say? It sounds a little crass, don't you think? Hi, Zoë, it's me; your ex who abandoned you at the worst time of your life. What are you doing these days?'

'Well, why did you bother to get her address in the first place?'

Richard sighs and puts down the tea towel. 'I *was* thinking of getting in touch but when I actually *could*, it didn't seem such a good idea. What would be the point?'

Julia stares at him. 'Do you think about her much?'

He shrugs. 'From time to time. Usually when I'm in my what-a-fuck-up-you've-made-of-your-life-you-tosser mood.'

'Can I have the address?'

'What for?'

'I might want to email her.'

'Email who?' Tom asks, coming into the kitchen with a tray of dirty coffee cups and saucers.

They ignore him.

'If you want, I suppose. But why?'

Julia dries her hands on the tea towel. 'Because she was nice, really nice, and brave, and because you and I – and Dad of course – shafted her.'

'Whom did you shaft?' Tom asks, unloading the tray onto the draining board.

'Zoë. Richard's ex.'

'I don't know that shafted is –' Richard begins.

'Ah,' Tom interrupts, 'all that. The unfinished business.'

They look at him and then at each other.

'Yes, well . . .' Julia says. 'Richard, leave the glasses, and go and get me the address, please. Put it up here on the message board.'

'But what will you say?'

'I don't *know*. Hello, Zoë, I've been thinking of you and I . . . I thought . . . I wondered if . . . Oh lord, I don't know. I don't even know if I'll do it but I want the address in case I decide to. Do it now, please, before you forget.'

'And the perpetrators return to the scene of the crime,' Tom says, rolling his eyes.

'Shut up, Tom,' Julia says. 'It's your turn to wash now.'

⌒⌒⌒

The beach at dawn is paradise: the sea, silky calm; pale, flat sand washed by ripples lace-edged with foam; the endless blue of the sky fading to a paler haze on the horizon. Gwen swims laps as though she's in a pool, her arms cleaving the water with surprising strength, feet alternating briskly and trailing ruffles of water in her wake. She always starts like this, at least when the water is calm. In winter, of course, when it's still dark at six o'clock, and the waves rear up and sling seaweed and bits of driftwood around, you often can't swim at all. You just flounder, treading water, pitting yourself against the current, hoping you emerge in almost the same place as you went in. Gwen knows that Justine worries about her swimming in the winter, and, most of all, doesn't approve of her swimming in the dark. But it's not as though she's alone; there are always others around, even on the worst days. Gwen has for more than a decade been one of the Polar Bears, the intrepid group of swimmers who take to the water at dawn all year round, irrespective of the weather. As she often reminds Justine, she may be seventy-four but there are several Polar Bears who are older than she is.

When she's done with her serious swimming, Gwen rolls onto her back and floats, moving her arms gently at her sides and watching Justine, who has joined her this morning, undoubtedly because she has something she wants to talk about. Dan is still asleep back at the house.

Justine is a messy swimmer, thrashing about with arms like windmills, legs totally out of sync, shaking her head and spluttering. It is, Gwen observes, an extraordinary performance for a woman who is so graceful on land, who walks like a dancer.

'Getting out now,' Justine calls from a distance. She crashes off through the water to the shallows and walks swiftly up the sand to where she left her towel.

Gwen rolls over and over in the water, dives down to the sandy bottom and floats up again, before turning to swim slowly back to the beach. Some of her fellow swimmers are heading up to the old lifesavers' building, where they usually have tea and toast. In winter, they hunch their shoulders into tracksuits and clutch warm mugs with both hands, savouring every bit of warmth. This morning they meander between the hut and the beach, talking, dripping sea water, contemplating a second swim. Gwen waves to a couple she knows well and turns along the beach to join Justine.

'I've told Dan,' Justine says from her seat on the towel, looking up at Gwen, who is drying her hair on a second towel. 'I told him about Mal a couple of weeks ago.'

'Everything?'

Justine shakes her head. 'Not yet. Just what happened to me, about you taking me to hospital and then giving up the farm.'

'But not . . .'

'No.'

Gwen's heart beats faster and she feels slightly dizzy. Dropping her towel onto the sand, she sits down suddenly. She has lived so long with her secret. 'And what did he say?'

'He was wonderful. Sad for me, of course, and for you, but totally understanding.'

'And when will you tell him the rest of it? Are you worried about it?'

Justine smiles and reaches out for her hand. 'No. And neither should you be. He'll understand, and if by the remotest chance he doesn't he won't be the man I want to be with.'

Gwen nods. 'It would be dreadful if what I did spoiled this for you.'

'It won't, Gwen. I'll tell him soon. And, anyway, you have to stop looking so worried and be happy, because he's asked me to marry him.'

'Marry him! Really?' Gwen says. 'And did you say yes?'

'Of course I did. With indecent haste, almost before he got the words out of his mouth!' she says, laughing.

Gwen flings her arms around her, their wet limbs slide together and water drips from their hair onto each other's shoulders.

'Darling Justine, I'm so happy for you.' She leans back on her haunches, her hands on Justine's upper arms, looking into her face. 'Dan is a lovely man, and he's also a lucky one.'

'I'm lucky too,' Justine says and a huge smile seems to take over her face.

'And you can cope with his job?'

She nods. 'I think so. It was really hard this time but maybe it gets easier. I've been thinking about it a lot, and I have you and the nursery, my friends; I've got a lot to sustain me when he's away. It's pretty scary but he's worth it. I love him to bits.' She puts her hand on Gwen's. 'You're sure you're okay with this?'

'Absolutely. When are you going to get married?'

'Not sure yet, maybe towards the end of the year.'

'When did he ask you?'

'New Year's Day.'

'So, who else have you told?'

'No one, yet.'

'What about Dan's family?'

'We're going to leave it a while. Wait until we're clear about our plans, about where we're going to live.'

Gwen looks away quickly to compose her expression. She has always known Justine would leave one day, but the length of time they've been together – more than thirty years – and the fact that Justine has never previously been in a serious relationship have lulled her into a sense of security. Without Justine, she is a solitary person, not entirely by choice. She has a full and satisfying life, but it is grounded in her privacy and solitude, and in her love for Justine and the knowledge they share. There have been times when Justine went away for long periods; a whole year working in the Pilbara, almost two years backpacking and working in Europe. But she has always come back; this is different.

'So you haven't decided where you'll live,' Gwen says now.

Justine shakes her head. 'No. But I . . . we wondered . . . and you must say if this is not okay . . . I wondered if we might start off downstairs.'

'In the flat?' Gwen says, her spirits taking a dramatic turn upward.

'If you didn't mind.'

'Mind! I'd love it, it would be perfect. Will the flat be big enough?'

Justine laughs. 'It's huge, Gwen. It's probably the only granny flat in existence with so much space, and a lovely balcony looking out over the water.'

The flat is the whole ground floor of the house, which in the seventies Gwen had turned into a self-contained unit for her mother. She had lived there for more than ten years before she died, and since then other family and friends have used it from time to time. Gwen is dizzy again, this time with pleasure.

'We could redecorate,' she says, relieved to find herself speaking of such normal and positive things, 'refit the bathroom and kitchen.' She pictures sunlight falling on gleaming paintwork, granite work tops, cedar blinds and mellow terracotta tiles. All warmed by the glow of Justine's happiness.

'Well, we don't need to do all that but we thought if you were okay with it, we might paint it before we move in. And we'll pay you proper rent, of course. It just seems it would be a good place to start. For me, too, when Dan's away . . . it's an easy way for me to ease myself into that life, having you there too.' She pauses. 'But I'd understand if you'd like to have the place to yourself after all these years.'

'I'd hate it!' Gwen says. 'I'd miss you dreadfully and, while I do know you'll go sometime, I'm delighted it doesn't have to be just yet.' She lays her towel flat on the sand now and stretches out. 'Do let's get it done properly; it would be such fun. Dan wouldn't mind, would he?'

'He'd love it,' Justine says with a laugh. 'He's raring to do a bit of one-legged DIY before he goes back to work.'

'And what about his family? They'll be pleased too, won't they?'

'Um . . . I think Archie will be, and the girls too . . . I'm not so sure about Zoë. I don't think she's feeling too comfortable about things at the moment.'

'She'll be fine,' Gwen says, her happiness breeding confidence. 'She probably just needs time. They must be very close; after all, it was just the two of them for years, wasn't it? And she's got used to him being single. I'm really looking forward to meeting her.'

'You're probably right,' Justine says, and Gwen thinks that she's about to say something else, before she repeats herself. 'You're probably right. Mothers and sons, it's a big thing, isn't it? She's just getting used to the idea.'

And, for an instant Gwen thinks she sees something in Justine's expression, but it is gone so quickly that she decides she must have imagined it.

'Oh, Jus, this is so exciting,' she says. 'I can't tell you how happy I am for you. Let's go home and wake Dan up and have breakfast, and we'll open up the flat and see what needs doing.'

TWENTY-FIVE

Rye – February 2000

Tom gets off the train and walks up the platform. The station is seething with people, all of whom seem to be in a terrible hurry. Why does everyone have to hurry these days, he wonders; why don't people take time just to be? This is how he used to be, rushing everywhere, commuting back and forth between Rye and London, hooked on the adrenaline and status of his corporate life. Now, of course, he wishes he'd quit the treadmill before, when Julia told him to, after his prostate operation. But back then, the idea of retirement, especially early retirement, had been far too scary; getting back to work was proof of life. Now, Hilary's death is another reminder that one must make the most of the time one has left, which is why he hates this annual trek to London; once you've had a brush with death you can't ignore it. He wonders if any of the hurrying people are on similar missions – blokes heading for their prostate examinations, women on their way to mammograms. Sometimes Julia comes with him but this time, her grief still raw after losing Hilary, he had told her he'd go alone. It would be easier, of course, if he went to a specialist nearer home, but he'd rather see Raheem. If it hadn't been for Raheem, Tom knows, he might not have made it.

Crossing the station concourse, Tom heads to the Underground to go to Raheem's rooms in Harley Street. It's the waste of time that annoys him; every time he's been back he's had the all-clear

223

but it costs him a couple of hundred quid and a wasted day. He straightens his shoulders and pulls in his stomach, in a conscious effort to pull himself together. A couple of hours and it'll all be over for another twelve months, and he can get back to Rye and call in at the travel agency before they close. He wants to book the holiday before Julia has a chance to change her mind. Having finally convinced her that he is not set on moving from England, merely wants to find a place for holidays, she has agreed to go to Portugal.

'Just a holiday, though,' she had said before he left this morning. 'A bit of sun. Don't read it as a signal that I'm ready for tennis or golf, or Mediterranean retirement.'

'We've been through all that, darling,' he'd said. 'Just a holiday, and the Algarve isn't on the Med. What's happened to your geography?'

Tom smiles now thinking of it; she is so stubborn, and so determined not to end up like Ralph and Anita. He inhales deeply at the prospect of Portugal – sun, sea and sand, the scent of garlic – and steps rapidly back from the sickening blast of hot, soot-scented air as the train arrives at the platform.

Hours later, the tickets and hotel reservations in a plastic voucher in his inside pocket, Tom retraces his steps back up the hill from the station to home. The solid steel grey of the afternoon sky has darkened depressingly early, to a merciless charcoal dusk, and the cobbled streets that lead up to Church Square seem particularly steep today. As he reaches the top of the hill, he hears the familiar rattle as the mechanism of the quarter boys ratchets up to strike quarter to six. He stops to catch his breath and watch these strange mechanical figures in the clock tower doing what they've been doing for the last three hundred years. Then he walks through the darkness of the churchyard, from where he can see the lights of home between the bare branches of the catalpa tree. The curtains are still open, warm and welcoming, and he quickens his step and lets himself in through the front door with a mixture of relief and dread.

'There you are!' Julia calls out, hearing him in the hall. 'You've been hours. I was starting to worry about you. Glass of wine or cup of tea?'

'Tea, please,' Tom says, unbuttoning his coat. 'In a big mug.' He walks through to the kitchen, sniffing. 'Smells good.'

'I made your favourite pork and bean casserole, as a reward for staggering off to that awful consultation on your own.' She crosses the kitchen and kisses him. 'How was it?'

Tom holds her, looking into her face, seeing again the complex traces of grief and exhaustion.

Julia tilts her head back and looks at him. 'Everything *was* okay, wasn't it?'

He hesitates, inhales deeply, makes a decision and then changes his mind. 'Of course,' he says, smiling. 'Clean as a whistle, same as always.'

She kisses him again and returns to the kettle, which has just come to the boil.

'Well it's always best to check.'

'Indeed it is,' Tom says. 'Watching our health has replaced religion and television as the opium of the masses.'

Julia laughs and pours water into the teapot.

He pulls the plastic folder from his inside pocket and drops it on the kitchen table. 'Got the tickets.'

She turns to him. 'Good. I'm actually looking forward to it now I've got used to the idea. I think we both need a break and some sun. When are we off?'

'Next week. Wednesday.'

'So soon . . . I thought . . .'

'Why wait? We need a break and there's nothing to stop us.'

She hands him the tea in his favourite mug. 'No, I suppose not. Marion's doing a great job with the business; hardly seems to need me. So, you booked for two weeks?'

'Three and a half.'

'Cheeky – I only agreed to a fortnight.'

'You know me,' he says. 'I need very little encouragement and I start taking advantage.' He wraps his arms around her waist. 'You are an amazing woman, my darling,' he continues. 'In all the years we've been together there has never been a moment when I haven't been aware how fortunate I am to be spending my life with you.'

Julia half turns to him and puts down the spoon she's holding. 'Goodness,' she says, 'you're very romantic tonight. Good thing you didn't come home with flowers or I might think you had a guilty conscience.' She kisses him then, firmly, on the lips. 'I love you too, Tomo, just as much as ever. Are you *sure* everything's okay? You look a bit off colour.'

'Just tired,' he says, 'bloody London. Don't know how I ever put up with it. Should've listened to you and retired earlier, waste of precious time.'

'Well, you've plenty of time now,' she says, 'so cheer up and sing to me while I finish off the soup.'

And Tom clears his throat and summons his flagging energy. '*Come fly with me . . .*' he sings as he opens the folder with the tickets and hotel bookings, and shuffles through them.

And Julia hums contentedly along with him.

⌒⌒⌒

Zoë drives down Finnerty Street looking for a parking space. All the bays are taken, so she parks in a side street. There must be something on at the Arts Centre; it's not usually as busy as this on a weekday. She has promised Rosie, who has gone off on a field trip for uni, that she will go in and buy the earrings that Rosie spotted at the weekend and then wished she'd bought. Earrings are Rosie's thing – large, unusual ones – for which, in Zoë's opinion, she pays far too much for a student whose only income is from working shifts in a local café. Rob's family are recent millionaires, winemakers from the Swan Valley and Zoë suspects that he sometimes gives Rosie money.

'I feel I should ask her about it,' she'd said to Archie this morning. 'It doesn't seem right.'

'You are *not* to ask her, Zo,' he'd said. 'It's not our business. Think how you would have felt if Eileen had asked you something like that.'

Zoë remembers how she was at nineteen. The freedom of

London, the way she hid everything she could from Eileen and resented the questions in those weekly calls.

'You're right, I would have hated it,' she'd said. 'I sometimes think I react to the girls just like Mum did to me.'

Archie held up his hands in protest. 'You have a very open and honest relationship with them, they can talk to you.' He'd put an arm around her shoulders and kissed her quickly on the top of her head. 'They're growing up,' he said. 'We have to learn to let go.'

He's right, of course, Zoë thinks now as she wanders into the shady grounds of the Arts Centre. Knowing you have to let go, though, is a long way from actually being able to do it.

There are some weird sculptures and a couple of large multimedia installations ranged across the lawn. They're ugly, she thinks, lumps of metal and wire, old tiles, and what look like bits of old baskets all stuck together and she walks quickly past them to the gift shop.

The earrings are easy to find; they are dangling clusters of sparkling purple and turquoise beads. Just as the sales assistant is about to close the case, Zoë sees another pair. They are similar to Rosie's, only not so large and the beads are lime green.

'And could I have a look at those too, please?' she asks.

Holding them against her ears in front of the mirror she knows she has to have them. They are unlike anything else she owns and they are perfect. She gasps when the assistant tells her the price – they are twice the price of Rosie's earrings, but she buys them just the same. Archie is always telling her she should treat herself more often. As she waits for the earrings to be wrapped, she walks across the shop to another jewellery cabinet, in which there are silver pendants, and, to her surprise, an oval pendant of blue and white enamel. It is larger than the heart-shaped pendant that was Richard's first gift to her, but the design and colour of the enamel are remarkably similar. For years after Dan's birth she locked it away, but she has never been able to bring herself to part with it.

Zoë decides to stop for a coffee in the courtyard café. Choosing a small table tucked away in a corner under the grapevines, she orders and waits silently, comfortable to be the observer. At the other end of the courtyard there are two women from her book club, they smile and wave but make no indication that she should join them and that's a relief. Zoë envies the easy friendships she sees around her, but her childhood isolation has created a barrier she feels unable to cross.

'You keep yourself to yourself, it's nobody else's business what we do,' Eileen had insisted. 'And don't go bringing those girls home after school.' Visiting friends' houses was largely forbidden too. 'You don't know what goes on behind closed doors, and you don't need to,' was the usual response when Zoë was invited to tea, or just to play. Even birthday parties were suspect and if she did manage to get Eileen to agree to her attending one, her mother would turn up to collect her long before the festivities were over; sometimes even before the cake had been cut.

Friendship was, and remains, too risky; there is only Jane and once, a long time ago, there was Julia. Even when she lived in the house in Delphi Street, she kept her distance. She circled around looking for ways in but never actually taking them. She had risked herself with intimacy, love and friendship and wouldn't risk losing everything again.

Zoë sips her coffee and nibbles on a little almond biscuit. Being a wife and mother may be considered unadventurous by some, but it has been entirely satisfying. Now, though, everything is changing. Dan disappearing frequently to dangerous unknown places; the girls growing up and planning to leave.

Finishing her coffee, Zoë walks out of the courtyard and into the cool, white-painted corridors of the main building. She is not inspired by the artwork on the walls, which lack the colour and action that she suddenly needs. She turns to leave and walks briskly across the highly polished timber floors into the passage. She has never been inside this part of the building before but vaguely remembers Eileen saying that it used to be the women's asylum. She walks on up a creaky staircase, past the State Literature Office. Then, ahead of her she sees a huge room, flooded with light from the high windows, in which a dozen or more people seated at easels are painting. At the far end of the room, a man, palette in hand, seems to be about to wind up the session.

'So, that's it,' he says. 'I hope you've enjoyed it, and if you want to go on, just call in at the office downstairs and they'll give you the info on the advanced classes.'

The painters shift in their seats and fiddle with their brushes. Zoë stares over their shoulders at the different variations of the same landscape. It's extraordinary, she thinks; some of them look really good, others look weird, but each is distinctly different. Is it because of the different levels of skill, or do they just see it in different ways?

People are rinsing out water jars, re-capping tubes of paint, drying their hands on rags or on their jeans. Zoë spots a familiar face; a woman who sometimes works in the healthfood shop in town is drying her brushes on a piece of old T-shirt. Glancing up, she sees Zoë standing in the doorway and smiles. Zoë walks over to her.

'Hi,' she says awkwardly. 'I was just watching. Your painting's beautiful.'

The woman pulls a face. 'Hardly,' she says. 'I'm a complete beginner but I'm better than I was twelve weeks ago, before this course.'

'Twelve weeks. Is that all?' Zoë asks in surprise. 'It looks really professional.'

'Whatever that means . . .' the woman says with a laugh. 'This is the beginners' class but Theo's a very good teacher. Do you paint?'

'Oh no. I don't even know if I could.'

'Nor did I until I tried. But it's enormous fun.' The woman straightens up from putting her pad and brushes away. 'And it's wonderfully restful. It feels quite self-indulgent because you get so wrapped up in what you're doing you forget about all the other crap going on outside. You get so involved that for a little while the painting is all that matters.'

'Really?' Zoë stares at her.

'Really. Well, that's how it is for me. You should try it sometime, I bet you'd love it. Excuse me, I'd better go and wash my palette now.' And, smiling, she crosses to the sink.

Zoë waits until only the teacher remains, writing something in a notebook. She hovers again near the doorway, hoping he'll notice her.

'Oh, hi,' he says, eventually glancing up and seeing her. 'Are you waiting for me?'

She steps into the room. 'Well, yes, if you have a minute.'

'What can I do for you?'

'I was just wondering about this class, the beginners' one. Whether I could join . . .'

'Today was week twelve; the last, I'm afraid,' he says. 'Are you sure you're a beginner, because maybe you could do the intermediate?'

'Oh no, I'm a beginner definitely. I haven't even held a paint-brush since primary school, and that's a very, very long time ago.'

'I don't believe it's *that* long,' he says grinning and, to her amazement, Zoë realises he's half flirting with her. She blushes.

'Anyway,' he says, 'there's a new beginners' class starting next month. If you're interested, you could check at the office down-stairs. I think there are still a few places.'

'And . . . is that . . . will you be . . .'

'Oh yes. I'll be teaching it. Theo,' he says, stretching out his hand. 'And you are?'

'Zoë.'

'Okay, Zoë. I look forward to seeing you.' And he turns back to his notebook.

Zoë walks out of the studio and downstairs, where she enrols for the course and pays. She leaves wondering why on earth she's done it and if she will actually be brave enough to turn up on the last Wednesday of the month.

TWENTY-SIX

San Francisco – March 2000

Richard walks briskly through San Francisco airport and out into the late afternoon sunshine to the line of waiting cabs. He is high on the chance to strut his stuff tomorrow at an international conference on the future of journalism. Martin Gilbert had top billing but, two days ago, he broke a leg, two ribs and a collarbone in a skiing accident. Tomorrow, Richard will deliver a speech on the challenges facing television current affairs, to an audience of the elite in the media industry. It is an opportunity to ensure that next time he will be the conference organisers' first choice.

'So you're well and truly plastered?' he had joked to Martin.

'I am, and I want your promise that *you* won't be plastered at the conference. Belinda will email you my speech.'

'I have one of my own,' Richard said, defensive now. It was only half a lie, as he'd been working on an article on the subject, which could quickly be adapted for the presentation.

'Okay, up to you. But stay off the booze the night before.'

'For fuck's sake, Martin, do you think I'm an idiot or something?'

'If I did, I wouldn't be asking you to step in for me. But I know what you're like when you're on the piss.'

'It's my business what and when I drink,' Richard said. He was sick of people hammering him about his drinking.

'Wind your neck in, Rich,' Martin said. 'I need to know I can rely on you.'

Now, two days later, in the back seat of a San Francisco taxi, Richard glances impatiently at his watch. He's put a lot of effort into his address, and he's edgy and hasn't been sleeping. On the spur of the moment after his conversation with Martin, he'd made another call to organise tonight's dinner.

The hotel suite is almost embarrassingly luxurious – more towels than he could use in a week, bathrobes, gold-wrapped chocolates, flowers, fruit and champagne. It's a long time since he's travelled like this and it's a comforting reminder of future possibilities if he gets it right tomorrow.

Richard pours himself a whisky from the mini-bar, unpacks his change of clothes, checks his laptop which has his Power Point presentation on it and then heads for the shower. Ten minutes later, he's dressed and wondering whether he has time for another drink before they arrive. Best not, he decides as the phone rings, and he unwraps a peppermint to mask the scent of the last one.

He is more than ever grateful for the room and all that it says about who he now is. He opens the door as they step out of the lift.

'Daddy!' Carly cries, stepping out ahead of her mother to throw her arms around his neck. 'You look so cool without that hillbilly beard.' And she kisses him several times.

'And you look stupendous, my darling,' Richard says, holding her at arm's length and looking her up and down.

'Stupendous,' Carly repeats, trying to mimic his English accent. 'My favourite word.'

Lily is followed by someone else; a stunningly good-looking man in jeans, white shirt and tailored black jacket, who looks like a youthful Sidney Poitier.

'It's good to see you, Rich,' Lily says, kissing him on both cheeks and not pulling away from his hug. 'Carly's right; you look cool.'

'And you look as beautiful as ever, Lil.' He puts an arm around her shoulder. 'And who's this?'

'Jason Lockyer, sir, I'm a friend of . . . well, I'm . . .'

'We're engaged,' Carly cuts in. 'We told Mom last weekend. I know you two are going to love each other. Jason's a journalist.'

'I thought I'd warned you about journalists?' Richard says, shaking Jason's hand with both of his, and using humour to mask the resentment that assails him.

'It's a pleasure to meet you, sir. I very much admire your work, and I'm looking forward to your keynote speech tomorrow.'

Richard smiles. 'So, you'll be at the conference. But if you're planning to marry my daughter, maybe I should interrogate you now?'

'Carly's mom already did quite a bit of that,' Jason says, smiling.

'Yes, she would,' Richard says looking at Lily. 'And it would be far more intimidating than anything I could put you through.' There is more kissing and hugging, and he struggles to muster the generosity of spirit that will enable him to overcome the fact that his daughter, whom he has already failed numerous times, has taken this step without telling him. There is a moment of awkwardness now that the greetings are over, and Richard wonders how he will manage the evening. He wants some time alone with Lily.

'Well,' he says, breaking the sudden tension, 'come on in and raid the mini-bar and then we'll head off out to the restaurant. I'll call and let them know there are four of us instead of three.'

They are suitably impressed by the size and opulence of the suite and wander around inspecting the facilities as he pours the drinks.

'You could've warned me, Lil,' Richard says softly a little later as they stand together by the window looking out across the Bay to the Golden Gate Bridge outlined against the blushing sunset.

'I wanted to,' she says. 'But they sprung it on me and when Carly heard you'd be here today, she wanted to surprise you. She made me promise not to tell.'

Richard nods, slightly mollified. 'He seems nice. How long has she been seeing him?'

'About three months, but they've known each other for ages. He's lovely; you're gonna like him, Rich. Try to be happy for her.'

'I am,' Richard says, turning to her. 'Really I am; if you approve, he must be a saint. It's just the shock.'

Lily surprises him by putting her hand reassuringly on his arm. She doesn't touch him much these days. 'They'll be fine,' she says, 'there's nothing to worry about. Just don't let your ego get in the way.'

She has him pinned again; there is no one who knows him better. Even Julia is not as brutally honest with him as Lily is and that suddenly seems more important than ever.

'Let's go to dinner,' he says, gripping her hand. 'I promise to behave nicely.'

'Really?' she says. 'That'll be a first.' But she's smiling when she says it.

Dinner calms him. Jason proves to be intelligent, articulate and clearly devoted to Carly. He is a reporter with the *Oakland Tribune*, he tells Richard, and his parents adore Carly.

'I guess I should be asking your permission, Mr Linton,' Jason says.

Richard shrugs. 'I'm sure you asked Lily, she's the boss around here.'

'My folks would really like to meet you, if you have time.'

'I'm flying back tomorrow evening,' Richard says. 'But maybe I should come down for a weekend soon, so we can all get to know each other.'

Carly engaged, Lily alone. This is the best chance he'll ever get. They have survived separations and reunions before, and this last separation has lasted more than a decade, but the chemistry is there, he's sure of it.

They are talking about a wedding – September, perhaps, or October. As he listens he watches Lily, remembering the day he first saw her cooking breakfast in the Black Panthers' kitchen. It was years later, after he had run away to Vietnam and then been posted to Washington, that he'd decided to look for her. When he was in California, following Ronald Reagan on the presidential campaign trail, he walked into the Panthers' office in West

Oakland, thinking he might find someone there who would know where she was. To his amazement she was there: a slight black woman with a wild halo of hair, her hands on her hips as she berated a guy built like a commercial refrigerator for dumping the leaflets he was supposed to be distributing. When she turned to look at him, Richard knew that he should have made the trip a long time ago. They were together for twelve years.

'Well, we're gonna leave you guys to it,' Carly says now. 'So, Daddy, you promise you'll come back in two weeks' time for the whole weekend?'

'Stupendous promise,' he says, pulling her to her feet and hugging her. 'I'm very happy for you, sweetheart. And you be nice to this guy; he seems okay.'

'He's more than okay,' she says. 'He's the one!'

And Richard walks them both to the door of the restaurant and turns back to the table, where Lily is putting on her glasses to read the conference program. He has been thinking about this for months, and knows he has a lot to answer for: the drinking, the outbursts of verbal abuse, the mood swings. He had loved her passionately and treated her abominably, been a lousy husband and a useless father. The day she ended it she'd warned him that if he didn't clean up his act, he would lose his job as well. But he was still convinced he could stop drinking whenever he chose to.

'So, when *will* you choose to stop?' she'd asked. 'You've been saying that for years. Join AA, or go get some counselling.'

'I don't need counselling and AA's for alcoholics,' he'd argued. 'I'm not a fucking alcoholic.'

'Really?' she'd said.

Richard takes a deep breath now and makes his way back to the table.

'Impressive!' she says, smiling up at him and taking off her glasses. 'Big stuff, Rich.'

He nods, gratified by her approval. 'You could come along, if you're free. I'm on at ten o'clock.'

She pauses. 'Okay, I'd like that. I don't have a lot on in the morning, just a meeting that I could move back.'

235

In the late seventies, she had done a degree in black history at Berkeley and, when he had walked back into her life, was just finishing a PhD. Now lecturing in the course she had previously studied, she is working on a history of the civil rights movement.

'I'll let the registration desk know to expect you,' Richard says, 'and we could have lunch before I leave?'

'We haven't finished dinner yet!'

'Let's order dessert,' he says, signalling a waiter. 'There must be something on the menu that will satisfy your chocolate addiction.'

His heart seems to have moved up into his throat. Should he say something now or wait until later? He has no idea where to begin. When they had reunited in 1980, despite the years since their first affair, she had taken him on trust. This time she is older, wiser, tougher, and she knows the best and the worst of him.

'I'll have the raspberry sorbet,' Lily tells the waiter.

Richard looks up quickly. 'Not the chocolate mousse?'

'I'm not completely predictable.'

He grins. 'Okay, then, *I'll* have the chocolate mousse.' He closes the menu and takes a deep breath, leaning towards her across the table. 'Lil, now that we've got the place to ourselves . . . there's something I want to ask you . . .' He panics and hesitates too long.

Lily waits, then says, 'I've got something to ask you too.'

Relieved to have time to get himself together, Richard indicates she should go ahead.

'Carly isn't the only one with good news,' she begins.

And, in that instant, Richard knows he's too late. He sees that while he has been blundering into and out of meaningless liaisons, someone of substance has walked into Lily's life. Each time they've met, he's told her about the women in his life, and she has listened, laughed, commiserated, and told him nothing. They've talked politics and world events, friends and acquaintances. They've talked of Carly, and often about his and Lily's work but never about her personal life. Richard sees that he has simply assumed that she would always be there for him and, that in the end, they will grow old together.

'So you see,' she says, 'after all this time, twelve years we've been separated now, I'd like a divorce.'

'But you never said you'd met someone,' he protests.

'It wasn't your business, Richard. I have my own life; so do you.'

'But we're friends, just the same, and I thought . . .'

'You thought,' she interrupts, 'that when you were ready to try again, I'd be waiting? That's not how it works.'

And then, of course, instead of just being gracious, agreeing to the divorce and wishing her happiness, he has to make it worse. Drinking, pleading, threatening, until, in the end, Lily gets up from the table.

'I told you back then that it was over. You're a good man, Richard, but when you're drunk, you're stupid, arrogant and a bully. How many people have walked away from you because of the drinking? Too many to count, but you always have some excuse. Now, go to bed, get some sleep. You have a job to do tomorrow.'

Richard pulls the pillow over his head to blot out the relentless ringing in his ears, but on it goes, penetrating his skull, until he realises that it's the telephone and reaches for it. Someone is saying something about a seminar. Suddenly he sits bolt upright, staring in shock at the luminous green figures on the clock telling him it is a quarter to ten. Fifteen minutes before he's on.

'Yes, yes. I'll be there,' he mumbles. 'Yes – it's Power Point, it'll only take a minute to set up.' And, slamming down the phone, he leaps out of bed, kicks aside an empty bottle and staggers for the bathroom door. It turns out to be the locked connecting door to another room, and he spins around bumping into the wall trying to get his bearings. A shower, get dressed, grab his gear and find the conference room on the thirty-second floor.

His head is thumping and his mouth feels like it's a sewer but, worse, his mood is leaden. Richard knows this side of himself all too well – the self-loathing, humourless, angry cynic, bent on self-sabotage – and he steps into the shower willing himself to wash it away. Ducking from the searing heat of the water, he slips, cracks his head on the stainless-steel frame of the shower screen, staggers and falls. Blood from a cut on his forehead runs down his face and swirls in pink rivulets over the white tiles as the scalding torrent of water pounds him. Swearing, he grasps at the taps and hauls himself to his feet, adjusting the flow to a gentle heat, and leans back against the wall. Deep breaths, he tells himself, the dizziness will pass, the water will stop the bleeding. Deep breaths. But as he steps out of the shower and stares at himself in the mirror, he can see that it is going to need some sort of dressing if he is not to deliver his presentation with blood running down his face. And he picks up the phone on the wall by the basin and summons help.

It is twenty past ten when he reaches the conference room, with a large surgical dressing plastered to his forehead, and his hands shaking, head thumping and stomach churning. Fortunately, there have been problems with the satellite link that was to transmit the introduction and opening remarks by the association's president, who is at a different conference, in Japan. People are drinking coffee and discussing the irony of a digital technology breakdown delaying the start of a conference about the future of a profession so dependent on its reliability.

Richard, feeling for once that there might actually be a god, hands his flash drive over to one of the technical crew, who tells him they will start with his speech and the president's message will be recorded and played before lunch.

Ian Stubbs, an old colleague from the BBC who now works for the ABC in Sydney, takes one look at him, raises an eyebrow and thrusts a cup of black coffee into his hand.

'How's the other bloke?' he asks, eyeing the dressing.

'We're burying him this afternoon,' Richard responds and gulps the coffee, hoping it will clear the fug in his brain and the pain in his head.

'You going to be okay?'

He nods, and the dizziness returns so that he has to put a hand out to the white clothed table to steady himself.

'Fine. I slipped in the shower. I'll be fine.'

The system is fixed, the delegates settle into their seats, the organisers apologise for the delay and the chair introduces him.

The title of Richard's keynote speech is projected onto the large screen and there is a mild round of welcoming applause as he walks to the lectern. Then, an expectant silence settles. He looks out across the roomful of people, most of them strangers, but a few well-known or at least familiar to him, and there, on the end of the third row, is Lily. He had completely forgotten he invited her and now her presence has the potential to destroy him.

She knows what an imposter he is. She will have taken one look at the telltale ashen grey of his skin, his bloodshot eyes and shaking hands, the hastily dressed head wound and known. How can he do this with her watching; she, who has witnessed so many other drink-induced failures? He glances at his notes, looks up at her again, clears his throat and hesitates.

'Good morning,' he begins in a tone, which, he hopes, exudes professionalism. In the corner of his eye as he looks around the room, he sees a movement. Lily is getting up, and now she walks quietly up the aisle to the back of the room.

'Good morning,' he says again, clearing his throat to get the croak out of his voice. 'It's a pleasure and a privilege to be here today, to stand in for my longtime friend and colleague Martin Gilbert . . .'

At the door, Lily stops and turns. She looks straight at him and then, without smiling, turns and gives him, as she has so often done before, the chance to save himself. She slips silently out and the door whispers to a close behind her.

TWENTY-SEVEN

The Algarve – March 2000

From her seat at a small café near the beach, Julia gazes contentedly out to where children are playing in the shallows and several people are swimming. A gentle breeze ruffles up small waves, and she can feel the sun and the proximity of the sparkling water working their magic on her. Tom was absolutely right; this is exactly what they both needed. She has just spent a very satisfactory hour browsing through the local shops, where she bought a purple leather handbag and a wrap in almost exactly the same purple but with an intricate design in shades of mustard with tiny flecks of charcoal grey and orange. She imagines describing it to Hilary. It's almost a relief not to have to, because, while it's absolutely gorgeous, it would *sound* hideous.

The blanket of grief that had almost suffocated Julia in the first couple of weeks after Hilary's death has certainly lifted, but only now is she ready to sample warmth and pleasure again. It is okay, she thinks; the sadness of bereavement never disappears but one moves slowly to a place of peace.

The long months of caring for Hilary before she went into the hospice were exhausting. She had been a sweet-natured, undemanding invalid, but Julia remembers the days when she felt that every ounce of energy had been drained from her. Tom had been wonderful, of course, but it had taken its toll on him too.

'It's the hopelessness of it,' Julia had told Richard, just before he flew home after the funeral. 'Knowing that however hard you try, there is nothing you can do to stop that relentless wasting away. I hope I never have to do that again.'

Sitting here now, watching the sun on the water, Julia can feel her grief thawing; Tom's idea of owning a place in the sun may be the right one. She even wonders if she wants to go back to working full-time. Tom is often right about things over which she has argued with him ferociously. Why *does* she argue like that? It's almost as though she does it on principle. Is it like the way she talks about his procrastination? He does procrastinate but not always; in fact, quite often he acts swiftly and efficiently, but she never mentions that.

Julia sighs, thinking that things seem to be changing between them since Hilary's death. They are gentler with each other; perhaps they have more left to give each other now that Hilary has gone. But then, Tom has always been gentle, thoughtful and generous with her and he makes her laugh. She, on the other hand, can be thoughtless, bossy and dismissive. Perhaps it is a throwback to the months when he pursued her after they had met again at Greenham Common. She had been offhand with him, imperious sometimes, making him work hard before finally agreeing to marry him. She had been determined he would see how different she was from the compliant, bored, rather ignorant girl he had known in Paris. She had challenged his views, although they were also her own, just to prove to him – and perhaps, most of all, to herself – that she now could. It wasn't enough that he loved her sufficiently to come back; she wanted his respect and admiration as well.

'But how could I love you if I didn't respect and admire you?' he'd asked.

'Easily, you did before. There was nothing about the person I was in Paris that you could respect or admire,' she'd responded. 'I was lazy, bored and ignorant.'

'You were simply on the brink,' he told her. 'I'm good at spotting potential.'

She realises that she still challenges him, almost as though she wants him to keep noticing who she is, when he has always known that perfectly well. Is this some sort of construction she's established for them; herself as capricious and bossy, bouncing off his steady, thoughtful reliability? Hilary, she realises, was part of this. Together they had established a dialogue about Tom and his lovable eccentricities. She wonders suddenly if her behaviour hurts him; whether he tolerates it because he loves her so much. She loves him beyond words, but her words are often dismissive. She had hated him once, but only briefly and only because hatred and anger were preferable to hurt and despair. Looking back, Julia decides she must change what is simply a way of behaving that is not very nice. She will show him she can be different.

On the table is her notebook, open at pages filled with her attempts to draft an email to Zoë. She can't seem to get it right. She starts another version now, though, because she is determined. A death makes you think of the things you wish you'd done better or not done at all; the small adjustments you wish you could make to history.

'I'm back,' Tom says, dropping a folder of papers onto the table and pulling out a chair. 'It's surprising how the adventure of setting out to look at houses starts off fun and so quickly becomes tedious.'

'Did you see anything nice?'

'A couple that are worth looking at again,' he says. 'I've made an appointment for us to go back this afternoon at five. How was the shopping? Is there any money left for the house?'

She hands him the carrier bag with her purchases. 'Have a look.'

He pulls out the handbag. 'Lovely colour, and this scarf thing matches it beautifully. Very nice – is that all you bought?'

Julia leans across and kisses him on the cheek. 'You are a very lovely man, Tomo. Most husbands would be moaning that I'd bought anything at all and demanding to know the price.'

'Hmm,' Tom says. 'Well, Simon wouldn't have, surely?'

'Simon was a millionaire. You . . . *we* aren't. I know about husbands; you don't spend thirty years in the women's movement without hearing an awful lot of stories about meanness and neglect. You, my darling, are a prince among men.'

He grins, signalling to the waiter. 'I don't know what I've done to deserve all this praise but, being a complete opportunist, I'm happy to accept it.'

'I think I've taken you for granted,' she says.

'Used and abused me,' he says with a laugh. 'Yes, that's me; poor old bugger, used and abused by women all my life.' He points to the notebook. 'Still farting around with that email?'

Julia nods. 'Just can't seem to get it right.'

'Want some advice from the expert procrastinator? Stop thinking it inside out and upside down. Just go into the café right now, sit down at their computer, write something and send it. I'll order some more coffee and you'll have sent the email before it arrives.'

'You think?'

'I know.'

'Okay,' she says, 'if you say so.'

And she gets straight up, picks up her notebook and heads into the café.

လာ

Tom shakes his head in surprise. Julia never fails to amaze him; she didn't even argue with him, must be going soft. He opens the file and pulls out the paperwork for the two properties he wants her to see. This whole business is proving harder for him than he imagined, because it's all about the future and, since Hilary's death and his visit to Raheem, all he seems able to think about is death.

The irony of his present situation is not lost on him. For once in his life, he wants and needs to take swift and decisive action, but he has to delay it. He knows he should have told Julia that Raheem said he thought there might be a problem which they should have investigated sooner rather than later. Forty-eight hours in hospital, a bank of tests, and then they'd have to look at the options: surgery, radiation therapy or, probably, both. But it would have meant postponing the holiday Tom felt they both needed. Bugger it, he'd thought on the train journey home. It was hard enough getting her to agree, so we're going and that's that.

When he had looked into Julia's eyes that evening, he had known that the one thing she could not cope with now was more illness, particularly his. Had he held back for himself too? Put off the day of reckoning because he couldn't cope either? She would raise merry hell if she found out, so he will have to make sure she doesn't. He is, after all, going to take Raheem's advice, just not as swiftly as recommended. That will give Julia a little more time to recover; meanwhile, he'd better start praying that it won't take her too long.

<hr />

On Wednesday morning, Zoë is getting ready for the art class; it's her fourth week, and the class calls to her with the relentless seductiveness of a new and illicit lover. The first time she brushed water onto paper and began to blend colours, something sprang to life within her. As the colours filled the paper, as the borders appeared between land, sea and sky, she was gripped with a heady sense of the power of what she was doing; creating something beautiful and uniquely her own, and feeling that she could do so much more.

'Wow! Zoë, you're a natural,' Theo had said as he wandered between the easels. 'Are you sure you haven't done this before?'

'Never,' she said, 'but I'll definitely be doing it again.'

That first weekend she bought an easel and some more paints, and, to everyone's amazement, set them up at home in a corner of the verandah. Then she settled herself on a stool from the kitchen and began to work the colours, blending, experimenting with different brushes, drying off each section with a hairdryer, before starting on the next. Zoë has ignored her family's surprise and mild amusement. She is compelled to paint, to discover what does and doesn't work, what she can and can't do. She forgets to do the washing, forgets to buy more milk, and when she finally remembers the washing, she forgets to hang it out. She is irritable on the days she has to go to work.

This morning she has a few minutes to spare before leaving for class and she decides to check her email, something she remembers to do about once a week. She can't understand people who check their inbox obsessively. The computer is in Archie's office, which is really the spare bedroom with a sofa bed for visitors, not that it gets used much. Gaby's friends sleep in her room, and Rob sleeps with Rosie. Zoë had felt uneasy about this but, as Archie had pointed out when it became clear that Rob and Rosie's relationship was serious, if they didn't sleep together at home they'd just do so elsewhere. So why not be open and accepting about it?

'What were you doing at nineteen, my love?' he had asked her.

Zoë thought about losing her virginity to Richard on Beachy Head and how, after protecting herself from the awkward gropings of boys at home and in London, she had come to believe that sex was the indisputable indication of love. How could she have believed that, despite everything else Richard did, the bruises on her thighs were proof of love? But she does still believe that he loved her; in fact, there were times in that roller-coaster relationship, especially in the months before Dan's birth, that it seemed he loved her quite a lot.

She logs on and immediately deletes the three offers to help her enlarge her penis, the profile of a Russian woman who wants to be her faithful, sexy bride, and an invitation to the opening of a new restaurant. There are three messages left, one of which seems to be from a stranger; she is about to delete it too when the phone rings. She takes a message for Archie, leaves her inbox open on the screen, grabs her bag of painting things and runs down to the car.

'It sounds like what you're experiencing is the discovery of your creativity,' Theo says when she talks to him at the end of the class. 'It *is* very exciting when you suddenly realise that you have this ability and you feel compelled to throw yourself into it.'

'It feels like magic,' she tells him. 'I just want to paint all the time, I can't leave it alone.'

'Then don't,' he says. 'Go with it, see where it takes you.'

Cyclone Zoë, Theo called her and he got the other students to crowd around her easel so that he could explain to them how, instinctively, Zoë had leapt ahead and used techniques that he would be teaching them over the next two weeks.

She had always claimed that she didn't have a creative bone in her body; her strength, she had told herself, was her practicality and her competence at running a home and looking after a family. Now, it seems, there is something else she can do and do it not at all badly, for a beginner. As she drives home, Zoë wonders what this might mean. Are there other things she could do if she tried? 'It's only an art class, after all,' she says aloud as she pulls into the drive.

To her delight, Dan's car is there. He's been spending a lot of time at Justine's place recently, doing some decorating, and so she's had very little time alone with him. Until painting got hold of her, Zoë had been trying to decide how much of her feelings were the natural response of a mother whose son was moving away from her, and how much was something more sinister. She has managed to convince herself that this relationship won't last. She has even – and she's not proud of this – hoped that Dan would soon be deployed overseas again and that this would be the breaking point. And yet, she can see that Dan loves Justine. This weekend Justine is bringing Gwen to the house for dinner, and Zoë realises she is nervous about it. Who *is* this Gwen anyway? She has avoided finding out anything about Justine's life, closed her ears to conversations and distracted herself with her painting, because it is easier for her not to know, but now she will have to. Is Gwen Justine's stepmother? Is she Aboriginal too?

Dan has, he says, been sorting some of his gear and has just returned from the barracks, where the medical officer has signed him on for Monday.

'And I was hoping I could use the computer quickly,' he says, pouring boiling water into the plunger so they can have coffee. 'But I didn't like to close your inbox.'

'I went out and forgot it,' Zoë says. 'Pour the coffee, and I'll go and do it now.'

As she sits at the desk, she looks again at the message she was going to delete. It's headed 'Hello' and comes from someone called Tom Hammond. She scrolls down to the signature.

'Coffee's getting cold,' Dan calls from the kitchen.

Zoë reads the email and then stares at the screen.

'Come on, Mum.'

She prints out the email and makes her way back to the kitchen as though she is sleepwalking.

'That's yours,' Dan says, pushing a mug towards her. 'Shall we take it out onto the verandah? Are you okay? You've gone white.'

She holds the sheet of paper out to him and he puts down his mug.

'What is it?'

'Read it,' Zoë says.

'Dear Zoë, I have tried so often to write this message, choosing words and sentences, erasing them and starting again. Now I've decided that there is probably no ideal way to say what I want to say, I just have to take the chance and hope that you will read this message in the spirit in which it is sent. Who the hell is this *from?'* Dan asks, looking up.

'Julia Linton, Richard's sister.'

'Shit!' Dan says. 'What the hell . . . are you okay, Mum?'

'Read it,' she says, 'just read it.'

'I have thought of you many times over the years, since that last awful time I saw you at the flat. That day stands in my memory like a judgment and while I have tried to make sense of it, to rationalise it, to make myself think that it was all right, I always come back to the fact that it wasn't.

'I can't begin to speak for Richard, I can only tell you that I bitterly regret my part in what happened, the way I failed you as a friend, as my sister-in-law, as another woman. I've tried telling myself I was too young, selfish and inexperienced to cope with something so complex and distressing, but it's only an excuse for something inexcusable. I know now that there were ways I could have stood by you as well as supporting Richard, things I could have done to make it easier.

'Perhaps it will seem facile to you if I say now that I am sorry, but I hope you will be able to see beyond these actual words to the meaning they carry. I have recently lost my dearest friend to a terrible, lingering illness; death has a way of reminding us that some things should simply not be left undone. And so I am writing to tell you I am sorry – sorry for what we did, for your pain and fear, and sorry that I let my love for and responsibility to Richard take precedence over my love for and responsibility to you as my friend.

'I would love to hear from you, to know about your life and to tell you about mine, but I will understand perfectly if you don't want to reply.

'I wish you love, happiness and joy in your beautiful son who is now a man, perhaps with children of his own. I hope that somehow, someday you may feel it in your heart to forgive me.

Julia.'

Dan drags his eyes away and looks up at Zoë, who is standing at the other side of the table as if she's carved from stone.

'I thought it was over,' she says, 'the shame of it, the hurt; but it isn't, is it? It's never, ever going to be over. One mistake, one false step, determines the course of your life. Here I am, fifty-two years old, and who I am today is the result of the night I slept with your father.'

<hr>

'You don't have to do *anything* if you don't want to,' Archie says. 'Nothing's different from the way it was before this message arrived. You can forget all about it.' He reads the email again. It seems genuine and heartfelt. And he's at a loss to understand why Zoë is so crushed by it. 'Julia is asking for forgiveness and she knows that may not be possible,' he says.

Zoë is curled into a corner of the sofa. 'It's like a scab,' she says, 'it becomes sort of tough and sealed; you can pick at it a bit and it doesn't hurt. But then it gets caught on something and rips off, and it's like all the old pain is there again.'

Archie sees the hurt and the shame in her face, and imagines again the struggle of a single mother with a black child, who is alone in the world. He sits down beside her and gently lifts her legs, cradling her feet in his lap.

'It's thirty years ago, Zo,' he says. 'More, in fact. They treated you badly, although many would have done even worse. Your son is a wonderful man, and he's that way because of your courage and strength. In other circumstances, he might have turned out a very different person. You can't regret that.'

'I don't regret it,' she cuts in. 'Of course I don't regret anything about Dan. But while I gained him, I lost so much else.'

'What did you lose? Richard? From all you've told me, I don't think he was any great loss. Harry? Well, my darling, he was never yours to lose.'

'My youth,' she says softly. 'My self-esteem. I lost all the ways I could imagine myself to be. I was twenty when Dan was born, a few months older than Rosie is now. I was alone with a new baby and terrified of what was going to happen to both of us. My mother told me not to come home, and Gloria and the others took me in but I didn't fit in with them. Every day was a struggle. I lost my youth to shame and humiliation. I know I only have myself to blame but that doesn't stop it hurting.'

Archie has never heard her talk like this before. Years ago when they met and she told him this story, it had been in a matter-of-fact way.

'I was stranded in a hospital where everyone knew that my husband had deserted me because I had a black baby,' Zoë continues now. 'People stared and sniggered, and came to look at me and Dan as though we were a side show. And then . . . and then Julia whisked me away in a flashy car and dumped me at the flat. I had no idea how to look after a baby; I could barely look after myself. And then they came back and tried to buy me off. I didn't think there could be anything more humiliating than what had happened in the hospital and then I found that there was. Richard was desperate to get rid of me.' She paused, breathless. 'I don't expect you to know how this feels. You just have to take my word for it.'

Archie grips her feet in his hands. They feel small and cold, almost as though they are shrinking, just as she is shrinking into herself.

'I do, my darling, I do,' he says. 'All I'm saying is that no one despises you or hates you *now*. No one thinks you deserve disapproval; not even Julia who's been agonising about this for years – maybe even decades. What happened in the hospital was awful but it is a sign of those times. When people look at you and Dan now, they see a beautiful woman – wise, mature, strong – who's raised a son of whom any parent would be proud. And if they do imagine your circumstances, they see only the courage it must have taken to get through them.'

'But –' she begins.

'But!' Archie says, holding up his hand to stop her. 'There is always a but, isn't there? Julia wants your forgiveness. You don't have to give it. But maybe it would be a step towards forgiving yourself.'

⁓

'So, how's your mum taken it?' Justine asks.

'Badly. Total freak out,' Dan says, as they sit eating fish and chips on the boardwalk by the harbour. 'I can see that it's upsetting for her, but it does seem like a bit of an overreaction. She can either ignore it, or write back and say fuck off, I never want to hear from you again, or she can accept that it's well meant and respond that way.'

'And do *you* think it's well meant?'

'Yes,' he says. 'I do. It seems genuine.'

'And what about you? You're at the heart of it; how does that make you feel?'

He pauses, shrugs and looks around him as if seeking the answer. 'I don't know. Strange, really, I suppose. Mum always said that Richard dumped her because of his pride. She says he couldn't cope with me being so obviously not his son. Apparently he was a bit of an activist at the time – you know, anti-racism, anti-the Vietnam War, all that late sixties stuff. But he didn't know how to walk down the street with a white wife and a black baby.'

'Mmmm. Well, I suppose that makes sense. Poor Zoë, it must have been so hard to cope with.'

'It's nothing to the hardship that your mum had to cope with,' Dan says.

'Knowing there are people who are worse off doesn't make one's own hurt any easier,' she says. 'But you still haven't told me how *you* feel.'

'Honestly?'

'Of course.'

'Hurt, really, and resentful, I suppose. What Mum said when she read the email, that I'm the result of one mistake that decided who she turned out to be, she might as well have hit me across the face.'

'But that's not how she meant it, Dan. She adores you, and it's obvious she's tremendously proud of you. You've always known how hard it must have been for her.'

'Yeah. But you didn't hear her,' Dan says. 'It felt like it was my fault, as though she was a victim because of me.' He gets up and pulls her to her feet.

'But you don't honestly think that's how she feels, do you?' Justine says, looking up at him.

'I never did before,' he says. 'But now I don't know. Come on, let's walk up to the cappuccino strip, and have coffee and ice cream.'

'Maybe we should postpone Sunday's dinner,' Justine suggests as they walk, arms around each other, across the park. 'Or, at least, not tell them our news just yet. Give Zoë time to get over this.'

'Absolutely not. It's Easter, and it was New Year when I asked you to marry me. We should have told them then. We told Gwen. I don't even remember now why you said we should wait. It's not as though we've got anything to be ashamed of.'

He's right, there is nothing to be ashamed of, and secrecy is not a good start to their life together, but Justine is still uneasy. Dan, Archie, Rosie, Gaby, all seem blissfully unaware of this thing with Zoë. Is she consciously playing a mind game, or just struggling to cope with things she doesn't like?

'I was only thinking it might not be the right time for your mum.'

Dan laughs. 'I don't think there will ever actually *be* a right time for Mum.'

They spot an empty table outside the Dome café and sit silently for a moment, watching the motley collection of tourists and locals strolling past.

He takes her hand. 'And it's time they met Gwen. Now we've got the flat ready, we can move in next weekend.' He lifts their joined hands to his lips and kisses her fingers. 'I'm going back to work, Jus; who knows what'll be happening from one day to the next? Wherever I go, just to the barracks or training at Bindoon, or somewhere on active service, I want to know that I'm coming home to you, to our life together. We'll tell them on Sunday. It'll give Mum something other than herself to think about; the future instead of the past.'

TWENTY-EIGHT

Fremantle – April 2000

*D*ear Julia, Zoë begins.
It's hard to know where to start, but perhaps I'll do so with the anger I felt when I got your message. I've lived my life in the shadows of what happened, the shame and rejection have shaped me, and in my worst moments of disappointment in myself I have blamed you and Richard. But of course I do know that I'm ultimately responsible for who I am and for what happened all those years ago. Yes, we were all young and confused. We were also proud and fearful. I think I still am.

You want me to forgive you? For that I'd need a cool head and a warm heart, and I don't have either at the moment. And yet I'm sitting here in the middle of the night, in a houseful of sleeping people writing to you. Why? Because I need to talk to someone who isn't part of my family and because it doesn't matter what I say. You've already thought the worst of me so I have nothing to lose, and perhaps this will help me to find out how I feel about the past as well as the present. So I'm making you my confidante, as I did once before, for no other reason this time than lack of choice and just writing this seems to help a little . . .

Zoë stops typing and leans back in the chair, stretching her arms above her head and flexing her shoulders. She's unused to writing long messages, and totally unused to writing about her feelings. Of course she's not going to send this, but it helps to imagine Julia as she writes, rather as though she is talking to her. She wonders suddenly what it would be like to talk to Julia again. But who *is*

253

Julia now? Why does she use an email address in the name of Tom Hammond? What's happened to Simon? And who is this friend whose death caused her to write that unexpected email?

No, she will never send this message, but somehow the feeling that she is speaking across the miles to the friend who supported her through the chaotic and painful weeks that followed the news of her pregnancy, seems to help. Briefly she can forget the Julia who walked away from the flat, who supported Richard in his desire to be rid of her, and remember instead the woman who had once briefly seemed like a sister.

I've recently started going to an art class, she begins again, with no idea why she is taking this tack. *I've never painted before but apparently I'm quite good at it. This might sound odd to you but creating something makes me feel powerful, which is something I've never felt before. What happened all those years ago battered me into a powerlessness from which I have never emerged . . .*

Whatever is she writing? Where is this all coming from?

And ironically, at the same time as I grasp the power of creativity I am trapped in a situation in which I am as powerless as ever and as full of shame and confusion as I felt back then.

The tea she has made turns cold in the mug as she types. She pushes it aside and turns back to the keyboard, rereads what she has written and then begins again.

Let me explain a little more so you can begin to understand . . . The words pour from her heart through her fingers as though something old and difficult is starting to uncoil.

⁓⁓

Dan can't sleep; he gets out of bed and wanders out onto the balcony, shivering slightly. The relentless heat of summer has given way to cooler nights and mornings, and it's a relief as well as something of a shock to feel the cool night breeze on his warm skin, the stark cold of the timber slats under his feet. It's only April but he can feel the change of season. He'd imagined there would be a joyful celebration when he and Justine broke their news. But in the end, he was so angry with his mother that he'd found it difficult to get through the evening.

It is a stunningly clear night, the sky a mesmerising mass of stars, the dark shapes of the trees around the house moving only slightly in the breeze. Dan stands at the balcony rail. Something strange has happened, that he doesn't fully understand and doesn't really want to be bothered with. He'd left home at eighteen to join the army, much to his mother's dismay, but mothers are always dismayed when their children leave home; Zoë perhaps more than most, because of how his life had begun. Starting off in Canberra, at the Defence College, he always went home on leave, and when he was posted elsewhere, he still returned. Later, when he was accepted into the SAS, he was based at the Swanbourne Barracks, close to Fremantle, so it made sense for him to live at home. Zoë's dismay at his choice of career was tempered by having him there. He should, he thinks, have moved out then and got a place of his own, but living at home helped him when operations were particularly tough. He had drawn strength from knowing the people he loved were waiting for him.

Now he wants to go home to Justine, and he'd assumed his family would understand, be happy for him, and they were – well, Archie was. He was over the moon, thumping him on the shoulder, hugging him and Justine, hugging Gwen, opening champagne. And his sisters were thrilled, teasing him, plying Justine with questions, asking Gwen about the Polar Bears. But his mother? She smiled and kissed them both, but it was tense and forced, and as the evening wore on, everything she did and said seemed to have a subtext that he didn't understand. Later, he followed her out to the kitchen to help with the coffee.

'Everything okay, Mum?' he'd asked, stacking some plates in the dishwasher.

'Fine, thanks, Daniel,' she'd said, which was weird because she never called him Daniel these days. 'It's just a lot to take in. I hadn't realised it was quite so . . . well . . . serious.'

He'd laughed then. 'It's serious, all right. Can't get more serious than this. But you're pleased, aren't you? Happy for us?'

'Of course I am. It's just . . .'

'Just what?'

'It's . . . she . . .' Zoë had flushed and looked away.

'She what?'

'Oh . . . it's nothing.'

'I don't think so.'

There was a long pause. 'I just wonder if this is really right for you.'

Dan remembers staring at her and suddenly hating her with the same intensity that he had hated her when he was a child and she refused him ice cream, or grounded him for some misdemeanour. He wasn't sure if she was upset about something and spoiling for a fight, or hurt. In that moment he had decided that he would not buy into it. He would not open himself up to her complicated feelings about the past or her attempts to hang on to him. This was something she had to sort out for herself.

'This is *absolutely* right for me,' he said firmly, holding her gaze. '*Justine* is absolutely right, I've never been more sure of anything in my life. So you'll just have to trust my judgment until you can see it for yourself.' And he'd picked up the tray with the coffee pot and cups, and walked back to where everyone was sitting at the table, leaving Zoë alone in the kitchen.

Dan knows he doesn't cope well with discord with people he loves. In the field, the barracks, in his social life, he is confident and competent. At closer quarters emotional upheaval disturbs him; Archie's the same, he thinks, they both like peace at home. He often backs down to avoid conflict but this is different. 'Stuff it,' he says to himself, 'this is *her* problem and she can sort it out for herself.' It's not just this evening that has upset him; he can't shake off his resentment at being cast as the cause of her shame. It is in total contrast to everything she has ever told him about himself.

It has not always been easy being the black son of a white single mother; as a teenager especially, he worried where he fitted, who he actually was. He has been teased for being too black and for not being black enough. His strength in dealing with that has come from what Zoë has told him about his father, and about his own importance in Zoë's life. Now he wonders how much of what she said was true. Has she always seen him as the root of her shame? A sense of responsibility for her feelings has always been a faint, uneasy background noise that he has never previously been able to define. And so much is happening now; his love for Justine, his new relationship with Gwen. He wants to be able to enjoy it all but feels trapped in the threads Zoë has woven. He wants to be free of this part of being a son. Surely, he thinks, gazing out to the gleaming surface of the moonlit water, sometime the mothering just has to stop.

∽◦∾

Justine dreams frequently of the day she found the map. She dreams that she is back in Mal Fitzgerald's office, planning her escape; memorising the pattern of the long winding road that linked the convent and the farm, counting off the things she will need for the journey. Then there's the moment when the pain and the nausea strike her. She feels the warm leak of blood and staggers, bent double, out onto the verandah and falls on her knees. That's when the reality of the dream changes to fantasy: instead of rolling in agony on the decking, instead of the heat and dust, the flies that settle on her face and in the trails of blood on her legs, the sound of voices and people running towards her, there is warmth and sunlight, and she is being lifted into some other, almost heavenly, dimension. When she wakes, as she does now, from the dream, she knows it is about freedom – the freedom of the moment that has brought her to this point. But sometimes she wonders whether there is more to the dream; when she was younger, she feared it meant that she might not be able to have a child. Now, however, she realises that her age makes this pretty unlikely anyway. Through the darkness she can see Dan standing on the balcony, silhouetted against the night sky. She wonders if he has thought realistically about this. They've never talked about having children; how will he feel if they can't? She knows he's out there going over his conversation with Zoë, and she'd like to comfort him but she holds back. This is something he alone can deal with; all she can do is complicate it.

She rolls over in bed, her back to the window and closes her eyes, searching again for the bliss at the end of the dream. In reality she was certainly lifted up, but onto the creaky old settee on which Mal Fitzgerald and Greg used to drink and smoke. The dusty upholstery, with its reek of tobacco and grog, made her heave. There was a seemingly endless journey in the back of the car, with her head in Gladys's lap and Gwen driving. And then the lights, bright lights, in her eyes, strange faces staring down at her, a mask over her face, the chill of metal instruments on her skin, the prick of a needle in her arm; and then darkness.

When she woke, it was to softer lights in a hospital ward, and Gwen sitting beside her bed, her face grey with exhaustion.

'You have nothing to be ashamed of,' she'd told Justine before she left the hospital to drive back to the farm. 'What's happened to you is terrible and none of it is your fault; it's his. And it's my fault too. I must have been blind. All I could see was that you'd changed and I didn't know why.' She left, telling Justine that she would be back in a few days. 'Tomorrow, Gladys will come and take you to my mother's house. It's by the sea. Have you ever seen the sea?'

Justine shook her head. 'I saw some pictures.'

'Well, now you'll see the real thing. You'll be able to see it from the window, and we can walk to the beach and you can learn to swim. You'll never see him again, Justine, I promise you that.'

It was this room they had brought her to, and she had shared it with Gladys until they were sure she would not wake in fear and wander onto the balcony. She has only a hazy memory of Gwen's return from the farm, a couple of weeks later, when she disappeared with a chalky white face and shaking hands, into her room for several days. It was almost five years before Justine learned what had happened back there.

Justine touches the shark's tooth that rests at the base of her throat. It's suspended now on a fine gold chain, the strip of black leather replaced long ago. She wears it always; a constant reminder that anything is possible even in the most unlikely circumstances. Dan comes quietly back into the room, and she feels the flow of cool air as he lifts the bedclothes and climbs back in beside her. He is, she thinks, a very fortunate man. He lost his father but has lived always in the warmth of his mother's unconditional love, and, later, the love of his stepfather and his sisters. Now things are changing and he has to adjust. Love makes her want to protect him from even this comparatively minor emotional hiccup but he must find his own way. She rolls over to face him, stretching her bed-warm body against the chilly length of his and laying her arm across his chest.

'Love you,' she whispers.

He pulls her closer. 'You are more than I ever dreamed of,' he murmurs against her hair. And he kisses her forehead and wraps his arms around her.

TWENTY-NINE

Fremantle – April 2000

In the space of a week, Zoë has become a person who checks her email several times an hour. Had she always meant to send the message? Would she have reread and changed it several times if she hadn't always intended to send it? Anyway, it's gone and the momentary relief of sending was replaced, when she reread it the next morning, with excruciating embarrassment. She might just as well, she thinks, have stood naked in the middle of the shopping centre. Still, it will only be read on the other side of the world, by someone whom she'll probably never hear from again. And yet . . . and yet, a vein of longing throbs in Zoë's temples; a nagging desire for completion, as though she has reached out a hand and only the corresponding touch of another can release her.

'You don't seem very pleased about it,' Gaby says, as they make their way around Coles with the trolley. 'You were always saying it was time Dan found someone and settled down, and now you're sulking.'

'I am *not* sulking!' Zoë protests. 'Who says I'm sulking?'

'No one; me, I thought . . .'

'Well, you're wrong.'

'I suppose it's, like, the empty nest thing,' Gaby says.

'What empty nest thing?' Zoë asks, mildly irritated by Gaby's interference.

'You know, like they say about women when their children leave home, that they get depressed. I heard it on *Sunrise*, some psychologist was saying . . . I think it's your hormones, and you feel useless or something.'

'My hormones are perfectly okay, thank you,' Zoë says, plucking a packet of digestive biscuits from the shelf. 'And with you and your sister still there, the nest is hardly empty – although sometimes I think it would be a relief if it was.'

'Charming!' Gaby says. 'So, does that mean I can go travelling after all?'

Zoë affords her a grin. 'You don't miss a trick, do you? Look, we've talked about all this before, Gabs. You *can* go, and Dad and I will help you, but you have to stay on at school and do your exams. You're too young. The best time to do it would be after uni.'

'But heaps of people do it in their gap year, and, anyway, I've told you before that I don't want to go to uni. Travel is an education in itself; Mr Wheedon said so.'

'Yes, well, Mr Wheedon's right. But I'm sure he didn't mean you should leave school and head off on your own without doing the TEE and trying to get into university. Another couple of years and you'll have a bit more experience, and you'll enjoy it more. If you don't do your exams, you'll always regret it.'

Gaby gives a huge sigh of frustration. 'You *always* say that but, you know, Mum, not everybody is suited to going to university. Some people learn by experience or get apprenticeships and stuff.'

Zoë raises her eyebrows. 'Mr Wheedon again or more wisdom from the *Sunrise* team of experts?'

'No, actually; we had this careers seminar thing, and this woman said that people should think about how they really want to spend their future, how they'd like their working days to be, and that that would help you work out what you wanted to do.'

'And your point is?'

'I thought I'd like to be, you know, travelling in Europe, seeing heaps of places and reading about them, and doing a bit of work, like being a waitress or picking grapes, or something.'

Zoë stops the trolley and faces her daughter. 'Well, the TEE won't stop you doing that, and nor will going to university. And at least you'll be able to get a decent job when you come back. Listen; darling, I used to say the same thing to your gran when I was your age. I nagged her rotten to let me go to London and in the end she gave in.'

'There you are, then,' Gaby says triumphantly. 'You were allowed –'

'But I wish she hadn't,' Zoë cuts in. 'I wish she'd made me stay at school, do my exams, go to university or get qualified for something, before I did it. I wish I'd been a bit more mature. I don't want you to make the same mistakes I made.'

'Well, you can't punish me for your mistakes. And I'm not even interested in having a boyfriend, so I'm not likely to go and get myself pregnant.'

'Gaby,' Zoë says, wounded by this but not wanting to let it show. 'Give it a rest; stop bludgeoning me.' The supermarket seems to close in on her. The bright lights and colourful shelves, the shoppers with their trolleys, the special offer signs, all make her feel as though her life has become some bizarre reality TV show from which she will suddenly be evicted for past mistakes, without anyone noticing that she's gone. 'I'm not trying to punish you, darling,' she says, as heat prickles her neck. 'I want you to have much more than I had, much, much more. But I want you to be ready for it, so you can get the best from it, be able to work out what's good for you and what's not.'

'Oh, my god, you're crying. Mum, don't cry,' Gaby says, stricken by the sight of a tear. 'I didn't mean to be horrible, please don't cry.'

Zoë sniffs and brushes her fingers under her eyes. 'It's okay, I'm not really crying. But I mean it, you know. I don't want to stop you, I really don't. I just want you to be older; a bit more prepared.'

'Yeah, yeah, sure, Mum,' Gaby says. 'I know, I was just – you know, having a whinge. Look, we've got everything now; we can put it in the car and go for a coffee, if you like.'

They pack the shopping into the boot, and walk to South Terrace, where the pavement cafés are busy with Saturday shoppers and day trippers.

'So, you are pleased for Dan, then?' Gaby asks as they settle at a table. 'I think Jus is brilliant. So's Gwen. She says I can go swimming with her and the Polar Bears, but I'd need to stay the night at her place because we have to get up at half past five.'

Zoë laughs. 'She's obviously never tried to get you out of bed at seven o'clock on a school morning.'

'Justine'll come too, she says. It's gonna be cool having her as a sister-in-law.'

'Mmmm. Well, let's see what happens. They may not even get married, you know; they haven't known each other very long.'

''Course they will. D'you think Justine'll ask me to be a bridesmaid?'

Zoë ignores the question, takes a twenty-dollar note from her purse and hands it to Gaby. 'Why don't you go and get the coffee? I'll have a flat white and a blueberry muffin, and get whatever you want for yourself.' She breathes a sigh of relief as Gaby leaves the table. 'If I haven't heard from her by this time next week,' she tells herself, 'I'll know she's not going to write back. And if she doesn't, I don't care; she gave up on me when I needed her most.' Only she knows that she does mind, and when she gets home, she goes straight to the computer to check her email but the inbox is empty – again.

⤤

Renovating the flat has put Gwen in the mood for spring cleaning, although it's autumn. She wakes early, goes to the beach for a swim, and returns to a hot shower, brown toast with Vegemite, and is raring to go. She knows she's lucky to have so much energy. People assume she's younger than she is; she, too, is sometimes pulled up short by the realisation that she is nearly seventy-five. It's her forties she clings to, because it was a time when everything changed for her, all of it for the better. A time when she discovered what she was capable of.

Today, she thinks, she'll clear out the old bureau desk. Dan has finally persuaded her to buy a laptop and fixed her up with a broadband connection. Having discovered the internet she feels like a child let loose in a toyshop: newspapers from around the world, books, everything is just a mouse click away. She wants a nice modern desk for her laptop but first the bureau has to go. It is stuffed with old correspondence, articles clipped from magazines, dress patterns, recipes she's never used and her old notebooks. She prefers not to call them journals, which she thinks sounds rather self-important; she's always been an intermittent record keeper. They're just slim exercise books, piled up in one of the drawers, their covers tatty, the dates scrawled across the front. If it were up to her, she'd dump them, but Justine would never forgive her.

'You must *never* throw them out,' she'd said, years ago. 'Please, Gwen; leave them for me, promise me you will.'

'Whatever for?' Gwen had asked, ready to drop them in the bin.

'Because they're your story, our story. Please, Gwen.'

And so now she must find a home for them, in her bedroom, she thinks, not down here on the bookshelf where someone might read them. She dumps the pile onto a chair, and the smooth covers shift and slide, and several fall on the floor. A piece of yellowing card glides down to join them. Gwen gathers up the notebooks and turns the card over. It is a picture of the Sacred Heart, one hand raised in a blessing, the other pointing to his, now somewhat faded, red heart. Gwen's own heart gives a leap and, she sits on top of the other notebooks and gazes at it. It's the picture Justine gave her the day they went to the convent to find her box.

She had realised, soon after she had married Mal Fitzgerald, that she couldn't bear to have his children. It was later, when she had paid a visit to the convent one day with her mother, who was a regular donor, that the idea of a young girl whom she could nurture came to her. The child would have to work, that was for sure; Mal would not stand for someone for whom he could see no use. But Gwen thought she could repay this work by giving the child a better life.

Even sitting here alone now, she blushes at her arrogance. But back then, she'd just thought she could give a child a home and have someone to care for.

'I knew it had to be you,' she'd explained to Justine, years later. 'There was something about you, something that wouldn't be crushed. That was why I was so frustrated when you became so quiet and unhappy. You'd been doing so well; the reading, the sewing, even with the arithmetic you hated so much. If only I'd realised . . .'

Browsing now through the pages of the notebook, she comes across the long gap between the week when Justine ended up in hospital and when the record begins again weeks later. Then there are pages and pages of painful detail about that last trip to the farm and about what happened with Mal. She certainly doesn't want to read all that, and she flicks ahead to the point that she and Justine went to the convent, several months later.

'Absolutely not, Mrs Fitzgerald,' Mother Superior had said, drawing herself up to her full height. 'The child is making a fool of you, I'm afraid. All her possessions were in her bag when you took her away. She couldn't have hidden anything; we wouldn't have allowed it. And under the water tank, of all places. Ridiculous.'

'Justine is very clear about it, Mother Superior,' Gwen had said. 'The things are in a cigar box under the tank, and we'd like to go there now and dig it up. It's very important to her.'

'I really can't allow it.'

Gwen felt, rather than heard, Justine's sharp intake of breath and sensed the droop of her shoulders. She looked around her, wondering what to do, and the sight of the crucifix on the wall gave her an idea.

'I believe the chapel is in need of repair,' she said, looking coldly at the nun as she put her handbag on the desk and drew out her chequebook. 'Perhaps a small donation might help.'

Mother Superior held her gaze for a moment and then looked down. 'That's very kind . . .'

'On the clear understanding . . .'

'Of course.'

Gwen wrote the cheque, tore it out of the book and handed it to her. 'There's no need to see us out. Justine knows the way.'

But Justine had grown too big to crawl into the space, and had had to run to where the gardener kept his tools and find two spades. Together they'd dug away at the earth and the tufts of grass so that she could wriggle through.

'This is for you, Mrs Fitzgerald,' Justine had said, handing her the picture when they were back in the car and she was wearing Norah's necklace. 'It's Jesus. It's a bit messy but it's the only thing I've got to give you. Apart from this necklace, it's the only special thing I've got that didn't come from you.'

Gwen looks again at the card. 'I'll keep it always,' she'd said then. 'And let's hope we'll be as lucky in our next search.'

Now she props the Sacred Heart up on the mantelpiece, scoops up the notebooks, and is heading for the stairs when there's a ring at the doorbell.

Gaby is standing on the porch, unrecognisable at first under her bike helmet. 'You said I could come over sometime,' she says, unbuckling the strap. 'Is now okay?'

'Well . . . yes, I suppose so,' Gwen says. 'It might have been better to call first, I might have been out.'

'But you aren't, so . . .'

'So come in,' Gwen says, stepping back from the door. 'Better bring your bike inside. Justine used to be able to leave hers on the verandah but you can't be too sure these days.'

'I'll chain it up,' Gaby says, pulling a chain from her backpack. 'Don't want to make tyre marks on your nice floor.'

Gwen smiles, the sudden irritation of this unplanned arrival dissipating as fast as it came. 'So,' she says, leading the way through to the kitchen, 'half term, is it?'

'It's a DOTT day,' Gaby says. 'Duties other than teaching,' she adds, seeing the question on Gwen's face. 'The teachers have a day to do their stuff; you know, planning more torture for us.'

'Ah! I see. You might as well make the most of it. Would you like some coffee, or tea maybe?'

'A glass of water, please,' Gaby says, looking around. 'This is a lovely house. Have you always lived here?'

'I lived here until I got married,' Gwen says, getting the water jug from the fridge. 'My father also owned a farm in the wheat belt, and, much to his disgust, I ran off with the farm manager, and married him.'

'What, like, eloped?'

'I suppose you could call it that.'

'Really?' Gaby says, looking at Gwen with new respect. 'So, did you live happily ever after?'

Gwen hands her the glass, laughing as she does so. 'We lived happily for a few weeks,' she says. 'After that it was all downhill. When we split up, I sold the farm and moved back here with Justine to live with my mother and an old lady called Gladys, who used to cook for us there.'

'Cool,' Gaby says again. 'A house full of women. Mum lived in a house full of women when Dan was born.'

'Really?'

She nods. 'They had a consciousness raising group, they were sort of the first of the second wave feminists, I think. We're doing the sixties in History.'

'History?' Gwen smiles. 'It's odd thinking of something you've lived through as history but, of course, it is. I didn't realise Zoë was a part of the women's movement then,' she says, gesturing Gaby towards the back verandah.

'Oh, she wasn't. No way. She's hopeless, doesn't seem to have noticed how awesome it was.' She shrugs and gulps the water. 'Those women freaked her out but she had nowhere else to go.'

'I see.' There are more questions Gwen would like to ask but knows that this is probably not the right time. 'So, what brings you over here this morning, Gaby?'

'I came to see you. You said I could.'

'Well, yes, I did. But . . .'

'But there *was* something.' Gaby flushes and sets her glass carefully on the ground beside her chair. 'I want you to tell me about Justine.'

'Justine?'

'Yes. Where she comes from, how come she's lived with you all this time.'

Gwen hesitates. 'Do you think perhaps you should ask Justine? She's going to be your sister-in-law, after all.'

'I know and it's just . . . I wouldn't want her to think I was asking because . . . well because it made any sort of difference.'

'Ah! I see. So why *are* you asking, then?'

Gaby sighs and scrunches her face up against a brilliant shaft of sunlight. 'Because of Mum, because she's funny about Justine and I need to know why. So I can, you know . . . make it all right.'

Gaby is the image of her mother physically, but there is a straightforwardness and determination about her that she must get from her father. Zoë is far more tentative and complex.

'Gaby, it's very good of you to want to make things right, but this may be more complicated than you realise,' Gwen says.

'I don't think so. Mum's frightened of Justine because she's different and she doesn't understand who she is. It's stupid, really, because, after all, Dan's different too, isn't he? It's the way Mum was brought up, Gran's . . . well . . . you must know how it was then, what people thought . . . Gran's always been funny about Dan. Now Mum's funny about Justine. Grandma's a hopeless case, but Mum isn't. She can't be – *I* so will not let her be. So I need you to help me, you see?'

Gwen nods slowly, impressed by Gaby's ability to cut to the crux of what she'd suspected. 'I do see,' she says, 'and, Gaby, I'll do what I can but it may be that the best thing *I* can do is not interfere.'

'That's okay,' Gaby says with a satisfied smile. 'You can leave the interfering to me. I'm good at that, my sister says so all the time. I just need to know what's what so it's sort of . . . well . . . educated interfering, if you know what I mean.'

'Educated interfering, I like that,' Gwen says smiling. 'I do indeed know what you mean. So, how long have you got? Would you like to stay for lunch?'

Struggling with her third attempt to wade through Zoë's long and rambling email, Julia stares at the screen and wonders what sort of can of worms she has opened. There are so many strands that don't come together: the past, obviously; the present sense of fear; the anticipation of loss. Zoë mentions panic attacks, hopelessness and, again and again, the word 'shame' appears. And yet, she writes too about her family: a thoughtful, loving husband; two beautiful daughters; a comfortable home; and Daniel being engaged to a woman with whom everyone except his mother is enchanted. What is Zoë asking her? Or is she not asking anything but just doing the email equivalent of thinking aloud? She writes as though some terrible sadness is poisoning her.

'Well, what did you expect?' Tom had asked when he read it.

'I don't know, but certainly not this. I'm not a therapist. What do you think she wants me to do?'

'Lord knows. She's going through a bad time, I suppose, just wants you to say something meaningful and wise.'

But meaningful and wise is not how Julia feels while trying to match the words to the voice and face of the Zoë she remembers. She sees her walking into the bar of the Branston, hand-in-hand with Richard, looking nervously around, impressed and intimidated by the surroundings, and desperate for acceptance.

'I don't think your parents liked me,' Zoë had said, disappointment and the fear of what that might mean written across her face.

'They wouldn't,' Julia remembers saying, 'you don't fit the bill at all.' And she wonders if Zoë remembers that moment and realises that she herself is now in Anita's shoes.

And, in a blinding flash, Julia sees that Zoë had always felt she didn't fit the bill; not the Linton bill – nor anyone else's for that matter – and maybe this is what's at the heart of this deeply sad and confusing message. She tries to remember what she once knew about Zoë's childhood, and, as she does so, she can also recognise the terrible sense of unworthiness that now seems to have characterised so much of what Zoë did, particularly her desperate attempts to cling to Richard even when he was at his most unpleasant. She was grasping at something, or someone, to validate her, and once she was married, her confidence grew as she was released from the merciless need to strive for something more. But it had all changed with Daniel's arrival. Julia sees now that what she had thought was Zoë's pride the last time they met was simply a desperate sort of bravado, and that she and Richard had trampled Zoë's self-esteem into the ground. They must have driven her into a space more emotionally arid even than that from which she had come.

And so, Julia begins to write, as she believes Zoë must have done, instinctively, thinking not about words and sentences, but drawing on what she remembers so well from her life with Simon, about how it feels to be a woman who senses somehow that she is always in the wrong.

Dear Zoë, she begins, *How I wish we could sit down together and talk face-to-face as we did when we first met. In our different ways we thought we knew what mattered, but after all this time it seems obvious that we knew nothing, the past looks so very different now . . .*

And so, in the ensuing weeks a conversation begins, one taking place across the globe and becoming daily more important. Confidences unfold and there are reassuring similarities, poignant memories, disturbing differences not fully comprehended, moments of hurt and profound affection. No phone calls are made but recent photographs are exchanged and, one day in May, the telephone rings in Rye and Julia answers it.

'It's Zoë,' says a shaky voice.

Julia, taken totally by surprise, hesitates. 'Zoë?'

'Yes. I want to see you. I've just booked a flight to England for next month, and now I'm worried that you won't be there or won't want to see me.'

'I'll be here,' Julia says, shivering with emotion at the sound of Zoë's voice. 'And of course I want to see you.'

THIRTY

After years of hesitation, indecisiveness and a preference for following Archie's lead, Zoë has taken two decisions and acted on them very quickly. With no planning or agonising about what she *ought* to do, she has handed in her notice. For the last eight years in her job at the tourist office, she had clung to the safety, predictability and the small regular income. But she had also felt she *should* have some sort of structure to her week, *should* do something outside her home.

She's worked for three decades; part-time, mostly, and with time off when the children were born, but she always went back. And she went back, she knows, because of her mother. Eileen had worked full-time for most of her life – in the laundry, and then in the biscuit factory – and she never let Zoë forget it. Now she thinks it would have been nice to have had more time at home with the children, especially when they were small. These days, Zoë thinks she is sounding more and more like her mother, so resigning makes her feel she is striking a blow for change.

'At last!' Archie says, hugging her when she tells him what she's done.

'I just thought I'd have a break. I'll find something else later.'

'Only if you want to. We can manage without the money. It'll give you more time to paint; you must keep that up.'

'Yes, but it's not only the painting,' Zoë says, hesitating. 'I've been writing to Julia.'

'Julia? But why? You were so upset and angry, I thought you'd decided to ignore her.'

'I did,' she says blushing, 'and then I changed my mind.'

'When?'

'A few days later.' And she holds back from telling him that it was on the night that Dan and Justine had announced their engagement.

Archie whistles, puffing out his cheeks. 'And?'

'We've been emailing several times a week. I needed to unload some stuff and I unloaded it on her.'

'What stuff?'

There is a silence and Zoë looks away. 'Oh, you know, just stuff about the past.'

'Big stuff, presumably.'

She nods.

Archie pauses, battling a sudden unease as this is so uncharacteristic of his wife. 'Anything I should worry about?'

She puts her arms around his waist. 'Absolutely not,' she says, leaning her head against his chest. 'Emotional house cleaning, that's all.'

'Okay. If you're sure. And the painting?'

'I love it. There's no way I'd stop now.'

He looks down into her face. 'Well, anything that works, I say. Did they beg you to stay on at work?'

'Yes, but I resisted. And,' she takes a deep breath, 'I've booked a ticket to England.'

There is silence and Archie's jaw drops. 'England, when?'

Zoë's chest is tight with tension. She doesn't want to hurt him, but she's determined to go and to go alone. 'Next month, for four weeks.'

Archie hesitates and Zoë holds her breath. 'Are you . . . did you mean both of us?' he asks cautiously.

'No. Please don't be hurt, Arch, but I need to go alone. I want to see Julia.'

'Of course I'm not hurt,' he says, looking mightily relieved. 'I couldn't have got away right now. And I think you probably do need to do this alone. But, Zo, I *am* concerned about you. You were so upset by the email and now you want to see Julia?'

'I overreacted,' Zoë says. 'It opened it all up, but now I think that was probably a good thing. A chance for me to get things in perspective.'

'And Richard, will you be seeing him?'

She shrugs. 'I shouldn't think so. We've barely mentioned him except in relation to the past. It's Julia I want to see; we had the beginnings of a friendship that seemed really special.'

Buckling her seatbelt as the aircraft begins its descent, Zoë peers down through the thinning cloud to the Channel coastline and the incredible green of the English countryside. She is under no illusions about what she's doing; she is running away, escaping briefly from things that she can't face at home, mainly the preparations for a wedding that she doesn't want to take place. The excitement generated largely by Rosie and Gaby, and into which everyone else has entered, oppresses her.

Beneath her are small towns and dense patches of woodland, and then the density of a large town and the perimeter of Gatwick airport, and she swings suddenly between fear and exhilaration. What will Julia be like? Will they be able to re-create the email friendship face-to-face, or will it be a disaster? The wheels touch the runway, bounce slightly, touch again and the aircraft races at terrifying speed towards something she can't see. Is this what she is doing, running blind at hundreds of times her normal speed? If so, she has now reached the point of no return.

From the airport she takes the train through fields and between steep wooded banks, and along the outskirts of small towns that she doesn't recognise. And later, from the back seat of a taxi, she sees Rye nestled on a hill: the ancient town dominated by grey stone buildings that survived the fourteenth-century French raids and the fire that razed the town to the ground; between them, the black-and-white wattle-and-daub and elegant Georgian brick of successive builders thread through the steep streets. And she remembers Richard bringing her here one day, explaining the history of the Cinque Ports, and taking her to see a strange clock in the church – or was it the town hall? – with odd little mechanical figures that jerked around in a high gallery striking the quarters of each hour. The driver weaves his way through the narrow streets, up the steep cobbled slope of Mermaid Street and draws up outside an elegant three-storey Georgian house, with a bed and breakfast sign just visible through the dense green creepers.

Her room is on the second floor off a gallery overlooking the breakfast room, in which portraits of previous owners and their ancestors survey the tables laid with white linen and willow pattern crockery. She is in another world, one of which she had previously caught only a glimpse. She booked this hotel for just one night, to give herself time to get over the journey, but she realises now she also needs a more profound type of recovery. She is exhausted by the enormity of what she has done. Quietly, she makes herself a cup of tea and lies down on the bed. Tomorrow she will meet Julia again, stay in her house; now she just needs time to get used to the idea. And Richard, what will she do about Richard? She is torn between the need to erase any thought of him and an increasing desire to see him, to find out . . . to find out what?

It's four in the afternoon when Zoë wakes, her limbs heavy, her mouth dry, feeling now the horrible effects of her almost sleepless night on the plane. Forcing herself up, she has a shower and puts on clean clothes, deciding to explore the town and perhaps find somewhere she can have a real English tea.

The cobbled street glistens in the sunlight that has followed the rain that fell while she slept, and she sets off in search of the café where, the receptionist has told her, she can get the best cream tea in town. The prospect of scones with jam and cream almost has her salivating; she hasn't eaten since the in-flight breakfast. Turning the corner at the top of the hill, she finds herself at the entrance to the churchyard and realises that she must be very close to Julia's house.

'It faces the churchyard,' Julia had said, 'and it's hidden behind the catalpa tree.' Zoë has no idea what a catalpa tree looks like, but it can only be this, with its long, low branches, leaves like saucers, and exotic bean pods. She walks on through the churchyard, through the dappled sunlight on the path, across the drenched and sparkling edge of the grass, between the gravestones that lean at rakish angles, speckled with moss, their legends unreadable with age, and realises she is standing almost directly in front of Julia's front door. The house is a double-fronted cottage of white Sussex boarding, two storeys high with what might be a third attic floor with little windows jutting out of the sloping roof. It would be so natural just to knock at the door and say hello. Zoë's heart beats furiously and she pauses to calm herself, taking in every detail. Is this unfair, she wonders? Maybe just leave it until tomorrow, as planned. But the temptation is too great. She steps up to the door, rings the bell, hears footsteps, and the door is flung open and she finds herself face to face with Richard.

⚬≈⚬

'I can't believe you didn't follow this up,' Julia says, pacing back and forth across the hospital room. 'You let it go so long.'

Tom, propped up on pillows, looks pale and sheepish. 'You were so upset at losing Hilary. I was too and I wanted us to have the holiday together, time to recover. It was only tests, and Raheem didn't actually say . . .'

'He said you should get the tests done as soon as possible. You didn't even tell me when we got back from Portugal.'

'No, I should have come straight out of Raheem's surgery and organised it then, but when we got back from the holiday, I felt okay. And I just dreaded going through all this again, so I, well, I just kept putting it off.'

'That is so stupid,' Julia says. 'You let it go so long, and now you have to be brought to London by ambulance and have an emergency operation. That is so irresponsible and so like a man . . .'

'Please, darling,' Tom says, reaching for her hand. 'Don't go on . . . I started out trying to do the right thing and then I just couldn't bring myself to . . .'

She is completely undone by this. 'Oh, I'm so sorry, Tomo,' she says. 'It's my guilt talking; I was so focused on Hilary, and then the stuff with Zoë, that I didn't even notice that you were worried.' She kisses him first on the forehead and then on the lips, and he holds her into the kiss, stroking her neck.

'I'll be fine. Raheem says it's a piece of cake, and you know what a bloody good surgeon he is.'

Raheem had not, in fact, said anything of the sort. What he had said, earlier that morning, was, 'You are a fucking idiot, my friend. I warn you when you come to see me. I send you two letters telling you get your frigging finger out and let me organise the tests, and what do you do? Ignore me. Now we are a very dodgy, complicated, elevated risk level for negative outcomes.'

'You mean, like dying?' Tom had said, keeping an eye on the door in case Julia came back from her trip to the cafeteria to get a coffee.

'If you want to put it like that,' Raheem said. 'You one lucky fucker, Tom, I am the best urologist in the known universe.'

'And modest with it.'

'That too. So, probably you are being okay. But you are too old for being so stupid.'

'But my heart's in good shape, and my lungs. I've got a good constitution. I'm otherwise very healthy and in good shape for surgery,' Tom had said, not sure whether he was reassuring Raheem or himself.

'These things are good, yes. Just your brain is obviously in question now.'

'You are the best urologist in the known universe and I love it when you're angry,' Tom had said with a half smile.

Raheem broke into a laugh and did some air punching. 'Okay, silly old bugger. We do the surgery at four o'clock, and I save your life and am a hero, okay?'

'It's a deal. But listen,' Tom says, lowering his voice. 'I know I'm an idiot but can you just tone it down a bit in front of Julia? I'm in enough trouble with her already.'

'Okay, buster.' Raheem's early knowledge of English came from reading *Biggles* novels. 'See you later when I am hero. Chin Chin.'

Fortunately, Raheem's and Julia's paths did not cross.

'So, they'll be along shortly to give you the pre-med, I suppose,' Julia says later. 'Did Raheem say how long it will take?'

'Up to four hours, barring complications.'

'I'll be here when you wake up. I'll stay up here, at Richard's place, tonight.'

'But Zoë's coming tomorrow,' Tom says. 'You wanted to go shopping, sort out the spare room.'

'Richard's driven down there to do the shopping and make up the bed, all that stuff.'

'That's kind; didn't he mind?'

'He minds about you and he minds that he might not get to see Zoë.'

'But he *might*; after all, she hasn't said she *doesn't* want to see him.'

'But she hasn't said she does, which I think is significant,' Julia says. 'And, anyway, she's married to someone who sounds really nice. Richard can't go through life hoping to kidnap his ex-wives.'

'There was only one other, and he *was* very upset about Lily.'

Julia sighs. 'But he was crazy to even *think* she'd have him back. I did warn him.'

'Well, now that he's back here and living in the flat, perhaps life will settle down for him,' Tom says. 'Maybe some wonderful woman will fall madly in love with him.'

'Mmm. Maybe, but it's more a question of whether she'll *stay* in love with him when she finds out about the drinking.' Julia looks at Tom and kisses him again. 'I do know how lucky I am, Tom,' she says, and tears spring up in her eyes again.

A nurse holding a medicine cup, tablets and a glass of water materialises between the curtains.

'I'll have to ask you to leave now, Mrs Hammond,' she says. 'Time for your husband's pre-med.'

'Could I stay just a little bit longer, if I'm nice to him?' Julia asks.

The nurse laughs. 'Well, five minutes, if you're very nice and very quiet. We want him really relaxed.'

'And ready for the slaughter,' says Tom, swallowing the tablets.

'I'll just sit and hold your hand,' Julia says, her voice wavering with emotion. 'And I'll be sitting here holding it when you wake up too.'

⁂

'So they had to rush him off up to London last night,' Richard explains, standing awkwardly in the doorway. 'And Jules asked me to pop down, and sort of tidy up a bit, and get the shopping and, well . . . look this wasn't meant to happen, Zoë, she made it clear that I should stay away unless you actually wanted to see me.'

'Yes, I see,' Zoë says, giving him an odd sort of half smile. 'It makes you sound like a leper.'

He shrugs. 'I can understand that you wouldn't . . .'

'Did *you* want to see *me*?' she asks, taking him by surprise.

'Very much and not at all, if you know what I mean.'

'Mmm. Exactly, me too,' she says. 'But, look, this is my fault; I took a room for one night and didn't even tell Julia I was going to be in Rye. And then I just saw I was close to the house, so . . . I thought . . .'

'Yes, of course.' Richard feels hyped up on anxiety and memories and thinks he must look insane. Knowing about Zoë's visit has had him on edge for a couple of weeks. He'd assumed she would avoid him and now she's here in front of him; so much the same and, at the same time, so totally different. More than thirty years older, for a start, but unmistakably Zoë and she's wearing black jeans and a red shirt, just like the red and black she was wearing that first day he saw her. He feels as though he's back in the foyer of Broadcasting House and that all the messy years in between have miraculously disappeared; he is twenty-eight again and full of hope.

'Look, tell Julia I can easily stay on at the hotel,' Zoë says. 'She'll want to be there with Tom – she mustn't come back for me. When's the operation?'

Everything Julia has told him about Tom's operation has disappeared from Richard's memory and he has to study the figures on his watch to focus himself. 'They were due to start about an hour ago,' he says eventually.

She nods. 'I hope it all goes well. Tell Julia I'll catch up with her later in the week. I'm staying at that place opposite the Mermaid.' She turns to go.

'You could come in . . . I mean, if you want to,' Richard stammers. 'I could make you some tea.'

She pauses. 'I was going to have a cream tea at the place on the other side of the church.'

He shrugs with a nonchalance he doesn't feel. 'It would take me two minutes to get scones from the bakery, cream was on Jules's shopping list and there's a cupboard full of homemade jam in the kitchen.'

For a moment she stands there looking at him; her eyes meet his, flick away and then back.

'Okay,' she says. 'Why not?'

And he opens the door wider and steps aside to let her in.

THIRTY-ONE

Cottesloe – June 2000

'Have you heard from your mother?' Gwen asks when
Gaby turns up late on a Friday afternoon with her
backpack.

Gaby nods, dumps the bag on a chair and goes to the fridge
to get herself a glass of water. She is quite at home here, and has
twice stayed overnight to go swimming with Gwen early in the
mornings. Gwen delights in her company, for, although Justine
and Dan are downstairs in the flat, she sees much less of Justine
now. She is cautious, though, about Zoë's reaction. What does she
feel about her daughter spending so much time here? Will it just
add to the indefinable tension between Zoë and Justine? But right
now, Zoë is away for a while, and presumably not keeping tabs
on the frequency of Gaby's visits. Archie, on the other hand, is
delighted and has promised to drive over with Gaby early one
morning to swim with the Polar Bears.

'Yeah,' Gaby says, 'she's having a great time. She's gone to visit
this woman, Julia, who used to be her sister-in-law.'

Gwen nods. Dan has filled her in on those past relationships,
along with some views of his own on what happened and why. He
is battling, she thinks, with the way he's always seen his mother
and the way he sees her now. Gwen is careful what she says as
he tries to probe the causes of Zoë's coolness to Justine. There
are, of course, many possibilities: age, race, the chaotic feelings of

mid-life, the symbolic separation from a particularly beloved son. Any, or all, of these, could be at the root of it.

Gaby has told Gwen that she has been 'working on' her mother, without success. She's been letting little bits of information and opinions about Justine drop into the conversation, asking pointed questions to which, it seems, there are no answers. She even went down to the Fremantle Library and brought home the huge hardback edition of *Bringing Them Home*, the report on the stolen generations, together with a book called *Mystical Menopause: Enjoying Your Mid-life Journey*. She had left them on the coffee table, where they sat, apparently untouched, for three weeks until she stuffed them in her school bag and took them back to the library.

'That wasn't very subtle,' Gwen had told Gaby in what she felt was a massive understatement. 'It might be best just to do nothing and see what happens.'

But Gaby took a lot of convincing.

'Well, I hope she enjoys her trip,' Gwen says now. 'She probably needs a break.'

'She's never been away on her own before,' Gaby says. 'She hardly does anything on her own, so we were all, like, totally amazed when she started going to that art class, and now she's gone off like this.'

'Really?' Gwen says, surprised. 'Why do you think that is?'

Gaby throws herself onto the sofa by the window and looks out across the garden, to the street and, beyond it, the ocean. 'She's frightened, I think.'

'Of what?'

'Oh, I dunno; it's like she's not sure who she is if we're not there.' She pauses. 'Anyway, I'm glad she's gone away, because she's upsetting everybody. We want to talk about the wedding and everything, and we can't do it with her around because she makes us feel guilty. Like, because we're all excited about it, we're not being loyal to her.'

'But has she said that?'

'Oh no, she never actually *says* anything. She's just *there*, making a weird atmosphere, being disapproving. So I don't talk to her about it now. I mean, what can I do? If it was the other way round, she'd be giving me a mega hard time.'

'What do you mean?'

'Well, if I'm yelling at Rosie if she's going somewhere, Mum's, like "Oh, Gaby, you're so selfish, spoiling it for Rosie," and everything. But it's okay for her to do it. But that's – well, that's parents, isn't it?'

 ⌒⌒

Zoë sits by the open window of her hotel room, watching pedestrians making their way up the steep street to gaze at the famous facade of the Mermaid Hotel. She had forgotten these long summer evenings, when it is still light at nine-thirty and the air is mild and gentle. She feels as though she is suspended in a life that is not her own, in which anything could happen, and, indeed, in which the strangest thing has *already* happened.

When Richard opened the door, her first reaction had been panic; she had even felt she might faint. That he was equally shocked was obvious from his expression. How long had they stood there, staring at each other as the past swam before her eyes like a series of slides? He looked older, much older, and, while he was still an attractive man, it was clear from his ravaged face that life had not been particularly kind to him. His hair, only a little shorter than it had been in the sixties, was almost completely grey and she had never seen him with a beard before – although this was more what Rosie would call designer stubble. He was wearing jeans and a blue-and-white cotton shirt, and his feet were bare against the polished floorboards. She remembered sliding down a stony beach on a late afternoon in summer, just like this one, and taking his cold feet in her hands, tickling them, and then, as he begged for mercy, kissing them, tasting sea water on his skin. It seems impossible now that she could ever have done that.

Zoë had so often wondered what it would be like, how she would feel, if they met again. She had even rehearsed the biting sarcasm she would employ, that would leave him crushed. And when he'd offered her tea she had almost refused, but something intrigued her; something about the way Richard was behaving and about the way it made her feel.

'Okay,' she'd said. 'Why not?' And she'd followed him down the central passage to the large light kitchen where shopping sat in carrier bags on a big scrubbed pine table. 'This is beautiful,' she'd said, looking around her and out through a glazed breakfast room to the garden and beyond, to where the land dropped steeply away to the sea.

She thinks she must have appeared comparatively calm and confident, but all the time she had been wondering why she was there in Julia's kitchen with Richard. He had moved around in confusion, unloading the shopping, attempting to make tea; clearly distracted, obviously wanting to stare deeply at her and through her into the past, in just the same way she wanted to stare into him.

'If you tell me where the bakery is, I'll go and get the scones,' she'd said, thinking it would give him time to sort himself out.

'But you *will* come back?' he'd asked as he'd pointed across the churchyard, and indicated that she should follow the path to the square and wouldn't be able to miss the bakery.

'I'm getting scones for both of us; of course I'll come back.' But she had taken her time, pausing once out of sight of the house to sit briefly on a seat against the church wall, in order to gather her thoughts. And when she got back, the tea was made, the table cleared of shopping, and Richard was spooning cream into a small dish that matched the one into which he'd already put the jam.

It wasn't the easiest of conversations, peppered as it was with awkward silences as they both struggled to keep it up, when it kept veering towards dangerous ground. She had told him about Archie and the girls, and about her mother, to whom he could remember having spoken a few times over the phone.

'And Daniel?' he'd asked, looking down into his tea, and Zoë thought she saw his hands shaking.

'He's well,' she said, swallowing hard, also unable to look up at Richard as she spoke. 'He's an officer in the Australian army; the SAS, actually.'

Richard's head jerked up. 'The army, really? I never imagined . . . although, of course, what would I know about . . .'

'I never imagined it either,' she said. 'And, frankly, I hate it. It's the last thing I wanted for him, especially his being in the SAS. Sometimes we haven't a clue where he is, even if he's alive or dead. The last time, he was away for about three months and then turned up out of the blue on crutches on New Year's Eve. His leg was broken in two places and he'd had two lumps of shrapnel removed from it.' She swallowed hard, determined not to cry in front of Richard, and unsure why she felt she might.

'It must be incredibly hard,' Richard said quietly, and she looked across at him and saw her own sadness reflected in his eyes. 'Where had he been?'

'East Timor.'

They sat in silence for a moment and then Richard said, 'You must be very proud of him. I have a daughter, Carly; she's a journalist, she works for a newspaper in San Francisco. And she's getting married in September.'

Zoë looked up at him. 'Dan's getting married then too. We're getting old, Richard.'

'Not you, Zoë,' he'd said then. 'Not you. I, on the other hand, am a wreck, for which I only have myself to blame.'

He did look wrecked, Zoë thinks now, sitting in the twilight, enjoying the feeling that she has survived this extraordinary encounter; in fact, enjoyed it. Had she known she would meet him, her fevered imagination would have conjured up a painful encounter fraught with recriminations and resentment. But all her long-held anger towards Julia had simply dissipated in the early days of their correspondence, and so it had today with Richard. The past was done and perhaps Archie was right; the person she really needed to forgive was herself.

Their conversation had finally been interrupted by Julia's call to say that Tom had come through the operation and the surgeon had insisted that everything would be fine.

'What are you going to do now?' Zoë had heard Richard ask. And, apparently, Julia had told him that she was going to stay a while longer at the hospital and then go back to the flat, and asked if he would be coming back there.

'No,' he'd said then. 'No, I'm not going to drive back tonight. I'll stay down here and drive up in the morning. And by the way, Jules, Zoë's here.'

There was a horrified squawk and then a fast, high-pitched torrent of indistinguishable words.

'It's okay,' he said. 'At least, I think it is, isn't it, Zoë?' he asked, raising his eyebrows. 'She's nodding and smiling, so it must be. We've had tea together and I might . . .' But Julia had interrupted and he had listened to her for a moment, shrugged and pulled a face. 'Okay,' he said, 'hang on. She wants to talk to you,' he said, handing Zoë the phone.

She had assured Julia that things were fine and they then spoke briefly of Tom. 'Don't hurry back,' Zoë said. 'I can stay on at the hotel, or maybe come up to London and meet you.'

'Let's talk in the morning,' Richard had interrupted. 'We'll know more about how Tom is by then.'

As she'd put down the phone, Zoë had suddenly felt her energy drain away, as though shock and emotion had sucked everything from her.

'I'm going to head off now, Richard,' she'd said. 'I'm really tired, but I'm so glad about Tom.'

'Me too,' he said. 'He's a lovely man, you'll like him, Zoë.'

'Not another Simon, then? Although I did rather like Simon, he was so . . . so . . .'

'Charming, bumptious and full of himself?'

'Well, yes, but in the nicest possible way.'

'I know what you mean. He's still much the same. He married twice, first to a very nice woman, one of his own kind, Jules says, and they had twin girls. Then more recently a very glamorous model. Look, let me walk with you.'

And they had strolled back through the churchyard and down Mermaid Street to the hotel.

'I'll give you a call in the morning,' Richard said. 'Let you know how Tom is and what Julia's doing.'

'Yes,' she nodded. 'Thanks for the tea. It's good to see you again.'

And they stood there, staring at each other, until Richard leaned forward and kissed her lightly on the cheek.

'You too,' he said, and he turned and walked quickly away.

⌇

By the time Archie arrives at the Thai restaurant with Rob and the girls, Justine, Dan and Gwen are already at the table. He'd invited everyone for dinner as part of his promise to Zoë that he'd ensure things didn't fall apart in her absence. In fact, things haven't looked less like falling apart for some time: the house is immaculately clean, thanks largely to Rosie; the fridge and pantry are well stocked, thanks to himself and Gaby having done a joint shopping expedition; and this morning he'd called in to see Eileen at the retirement village and taken her out to lunch. As always when they were alone together, things had gone very smoothly until she'd started on Zoë.

'So, have you heard from her ladyship?'

Archie was so infuriated that he wanted to punch her right on the nose.

'If you mean Zoë, yes, I have,' he'd replied coldly. 'She's fine, sent you her love. Everything seems to be going well.'

'I can't imagine why she had to go gallivanting off to England anyway,' Eileen had said, examining her toasted sandwich. 'A waste of time and money, if you ask me.'

'Well, I didn't ask you, Mum, and I disagree. As far as I'm concerned, Zoë's more than entitled to a holiday, and if she wants to take it in England, that's fine by me. It'll do her good, cheer her up.' He could've bitten his tongue for saying that and, sure enough, Eileen pounced on it.

'I don't know what she needs cheering up for. She has a lovely home and family, and you are a wonderful husband, Archie. Zoë's very lucky.'

'We both are,' Archie said, reaching for his beer. Eileen's canonisation of him, always to Zoë's detriment, riled him again but he recognised that it had its advantages. He was the only one who could talk Eileen round when necessary, and he knew that without him, Zoë and her mother would no longer be on speaking terms.

He's looking forward to this evening. He hasn't see Dan or Justine for a couple of weeks, he loves Thai food, and Rob had turned up at the house with a case of the best semillon from the family's estate. Zoë has been gone for a week and is obviously fine. The uncharacteristic nature of her behaviour is not lost on him but its impact is blurred by his relief at being without her for a while. He wouldn't admit this to anyone, but her recent moods have exhausted and infuriated him. While he's happy now, he's tired of being in charge, and Dan seems to sense it, and opens the wine and chivvies everyone to sort out their orders so they can all share the dishes. Archie thinks, but only fleetingly, that maybe it will be nice when the time comes that he is the elderly relative who gets looked after, instead of being the one who does the organising, but, just as quickly, he knows he'll hate it.

The food is delicious, and wine and laughter flow freely until the waiters remove what's left of the main course. Then, as they pause to consider dessert possibilities, Gaby leans forward, her arms folded on the table.

'Now that we've eaten,' she says, 'we need to talk about Mum.'

Archie chokes on his wine, Justine and Gwen freeze, and Rob decides he needs to go to the bathroom.

'Shut up, Gab,' Rosie says, flapping her serviette at her sister, 'I told you not to.'

And Dan shrugs, giving Archie a wry smile.

'Yes,' says Gwen, coming to the rescue. 'Do let's; how is she, Archie? Having a good time, I hope? You must all miss her.'

Archie draws a grateful breath and delivers a quick update, after which there is another, longer silence.

'Well,' says Gaby. 'That's nice but it's not what I meant. We have to talk about Mum being so weird about Dan and Justine.'

Archie groans and puts his head in his hands, and Justine, who is sitting next to him, puts her hand on his arm.

'It's okay, Arch,' she says. 'Gaby's just trying to help. I mean, I do realise Zoë's not too happy about us being engaged.'

Dan, who appears lost for words, puts his arm around her shoulders.

'Well, she *should* be happy about it!' Gaby says.

'I told her not too, Dad, honestly,' Rosie says, her face flushed. 'I told her she shouldn't say anything. You're just making it worse, Gaby, shut up.'

'Shut up yourself,' Gaby says and turns to Archie. 'Justine's right, Dad. I'm trying to help. We need to talk about this before Mum gets back because if we don't, it'll just be like it was before she went and it's horrible. I've done everything I can and you've all . . . well, you've done nothing about it, as far as I can see. We need a plan, we all need to sing from the same hymn sheet . . .'

'Where the fuck . . . sing from the same . . .' Dan says.

'What? Oh, Mr Wheedon always says it. And we do need to sing from the same sheet, otherwise, instead of it being a really lovely wedding, it's going to be awful, or there won't be a wedding at all because everyone's afraid to talk about it.'

Justine sucks in her breath.

A birthday cake is delivered to the next table and, fortunately, the diners there have very loud singing voices. Dan sees Rob emerging cautiously from the men's toilet and shakes his head, and Rob raises a grateful hand and wanders off outside to sit on the verandah.

'Christ,' says Archie. 'I hope Mr Wheedon doesn't suggest a career in the diplomatic service.'

THIRTY-TWO

Rye – July 2000

The house is peaceful, a blessed relief after the constant clatter and action of the hospital. It was always its tranquillity in proximity to vibrant activity that Julia loved. From the kitchen window, the view of the sea suggests that at the end of the garden, the land drops sharply to the water. It's an illusion, because behind the plumbago hedge that badly needs a trim, there is a footpath and a low wall, and beyond that, the slope of the land is tiered gently and the path follows it down across long reclaimed expanses of flat land to the water. It was this natural *trompe d'oeil* that had compelled Julia to buy the house when she and Hilary came home from Paris. At the back, you could be miles from anywhere, and from the front door, where she is standing now, the life of the town is comfortingly apparent. In fact, right now, against the backdrop of the huge catalpa tree, a bride and groom are posing for photographs while their guests stand by. The catalpa is Julia's personal landmark; the one she uses to direct visitors to the house and the one she had used to guide Tom when he turned up at Greenham Common.

'It's easy to find,' she'd told him, 'and Hilary'll be thrilled to see you. It's in the highest part of the town, behind the church. Find the catalpa tree in the churchyard, it's between that and the sea.'

He'd come down here the next day, and then back again to the peace camp the day after that, and then done so time and again in his relentless pursuit of her, his effort to resolve the past and capture the future. Months later, when she'd left the camp and he was still attempting to chip away at the rock of her resistance, she and Hilary had invited him to Rye for Christmas. On Christmas Eve, as the first flakes of snow were starting to fall, he had appeared in the kitchen. She was working there at the table because the kitchen was the warmest room in the house. She was reading the applications for the position of secretary for the language school, which she and Hilary had moved into its own premises, down near the station, some weeks earlier.

'Would you come with me for a moment, Julia?' Tom had asked. 'There's something I want to show you.'

'I'm busy now, Tom,' she'd said. 'Can't it wait?'

'Probably, but I'd rather it didn't.'

She got up, with a theatrical sigh. 'It better be worth it.' And she'd let him take her hand and lead her across the churchyard and into the spectacular red-and-gold decorated interior of the church in which the scent of pine needles from the Christmas tree mingled with incense and the sulphur of recently extinguished candles.

'Isn't it glorious?' he'd said softly, holding firmly onto her hand.

'Yes, but I've seen it several times already,' Julia said. 'Hilary sprayed all those fir cones with gold paint in our shed, and sprayed most of the garden tools at the same time.'

'I know,' he said. 'But look at this.' And he drew her with him along the aisle to a small memorial plaque in the tiling. Releasing her hand, he crouched beside it and pointed to the inscription. 'See what it says – "on the ruins of yesterday we build the foundations of tomorrow".' He stood up and took her hands in his. 'That's what we can do; we have a second chance and some people would give their right arm for that. We're older now, and wiser. Say you'll marry me, Julia, like you did before – and this time I won't let you down.'

'I've *been* married, Tom,' she said. 'It didn't work for me, I'm not good wife material.'

'Maybe not for Simon, but you are for me.'

She shook her head. 'I've been a caged bird, I can't do it again. And I'm not the woman you proposed to in Paris.'

'Do you think I'm blind?' he'd said then, gripping her shoulders, and a couple wandering along one of the side aisles turned to look at them. Tom lowered his voice. 'You're the woman I loved then, and so much more. I don't want a caged bird, I want you, Julia; an eagle to fly with.'

'Don't be so embarrassing, Tom,' she'd whispered, flushing and glancing around over her shoulder, confused about how she really felt. 'An eagle . . . flying!'

'Fly with me, Jules,' he'd said and then, softly, *Come fly with me*. If you say yes, you won't have to keep thinking up more reasons to turn me down and you can concentrate on your work again.'

And she'd paused and closed her eyes and, as they stood there in the silent church, she wondered why she was fighting it. Tom had more than proved himself this time around, not just through his persistence. He loved her for who she was; she could be married to him and still be herself. She laughed, softly at first, and then joyfully. 'Okay,' she said, loudly enough that the other couple, and a few more visitors who had wandered in from the cold, stopped and looked around. 'Okay, Tom, yes, I will marry you.'

'Yes!' he had cried aloud, punching the air with his fist, and in the ensuing silence of their kiss there was a smattering of applause.

'I have witnesses now,' he'd said. 'And I mean it; this time I won't let you down.'

And, of course he hasn't, not once; even now he hasn't. He has refused to be beaten and is home here with her seven days after a major operation; padding experimentally around the house in his pyjamas, taking the stairs with caution, having red wine in moderation, and taking himself no more seriously than he ever has. And all that Julia wants now is to be alone with him. But, for the moment, they have Zoë's presence to contend with, and, while she had anticipated it with enormous pleasure, the reality is more complicated. Perhaps it was all there in the emails and she had just failed to see it, but it's certainly clear to her now that Zoë has not made the huge leaps of consciousness that she herself has made. She is, in so many ways, the Zoë of the sixties.

Even so, it is a delightful rediscovery of friendship, and she is enjoying learning about Zoë's life. Her world is so very different from Julia's own, and one so obviously determined by the presence of children. Julia has never regretted her decision not be a mother, and being with Zoë hasn't changed that. Her marriage to Tom, her friendship with Hilary and others have been, she thinks, all she needed and more than she deserved. And Zoë, despite what seems to Julia to be a tangled web of responsibilities and demands that enmesh her, has obviously been extremely content with her own situation. For both of them it is their relationships with the people they love that are the spine, the muscle and soft tissue of their very different lives. But Julia is still concerned about Richard's capacity to rock the boat.

'Don't push your luck,' she had told him the day after Tom's operation, when he drove Zoë to London and took them both to lunch at a restaurant near the hospital. Zoë had stopped to buy postcards and they were waiting for her outside the shop. 'You still have to have a very difficult conversation, about Lily, and about what happened when you met all those years ago.'

'Of course,' he'd said. 'I just have to find the right moment.'

'Well, make sure you do,' she'd said, watching Zoë inside the shop, fumbling in her purse and then peering at the unfamiliar coins in her hand. 'The shame of that whole business has haunted her for years. Part of it is that she betrayed you, so letting her know that you weren't entirely blameless yourself is the least you owe her.'

'I know,' Richard said. 'I'll tell her, really I will.'

Julia had decided to stay another night in London, and Richard had driven Zoë back to Rye and moved her luggage from the hotel to the house. When she arrived home the following day, she was surprised to find Richard still there, and he and Zoë in the garden eating bread and cheese and tucking into a bottle of claret.

Later that day he had left, and would be occupied for at least another week on some project for the BBC. And now that Tom is well enough to be left alone in the house, she and Zoë are going to Hastings, to Marks & Spencer, where Zoë still believes she will find the best underwear in the world. Julia hasn't the heart to tell her that M&S is not quite the groundbreaker it used to be.

Julia can hear Zoë at the top of the stairs talking quietly with Tom through the open door of the bedroom, where he is sitting up in bed, reading the paper.

'I like her very much,' he'd said the previous day. 'She's not at all as I expected. It's hard to imagine that she and Richard were ever an item.'

'So, what did you expect?' Julia had asked.

'Oh, I don't know; someone a bit more carefree, I think. There's something quite burdened about her,' he said. 'It's in her manner, and in her body too, in that droop of the shoulders when she thinks no one's looking at her.'

'You're very observant,' Julia said. 'I think she *is* burdened, and, one thing's for sure, Zoë isn't, and wasn't ever, carefree.'

'Come on, Zoë,' Julia calls now from the front door, 'let's get going. We'll only be a couple of hours, Tomo.'

And Zoë runs down the stairs, and together they walk out and down the path to the car.

'So, tell me about Richard's second wife,' Zoë says, as she waits, laden with knickers and bras, in the queue for the cash register.

'Oh!' says Julia, flushing with embarrassment. 'Lily. She lives in Oakland now. They have a daughter, Carly.'

'Yes, he told me that,' says Zoë, handing the underwear over to the assistant. 'But what about Lily?'

Julia feels as though her face is on fire. What Richard has told, or will tell, Zoë about Lily is really none of her business, but her knowledge feels like a neon sign flashing above her head.

'Well, she's a lovely woman, very smart; she's a lecturer at the University of California. I like her a lot. She's tough and funny, and doesn't stand any of Richard's bullshit. They're quite good friends still.'

The saleswoman has totalled the underwear and, to Julia's relief, Zoë is focused now on completing the credit card transaction.

'Well, M and S things still look pretty good to me,' Zoë says as they make their way out into the street. They head for a nearby café and settle at a table.

'So, what does she teach?' Zoë asks, after their food arrives. 'Sorry, I mean lecture; what does Lily lecture in?'

'Oh, black history,' Julia says.

'Black history? But she's not actually black herself?'

'Yes, she is.'

Zoë looks amazed. 'Richard didn't tell me that.'

Julia, her mouth full of tuna and cucumber, feels she needn't respond.

'Don't you think that's odd?' Zoë asks.

Julia swallows her food. 'Not really; did you tell him Archie is white?'

'Well, no, but it'd be sort of obvious, wouldn't it?'

'Not necessarily. Not after Harry.'

'Okay, I see what you mean. Just the same, I . . .' She hesitates and then says, 'So, their daughter . . . she's . . . I suppose she's like Dan, then. And Justine, Dan's fiancée, has a black mother and a white father.' She measures some sugar into her teaspoon and lets it slide slowly through the froth and into the coffee. 'I don't know whether you know this but there were a lot of Aboriginal children who were taken away from their families by the government, because they were of mixed parentage. It was a terrible business and it went on for decades; they're called the stolen generation. Justine is one of them.'

Julia leans forward attentively. 'Yes, I've read about that. So, Justine is half Aboriginal?'

Zoë nods.

'And that's why . . .' Julia pauses, not knowing how best to frame her question.

'You were going to ask if that's why I don't want her to marry Dan?'

'Well, is it?'

Zoë shrugs and shakes her head. 'It's part of it, I suppose, but only a part. I feel so muddled and upset, it's hard for me to sort out the different parts of what I feel. It took me by surprise, you see; he came back from overseas and told us he'd met someone months earlier. He hadn't said anything about her until then, but she'd known about us all that time. Then, when he brought her to the house, I found I knew her. She runs the nursery where I buy my plants. A couple of months before Dan brought her home, while he was still overseas, I'd been in there talking to her about a plant and she'd given me some plant food. She said it was a gift and at the time I thought, how nice. And then later, I thought, how sneaky. She must've known I was Dan's mother and was just being patronising; knowing about me and me not knowing about her. I felt she'd had one up on me all the time.'

'So, *did* she know you were Dan's mother?'

'Well, she did seem surprised when Dan introduced us, but she must have known.'

'How would she know?'

'He must have shown her a picture or something.'

'Did you ask him, or her?'

Zoë shook her head. 'No, of course not.'

'Why not?'

'Because I won't get involved in all this secrecy. It's like the army, that's bad enough, and now he starts being secretive about this too.'

'But it's very different, surely?' Julia says. 'He doesn't have a choice about the army's rules. And maybe he just kept this romance a secret until he was sure that it was going to work out. You know, Zoë, even if Justine *did* know it was you, it's hardly a crime that she wanted to give you something. She was probably dying to introduce herself. It just seems like a nice gesture.'

Zoë sits back in her chair and folds her arms, and Julia feels as though she is struggling with the plot of an Agatha Christie mystery, having missed several crucial chapters.

'Sorry, I'm having difficulty understanding this,' Julia tries again. 'You don't mind her being part Aboriginal, it's just the secrecy that's the problem; is that right?'

'Well, it's a bit of both and then there's her age. She's forty-three, almost forty-four; that's only nine years younger than me. How can Dan . . .'

Julia puts a hand on her arm. 'Stop, Zoë, stop it, please. Don't do this to yourself, don't do it to them.'

'I *can't* stop it,' Zoë says, burying her face in her hands. 'That's the trouble, I don't know how to change how I feel. I don't *want* to be like this, Julia, really I don't. Her age – it's too much. The secrecy – well, maybe you're right. Being Aboriginal, it's not that I actually mind that, I just think it makes it all harder . . . for Dan. He's always had to cope with that and now – it's like a double whammy to cope with. A lot of people in Australia are really hostile to Aboriginals.' She looks as though she might cry, and rummages in her bag for tissues.

Julia pulls a package from her own bag, rips off the top and hands it to her. 'But Dan must know this, Zoë,' she says. 'And, as you know very well, there's always been hostility to the idea of black men with white women, so he'd have that to cope with anyway. Look, I don't know Dan or Justine, but it seems to me that, as well as the fact that they are obviously in love, they must find great strength and comfort in being with someone who has learned to live with that experience.'

Zoë shrugs and presses the tissues against her eyes. 'Maybe; probably, I suppose. But Justine, she's . . . she is just not the person I wanted Dan to marry.'

'So what *are* you saying, Zoë? Just that she wouldn't have been your choice as a daughter-in-law? Because, if so, I'd have to say that I think at least half the mothers in the world are in the same situation. I'm not a mother, but I'm sure that if I were, I'd have fixed ideas about who I wanted for my kids, and it probably wouldn't be the person they chose for themselves. But you can't make those choices for them.'

'It's more than that,' Zoë says, blowing her nose. She looks around her as though seeking a way out. 'I know it's difficult for you to understand – you're not a mother, and you're so much more confident than me anyway – but the fact is, Julia, I'm frightened of her.'

'*Frightened?*'

Zoë nods. 'Yes. You see, I always thought Dan would end up with someone like his sisters or their friends; young, still sort of needing to be looked after a bit, learning about life. But Justine – well, it's not just her age. She's travelled, she runs her own business; you can tell just by looking at her that she's mature and confident and independent. She's so thoroughly grown up.'

'So, are you saying you hoped Dan would marry someone who's less than that; somebody who isn't grown up?'

'I told you it was difficult to understand.'

'It's bloody impossible at the moment.'

'The thing is, Julia, I thought, that when Dan got married I'd be getting another daughter; someone like my own daughters, who would need me – or, at least, appreciate me – as a sort of mother too. I thought that would keep me safe.' She flushes now, and takes a huge breath. 'The family, you see; it's all I've got. I don't have a career, I don't really have any close friends. The family is what I do – I am the heart of it, I keep it together. I thought that adding a daughter-in-law would reinforce that for me. But a woman like Justine, she doesn't need *me*. They love her: Archie, the girls, not just Dan. They all think she's beautiful and clever, and an amazing cook and . . . lovely, really. And she is. And I'm frightened she'll . . .' She stops, looking down at her hands twisting the tissues to shreds.

'You're frightened she'll usurp your position in the family,' Julia supplies.

'Yes,' Zoë says, able now to look her in the eye. 'Justine, she's . . . somehow more than me, stronger, more . . .' She hesitates. 'More together, more intelligent, all the things I'm not. My family, it's all I've got. And now I'm losing it, because I'm going to have to share it with her.'

THIRTY-THREE

London – July 2000

In a pub in Soho, Richard plants a light kiss on the lips of a beautiful young woman in a halterneck dress, and slides his hand down her bare back, speculating fleetingly on the wonder of breasts that need no visible means of support. He walks with her to the door, holds it open, and she smiles at him over her shoulder and steps into the street. At the bar, he orders two pints of bitter and a whisky chaser, and carries the drinks back to the table.

'Keeping the blood/alcohol level topped up, I see,' Charlie says, nodding to the whisky.

'Don't *you* start,' Richard says, pushing a beer across the table to him. 'Everybody seems to be an expert on my level of consumption.'

'And the expert consensus is that it's too high. Cheers.'

They've met several times for lunch since Richard moved back to London, where Charlie is now principal of an exclusive sixth form college in the city.

'Cheers. So, what do you think of Amanda?'

'Delightful. How long has this been going on?'

'Five, six weeks.'

'And she's how old, exactly – twelve?'

'Gimme a break, she's twenty-six.'

'And just remind me again how old *we* are.'

'*We* are sixty this year. You first, as you may recall.'

'And you don't see a problem with that?'

'Well . . . I can see that . . .'

'Don't bullshit me, Richard. She's young enough to be your daughter, almost young enough to be your granddaughter. You're turning into a cliché. Next thing, you'll be getting your ear pierced and buying a Harley-Davidson. How would you feel if it were *your* daughter with a sixty year old?'

Richard delays his reply by taking a long swig of beer. 'She's getting married, my daughter – Carly,' he says, seizing the chance to change the subject. 'Did I already tell you that?'

'Twice,' Charlie says. 'I meant what I said about Amanda. She's lovely, but what do you have in common?'

'Well, media, of course. We're in the same business.'

Charlie looks skeptical. 'She's a junior feature writer on the beauty section of a women's magazine; you're an ageing and fairly distinguished overseas correspondent and documentary maker – forgive my cynicism. What do you talk about, you two?'

Richard grins and tosses back his whisky. 'Who needs conversation?'

'Well, *you* do, actually, and your perennial problem seems to be that you persist in pursuing women with whom you can't have the conversations you want. You're still doing it.'

'Amanda's not stupid.'

'I didn't say she was but I doubt she's ever going to debate US politics or Middle East tensions with you. The only woman you've ever had a relationship with who would, or could, have those conversations was Lily.'

Richard fidgets in his chair and then sits back, crossing his legs. 'If we're on the subject of ex-wives, I saw Zoë last week.'

Charlie puts down his drink and leans forward. 'Good heavens. How did that happen?'

Richard explains Zoë's renewed friendship with Julia, her visit and the circumstances of their meeting.

'Interesting,' Charlie says. 'I always liked Zoë, she was far too nice for you. Tried to chat her up myself once but she was too besotted with you to notice I was doing it. How is she? What's she like these days?'

'Married, with the son, of course, who's now thirty-one, and two daughters. In many ways, she's just an older edition of who she was – very sweet; warm; a bit more confident; cautious, I think; and a bit sad.'

'Aren't we all,' Charlie says. 'Actually, I think that a bit of sadness is a rather fine quality; attractive.'

'Yes,' Richard says thoughtfully. 'It can be, I suppose. Zoë is still quite attractive, and, even though I don't think she realises it, quite sexy.'

'You, of course, find any woman sexy as long as she's breathing,' Charlie says, finishing his beer.

'Not really. Margaret Thatcher never did it for me. Neither did Madeleine Albright.'

'I'm sure they'll both be devastated to hear that,' Charlie says. 'Anyway, I must be off, meeting to go to.' He gets to his feet. 'Give Zoë my love if you see her again and, remember, beautiful girls with perky breasts and perfect skin are ten-a-penny. Wise, loving and attractively sad older women are not, and they make better companions; you're shopping in the wrong mall.' And, thumping Richard on the shoulder, he squeezes out between the tables and heads off into the street.

Alone again, Richard contemplates his friend's parting remark. Charlie may well be right, he thinks, but it's easy for him. He's been married for years to a lovely woman they both knew at university; it's the sort of rich, lively and loving relationship that Richard would give his right arm for but how will he find it at this time of life? Not long ago, he tried internet dating with women of his own age, but most of them just seemed to be looking for someone who'd take care of them financially. Even on a first meeting, they asked him what he earned, if he owned his own home, if he was internet dating with a view to marriage. After meeting several pleasant, but uninspiring, women who seemed to see sex and cooking as a sort of barter for financial security, he gave up. That was when he had started thinking about the possibility of getting together with Lily again. Some of the best times of his life had been with her; even the rows were exciting, and the conversations were incomparable.

Over a long career, he has learned that the media – and television, in particular – has for some women a glamour attached to it, and that having a face that is even remotely familiar from the television screen gives him choices other men would kill for. Sadly, he's found that the people it attracts are often vacuous, juvenile wannabes. Amanda is certainly not one of those. She's smart and good company. Besides, there are other perks: the ego boost of being seen with a beautiful, and much younger, woman, the mindblowing sex and being flirted with by her friends. But Charlie is right; he does yearn for something deeper and more satisfying, and for the comfort of a different sort of companionship – something he'd considered a hopeless cause after the recent shock of finally losing Lily. Was Charlie encouraging him to pursue Zoë? Surely not . . . and does he want to, anyway? She is married, after all, seemingly happily married, with a life and family on the other side of the world. Where could it possibly go?

He orders another double scotch and turns his chair to the alcove window so he can watch the passing parade outside. Girls in flimsy summer dresses, the sunlight shining through their skirts just like in Princess Diana's first press photograph; backpackers, in tiny shorts and cropped tops that leave little to the imagination; and the occasional elegant young professional in linen and silk who would distract the attention of an entire boardroom. Women, women, women – what is he supposed to do? Spend the rest of his life alone, a boring old fart, forgetting to wash and shaking his fist at potential intruders?

He'd thought that if he and Zoë met it would be brief and prickly, but it had been easy and fun. And it was spiced somehow with the curiosity born of an intimate shared past. It had seemed almost risqué, sitting with her in Tom and Julia's garden, walking her home, driving her to London and back again, and spending the following day with her. How easily, Richard thought now, with two pints of bitter and a couple of double shots of whisky under his belt, how easily it could have developed into something more. How easily it still might.

❦

It is still pitch dark when Archie's alarm goes off on Saturday morning. As he stretches his arm out to silence it, his heart sinks at the sound of rain and wind whipping through the trees. He buries his face in the pillow and groans; what madness made him agree to this? But he is a man who keeps his promises and, rather than risk falling asleep again, he puts on the light, gets up, steps straight into his swimming trunks and a T-shirt, and pulls on his tracksuit. In the ensuite, he sluices water over his face and brushes his teeth. It is ten past five and he can hear Gaby's alarm clock. Rubbing his hands through his hair, he goes to her room, switches off the clock and puts on the light, adjusting the dimmer switch to a low level.

'Come on, Gabs,' he says. 'Time to get moving.'

An irritable grunt comes from the mound in the bed but there is no movement.

'Come on, love,' he says, gripping the curve of her shoulder through the duvet. 'Don't go back to sleep.'

'*Okay, Dad!*' Gaby says sticking a disgruntled, sleep-blurred face out from the covers. 'Okay! I can hear.'

'Well then, get up and get moving, or we'll be late. I'm going to make some tea.' And he heads off to the kitchen, stopping on the way to collect the newspaper from the front step, and reassuring himself that in a couple of hours this caper will be over. He can come home, have a nice hot shower and plan his day. He makes two mugs of tea and, peeling the cling film off the *West Australian*, starts to read the front page story, about a scandal involving finance brokers. Sipping his tea, he turns to the rest of the story on an inside page and then to a related double-page feature. By the time he's finished it, he's drunk his tea, and is horrified to see that it's five-thirty and there is no sign of Gaby. He taps on her door.

'Come on, Gabs, time we left.'

There is no sound from the room. He tries again and, when there is no response, opens the door. Gaby has switched off the light and disappeared back under the duvet.

'Gabs!'

'Shut *up*, Dad,' she mumbles. 'I'm not going; it's cold and wet out there.'

Archie, in the doorway, tosses up whether to drag her out and face the resulting hassles or leave her behind. He decides that the latter is easier and, grabbing a towel from the linen cupboard, he steps out into torrential rain and runs to the car.

In the windswept car park near the surf club, a couple of people shrouded in rain capes are running through the puddles to the hut where the Polar Bears meet. Gwen's car, he notes, is parked as close as possible to the hut. Archie takes a deep breath to steel himself for the ordeal ahead, opens the car door and runs, head down, to the hut. It's warm inside and the light is dazzlingly bright. At one end of the small space, a woman whose wet hair is dripping onto the shoulders of her tracksuit is making toast – a reward, presumably, for surviving the ordeal of the ocean; others stand nearby stamping their feet, their hands clasped around mugs of tea or coffee. At a glance, it appears to Archie that everyone in the hut is his age or considerably older, and he wonders what on earth it is that compels them to turn up here almost every morning of the year to hurl themselves into the water. In summer, yes – but in mid-winter?

Just inside the door, Gwen is leaning against a cabinet and chatting animatedly with a couple of burly older men in swimming trunks who are yet to take to the water.

'Ah! Here he is,' Gwen says. 'Hello, Archie, I was just starting to think you'd chickened out.'

He rubs his hands together. 'Not me! But Gaby has, I'm afraid. She's still glued to the bed.'

'That's the young'uns for you,' one man says. 'Faint hearted. Not stoic like us. Nice to meet you, Archie. This is Derek, I'm Bruce. It's pretty rough, so we thought we'd wait and go down with you, as it's your first time. Shall we get going?'

Archie takes off his tracksuit and, acknowledging to himself that nothing can save him now, follows Gwen and the two men in a cautious jog to the water's edge, feeling unusually vulnerable. It is still pitch dark, and barely possible to see where the sea stops and the sky begins, but the distant lighting in the car park reaches far enough for him to see that the waves are enormous.

As a young man, Archie was a keen surfer and for years, the beach was his second home, but other things have slowly taken over his life. Marriage, children and all the responsibilities they create, advancement in his engineering career and the different lifestyle that has brought, have all gradually squeezed out his first love. Walks on the beach, a bit of swimming in the summer, and the occasional fishing trip are all he manages to fit in around the competing claims of work and family. And on this cold, dark morning, with the wind and water roaring in his ears and icy spray hitting his body, his youthful comfort zone is a horrible challenge.

'Are you a strong swimmer, Archie?' Gwen shouts above the wind.

'Used to be, but it's a long time ago.'

'Best if we stay close together, then,' she says, and gestures to the other Polar Bears to stay one on each side of him.

The water is breathtakingly cold and he yells in shock as a wave hits his crotch. Immediately, another huge wave rears up and punches him in the chest, hurling him up and then down into what is surprisingly deep water. Archie wonders where and when they will find his body, and bizarrely hopes that when they do, Gaby will feel really bad about having left him to do this alone. A large clump of seaweed wraps its thick slimy fronds around his legs and he kicks to free them, only to yelp in pain and swallow seawater as his foot connects with a lump of driftwood entangled in the weed. But he's free now and he rises, spluttering, to the surface, gulping air, his heart pounding, and he breaks the surface suddenly, hugely exhilarated, as though he has achieved something amazing.

'All right, mate?' Bruce yells.

'Brilliant!' he calls back. 'Bloody brilliant.' And he swings his arms and kicks his legs in an attempt to swim either with or against the swell. Not far away, he spots Gwen, tossed on a wave but righting herself and struggling to swim again. And, with his eyes now accustomed to the darkness, he sees the bobbing heads and flailing arms of other swimmers and feels as though he is part of a heroic collective struggle against the elements. Actual swimming is well nigh impossible, but being there, thrashing around in the water, revives the exhilaration of launching his surfboard into the path of the perfect wave and hurtling towards the beach. Now he wants to stay here for hours. He is sixteen again; flying, balancing, re-balancing, tumbling into the tunnel of the waves, thrilled and fearless, cruising finally to the shore. Ahead of him, he can see Gwen standing up, shaking her head to clear the water from her ears and taking the last few steps out of the water.

'Marvellous,' he cries, running up, throwing his arms around her and lifting her off her feet. 'Bloody marvellous. I can take on the world! I might go back in.'

'We must have been in for about fifteen minutes,' Gwen says, 'long enough for me on a day like this, and long enough for a first timer.'

He nods reluctantly and they run side-by-side up the beach to the hut.

∽∾

'Eggs, bacon, baked beans and toast,' Gwen says later, setting a heaped plate on the table as he emerges from the shower. 'And the coffee won't be a moment.'

Archie pulls out a chair. 'Not just for me, I hope,' he says. 'You're eating too, aren't you?'

'Of course,' she says, putting her own, more modest, serving on the table and bringing over the coffee plunger. 'We both deserve it. You know, Archie, I didn't like to tell you when you arrived but it's the worst morning so far this year, so you did do well. It's exciting, isn't it?'

'Sure is,' he mumbles through a mouthful of toast. 'I'd forgotten the thrill of the ocean. But it's a bit hazardous, Gwen. Are you sure you ought to be out there on your own on mornings like this?'

'Oh, don't *you* start,' Gwen says. 'Justine's always on at me about it. But I'm not on my own. In the winter, when it's dark, I always wait to go in with a couple of others nearby. Besides, I like the risk, one needs a bit of excitement at my age. And, to be perfectly honest, I don't usually go when it's as bad as this morning, but I was showing off for you.'

He laughs. 'Well, I was suitably impressed, and I feel so good I'll definitely be back.' He feels surprisingly at home in Gwen's bright, warm kitchen. They eat ravenously, and mainly in silence.

'More coffee?' Gwen asks eventually, pushing the plunger towards him.

He refills his cup and leans back in his chair. 'What am I going to do, Gwen?' he asks; the sudden, unplanned question sneaking unbidden into the warmth and intimacy of the kitchen.

'About what, Archie?'

'You know about what. Zoë, of course; Dan and Justine, the wedding, all of it. Gaby blew it all open the other night but, after that, we all backed off again.'

Gwen raises her eyebrows. 'Yes. An opportunity lost; but then, it's a very sensitive situation. What do you think is behind it?'

He shrugs. 'I wish I knew. Zo's been going through a rough time, mood swings, panic attacks, hot flushes; I think she's a bit depressed. Maybe it's just the nest beginning to empty, but something tells me it's more than that. She's always known Dan would get married one day; they all will, or they'll leave in some other way. But it's almost as though she'd made up her mind about the sort of woman she wanted for Dan, and Justine's not it. And she can't get her head – or, more importantly, her heart – around it.'

'Justine thinks it's about race,' Gwen says.

Archie sighs. 'I was afraid she might, but I really don't think it is. I've known Zoë for a very long time, so I think I'd know if it was that. I mean, you know how it was when we were young. I was terrified of the Aboriginal people I saw as a kid. It's how we were brought up, the fear and the distrust. But times change; you learn the history and you learn about yourself. If you care anything about people and justice, how can you *not* change?'

'Well, very easily, apparently. I mean, it's pretty clear that a lot of people simply don't want to change. But I don't know about Zoë. Maybe this holiday will help her sort out her feelings. We can only hope that things are different when she gets back. If not, you may have to be the one to open the can of worms.'

Archie nods gloomily. 'I guess you're right about that.' He gets up from the table and starts to clear the plates, glancing as he does so at a framed photograph on the wall. 'Is that your old farm?' he asks, setting the plates on the draining board and crossing the room to take a closer look. 'Beautiful place; don't you ever miss it?'

'Never,' Gwen says. 'I'd prefer to forget all about it. The photograph is up there because Justine wants me to keep it. I must take it down and give it to her, although I can't imagine why she, of all people, wants any sort of memento of her time there.'

'You rescued her from the convent, didn't you? Not surprising that she wants to remember that.'

Gwen is silent, poised at the point of revelation. The sudden need to unburden herself after decades of silence is compelling.

'What was done to those kids and their parents was bloody dreadful,' Archie continues, 'but Justine had a good home. A lot of those children went to people who treated them like shit. Justine was lucky, she wouldn't be with you now and as close to you as she is, if you hadn't been like a mother to her.'

Gwen hesitates; will she give him the simple explanation, or the whole truth? She puts a hand on the edge of the table to steady herself. She has kept her secret for more than three decades and has avoided friendships, fearing the compulsion to share her past. But the silence has become a burden. Perhaps the time has come for an honest conversation with a person of integrity; someone whom she can trust but who is not bound to her by love, as Justine is. It's a risk, in a whole lot of ways, but it is one she wants to take.

THIRTY-FOUR

London – July 2000

Zoë has escaped to London. It seems ungrateful to think in those terms, in view of Julia and Tom's warmth and generosity, but Julia's apparent compulsion to look after her, despite many other commitments, was making her uneasy. Tom is a cheerful and undemanding patient and is making a good recovery, and Zoë has helped as much as she can. But Julia still has a lot to cope with and, to make matters worse, there are ructions at the language school. Two teachers have run off together and can't be found. Replacements had to be recruited and, for some reason, the spouses of the missing couple both seem to think the school is in some way responsible for finding them. Zoë can see that Tom and Julia need time to themselves. Richard, who put in an unexpected appearance at the weekend, has given her a key to the flat. He will be away until Thursday, he'd said; she should use it. Julia's jaw dropped when Zoë had told her where she was going.

'You're actually going to stay at Craven Terrace?'

'Why not?' Zoë had said. 'Richard's going to be in Birmingham.'

'It's just . . . it's not what I expected. I mean, I didn't think you'd want to see Richard at all, or the flat. Bad memories, I suppose.'

'I didn't think so either. But I did see Richard and it was fine. No drama, no drugs, no therapy, no lobotomy.'

'Well, that's good, more than good; it's wonderful, actually,'

Julia said. 'Now all we need is for Richard not to bugger it up with his usual flair.'

'Oh, I think I can handle Richard rather better now than I did in the past,' Zoë said, smiling. 'I know you think I haven't changed much, but I'm not the doormat I used to be.'

And, as she takes an early train to Charing Cross and then the Underground to Lancaster Gate, she wonders about this sudden and dramatic change. How can something that has haunted her for so long just disappear? Was it a monster of her own creation, that she had clung to, thinking it was indestructible and letting it define her?

The walk from the station is surprisingly unchanged – a few different shops, a nice-looking café, and the building itself entirely recognisable, despite obvious refurbishment. As she turns the key there is a painful moment as she recalls arriving here in a Branston car with Julia and Dan, paralysed with misery and with the fear of what lay ahead. The interior of the flat is completely changed. It had been renovated, Julia had explained, several years earlier.

'Until then, we all – me, Tom, Richard, even Hilary, on occasions – used it as a place to stay in town when we needed it. But it was crying out for a makeover, so we thought it would make sense for us to do it up and rent it out for a few years. Then, when Richard came home this year, he tarted it up a bit more. I suppose it must have seemed a bit faded after Manhattan.'

Zoë wanders through the hall, which is brighter now, thanks to the addition of a skylight, and into a new and, initially disorienting, space, which was once the rather small lounge. It has been opened up to incorporate the kitchen and dining room in one large living room and is familiar only because of the window seat, which she had always loved, and the view across the rooftops. She cautiously opens the door to the second bedroom. Charlie had once occupied it, and later she and Richard had painted it yellow, stencilled Beatrix Potter characters onto the walls and pasted a frieze below the picture rail. But the stencils and the picture rail are gone, and there are shelves packed with books, fitted cupboards and a large desk littered with papers and files. There is a fax machine and a computer, the frame of its screen dotted with

Post-it notes. It is quite a relief to find it so changed; so entirely free of reminders of a past life.

Walking back to the kitchen, which is a mass of granite, brushed stainless-steel and state-of-the-art appliances that look as though they are rarely used, she spots a note addressed to her leaning against the kettle.

Zoë

Make yourself at home. There is food in the fridge and wine in the rack. Help yourself.

I suggest you sleep in the main bedroom, I've changed the linen. But the single bed in the office is made up too if you prefer. Enjoy London!

Rich x

She opens cupboard doors and then the fridge. There is camembert, always his favourite; two different types of cheddar; bacon and eggs; Fair Trade coffee; milk; a couple of packets of smoked salmon; double cream; watercress; raspberries and two large bars of chocolate. In the freezer there is bread, a couple of steaks, a packet of prawns and some frozen vegetables. All it tells her about Richard is that he is a more extravagant shopper than he used to be.

She fills the kettle and while she waits for it to boil opens the door to the main bedroom. This, too, is changed beyond recognition: the old-fashioned bed, and the bedside table always groaning under books, newspapers, dirty cups, overflowing ashtrays and forgotten, wizened pieces of fruit, have made way for a queen-size bed, a fitted wardrobe, matching cabinets, and a large, and rather overbearing, work of abstract art in shades of red, mustard and charcoal that is on the wall facing the window. Zoë opens the wardrobe and surveys the row of suits and jackets, the shelves of neatly folded shirts and sweaters, the rack of ties and, beneath them, the rows of shoes. She runs her hands over the shoulders of the jackets, and then takes down a soft yellow sweatshirt and holds it up to her face. It smells of fabric conditioner but also of Richard; an intimate, vaguely remembered smell that brings her out in goosebumps. She wonders if there is a woman in Richard's life – she suspects not; at least, not one who is here on a regular basis.

Zoë walks to the edge of the bed and sits down, feeling, at last, some sadness at the lack of evidence of the past; a sense of something precious having been ripped away, and memory obliterated by such mercilessly different décor. But incongruously, the old ceiling rose has been left in place and she lies back on the bed, staring up at it, remembering the many times and different moods in which she has lain here. She wonders what it would be like to make love with Richard now. He is – was – such a different lover from Archie, and she has only ever made love with three men. How would it have been if things had gone as planned? If she and Richard had stayed together, had more children, bought a house in a leafy suburb, as they had talked of in the last months that they had spent together here? Richard had been gentler then, more involved with her than he had been at any time since their early days together. It had felt as though the dropped stitches in their relationship had been picked up. Zoë sits straight again, clasps her hands and stares down at the floor. Regret is so complicated. She would not have Dan any other way, nor Archie and the girls; she would not change her life. But there *is* regret just the same, and a haunting curiosity about what might have been.

Sighing, she shakes her head to free herself from this maudlin speculation and gets up. When she has made and drunk a cup of tea, and taken a loaf out of the freezer for later, she takes her bag to the office, hangs a few things on the back of the door, lets herself out of the flat and walks to the corner to catch the bus to West Hampstead.

It is the sameness that strikes her as she turns into Delphi Street but, as she strolls along the pavement, she becomes aware of the changes. These houses, once occupied by the last surviving members of families and long-term sitting tenants, are now home to very different people. The Victorian character has been preserved by the tasteful renovations, yellowing net curtains replaced by fashionable cedar blinds or calico looped into elegant scallops. There are miniature trees and tall roses in glazed pots, burglar alarms, doors painted in rich colours with gleaming brass fittings. The battered Ford Prefects and Minis are gone; instead, there are BMWs, a Mercedes sports car, a VW Golf, and some trendy Japanese cars, with names she's never heard of. The rusty swings and creaky roundabout in the park opposite, where Dan had so often played, have been replaced by a small playground equipped with brightly coloured cubes, climbing frames, swings and a slide, all safely fixed into artificial ground cover that softens falls.

She is outside number thirty-one almost before she realises it. This one, too, has been renovated: its dreary brickwork cleaned and repointed, the front door painted a deep crimson, window-sills now gleaming white, and stacked with troughs of lobelia and geraniums. Zoë steps back from the pavement into the road to get a better look, glancing each way as she does so to check if anyone is watching her. For a moment she stands there, wondering who lives in it now, what voices fill the high-ceilinged rooms, who sits on the seat in the bay window, and whether the old range is still in the kitchen. Taking her camera from her bag, she adjusts the lens, taking the photographs she knows Dan will want. And, as she refocuses, the light catches a brass plate on the fence adjacent to the gate. Is it a doctor's surgery now, perhaps? If so, she might go inside on the pretext of making an appointment, she would, at least, get a glimpse of the interior. She puts the camera away and walks to the gate to read the name on the plate.

Dr Gloria Laverne BSc.(Hons) PhD. MBACP
Counselling, Psychotherapy, NLP, Stress Management

Zoë's mouth goes dry and she takes a step back, torn between the desire to run away and an overwhelming curiosity to see the person who had rescued her but who, even in memory, remains intimidating. As she stands there, the door opens and a woman comes out, closing it behind her, and walks briskly to the gate.

'Excuse me,' Zoë says. 'Is Dr Laverne in at the moment?'

'Oh yes, I just saw her. I think I was her last appointment for the day. Are you a client too?'

Zoë shakes her head. 'No. I was wondering . . .'

'Don't wonder, don't hesitate,' the woman says, putting a hand on her arm. 'She's the most wonderful therapist. You won't regret it, I'm sure. She's absolutely changed my life.' And she turns and walks off up the street.

Zoë stands for a moment, watching her confident manner, hearing the click of her heels on the pavement, catching the scent of her perfume still hanging in the air. And, feeling almost dizzy with anticipation, she opens the gate, walks up the path and rings the bell.

⚮

It is nine-thirty when Richard gets back to the flat to find it in darkness. This is not the way he planned it. He knows he's been shifty, saying he was going away, giving Zoë the key and planning to turn up pleading a change of schedule. But he believes his intentions are good. He wants more time with Zoë, wants to get to know her again; something he can't do with Julia watching them with all the subtlety of a Stasi agent. And he needs somehow to find the right moment to own up about how and when he first met Lily. Julia is quite right; he owes it to Zoë.

He switches on the lights and walks through to the lounge, wondering if perhaps she has changed her mind and is still in Rye. But then he sees that the note he left her has gone and there is bread defrosting on the counter, and, having checked the bedroom, he goes to the study and sees her open bag on the bed. In opening the door, he dislodges something hanging on the hook at the back and bends to pick it up. It's a blouse, soft green silk. Richard looks at it and holds it to his face, and detects something old and familiar: *Je Reviens*, of course. 'Ah yes,' he says aloud, in his best Maurice Chevalier accent, 'I remember it well.' Hanging the shirt back on its hanger behind the door, he walks over to the bed and stares for a moment at the contents of the open suitcase.

He is about to switch on the computer to check his email when he sees a satin jewellery roll open on the edge of the desk.

Intrigued, he sits in his revolving chair and unzips the pocket. There is not much there; only some simple gold and silver earrings, and another, surprisingly flamboyant pair made of lime green and silver beads, a gold bangle and bracelet of red enamelled silver, with a swirling design. It is only as he is about to turn away that he sees it – a small, and once familiar, piece of nineteenth century enamel jewellery, a heart-shaped blue and white enamel pendant.

'I love it,' she had said as he fastened the clasp at the back of her neck. She'd told him it was the best birthday present she'd ever had, and that she'd keep it forever. And she has. What does that mean? In the darker moments of other relationships, Richard has often speculated on the ways his life might have unfolded had he and Zoë lived it together; whether this could have been the one relationship that didn't degenerate into bitterness. He remembers their last months together in this flat, the plans they made; the way in which their life together began to become as important as his ambition and political commitments.

Later – years later – he had been forced to face the fact that railing against injustice in the world meant very little unless you could actually apply aspects of that passion to the way you lived your life. He had learned this from Lily, but only after she had kicked him out; it's a lesson he has not forgotten. Since then, he has tried to balance his burning concerns about the state of the world with greater focus on his own little corner of it. By the time he tried to win Lily back, it was too late. But what about Zoë; what does she think of him now?

For a while he sits there, feeling the smooth planes and curves of the pendant. And then, recognising that this is an invasion of her privacy, he replaces it, turns off the light, and goes out to the kitchen. He pours himself a large whisky, makes a toasted cheese sandwich and sits down to watch the ten o'clock news, wondering where she is.

By quarter to eleven, he's worried. She doesn't know anyone in London; could she have had an accident? The minutes drip away and he wonders if he should be doing something to find her. London is not the safest of cities, especially compared with Perth, and

Zoë no longer knows her way around. At eleven, he picks up the phone.

'Haven't a clue,' Tom says, through a yawn. 'Hang on, I'll ask Jules.'

'What are you doing there, anyway?' Julia asks irritably when she comes to the phone. 'You're supposed to be in Birmingham.'

'Oh . . . well, yes, I was, but there was a sudden change of plan.'

There is a long silence at the other end. 'I don't believe you,' she says. 'You rigged this, didn't you?'

Now the silence is at Richard's end. 'Okay, I did, but only for the best possible reasons. I just wanted to talk to her, get to know her a bit better, and then I thought I could tell her about Lily.'

'Bloody hell,' Julia says, 'you really are the pits, Richard. You just be careful; sometimes I think you should have a warning sign tattooed across your forehead.'

'But do you know where she is? I'm afraid something might have happened to her.'

Julia sighs. 'She's a grown woman, she's made it from Perth to London. I'm sure she can find her way back to the place she used to live.'

'But you know what London's like . . .'

'Rich, she's probably taken herself off to the theatre or a concert, and she'll turn up in a taxi any minute. Now, just mind your own business and go to bed.'

But Richard is not satisfied. He pours himself another drink and sips it, pacing back and forth parallel to the window and looking down into the street, hoping for the sight of a taxi drawing up outside. It's then that he remembers Zoë has given him the number of her mobile phone. He hesitates, presses call and waits as it rings. He is about to hang up when the call is answered. There is a lot of scuffling and some muffled giggling, and finally, Zoë's voice.

'Zoë?' he says. 'It's Richard – where are you? Are you okay?'

'Richard?' she says, sounding distinctly odd. 'I thought you were in Birmingham.'

'Had to come back. Are you okay?'

'I'm fine,' she says, and there is a trill of laughter and some more mumbling in the background. 'I am totally, completely, perfectly fine; splendid, in fact.' More laughter.

'Where the hell are you?'

'You'll never guess. Go on, guess. I bet you can't.'

'Of course I can't fucking guess where you are,' he says, angry now, thinking he sounds stupid. 'I'm worried about you; tell me where you are. You sound as though you've been drinking; I'll call a cab, and come and pick you up.'

There is more laughter now and he can hear music – the Seekers – faintly in the background.

'Okay,' Zoë says. 'You give up?'

'I give up. Tell me where you are.' Richard is not used to being the most sober person around and he isn't particularly enjoying the experience.

'Well,' she says in a whisper before going off into a burst of laughter again. 'Actually, Rich, I'm at thirty-one Delphi Street, and Gloria and I have just been having a little smoke. I think I might be just a tiny bit stoned.'

THIRTY-FIVE

Perth – July 2000

Justine and Gaby are shopping in the city. Rosie was supposed to go with her sister to help her choose something special to wear to a party, but she reneged in favour of spending the weekend with Rob at the winery.

'I can go with you, if you want,' Justine had offered when she had popped upstairs to talk to Gwen and found a gloomy Gaby. 'Tomorrow, if you like.'

She feels a special affection for Gaby since her outburst in the restaurant. It hadn't resolved anything but had put the issue out in the open and she no longer feels that the problem is hers alone.

'Let's go in here,' Gaby says. 'This place is cool. Rosie said I should get a dress but I thought jeans, maybe, with a sparkly top. There's this guy from school who told my friend he really likes me.'

'I thought you didn't have any time for boys,' Justine says.

'Well, I don't but he's not rancid, like most of them.'

This is another world for Justine, like having a younger sister. It seems full of delightful possibilities but she's also cautious. There is, she senses, a level of risk in getting involved with Gaby and Rosie as it can only deepen Zoë's hostility to her.

'It'll be all right in the end, you know,' Gaby says, flicking through racks of sequined tops.

'Oh, I'm sure you'll find something lovely, and there's heaps more shops in Hay Street.'

'No, I mean Mum, she'll be all right. We all love you. But Mum . . . well, I don't know, maybe it's the menopause thing, or maybe she's just jealous because Dan loves you. But it'll be okay; I felt better after I said that stuff the other night.'

'So did I,' Justine says. 'Much better, and anyway, there's nothing I can do about it.'

'Mum's always going on about how important it is to be honest and open, but she never is. She's always pretending things are okay, or saying she doesn't mind when you can tell she does. Now she's shitty with everyone but she won't come out with it. Parents!' She hesitates and blushes, looking at Justine, 'Sorry, I forgot you haven't . . .'

'It's okay,' Justine says. 'I know what you mean.'

'Lets go to Hay Street,' Gaby says, taking her arm as they walk out of the shop. 'Gwen told me about how you were taken away. We learned about the stolen generation in Year Ten. And Gwen told me about going back to find your necklace at the convent and then trying to find your mum.'

'Gwen was wonderful to me, she always has been,' Justine says. 'I'm so lucky, Gaby; much luckier than most of the others who were taken away.' They are strolling through one of the arcades that leads to Hay Street and she points to a café. 'Would you like a coffee or a milkshake, or something?'

'So, did you just go up there and drive around looking for her? Your mum, I mean,' Gaby asks when they are sitting down.

'Yes, that was more or less it. Gwen did a bit of detective work first and managed to pin it down to a couple of places in the Pilbara. Then one day she just said, "Come on, Justine, pack your bag, we're going to find your mum", and off we went.'

Gaby swirls the straw around in her banana milkshake. 'Cool. Gwen's brilliant, she does everything. Like the swimming and she does classes too, doesn't she?'

'It's called the University of the Third Age,' Justine says. 'She goes to a writing class and one on art history.'

'Mum should do that,' Gaby says. 'It would give her something else to think about.'

'Well, she *is* going to an art class now,' Justine says, surprised to find herself suddenly defending Zoë.

Gaby shrugs. 'Whatever. So, what was it like seeing your mum again, was it amazing?'

'*Totally* amazing. She was sitting on some steps outside where my auntie lives, and we drove up and they just stared at us.' She pauses, remembering the days on the road in the big four-wheel drive that Gwen had hired; the anxious waiting while Gwen stopped to ask questions, her frantic longing for the search to be over. 'I got out of the car and I was so scared, I just stood there.'

'Scared?'

'Mmm. Well, I thought maybe Mum would be upset with me because I took so long to find her. Silly, really, but I'd been planning to run away for years, first from the convent and then from the farm, and I sort of felt she must've known that and, because I hadn't done it, I'd let her down. It was seven years, you see, from the time I was taken to the time Gwen took me back there.'

'And then what happened?'

Justine smiles. 'We just stared at each other and I thought maybe she didn't know it was me because I'd grown so much. I was wearing the necklace and, I don't know why, but I just put my hand up to my neck to touch it, and she got up and almost flew off those steps and we ran towards each other at the same moment.' She laughs now, pressing her fingers to her eyes. 'Sorry, I always cry when I think about it. It was so wonderful to find her. Like magic.'

'So, have you got a picture of her?'

Justin pulls her wallet from her bag and hands over a battered colour print of a dark-skinned woman in a floral dress. The wind is blowing Norah's skirt and she is holding it down with one hand and looking shyly into the camera. 'It was taken that day,' she says. 'The same day we found her.'

'Why did you stay with Gwen, then?' Gaby asks.

'Well, Gwen said it was up to me and Mum what happened but that if I wanted, I could live with her and she'd see me through school. It was the holidays, so I stayed on up there with Mum, and I met all my aunties and uncles, the cousins, everyone. But

Mum said I should go back to the school here. I think she was just so happy to see me again, and know I was safe and that I'd wanted to come back. But she was really proud when Gwen told her I was smart and doing well. I think she trusted Gwen because she'd brought me back and she felt I'd be safe with her. So I wrote to Gwen, and she came and got me at the end of the holidays.'

'Do you wish you'd stayed there with your mum?'

Justine shakes her head. 'No. I loved living with Gwen and I loved going back for my holidays. And, years later, before I took over the nursery, I went and worked up there for a while. Then Gwen persuaded Mum to try living down here in the flat, where Dan and I live now. She was getting sick and Gwen thought we could look after her. But Mum couldn't settle; she just pined for her own place and for the aunties, so we took her back. It was . . .' she stops. She had been going to talk about what it had meant to her to find Norah and the aunties, to be there in her own country with them and to learn about her family. She wants to describe the extraordinary power of discovering the traditions, hearing the stories, understanding her history and her place in the world. But Gaby's attention is drifting; the call of the fashion shops is just too strong. 'Anyway,' Justine says, getting to her feet. 'I'll tell you more about it another time.'

'So you've got three families now – your own, Gwen's and ours,' she says. 'I love it that you're my sister. It's so much better than just having Rosie.'

'I love it too,' Justine says. 'But it'll be better when it all settles down.'

'So, how was the shopping?' Dan asks that evening. 'Did Gabs wear you out? She can be a bit full on.'

Justine smiles. 'You can say that again. But I do love her, she's so honest. She was interrogating me about my past.'

Dan pours two glasses of wine. 'I hope you didn't tell her your darkest secrets,' he says, handing one to her. 'Was she going on about Mum again?'

'Yes, we did talk about that a bit. She assures me that it'll be all right in the end. She was sort of implying that Zoë has trouble coming out with what she really feels.'

'That'd be right. She does do some funny stuff, saying everything's okay when you can see it's not. But I've never seen her quite like this before.'

'What do you think, then? When she gets back, are we still going to be planning the wedding in whispers because we're scared of upsetting her?'

'I'm not sure that scared is the right word,' Dan says, flopping down on the sofa.

'It's the right word for me. I've been scared since New Year's Day,' Justine says. 'And it's just got worse since then, because, as Gaby said, none of us is prepared to talk about it.'

Dan reaches up for her hand and draws her down to sit beside him. The tension in her face revives the hurt and frustration he had felt before Zoë went away. 'I'm so sorry, sweetheart. I know it's really hard, and I was so thankful when she went away that I suppose I'd sort of put it on the back burner. But you're right, it's a ridiculous situation; we can't let her intimidate us like this. We'll see how she is when she gets back but if things haven't changed, she'll just have to put up with it. We'll organise the wedding, include her in the conversations, and if she doesn't like it, that's her problem. If she doesn't want to be a part of it, that's up to her.'

'But you two have such a special relationship.'

'We did, but I can't talk to her anymore. I know it's hard for her to let go of me, but she must've known that it would happen sometime. And as for the rest of it – well, I can't make up to her for the past, I shouldn't have to, and I'm tired of the guilt trips she lays on me for choosing the army. I'm a grown man, I've always tried to do the best thing by my family, but I have a right to make my own choices, even if they don't suit my mother.'

'Of course,' Justine says. 'But it's a bit like an iceberg, Dan, the crucial, dangerous part is hidden under the water. It's true, she's always known that you'd go eventually. What she can't cope with is that I'm the catalyst. It's fine for me to be the helpful woman who runs the nursery and advises her on plants, but it seems that it's not fine for me to be the woman you love. And that scares me.'

Dan kisses her forehead. 'There's nothing to be scared of. We're getting married, with Mum or without her. This is not going to come between us; you have to trust me on this. I love you. You surely don't think that's so fragile it will crack under pressure from my mother?'

Justine smiles. 'No, but it's like some virus that's affecting all of us, and I want things to be right in every way. I hate coming between you and Zoë as though you have to choose between us.'

'No, that's not going to happen. Gaby's right, Mum'll come around eventually and you know why?'

She shakes her head.

'Because, in the end, the price of not doing so will be too high. She knows that if I had to choose, she would be the loser.'

Justine leans her weight up against him, tucking her legs underneath her. 'I love you, and I don't want there to be any losers,' she says. 'Look, while we're being so serious, there's something else I need to talk to you about, something I should probably have told you earlier.'

'Oh lord,' Dan says, laughing and topping up their glasses. 'What's this, your criminal record?'

'Not exactly,' she says, with a tight smile.

'Okay,' he says. 'You can tell me anything at all, unless it's that you've changed your mind.'

'You don't escape that easily,' Justine says. 'And it's not about me . . . well, it is, I suppose, but only indirectly. It's about Gwen, and what happened the day she left me at the hospital and went back to the farm.'

THIRTY-SIX

Rye – July 2000

'A re you sure this isn't just an excuse to read old newspaper cuttings?' Julia asks, putting a mug of coffee down beside Tom's box of papers.

'And what if it is?' he asks. 'You sound like the woman who runs the poorhouse in *Oliver Twist*. Please don't punish me, Mrs Whatever, I'm just a poor frail old invalid. I am actually doing research, but I apologise if I appear to be having fun doing it. How long do you intend to pace back and forth; you're almost foaming at the mouth.'

'I'm worried about Zoë,' Julia says, 'Zoë and Richard. There's no answer from the phone at the flat and they've both got their mobiles switched off. What am I to do? Anything, literally anything, could be happening.'

'It's only ten o'clock. And they're two grown-up people, Julia,' Tom says. 'If there were a problem, if Zoë had had an accident, or something, Richard would have called. He called last night and you, quite rightly, told him not to be silly. Zoë probably turned up five minutes later, just as you predicted. All you're worried about is that Zoë might be having wild sex with your brother, which, frankly, I think is most unlikely.'

'But I feel responsible for Zoë. I started all this by writing to her.'

'Yes, darling,' Tom says. 'And it was a lovely thing to do and Zoë told me herself how much it has meant to her.'

'But you know Richard and women; he's like some sort of hazardous substance. They always fall for him, and then it all congeals into something nasty, and he drinks more . . . and . . . oh lord, I wish they'd answer the phone.'

Tom grabs her hand as she paces past. 'Come here,' he says, pulling her down to sit beside him. 'Zoë's perfectly able to look after herself and if she fancies a bit of a fling with her ex-husband, it is none of your business. You are such a control freak.'

'I know, I'm sorry, but it's going so well. I know this is all frightfully important for Zoë. I just don't want Richard to stuff it up.'

'Your brother isn't a complete bastard, Jules. So, women swarm to him likes moths to a lamp and he doesn't know how to do relationships. You should worry more about what this might do to *him*. Zoë, I suspect, is well able to look after herself, and she has a very nice husband, so I don't think she'll be leaping into Richard's bed.'

Julia shrugs. 'It's a difficult time of life for women; they do often need some sort of affirmation of themselves as sexual beings.'

Tom puts his arms around her. 'Would you like me to affirm you as a sexual being, my darling?'

'Raheem said not for four weeks.'

'Oh, bugger Raheem. Seize the day, I say.'

She leans against his shoulder. 'Just cuddle me – I feel exhausted. Do you think life from here on is going to be one of us getting sick all the time? You know, measuring out our days with medication, doctors' visits, incontinence pads and zimmer frames?'

Tom laughs so hard that it makes him gasp with pain. 'Raheem should have banned laughing,' he splutters. 'No, it's not going to be like that. But I think you might enjoy it more if you unload some of your commitments and relax a bit. Taking things more easily doesn't actually mean immediate admission to a nursing home. It just allows you to pick and choose what you do. And, as I remember it, that's what you said to me after the first operation, and it's why I eventually decided to retire when I did.'

Julia is silent. Eventually, she says, 'I've been thinking that maybe we should sell the business.'

Tom tightens his arm around her shoulders. 'Thank you, god,' he says. 'And thank you, Hilary.'

Julia smiles. 'She did keep going on about it.'

'Yes, we talked of it often, and about how hard it would be to get you to give it up. We agreed that you had to arrive at the decision on your own.'

'I know, but, as I kept explaining to her, it would feel – *does* feel – like giving in to age.'

'What? You mean there's something youthful and magnificent about consistently hurling yourself at something that has already sucked you dry?'

She laughs. 'I wouldn't put it quite like that, but it does seem like a step nearer death, doesn't it?'

Tom sits up straighter, takes her by the shoulders and holds her away from him. 'Absolutely not! Oh, you are so exasperating. This is not a stage of deterioration, unless you choose to make it so. It's just another one of life's changes and change means opportunity. D'you really think that bloody language school is somehow holding the grim reaper at bay? It's ridiculous; you're only fifty-five and it's far more likely that it'll drive you into an early grave. You've stopped enjoying it, stopped being excited by it – it's become a burden. Think of all the things you and I could do if you were free. The school is a wonderful achievement, but does it still make the earth move for you, Jules?'

A few small tears squeeze their way out of Julia's eyes, against her will. 'No,' she admits, shrugging and clearing her throat. 'No, I'm sick of it. I was going to go back as soon as you're better but I really don't think I can bear much more of it.'

'Well then?'

'At the same time, selling it feels like stepping into a void.'

'But there is so much more that you want to do.'

'But suppose I end up not doing anything, or failing.'

Tom winces again with the pain of laughter. 'It's most unlikely,' he manages to say. 'And what would it matter if any, or all, of the things you or I do fail? We have nothing to prove, and we will at least have the satisfaction of having tried. Listen,' he says, stroking her cheek, and, getting to his feet, he walks to the bookshelf and runs his fingers along the spines.

'You were doing that the day we met,' she says. 'Looking for a book.'

'The score of *The Magic Flute* was what I was looking for that day. And instead of that, I found you. If I'd kept on looking, and ignored you and your egg and cress sandwiches, we wouldn't be here now. Life hinges on such small events, and sometimes you have to take your eyes off one thing before you can see others.'

'What are you looking for?'

'William Hazlitt.'

'Dreary,' she says, picking up their mugs.

'Not at all,' Tom says, pulling a slim volume from the shelf and flicking through the pages. 'Hazlitt is timeless; listen to this. Leave the mugs and sit down and listen properly. *"The only true retirement is that of the heart; the only true leisure is the repose of the passions. To such persons it makes little difference whether they are young or old."* '

Julia looks at him. 'I always loved you, you know,' she says, 'even through the dramas in between. It was always you.'

'You too,' he says, closing the book. 'Every minute of every day, although your reluctance to say yes the second time was somewhat testing. You just didn't get it, did you? You were supposed to fall straight into my arms when I turned up at Greenham Common, not keep me hanging around like a puppet on a string for more than a year.'

'I needed to be . . . damn . . .' Her mobile rings and remembering she left it on the hall table, she goes out to answer it. 'Hopefully, that'll be Zoë or Richard.'

Tom returns Hazlitt to his place on the shelf, pausing briefly to enjoy a small moment of satisfaction that he has gone at least part of the way in creating a change. Hilary, he thinks, will be cheering him on from heaven, and he looks upward and gives her a thumbs up.

'That was Zoë's husband, Archie,' Julia says, coming back into the room. 'He sounds awfully nice, but he's worried too. Her mother's been taken to hospital; it's not serious but he thinks she ought to know. He's been trying to call her mobile for hours. What am I to do? Do you think I should drive up to town and see if everything's all right?'

'If you even attempt to do that,' Tom says, 'I shall have to forcibly restrain you. You've got tangled up with the two of them before and you've always regretted it. You can't honestly think that I'm going to stand by and let you do it again. Come on, we're going somewhere nice for lunch to finish the conversation about the school, and you can leave that bloody phone behind. You'll have to drive, though; that's the other thing I'm not supposed to do for four weeks.' And, picking up the car keys, he urges her out the door and pulls it closed behind them.

'Pretend we're on a date,' he says, maneuvering himself awkwardly into the passenger seat. 'You know, focus on me, look into my eyes adoringly, agree with everything I say, and I'll get you drunk and try to seduce you, although consummation will take another week or so.'

'Is this what it would be like if we had more time?' she asks, starting the engine. 'You being the bossy one and me quietly doing as I'm told?'

'It's an attractive thought,' he says, 'but somehow, even in my wildest imagination, I can't see it happening.'

❧

Honeysuckle is still growing against the back fence, and now a trellis covered in what looks like a vine but is actually hops covers the path. Hops in West Hampstead; she takes some more photos for Dan. Pictures of the scrubby patch of grass where he and the other kids played, which is now a neatly mown lawn, the cracked paving stones replaced with rosy old bricks, and the large pots overflowing with pansies, pink geraniums and white lobelia, grouped together in the spot where the old outside toilet used to be. At the bottom of the garden, she turns to photograph the back of the house, changed now by the addition of a glazed extension in which they are about to have breakfast.

Strolling beneath the hops, Zoë wishes desperately that Dan were there to see it. Here in this place where they spent his first five years together, she seems able to ignore the present and think of him again as he was in the days when she could decide what he did and where he went, what he wore, who he played with.

Nostalgia for the time when it was just the two of them against the world almost chokes her, and she has to remind herself that it was hard, exhausting, and frighteningly precarious.

The house is changed even more radically than the garden: walls knocked down; a well-fitted kitchen; a second bathroom; all so much lighter and brighter than it had been in her day. It is the result of Gloria's professional success and, as she had conceded last night, her marriage to a Jungian therapist, who had died suddenly of a heart attack in his sixties. It had amazed Zoë to learn that Gloria had been married.

'You actually got married to a man?' she'd asked. 'But you were . . .'

'A feminist, sure thing,' Gloria said. 'But I didn't have anything against men per se, Zoë; just the system, the politics.'

'But I always thought you were . . .' she paused, blushing.

'A lesbian?'

'Well, yes.'

'No, hon, not me. But Claire and Marilyn ended up together.'

'But they'd both been married,' Zoë said.

Gloria laughed out loud. 'It happens,' she said. 'Women find things out about themselves as they get older. They're still together, although Marilyn's not too well these days. She never did give up smoking and she's just turned eighty, and it looks like the emphysema is going to win. You should give them a call; they live in Fulham and they'd love to see you again.' She paused, leaning forward and looked hard at Zoë. 'I know you never had any time for women's politics, but they were good days and we achieved a hell of a lot. I often thought that if you hadn't had so much else to worry about, we might've won you over. It was all so relevant to your situation.'

'I know I'm a disappointment to you,' Zoë said with a smile, 'and to my younger daughter as well. Gaby can't believe that I let the women's movement pass me by.'

'Well, you send her over here to me, and I'll make sure she keeps the torch burning.'

'You and my former sister-in-law,' Zoë said. 'Do you remember Julia?'

'The poker-faced dame in the Chanel suit at the hospital?'

Zoë laughed. 'Yes, only she's not poker-faced and these days, she shops in the high street. You and she would get on well now. She spent quite a long time at the women's peace camp at Greenham Common.'

'You're kidding? But wasn't she married to some rich guy in Paris?'

'That's right, Simon Branston, but they were only married for a few years. Julia joined a women's group in Paris, what was it now . . . *Jeunes Femmes*, I think she said.'

'*She* was in the *Jeunes Femmes*?'

'Yes. Have you heard of them?'

Gloria rolls her eyes. 'Is the Pope a Catholic!'

'Oh well,' Zoë shrugged. 'I hadn't, but then, I wouldn't have. Anyway, she left Simon, and came back here with a friend and started a language school in Rye. I've been staying with her this week.'

It seems so much easier to talk to Gloria now; Zoë's not sure if it is just that she's older or if it was her reliance on Gloria for a place to live that made her so intimidating. Strangely, since she walked in here yesterday afternoon, she has felt free to say what she thinks without fear of judgment. 'What I said earlier,' she had ventured later in the evening, when they had finished drinking Gloria's iced tea and were well into a bottle of wine, 'you know, about disappointing you and Gaby. Well, the person I've disappointed most is myself.'

'Yourself?'

She nodded. 'I don't mean about the women's stuff, but because when I first arrived in London, I was so full of hope and ambition. You know, my mother's only ambition was that I wouldn't get into trouble or get above myself. I thought that coming to London would let me get free of all that.'

'And you think it didn't?'

'No. Once I'd met Richard my only ambition was to hang onto him and, of course, I *did* get into trouble, in just the way Mum had feared. And so, I got drawn back onto that narrow path of survival; different in many ways from hers, but so often I behaved just as she had done. Marrying Archie was my salvation and so I've never really had to worry about my lack of ambition; my complete failure to focus on anything other than my family. Except, of course, until now.'

Gloria shook her head. 'Family's precious, Zoë; it takes strength and commitment to raise three kids and maintain a long relationship. Don't underestimate what you've done, or what you've got.' She poured the remains of the wine into their glasses.

'I don't underestimate what I've got,' Zoë said, picking up her glass and swirling the wine. 'It's my life; that's why I'm so scared of it slowly being taken to pieces. Why it seems so dangerous to let anyone else in.'

By the time Richard called, they had been out for a meal, smoked a very large joint, and were well on the way through a second bottle of wine. And when he arrived in a taxi, they sat talking for hours until they noticed that Richard, stretched out on the sofa, had fallen asleep.

'He's had it and so have I,' Gloria said. 'Two-thirty, way past my bedtime. The bed in your old room is all made up, Zoë. You might as well stay the night, what's left of it.'

And so, she had lain down in that same room trying to remember herself and Richard as they were, trying to see things clearly as an outsider might do; trying to free herself from the judgments and emotions that had accumulated over the years. And this morning she had woken, fully dressed, and wandered downstairs to find that Richard and Gloria had been up for some time and were cooking breakfast together.

'C'mon, Zoë,' Gloria calls from the kitchen, 'breakfast is ready, and I've got my first client at ten.' Now well into her seventies, she is half the size of the old Gloria. The voluminous tent dresses and fringed shawls have given way to more sophisticated, but colourful, long skirts and flowing blouses.

The table is loaded with fruit, croissants, toast, coffee and cream, and the smell of bacon wafts through from the kitchen.

'You look worse than I feel,' Zoë says to Richard, smiling as she piles melon and raspberries onto her plate.

'Thanks,' Richard says. 'I always look like this in the mornings.

You don't look your best either but then, you were totally off your tits on weed.'

Zoë smirks. 'First time in decades,' she says. 'No wonder I warned my kids off it, it's far too nice.'

'I tried to get you to try it and you never would. Archie must have been more persuasive. You were always such a prude about drugs.'

'Scared stiff,' she says, through a piece of melon. 'Still am, really, so god knows what got into me last night.'

Gloria puts an oval platter of bacon, eggs and tomatoes onto the table. 'Well, who'd ever have thought I'd have you two under the same roof all these years later,' she says. 'Especially you, Richard.'

'Last time, as I remember it, Gloria, you virtually slammed the door in my face,' he says, helping himself to bacon. 'Not that I blame you, I deserved it.'

'When was that?' Zoë asks.

'When you went to Glasgow,' Gloria says. 'Is that the time you're thinking of, Richard?'

'When I went to Glasgow – you came here?'

Richard nods. 'I came to win you back with a ticket to the film and TV awards.'

'You came to get me back?'

'Yep. But clearly I missed the boat.'

There is a sudden and subtle change in the atmosphere. 'I didn't know,' Zoë says, looking at the two of them, bewildered.

Richard sees the confusion in her face, the furrows forming between her eyebrows. He looks at Gloria.

'Did you tell her?'

'I sure did.' She looks at him and then at Zoë. 'Yes, hon, I really did. When you got back a coupla days later, I told you that Richard came and asked you to call him. Maybe you don't remember.'

Zoë pauses, shakes her head and puts her hand to her forehead. 'No, it's so long ago. Did you tell me he'd come to get me back?'

Gloria laughs. 'Well, *no*, because I didn't know. He wasn't gonna tell *me* that, was he?'

Zoë looks at Richard. 'What *did* you say?'

'Christ, Zoë, it's donkey's years ago; I can't remember the actual words. I'd spent weeks mooning around getting drunk, knowing I'd made a mistake, wanting you back. I'd convinced myself I could be a father to Daniel. And then we heard we'd been short-listed for the award, so I got really sober and put the invitation in my pocket, and came over here to ask you to go to the ceremony with me. I thought it might be a start, that maybe we could try again. But when I got here, you'd gone off to Glasgow.'

There is a silence and they face each other across the breakfast table, eyes locked.

'You *didn't call*,' he says, suddenly feeling the waste of it.

'I *didn't know*,' she says, in what is almost a whisper. 'I was stunned by what had happened to Harry. I suppose . . . well, I suppose that when Gloria told me I must have thought it was about the divorce, or that if it was important, you'd call me.' She looks across at him, confused still. 'But you didn't call; you didn't come again.'

'You didn't call *me*. I thought that meant you were with Harry,' Richard says. 'I didn't find out about all that until years later. When I got back from Vietnam, I bumped into Claire one day and she told me. For years I thought I saw you together with the baby, I thought . . .' He stops and looks up. Her face is ashen and her eyes are searching his. He wonders if he has misunderstood. 'Are you saying that you would have . . . in spite of what had happened, and in spite of the way I'd . . . you would –'

'Yes,' she cuts in. 'Of course I would. In spite of all that. I loved you and I hated you, but . . . of course I wanted you back, Richard. Of course I did.'

THIRTY-SEVEN

Fremantle – July 2000

When Dan arrives at Clancy's pub, Archie is already there and halfway into his first beer. Dan pauses for a moment watching him sitting on a stool and staring gloomily down into his drink. For the first time, he notices signs of age. Archie is an outdoor sort of man: tall, big boned, with a fair complexion tanned by years in the sun, his hair an unruly mass of reddish curls now increasingly threaded with grey. It strikes him suddenly that Archie, always so youthful and energetic, so endlessly resourceful and generous, is getting old. Shoulders slumped, lost in thought, he seems vulnerable, as though he has suddenly lost his grip, and Dan feels the shock of recognising that one day he will lose him; this father whom he loves and admires so profoundly. He walks over quickly and puts his hand on Archie's shoulder.

'G'day, Arch, can I get you another one?'

And as Archie looks up and sees him, the years seem to drop away and he is the familiar Archie again – except he's not, not quite.

They take their drinks out the back, where it's quieter, and sit down. Large moths hurl themselves at the old street lamps that light the pub terrace, and out on the grass a couple of kids are rolling with a dog while their parents watch from a nearby table.

'Thanks for coming, mate,' Archie says, and they are silent again.

Dan knows he's been asked here for a reason. They often have a beer together, but this is much later than they usually meet and Archie is different.

'I went across to the hospital,' Dan says. 'Saw Rosie there. Gran seems okay, doesn't she? I mean, it wasn't a bad fall.'

'No, she'll be fine. They're just going to keep her in a couple of days to be sure. Heard from your mum?'

Dan shakes his head. 'Not since she left. I'm in the dog house anyway so I didn't really expect to. What did she say about Gran?'

Archie sips his drink, looks out at the playing children, up at the moths and then at Dan. 'She doesn't know yet,' he says. 'I haven't been able to get hold of her.'

Dan raises his eyebrows. 'Did you try the mobile?'

'Dozens of times, it's switched off.'

'Probably she forgot to switch it on. You know what she's like with it. You could call whatsername, Julia, where she's staying; you've got that number, haven't you?'

'I've done that and she's not there. She's in London and they can't get hold of her either.'

'That's odd,' Dan says. 'I thought she was staying with them all the time. She just said she might go up to London to look at the house in Delphi Street – you know, where we used to . . .'

'Yes, I know.' Archie pauses and turns to face Dan. 'Did Zoë tell you she was going to see Richard?'

'Richard! Bloody hell, no. Has she? I thought she never wanted to see him again.'

'Well, according to Julia, Zoë's staying in London in Richard's flat while he's away. Julia gave me the number. She's left a message there but Zoë hadn't got back to her. That number's still not answering, Zoë's phone's still off and so, according to Julia, is Richard's.'

Dan whistles through his teeth. 'That's pretty weird.' He looks up at Archie and sees what looks like desolation in his face. 'Hey, Arch, you're not thinking . . .'

'What else can I think?' Archie says. 'And I know it's not fair to be laying this on you, Dan, but it's ten o'clock and her phone's been off for almost twenty-four hours.' He puts his glass on the table. 'I must sound like a bloody idiot, but I don't know what to do, and I don't want to talk about this to anyone else. But you've got to admit . . .'

'No, Arch,' Dan says, putting a hand on his arm. 'I know what you're thinking and there's no way. Mum wouldn't; she just wouldn't.'

'She's been very odd lately about a whole lot of things. You know that.'

'Yes, but not this, not Richard. Look, it's odd, I'll grant you, but there's probably some simple explanation. She's gone out, she's forgotten her phone's off or maybe she just forgot to charge it. And, anyway, didn't you say Richard was away?'

'Yes, but . . .'

'Well, there you are, then. Forget about it, Arch, I'll get us another round. Any minute now she'll be on the phone, telling you she's sorry she forgot to switch it on.' And he takes the empty glasses and carries them inside, orders two more beers and, while he's waiting at the bar, wonders if he's wrong.

∽∾∾

There's a glorious view from where they sit on a bench at a high point on Hampstead Heath, looking out across the tree tops to the russet and grey of distant buildings blurring in the hazy light.

'We could get a cab back to the flat,' Richard had suggested as they walked down Delphi Street, 'but it might be quicker to take the tube.'

'Couldn't we just walk somewhere?' Zoë had said. 'I need air and exercise.'

And so they had taken a bus to the heath.

'It seems such a small thing,' she says now, still wrestling with the fact that it was, in the end, just a minor trick of fate that kept them apart. 'If only I'd . . .'

'It's not your fault, I should have –'

'It's not yours either,' she cuts in. And they sit on in silence. Zoë feels sick and shaken, by the debilitating cocktail of too much wine, the other-worldliness of her marijuana hangover and the shock of discovery.

Richard stretches his legs out in front of him and lays an arm behind her along the back of the seat.

'What would we have become?' he asks. 'A happy family, a broken family, a divorced couple lost in misunderstandings?'

'Well, we were that anyway. But maybe we could have been a family.'

'Who knows?' he says. 'But I haven't proved a stayer in relationships, although that hasn't been my choice. I've mainly been the one who was given, rather than giving, the marching orders.'

'Perhaps it would have been different for us. What sort of people would we be now? Would we be similar, different, and what about our children?'

'This is no good, you know, Zoë,' he says moving his arm firmly around her shoulders. 'It's done, and what we lost may not have been as good as what we have, particularly in your case. Come on, let's walk down to the pub and have a drink and some lunch. Then, I don't know about you, but I'd like to go home and change my clothes.'

It's as he stands at the bar waiting to pay that Richard realises that his phone is off and after switching it on, discovers several messages from Julia asking him to call. He decides to wait until later and switches it off again.

It is a strange afternoon, too bright, too hot, too noisy, and the bus ride back to Craven Terrace is too long. Zoë and Richard hold hands most of the time, not in the way of lovers but as two people united by a discovery that has left them lost and bewildered.

'Would you like me to drive you back to Rye tonight?' Richard asks much later, when they are back at the flat and he has returned other calls and checked his email. Zoë has made tea and is sitting on the window seat with her mug, gazing down onto the street below.

'No thanks. I'd prefer to stay here, if that's okay. I don't think I can cope with anyone else at the moment.'

'What would you like to do?'

'Walk a bit more, maybe,' she says. 'That walk we used to do in the evenings when I was pregnant.' She swallows, clears her throat and looks up at him, her eyes shadowed with sadness.

Richard nods in agreement but finds he daren't open his mouth because he can't trust what might come out of it. Looking down at Zoë, he thinks that Charlie was spot on when he said something about the appeal of sadness; he realises that it was part of what had attracted him to Zoë all those years ago. Behind her apparent lightheartedness and her efforts to please him was the sadness, and he had been confident he could fix that, among other things. How arrogant, he thinks now, as though he were a sort of Svengali who could make her happy and, most of all, make her different. And now? He wonders what he's learned in the intervening years, and whether it is enough to bring her back to him. Despite all the evidence that Zoë is totally committed to her husband and children, Richard still entertains a sliver of hope. Is it just his arrogance again, he wonders; is he doing now what he did back then, feeling he can fix her life to suit himself and this time make her happier than the people whom she so clearly loves?

Richard clears his throat. 'Okay,' he manages to say. 'A walk, it is.'

They walk later, still largely in silence. They sit outside a pub by the park and watch the passing parade.

'I'd forgotten how beautiful these long evenings are,' she says. 'There's a sort of magic about them. England feels like another country on summer evenings, somewhere peaceful and exotic.'

'You could always come back,' he says watching her, only half joking.

'No,' she says firmly, stopping to look at him. 'No, Richard, I couldn't do that. It's far too late for that.'

Back at the flat, Richard grills steak, makes a salad and opens a bottle of wine. They eat at a table near the open French windows, and then move their chairs onto the balcony, looking out at the first stars in the darkened sky.

'My life is falling apart,' she says quietly.

'Zoë, you mustn't let this . . . this flashback ruin . . .'

'No.' She stops him. 'It's not that, not what you told me today. It's at home, what's happening there. Somehow I thought that coming here would help and, in some ways, it has. It's helped with the past. But in a few days I'll be back home, in the present, in the same situation I left behind.'

'But your family,' he says, puzzled. 'You have so much . . .'

'I have had,' she says, and slowly she begins to tell him what she told Julia.

He listens attentively. 'And now it's falling apart?'

'It's all changing, being taken over, and what will be left? I can't bear to think about it but I *do* think about it – all the time. Your kids go from needing you one hundred per cent to the point when you wake up one morning and they're making their way out the door. And then, worse still, someone so wrong comes along to speed it all up, to chip away what might have remained, and to push you out of the way.'

'Poor Zoë,' Richard says and, in the light from the street lamps, she sees a flicker of amusement on his face.

'You're laughing at me.'

'No,' he says. 'No. I'm just remembering a weekend I usually prefer to forget, the time I took you home to meet my parents.'

Zoë sighs. 'I remember it well.'

'Do you? Do you really? Do you know what it was all about? Not the argument at lunch but all the rest of it?'

She shrugs. 'They didn't like me. Your mother, in particular, hated me because I was so unsuitable. Australian for a start and my skirt was too short, I said all the wrong things, I shared a house with a black man. I was entirely unsuitable.'

'And you forgot the bit about being descended from a convict. Yes, you were entirely unsuitable. My parents, especially my mother, had a very clear idea of the sort of girl I should bring into the family.'

'Yes,' Zoë laughs. 'Definitely not Australian. I was supposed to be upper class, and probably living with my parents somewhere in Surrey; someone, a bit like Julia, I suppose. Like Julia as she was then.'

'Exactly! Someone bland and unthreatening; a girl who would slip nicely into the family without dislodging my mother from her domestic throne. I could only see it years later, Zoë, the reason why everyone I took home was bound to be wrong. I was just never attracted to the sort of girl my mother needed me to marry.'

There is a long silence.

'You mean,' Zoë says eventually, 'that I'm doing the same thing.'

'It does sound that way.'

'But I'm *not* like her, I'm *not* like your mother. I had a job until a few weeks ago. I'm really busy, I do things with the girls, like I used to with Dan; it's not the same.'

'You are not remotely like my mother,' Richard agrees, 'nor your own mother, for that matter. But they were both women who were totally focused on protecting their territory, irrespective of how that felt for Jules and me, or for you. Zoë, you're an entirely different sort of person and I'm sure you have the sort of relationships with your children that Julia and I would have given our right arms for, but you are doing just what our mothers did. Daniel's fallen in love with someone whom you find entirely unsuitable because she's so different from what you wanted. Have you wondered why Archie and your daughters love her and you don't? Could it possibly be that, despite decades of loving and raising Daniel under difficult circumstances, you are no longer the best judge of what's right for him?'

～～～

Archie sits alone in the darkness out on the deck, where he has sat most of the night, watching the first slivers of dawn lightening the sky. Gaby is sleeping over at Gwen's place, and Rosie staying with Rob's family at the winery. The place is horribly still; everything is still except for his head, which is seething with anxiety and resentment, and aching from lack of sleep. There is no point in calling again; he can't bear to hear the recorded message and, in some ways, doesn't even want to talk to her. He prefers to reflect on how it was when they first met all those years ago, when he saw her on the jetty trying to bait Dan's fishing line hook. She'd been so defensive that day, as though she wished he'd disappear once the problem of the bait was solved. It had been Dan who kept him there, kept asking things, and eventually he'd caught a very small fish. Archie knew it should have been thrown back, but hadn't had the heart to make him do it. He was a lovely kid and Archie didn't want it to end in tears; in fact, he didn't want it to end at all.

'We should celebrate your catch with an ice cream,' he'd said and, over Dan's head, saw Zoë's reluctance.

'Go on,' he'd said. 'It's only an ice cream. Live dangerously.'

And she'd given him a half smile, shrugged, and followed him and Dan along the jetty back to the kiosk. Later, weeks later, when she had finally told him her story, he could only admire the determination and strength of character it must have taken for her to raise her child. As he grew to know her better, he could imagine no one less equipped to withstand the shame and rejection that had been dealt her.

Archie knew he was at his best as a loving protector; it came easily to him. Now he wonders if this has been bad for Zoë. Perhaps he should have pushed her to test herself in other ways; to get a more demanding job, to study for something, to venture out of her comfort zone? He has always thought they had a fortunate life together, but perhaps she has wanted more. Has he failed to notice because the situation suited him too well? Is this his come-uppance? He remembers the anger he saw in Zoë after Julia's email arrived, anger that he suspected was not directed just at Julia and Richard, but at herself. Now he wonders whether he, too, is part of the cause.

The sound of the phone jolts him from his thoughts and his heart rate doubles instantly. Perversely, he now wants to ignore it; he has no desire to speak to her while she is in this black hole that he is trying not to imagine. There is the matter of Eileen, though, so he picks up the phone.

'Arch,' Zoë says. 'I'm so sorry, I forgot to put the phone on and when I did go to check the messages last night, the battery was almost flat and I'd forgotten to bring the charger with me to London. I had to borrow a charger, so I only just got your messages. How's Mum?'

Eileen, he tells her, is okay. She tripped on the step coming out of her unit, and although she has a badly grazed knee and elbow, and is very dizzy, there appears to be nothing more serious.

'So why is she in hospital?'

'They thought at first that the fall might have been caused by a slight stroke,' he says, 'so they're doing some tests, and keeping her in for a couple of days to observe her.'

'I don't need to rush back? I'll be home on Friday anyway.'

'No need to change it,' he says.

He wants to ask her where she is, and, more importantly, who she's with but he doesn't want to know the answer.

'Are you okay, Arch? You sound a bit odd. Are the kids okay?'

'We're all fine.' He is incapable of having a conversation.

'Good. Well, let me know if anything else happens with Mum, and if not, I'll see you at the airport on Friday.'

'Sure.'

'Um . . . okay then. Give everyone my love.'

'Will do.'

'I love you, Arch.'

But he hangs up, unable to cope with any more words. He is imagining her in London, and in the background the shadowy image of a man whom he has never met, but always despised and now fears.

THIRTY-EIGHT

Rye – July 2000

It has been a testing time for Julia. Tom's illness, Zoë's presence, her own concerns about Richard putting his foot in it, and the inevitable raking over the past have been exhausting. And Zoë is leaving tomorrow and she wishes they had more time together. Despite their differences, Julia has felt the threads of that precious early friendship strengthening again; felt herself grasp at them across the years and across the cavern left by Hilary's death. As she walks back up the hill from the town towards home, she thinks they have spent too long dwelling on the past. What she wants is to nurture this friendship that was so painfully cut off at the root.

As she nears the house, Julia sees that the front door is open and Zoë is standing where she herself often stands. She is looking out across the churchyard, her arms folded, leaning against the door jamb.

'I'm storing it all in my memory banks,' Zoë says as Julia arrives alongside her. 'I love it here. This has been so important to me, Julia. I'm remembering everything you once began to teach me about friendship, about it being safe to trust it.'

'It's a pity I couldn't live up to it when the going got tough,' Julia says wryly, threading her arm through Zoë's. 'But we have a second chance. I've stuffed up enough things in my life, Zoë, and this is precious to me too. We've done the past to death; time to start on the future, don't you think?'

Zoë nods, squeezing Julia's arm against her side. 'It really is. I'm going to miss you so much but going home . . . well, it doesn't seem like an ending, more like we've picked up where we left off.'

Julia nods. 'Thank god for email,' she says.

'And cheap phone calls.'

'And most of all . . .' Julia says, struggling with the feeling that her throat is full of tears, 'most of all, thank god for a second chance.'

∽∾

Justine, against her better judgment, has agreed to help Rosie and Gaby prepare a celebratory meal for Zoë's return. She is torn between pleasure at their request, and anxiety about how Zoë might view her involvement.

'I'll leave the nursery early and go and help, and I'll come home when Archie goes to fetch her,' she had told Dan before he left that morning. 'But *you* should go. Have dinner together with them, like you all used to do; just say I had something else on. Maybe having a family dinner will help things along a bit.'

'I don't know,' he'd said. 'Might be best if I stay away. And, anyway, I don't *feel* like doing it; especially without you there, it doesn't seem right. And you shouldn't have to help, not after the way she's treated you.'

'I'm helping for Gaby and Rosie,' she says, 'and because I want to. It's fun doing stuff with them, they treat me like a big sister. And it would be nicer for them if you go too. Go there straight from work, Dan. Don't sulk. Do as we agreed – go ahead with what we want to do, then it's up to Zoë what she does. Just do the right thing, darling.'

Dan puts his arms around her. 'I spend my days planning to outwit fanatical terrorists, and somehow it seems easier than dealing with my mother. But you're probably right. I'll see you later, if I survive it.'

The menu the girls have planned is elaborate, and with Gaby at school and Rosie in a lecture until four, it's up to Justine to do most of the shopping. Archie has offered but the girls don't trust him to get everything on the list. So Justine goes to the supermarket and stops outside the school to pick up Gaby on her way to the house. Cooking with them is fun but unnerving; they want each stage of the process to be admired, and they play loud music and sing a lot. Justine is quiet, efficient and orderly in the kitchen – almost clinical, Gwen says – and she is agitated by the burgeoning chaos of pots and pans piling up, flour and icing sugar creeping mysteriously across the work surface, and nothing being done in what she thinks is the right order. Eventually she gives up trying to control what's happening, issues some instructions, turns up the music, and while Rosie and Gaby put the final touches to the cake, makes an attempt to clear up after them.

⁓

The remainder of the flight stretches ahead like an eternity. Zoë, squashed into her window seat by the beefy arms and overlapping rolls of fat of the man in the seat beside her, longs to stretch her legs in the aisle, but negotiating a passage over his sleeping bulk earlier had been a monumental task and she can't face it again. Sunlight reflecting back from the bed of white cloud beneath them blinds her with its brilliance, and she pulls the shade halfway down and closes her eyes. In England, time slipped like sand between her fingers; now it feels as though she has been away for ages. She had felt as though she were discovering a different self. The fluctuating hormones, the fear of loss, and the sense of inadequacy that had overwhelmed her had all seemed to recede. Now they cast their shadows once again.

'I guess it's a difficult time of life for all of us,' Richard had said as he drove her back to Rye. 'We go on for years believing that one day we'll be grown up and know the answers, but the years roll on and suddenly we're past the halfway point – probably well past it – and all we know is how little we know. Wisdom and maturity just seem like illusions.'

'It all seems so hard,' she'd said. 'Especially with one's children. It must be the same with your daughter.'

Richard shrugged. 'Yes, but it was a bit different. You see . . .' He paused and Zoë sensed a sudden charge in the atmosphere.

'Go on.'

He hesitated again. 'Well,' he began, 'you see, it's more complicated . . .' He paused. It's different. When Lily and I split up, I moved away and immersed myself in work, so I relinquished my rights to that sort of fatherhood.'

She looked hard at him, waiting for something else. 'I suppose so,' she said eventually. 'And I realise you might be right about what you said that maybe I don't know what's best for Dan. But what if I *am* right? What if it's all a terrible mistake?'

He gave a small mirthless laugh.

'Then it's *his* mistake, Zoë – *their* mistake and they'll have to work it out. Is it that you don't trust Dan's judgment or would it be more honest to say you simply want to be able to make his decisions for him? This is a failure of imagination on your part. You think Justine is going to steal something from you. It's unlikely, I think, but, even so, setting up barricades is hardly the most imaginative way to deal with it.'

'What do you mean?'

'Well, Daniel's a man and he'll do what he wants to do. You can resist, you can poison the water but the smart and compassionate thing to do is to change yourself instead of trying to change him.' He took his eyes off the road briefly to look at her. 'Years ago, I put a lot of effort into wondering how I could change you, when what I should have been doing was thinking about changing myself. Remember what you said about your art class – that it showed you there were all sorts of ways of seeing the same thing? Try to see this in a different way; take a risk, opt for generosity and trust.'

The inflight PA system crackles to life now and the pilot announces that they are commencing their descent. Zoë returns her seat to the upright position and it is only as she adjusts her watch to local time that she realises she has messed up by giving Archie an arrival time that is two hours later than their actual arrival. She thinks she will phone him when they land, and then decides it might be fun to take a cab and surprise him.

As Zoë pulls her suitcase along the drive and lets herself in through the side gate, she can hear music coming from the kitchen. She leaves her case, walks briskly up the steps of the verandah and peeps in through the kitchen window.

Archie sits on a stool playing mock drums on the benchtop. On the other side, Rosie and Gaby are singing along and dancing to the music. At the sink is Justine.

Zoë gives a little gasp, steps back from the window and puts her hand against the lattice to steady herself. The star jasmine has had a growth spurt in her absence and is making tracks up the brickwork. She stares at the plant, her stomach churning, her mind a panicky mass of jealousy, fear and resentment at seeing Justine in her kitchen with her family. Leaning back, she flattens herself against the wall, with her eyes closed.

Do it differently, Richard had said; imagination, generosity, trust. As she stands there pressed against the wall, a sweat breaking out all over her, it seems too much to ask. He's right, though, it will be her loss if she can't make that leap.

As she waits and watches, nervously willing herself to uncurl, she notices that even though Justine is smiling, she looks exhausted.

As Zoë moves away from the window and into the doorway Archie is on his feet, bopping, while Rosie and Gaby are all hip thrusts and pumping arms, totally into the music and unaware of her. And then Justine turns away from the sink, sees her and stops, the words of the song dying on her lips.

At the sight of Justine's face, Archie looks around. Rosie and Gaby, their backs to her, are gyrating, singing louder than ever as Zoë looks from Justine to Archie and back again to Justine, who looks as though she wishes she could disappear into the ground.

And then Rosie spots her. 'Mum!' she yells, and runs to Zoë, followed immediately by Gaby. Their voices are a babble lost in the music as she hugs them and then kisses Archie.

Justine rinses her hands under the tap, takes off her apron and steps out from behind the bench top.

'I'll get out of your way, Zoë,' she says. 'I hope you had a good holiday.'

But Zoë shakes her head and reaches out to take her hands. 'Don't go, Justine,' she says. 'This is meant to be a family celebration.'

2001

THIRTY-NINE

Rye – 3 July 2001

Dear Zoë
Almost a year since you left here and today the postman knocked
for a signature for an overseas package. I could hardly wait to rip
off the cardboard and bubble wrap but Tom, the great hoarder and
recycler, insisted that it all had to be removed intact. Well, the
contents were so worth waiting for. We are thrilled with your
wonderful painting. Thank you so very much.

I didn't realise it was your own work at first, I just thought
how amazing that you had found someone who could capture the
house like that through the branches of the catalpa tree. Then Tom
said, 'Don't be daft, she did it herself, Zoë painted this for us.' It's
brilliant, Zoë, we had no idea you could paint like this.

We are so grateful. Tom says he's writing a real letter, to say his
own thank you. He immediately took down the two etchings on the
wall by the fireplace and hung your painting there.

I hope you are going to keep on with the art classes, you obvi-
ously have enormous talent. And what an amazing year it's been
since you got home; Dan and Justine's wedding, Rosie going off to
Vietnam, and you and Archie becoming grandparents. I was feel-
ing that my life was standing still by comparison but now, after
a few false starts, we have signed off on the sale of the language
school. It's been rather protracted and very sad. I kept putting it
off, the school was so much a part of my friendship with Hilary

that getting rid of it felt like betrayal, although she would have thought that ridiculous. When the deed was done I had a couple of very bad weeks of grieving, not for the school itself but for Hilary and what it had meant to both of us when it started. Fragments of bereavement lurk for a long time and show up when you least expect them. Anyway I seem to be through that now and I know it was the right decision.

We're still thinking about a holiday place in Portugal, and the money from the school will help, especially now that we are both unemployed!

The people who bought the school have introduced classes in Portuguese and so I've enrolled! It's an odd feeling to sit in the classrooms there after all this time.

Has Richard told you about Bea? Well, in case he hasn't I'm going to.

The pleasant but inappropriate Amanda has taken herself off to Milan and Richard has a lovely new companion. He knew Bea back in his university days and they met up at some sort of reunion at Easter. She's a theologian. Yes, I can see you reeling in shock that a theologian should be involved with someone as godless as my brother, but, as she herself pointed out, a scholar of theology is a student of the nature of the divine, and doesn't necessarily have to be a believer. She's very nice, great sense of humour. Richard is drinking less, is more tolerant and less grumpy. I think we have Bea to thank for that, they obviously have robust conversations in which he doesn't always get his own way, which is very good for him.

I hope everything is going well with you and Archie.

Much love

Julia xx

PS. Can't wait to show Richard the painting. He loves that tree and wants his ashes scattered under it. If/when the time comes I shall have to do it under cover of night as apparently you can't just scatter your loved ones at will, even in a graveyard.

4 July

Dear Julia

Great news about the school, it did seem to be wearing you down and I know Tom will be relieved! I can understand how it would have revived your grief about Hilary, but you must have some wonderful memories of your time together setting it up.

I'm so glad you like the painting; I worked from a photograph I took on the last day I was there.

I laughed about Richard and his ashes. Remember when he used to say he wanted to be buried in the basement of Broadcasting House? But that was in the days when we were young enough to think we'd live forever.

Harry seems to grow daily; he's the image of Dan as a baby and we all adore him so he's at risk of becoming horribly spoiled. Justine is wonderful with him; she thought she had missed out so he came as a bit of a surprise, the best ever surprise for all of us really. Justine is back at the nursery three days a week and Gwen and I are sharing the childcare. The more time I spend with Gwen the more I like her, we are becoming great friends.

Richard hasn't mentioned Bea to me yet, but it's at least a couple of months since I heard from him. I do hope it works out for him this time.

I'm still loving the art classes and I'm trying to stretch myself a bit. Theo, who taught the three courses I've done so far, is running a group for people who want to go further. It's very informal and great fun, there are five of us, and talking about what we're doing and working together is really motivating. I wish I'd started years ago! So what with that and helping with Harry I haven't done anything about finding a job, but I guess that'll be the next thing.

Love to you both
Zoë xxx

2 August

Dear Zoë

Apologies for being the world's worst correspondent. My cutting down on work with the BBC has somehow resulted in me working harder and longer but for less money. But the production company is going really well and I'm doing things I really want to do and thoroughly enjoying it.

I'm writing because I was down in Rye last week and saw your wonderful painting. I had no idea you were such an accomplished artist. I had a friend with me at the time (I know Julia's told you about Bea), and she's something of a connoisseur, in fact she has a fine collection of watercolours, mainly of English churches. She was tremendously impressed.

As Julia's probably told you, Tom is a new man now, so very much better than when you saw him, and we battle on with our project for 2008, the book and the documentary. It gives us both enormous satisfaction.

Take care and keep painting!

Affectionately

Richard

29 August

Dear Richard

Thanks for your message, I'm glad you like the painting. The best thing about the art classes is first that I love painting, equally important is that it's changing the way I feel about myself. At last there is something I'm good at other than looking after a family. I feel so lucky to have discovered this at a time in my life when I needed it most.

I'm attaching the most recent photograph of Harry taken last week, he is so like Dan. As you can imagine my mother has been struggling – a black grandson was bad enough for her so you can guess her reaction to having a black granddaughter-in-law and great-grandson. She is ruthlessly insensitive and I frequently want to smack her! But, hey, a year ago the whole family wanted to smack me for not wanting to let Justine in so I should try to be more tolerant. I'll always be grateful for what you said.

I'm so pleased to hear about Bea and will be pumping Julia for more details as I don't suppose I'll get them from you!

Look after yourself,

Zoë x

Dear Gloria

Thanks so much for letting me know about Marilyn. How very sad, I'm sure Claire must be beside herself, they were obviously devoted to each other. I'll never forget Marilyn teaching me how to sterilise Dan's bottles, and how she met me at the gate the day I got back from Glasgow. I've posted a letter to Claire today.

And I want to ask you a favour. I told you a bit about my younger daughter, Gaby. She finishes school in November and is absolutely determined not to go to university, at least at present. She wants to travel, most of all she wants to go to London, and although she's pretty sensible Archie and I are naturally nervous of letting her loose on the world. How history repeats itself! She's talking about getting a job as a nanny in London. I think it'll be harder than she imagines, but we've convinced her that it will be better to get there and then go to an agency rather than fix it up online. At least then she'll be able to meet the family before committing herself to them.

So, I'm wondering if you would be willing to keep an eye on her when she first arrives, and if perhaps she could stay with you until she finds somewhere to live, or a family to work for? We would, of course, pay for her accommodation and she'll have more than enough to contribute and to keep herself until she finds something. She's interested in all the things that you were doing in the sixties and beyond.

I know this is a cheek; you gave me a home when I most needed it and now I'm asking you to take in my daughter, but it really will only be for a very short time. I hope you don't mind me asking, please don't hesitate to say if you'd rather not.

I hope you're well and will be thinking of you next week at the funeral.

Love and thanks
Zoë x

8 September

My dear Zoë
Yes, yes, yes! It would be swell to have Gaby come here. I will love to have some young company and I can pollute her mind with my horrible feminist ideology, and tell tales about her mother as a young woman. I can hardly wait. Tell Gaby to email me and we can get to know each other a little before we meet.

She can stay as long as she likes, it can be her London home. She can have your old room. What fun!

Claire is devastated, she may come and stay with me until after the funeral. It's so very sad, but we are all getting older rather fast.

Love and hugs
Gloria

9 September

Dear Dr Laverne (or can I call you Gloria?),
My mum has told me that you said I could stay with you when I come to London.

I am so grateful, it's so good knowing I have somewhere to go. I'm really excited about meeting you and London and everything.

Is it okay if I come before Christmas? It would be awesome to have Christmas in England, you don't have to get me presents or do anything special but I want to see the London lights, and maybe it might snow.

I'm going to send you some pictures and an essay I wrote on

the women's movement, but I just wanted to send this quickly to
say thank you.

I am dying to meet you, I can hardly wait.

Love

Gaby xxxxx

FORTY

Cottesloe – September 2001

D an is replacing sections of the shadecloth at the nursery; loading plants onto trolleys, to clear a space, brushing down the inside of the timber framework, then climbing up the outside, ripping off the old shadecloth and fixing the new. Kevin is his sidekick for the day. He's reliable, does exactly as he's asked and, most of all, Dan likes him, likes his directness, and the fact that he only speaks when he has something to say. Now, as Kevin stands at the top of the platform steps handing nails up to him as he kneels on a crossbeam securing the last section, Dan is thankful for someone who knows when to move the ladder, and doesn't moan at him when he drops nails, which he does quite often.

'Last section, Dan,' Kevin says as they reach the end nearest the wall. 'Then I'll sweep up before we put the plants back.'

Dan grunts approval through a mouthful of nails, and Kevin waits to hand up the last few.

'Looks pretty good, doesn't it?' Dan says, when he's back on the ground. 'Let's have a tea break before we clean up.' He stands back, brushing dust, leaves, moss, splinters and dead insects from his hair and clothes, and sits down on a crate to wait for Kevin, who has gone to get the tea.

'You've done a great job today, mate,' he says when Kevin returns with two mugs. 'Very organised, very efficient, you'd make an excellent soldier.'

'Yeah, but I wouldn't want to be. I'd rather work in the nursery,' Kevin says.

'Good decision; I'm not sure I wouldn't rather be doing that myself.'

'But you like it; Justine said you'd want to be a soldier forever.'

'Hmm. Did she? She might just be wrong about that.'

'Justine's never wrong, she's really clever.'

'She sure is, but she could be mistaken this time.'

'You went to the Olympics to look for terrorists. I'd like that bit.'

'The Olympics was okay,' Dan admits. 'But most of it's not like that.'

'So when you were away last time, where were you?'

Dan dips his biscuit into his tea. 'At sea, on that big ship with all the refugees, it was on the TV news.'

'Yeah! The *Tampa*, I saw that,' Kevin eats a biscuit and they sit for a moment in silence. 'I didn't like that, Dan.'

'No? I didn't like it much either.'

'You see, when there's a whale that gets lost and stuck on the beach, people go out and stay with it all day and all night, and they pour water on it, and try and move it into the water. They help it. Y'know what I mean?'

'Well, yes,' Dan says, puzzled, 'but I'm not sure what you're getting at.'

'No, but I haven't said it yet. You see, Dan, people go and do all that to save a whale, but all those people on the boat hadn't got anything, and they were lost and nobody wanted to help them. They just wanted them to go away. That doesn't make sense to me.'

'It doesn't make a lot of sense to me either, Kev,' Dan says, 'especially put like that. But not everyone wanted to send them away. It was a bit more complicated than the whales.'

Kevin shakes his head. 'I don't think so. Anyway, I suppose you don't want to be a soldier because of Harry. Now you're a dad, you don't want to get shot or anything.'

'Who doesn't want to be a soldier?' asks Justine, who has suddenly materialised behind them.

'Oh, er . . . Kevin, I was telling him he'd make a good one,' Dan says, getting to his feet. 'Must get on. See what we've done; just the cleaning up to go now.'

'Dan doesn't want to be soldier either, he said so,' Kevin says, picking up the cups.

'Did you say that?'

'I might have . . .' Dan stops and Justine waits. 'I think I implied that I could be having second thoughts.'

'Really? Well, if you have any third or fourth ones, I'd appreciate it if you told me first rather than Kevin, or any of the rest of the staff,' Justine says. 'And the shadecloth looks great, which is what I came to say, and that Archie rang to ask us for dinner. He's cooking.' And she walks off towards the glasshouses.

'Shit,' Dan says aloud and, picking up the broom, begins to sweep the paving. 'Shit, shit, shit.'

⌇

Archie is cooking on the verandah. One day, he thinks, when he has more time, he might do some cooking classes; meat dishes would be best, and soup maybe and interesting things with vegetables. Out here on the verandah with a beer, looking out onto the darkening garden is the perfect way to cook, with none of the women fussing around, interfering and telling him better ways to do things. He's baking three whole snapper in the barbecue kettle and firing up the grill plate so he can oil it for the vegetables. Dinner was a spur of the moment thing; he'd wanted an evening with his family around him. They are minus Rosie, who's volunteering in a baby clinic in Saigon while Rob is working with a Vietnamese farmer. Archie is proud of Rosie but misses her horribly. Now that Dan's moved out, the dynamics in the house have changed completely. He's never thought three is the best number for cohabitation, and in this particular case, it's made him more aware of his own discontent.

Things are better, of course; much better than they were a year ago. Back then, he'd wondered how they would ever get through Zoë's menopause. Thank heavens for Gwen's naturopath, who helped to sort *that* out. And now, they have Harry. Becoming a grandparent is one of life's turning points and he's relishing it. But

Archie is still haunted by that black hole of silence during Zoë's holiday in England. She left home fragile and needy, and returned stronger, less moody and more confident. Archie knows this can only be a good thing but now he is the needy one, wanting her to toss him some crumbs of reassurance. It's ridiculous to fear a man who lives on the other side of the world and he despises himself for not being able to ask the question outright, because he is afraid of the answer.

Archie lifts the lid of the barbecue and unpeels the foil wrapping to check the progress of the fish. It's looking good, and he folds the foil back and lowers the heat.

'Can someone bring me the olive oil, please?' he yells in the direction of the kitchen. Dan emerges with a beer in one hand and the oil in the other, followed by Justine.

'Smells fantastic,' Dan says, handing over the oil. 'You okay, Arch. You look a bit off colour.'

'Fine,' Archie says. 'Couldn't be better. Can you oil the grill plate and spread out those slices of zucchini and eggplant?'

Justine puts her hand on Dan's arm. 'I'll do the veggies; you tell Archie about your second thoughts.'

'What second thoughts are those? Fremantle might beat West Coast? In your dreams, mate.'

'Second thoughts about the army,' Justine says.

'You're kidding me?'

Dan clears his throat and looks awkward. 'No. Not really. I've been wondering if it's really where I want to be.'

Archie raises his eyebrows. 'Well, that's a surprise. I thought you were in it for the long haul.'

Dan shrugs. 'Blame Justine and Harry. It does feel a bit different when you stop being a carefree single bloke and become a husband and father.'

'I'm happy to take the blame,' Justine says. 'But it's been so important to you that you really do need to be sure.'

'Absolutely right,' Archie says. 'And, look, until you've made up your mind, best not tell your mother or she'll be down there trying to buy you out, or whatever you have to do, before you've had time to think about it.'

'I know,' Dan says. 'There's no way either of us will say anything to Mum at this stage. But I wouldn't mind chewing it over with you, Arch, sometime soon.'

'Sure thing,' Archie says. 'Give me a bell whenever.'

At the kitchen table, Eileen is sitting opposite Gwen, who has just finished giving Harry his bottle. 'He's a lovely little baby, considering . . . everything,' Eileen says grudgingly.

'He certainly is,' Gwen says, winking at Zoë, who has flushed scarlet with embarrassment. 'Considering absolutely everything and nothing at all.'

'Didn't catch that,' Eileen says, leaning forward. 'My hearing's not what it was, I miss a lot these days.'

'For which the Lord make us truly thankful,' Zoë says quietly and Gwen smothers a grin.

'My turn,' Gaby says. 'I've finished making the salad, so it's my turn with Hank.'

'His name is Harry, Gabrielle,' Eileen says. 'It's a perfectly good name; I don't go for all this shortening of names. Look at Zoë – you couldn't have a shorter name than that, could you, and yet what does Archie do? Shortens it to Zo, that's what. Time's getting on. Shouldn't you be doing something about the dinner, Zoë?'

'Archie and Gaby are in charge,' Zoë says, 'I'm just passing through.'

'Yuk!' Gaby says, holding Harry out to her at arm's length. 'You can have manky Hanky. He needs changing.'

'Five minutes,' Archie calls through the kitchen door. 'Have you laid the table, Gabs?'

'There you are, you see,' Eileen says to Gwen. 'Gabs – what sort of a name is that for a girl?'

⁓∾⌢

The fish is perfectly cooked – the skin crisp and tasty, the flesh white and tender – the vegetables golden and delicious. When Gaby produces a lemon meringue pie, Archie opens a bottle of dessert wine and fills tiny crystal glasses.

'I made this because it's your favourite, Mum,' Gaby says. 'And

I really hope it's okay, because I'm never going to make it again in my whole life ever – it's much too hard.'

Zoë pronounces the pie the best she's ever tasted. This evening would be perfect if Rosie were here, but Zoë's getting used to her absence and to the fact that Gaby, too, will soon be gone. She knows now that what she and Archie have created isn't coming to an end, it's growing, and so is she. Painting has helped her to see beyond herself and it's still helping her; pushing her to change. The damage of her early hostility to Justine is still not fully repaired, but their relationship is growing stronger, as they take small steps towards each other.

'I must be extraordinarily dim and very selfish,' she had said to Archie recently. 'I thought it was all about me and that because I'd sorted myself out everything would be okay, but it's not. I was almost wilfully blind to how much I'd hurt Justine.'

'But you two get on okay now, don't you?' Archie had asked.

'In many ways we do, but I don't think she trusts me and, frankly, I don't blame her. I'll just have to be patient.'

It's after eight when Dan offers to drive Eileen home and, once they have gone, Zoë, Justine and Gwen begin to clear the table. They stay talking in the kitchen while Archie and Gaby slump in front of the television.

'Coffee, just what I need,' Dan says coming in through the back door. 'Shall I take the tray through?'

'Bloody hell!' Archie yells from the lounge. 'Come and look at this.'

Zoë grins at Justine. 'Footy, probably.'

'Oh no!' Gaby cries. 'What is it, Dad . . . what's happening?'

The cups rattle as Dan dumps the tray on the coffee table. 'Christ,' he says. 'Look at that, what the hell . . .'

The women exchange a glance, shrug and abandon what they are doing.

On the television screen, dense clouds of grey smoke are belching from a gaping black hole in the side of a skyscraper, and there is a clamour of sirens, screams and panic-stricken voices.

'What is it? What's happened?' Zoë asks.

'It's New York, the Twin Towers, a plane flew into the side of the World Trade Centre about ten minutes ago; they just replayed it,' Archie says without taking his eyes off the screen. 'Just, just flew into the side of the building . . .'

Shafts of flame dart out from the darkening smoke.

'There are people in there, Mum,' Gaby says. 'Look up at the windows. What *are* those buildings, Dad?'

'Oh my god,' Dan says, in a low voice. 'Oh no, not another one . . .'

And, as they watch, a second plane hurtles towards the adjacent tower as if it will pass right through it, ripping into the concrete as though it's cardboard and exploding in a massive ball of flame against the clear blue of the morning sky.

They sit, huddled together, watching the horror unfold on the screen. They watch as desperate people hurl themselves from the towers and fall like discarded dolls to certain death, and as others run blindly through the dust, until eventually the two buildings collapse, burying the streets, the traffic, the fleeing pedestrians in clouds of smoke and rubble that falls like some monstrous waterfall. And then it is replayed, again and again.

Archie looks across at Dan and buries his head in his hands.

'Everything will change now,' Dan says softly, putting his arm around Justine. 'Everything will be different.' And he gets up and wanders out through the kitchen to the verandah and the cold darkness of the garden.

A great cold stone drops into Zoë's heart, and Gaby huddles close to Gwen on the sofa, tears running down her cheeks.

⌘

Dan's head is a mess. Images from past deployments race through his mind, muddled and out of sequence. He prickles with a cold sweat, his gut churns with nausea, and a bolt of pain shoots through his leg at the site of his wound and stays there, throbbing, as though the horror he has just witnessed has reminded his body of the circumstances of its injury. Is he losing his nerve? Is this a warning that somewhere ahead there is a fatal split second when he won't be able to make a life-or-death decision.

'Are you okay?' Justine asks, emerging from the light of the kitchen.

'Not really,' he says, getting up and putting his arms around her. 'You?'

'No, of course not.'

They stand in the darkness holding each other, seemingly unaware that it's almost eleven o'clock and the temperature has dropped dramatically.

'What does it all mean?'

'At this stage, it's anyone's guess. From here on in, it'll be one day – perhaps one hour – at a time. Let's go home.'

Very early the next morning, Dan gets out of bed and walks over to the cot in which Harry is sleeping flat on his back, with his arms thrown above his head, tiny hands curled into loose fists, legs tangled in the blanket. He is so small, so beautiful, so defenceless, that Dan can hardly bear to look at him. Briefly, as he stands there struggling to breathe, he wonders how it was for his mother; what it must be like to hold your child in your arms and know that there is no one with whom to share the love and responsibility. Then he lifts Harry from the cot and carries him back to bed. Harry snuffles and wriggles, and settles in with a whimpering sigh. Justine turns towards them and Dan pulls them both closer to him.

'I don't know if I can do this,' Dan says. 'And I don't know how not to.'

Justine threads her leg between his and puts her hand on his face, which is tense and hot as fever.

'I love you, Dan,' she says. 'Whatever happens, whatever you have to do, you know we'll be here waiting for you.'

FORTY-ONE

Rye – December 2001

J ulia stamps her feet on the icy platform and looks down the length of the London train that has just drawn into the station. As the sliding doors open, weary commuters and Christmas shoppers step out and hurry to the exit, disappearing into the darkness of the car park. At the far end of the platform, a young woman in jeans and a red anorak pulls up the handle of her suitcase and looks around her. Julia walks quickly towards her.

'You must be Gaby,' she says.

'Oh wow, yes! You came to meet me,' Gaby says and surprises Julia by throwing her arms around her neck and kissing her. 'That is so nice of you. I could've got there on my own. I looked at the map and it's not far to your house.'

'It's nice to be met, though,' Julia says, 'and it's awfully cold, especially for you.'

Gaby pulls a face. 'It's freezing! Do you think it's going to snow?'

'Tomorrow, apparently,' Julia says. 'Can I help you with something?'

Gaby hands her a large lightweight canvas bag. 'Christmas presents from Mum,' she says, throwing a backpack over her shoulder and dragging her case along. 'I can't get used to it getting dark so early; it's not even half past four yet.'

'Horrible, isn't it? Ghastly for people who have to go to work and come home again in the dark. Zoë used to hate it when she lived in London. Come on, let's get out to the car and home. Tom'll have the kettle on. We thought you might like to toast crumpets in front of the kitchen range. It's a traditionally English sort of thing to do.'

'Brilliant,' Gaby says. 'And thanks so much for inviting me. Gloria's gone to Boston for Christmas. I'm so lucky she's letting me stay there. I don't have to move if I don't want to. Gloria's really cool – do you know her?'

'I only met her once, just after your brother was born,' Julia says, opening the boot. 'But Zoë brought me up to date last year.'

Gaby puts her bags in the boot and closes it. 'Well, she says she's happy to have company. D'you know, I've got the same room that Mum and Dan had?'

Back home, as she watches Gaby capturing a crumpet on the old brass toasting fork, Julia tells Gaby how like Zoë she is.

'I'm taller, though,' Gaby says. 'I get that from Dad, but otherwise, I'm more like Mum. Rosie's just like Dad, though; lots of curly blonde hair and freckles, she hates it. She and Rob are going home for Christmas, so Mum's over the moon. In fact, they're probably there by now.'

'And your brother?'

Gaby pulls a glum face. 'He's in Afghanistan. We haven't heard anything from him, and it's awful for Justine. But it's a good thing too because . . . well, because if anything *had* happened to him, we *would* have heard.'

'It must be horrible, not knowing,' Julia says, watching her closely and seeing so much of Zoë in her. She wonders with a sudden and totally unexpected sense of longing, what it would be like to have a daughter who is almost a double of yourself at the same age, trekking off all alone to the other side of the world. Mothers, as she has always thought, must have a wealth of patience and emotional fortitude that she has never possessed. 'Is Zoë okay?'

'Sort of. She hates the army, she takes it all very personally. I mean, it *is* personal, of course, but she holds the army responsible for Dan having to take risks, when it's his choice and he loves it.

That's the weird thing, I think; him wanting to join up in the first place. But Mum's a bit different this time. I think she feels she has to be strong for Justine because *she's* really upset, what with Harry and everything.'

'Bloody dreadful,' says Tom from his seat at the kitchen table, where he is buttering a crumpet. 'Afghanistan's already been bombed to the stone age. But don't get me started on it.'

'No,' says Julia with a grin. 'Don't get him started. Next thing he'll be rehashing Vietnam and telling you about his nineteen-sixty-eight project.'

'Really?' Gaby says, almost dropping a crumpet. 'I'd love to know about that. I did a huge project on it for school last year, and had to do a lot of research. I keep trying to talk to Mum about it but she sort of glazes over, like it all passed her by or something.'

'Splendid,' Tom says. 'When we've finished stuffing ourselves with stodge, I'll show you my collection of cuttings and photographs. I'm writing a book, and Julia's brother, Richard, and I are writing up a proposal for a documentary to be ready for the forti-eth anniversary in 2008.'

'Oh my god, that is so cool,' Gaby says, bringing a plate with the last of the crumpets to the table. 'Do you really have the *original* cuttings?'

Tom nods. 'I have everything. Newspapers, photographs, torn posters and handbills from Paris and London. I've also got some stuff that a friend in Prague found for me. And Richard has materials from the Black Panthers and the Free Speech Movement in California. His second wife was in the Black Panthers. He'll be here tomorrow too, so you can talk to him about it; he was very active in sixty-eight.'

Julia looks from one to the other. 'Oh lord,' she says. 'Now there are going to be three of you spending Christmas drooling over yellowing newspaper cuttings. I hope we've got a good sup-ply of red wine to keep my spirits up.'

⌒⌒

Justine hadn't expected it to be quite so hard. Since September 11, her anxiety had increased, along with frustration that decisions taken elsewhere would have profound implications for her family. She listened resentfully to the rhetoric of prime ministers and presidents, to commentators and clerics, to the rabid and the moderate, and waited, as did mothers' wives and daughters around the world, in fearful anticipation. Her own brutal experience of decisions being taken by men conveniently distant from the people whose lives they were determining, gave her little hope that humanity would prevail. But she had promised both Dan and herself that she was tough enough to cope with the stress of being married to a very particular type of soldier. It had seemed an easy promise to make but living with it is much more difficult, especially now she knows that his heart is no longer in it.

'I'll write,' Dan had said the day he left. 'You know I'll write whenever I can, and if they can get the satellite working, I may be able to phone, but don't panic if you don't hear. I may be out of touch for weeks at a time.'

Dizzy with fear, too paralysed even for tears, Justine had watched him go, knowing that he would not turn around because he couldn't bear it. Was this worse than being torn away from Norah? But what was the point of comparing them when both seemed unbearable?

Now, on this warm Christmas Eve morning, as she sits in the shade of the peppermint tree with Harry curled beside her on his mattress, there is the sound of a car at the front of the house, and she hears voices. Justine shifts in her chair and closes her eyes, hoping that the visitors are for Gwen, she feels incapable of talking to anyone else. But from inside the house there is laughter and the sound of footsteps across polished floorboards.

'Here she is!' Rosie cries, from the steps outside Gwen's kitchen. 'She's hiding under the peppermint tree.'

'Rosie?' Justine opens her eyes. 'You're back?'

'I'm back,' Rosie says, running barefoot across the warm grass, the metallic threads woven through her crushed cotton dress glinting in the sunlight. 'We flew in last night, Jus. Oh, it's so good to be home.' She drops to her knees on the grass beside Justine's chair. 'I had to come and see my nephew for the first time. My god, he's huge; I was expecting a tiny baby.'

'He's seven months old,' Justine says, 'and he gets bigger and better every day. You just missed the boring bits.'

Harry stirs and opens his eyes as Rosie crawls beside him onto the mattress. 'He is *divine*,' she says, as his fingers curl around her own. 'Hello, Harry, I'm your Aunty Rosie. May I pick him up?'

'Of course,' Justine says, getting out of her chair to join her on the ground. 'He'll soon let you know if he doesn't approve.'

But Harry approves wholeheartedly. He grabs at Rosie's long hair and tugs, and gurgles with pleasure. Justine feels her own surge of pleasure seeing Rosie holding him, nuzzling his cheek and kissing the top of his head.

'We've come to kidnap you,' says Archie, who is walking towards her with Gwen.

'Kidnap?'

'Yes,' he says. 'You, Gwen and Harry.'

'Mum sent us,' Rosie says. 'She says it's silly waiting for Christmas to start, that you should come now and stay, so we'll have Christmas Eve together as well. You and Harry can have Dan's old room and Gwen can have Gaby's; Mum's already made up the beds.'

Gwen looks at Justine. 'What do you think?'

Justine hesitates. 'Well, I . . .'

'Oh go on,' Rosie interrupts, 'please come. It'll be fun; we can wrap presents, and do all the cooking preparation, and sing carols and watch rubbish on television.'

'And you shouldn't miss the annual treat of watching Zoë get tipsy from making the brandy butter,' Archie adds.

'Please, Jus, say you'll come,' Rosie says, getting up with Harry on her hip. 'See how good I am with babies? I've had a lot of practice, working in that clinic.' She reaches out a hand to pull Justine to her feet.

'Does this mean yes, then?' Archie asks.

'It's yes for me,' Gwen says.

'And for me,' Justine replies. It's an effort to enter into their mood, but that, she thinks, is probably what she needs. The current of Dan's absence connects them; perhaps this will douse her fear, for a while at least.

∽⌒∾

Richard and Gaby are shopping. Julia has dispatched them to get all the last-minute bits and pieces: extra gift wrapping, another roll of sellotape, a jar of cranberry sauce, and the chocolate peppermint creams and Turkish delight that she had forgotten but now believes are essential. Rye is overhung with the dense pale-grey cloud that promises snow; it adds to the Christmas fever, the shops bright with decorations, coloured lights strung across the streets, and shoppers hurrying over the cobbles. Halfway along the High Street, Father Christmas, assisted by two elves, is ringing a large brass bell and calling out to children to come and get a present.

'It's like a Christmas card,' Gaby says. 'Back home, this is how Christmas *looks*, but not how it *is*.'

'I know,' Richard says, thinking how similar Gaby is to the Zoë he first met. 'I was in Queensland once for Christmas; talk about culture shock. Have you been into this café for tea yet?'

Gaby peers in through the window to where logs blaze in the huge open fireplace, the flames reflecting off copper pans and kettles. She shakes her head. 'I only got here the day before yesterday, and we cooked crumpets on the range.'

'Come on then,' he says, 'it's time you had a cream tea.'

'What about Julia . . . won't she . . .'

'She'll be fine – glad to have us out of the way.' He pushes open the door and ushers her inside.

'I totally love England,' Gaby says, when they have ordered their tea. 'It's amazing.'

'When did you get here?'

'Four weeks ago, all of it in London until I came here. The Christmas lights in Oxford Street were awesome, and there were people singing carols on the street corners.'

'And you're not missing home?'

'No way. I mean, I miss them all, but I don't wish I was there, because this is so brilliant.'

'There is something particularly lovely and traditional about it,' Richard concedes, 'although the older I get, the more I tend to compare it with how much better it all was when I was young.'

'Old people do that wherever they are,' Gaby says.

'I'm *not* old,' Richard bridles and then leans across the table smiling. 'Well, not *really* old. The fact that I was a grown-up person in nineteen sixty-eight doesn't make me a fossil.' They have spent all morning with Tom in his study, exploring his treasure trove of memorabilia.

'I know,' Gaby says. 'But you're older than Mum, you're probably the same age as Dad.'

'Tell me about your dad.'

'He's great,' Gaby says, leaning sideways so the waitress can put a plate of scones on the table. 'He's an engineer, a civil engineer; he's doing stuff on the freeway extension, managing some of the construction, I think. He likes that. He'd rather be strutting about in work boots and a hard hat than having to put a suit on and go to meetings, but he has to do that too.' She pauses, helping herself to a scone and then looks up, as though thinking of what to say next. 'He's funny, he's cheerful, um . . . he likes fishing, and the footy, and he reads a lot of books about history.' She puts down the scone, reaches for her bag and pulls out her wallet. 'Here,' she says, handing Richard a photograph. 'I took this just before I left.'

Archie is sitting on the steps of a verandah, hands clasped on his knees and smiling into the camera. He is a well-built man with blue eyes and a fair, freckled complexion. He is casually dressed in khaki pants and a white shirt, sleeves rolled halfway up his forearms. He looks perfectly at ease, open and friendly, and he's looking at the camera in a way that makes it absolutely clear that he loves the photographer. Richard is taken aback. How arrogant, he thinks, that he had always assumed that Zoë would pick someone who was physically similar to him. Archie is his direct opposite; probably height is the only physical characteristic they share.

Gaby hands him another photograph. 'Here's one of him and Mum.'

Zoë is sitting beside Archie, his arm around her shoulders.

She's wearing a denim skirt and a white T-shirt, and she's smiling too, but with that characteristic anxious little furrow between her eyebrows – the furrow Richard knows so well – and she is wearing the enamel pendant. Richard is about to mention this to Gaby but changes his mind.

'Do you have a picture of your brother?' he asks instead.

Dan's likeness to Harry is striking; it's almost like looking at Harry himself, the slightly lighter skin tone is the only difference. 'Wow,' Richard says, 'he's so like his father.'

'What was he like, Dan's father?'

He hesitates. 'He was a genuinely lovely man. Kind, probably wise beyond his years.'

Gaby keeps looking at him thoughtfully, until he averts his eyes and looks down again at the photograph. Justine is darker than Dan, with glossy black curly hair that is pinned up. When Zoë talked about Justine she hadn't mentioned that she was beautiful – perhaps she had failed to see it. Richard hopes she can see it now. Between them, a chubby baby sits looking into the camera, slightly puzzled.

'And this is Harry junior.'

Gaby nods. 'Isn't he adorable? I'll miss his first Christmas but Mum says he won't really notice much of what's happening, he'll enjoy it more next year.' She hands him another photograph, this time of herself and a blonde girl who is very obviously Archie's daughter. They are standing, their arms wrapped around each other on the same verandah. 'Me and my sister,' she says. 'Didn't Mum show you any photographs when she was here?'

'No.'

'Why not? Didn't you want to see what we looked like?'

He pauses, thinking about it. 'I did,' he said, 'but not until it was too late and I wasn't going to see her again before she left.'

Gaby taps the edges of her photographs together and puts them back into her bag. 'Did you show her pictures of your daughter?'

He shakes his head. 'She didn't ask.'

'That's weird.' She picks up the milk jug and pours some into their cups. 'I thought that was what people did when they hadn't seen each other for years, bragged about their children.'

'I suppose it is but . . .' he hesitates, wondering how to explain. 'I think there was too much of the past hanging over Zoë and me. A lot of unresolved things; I guess we needed to sort all that out first and then the time just ran out.'

Gaby pours the tea and hands Richard his cup, looking him directly in the eyes. 'Were you pleased to see her?'

'Absolutely delighted. It's one of the best things that's happened to me in years.'

'Did you have a fight?'

He looks surprised. 'What, last year or in the past?'

'Last year, of course; I know you must've had fights in the past.'

'No, we didn't have a fight last year. We talked a lot, about the past, about how young and confused we were. About the bad decisions we – well actually *I* made – about how things might have been different.'

There is a long silence while Gaby plays with scone crumbs on her plate. Neither of them has started to eat.

'So, what else did you do apart from talk?'

'We had dinner here in Rye, and one time we met up at Gloria's place and your mother had got very stoned, which was funny because she wouldn't have gone near a joint in the old days.'

Gaby smiles. 'She told us about that but I didn't know you were there too. What else?'

'We went for a walk on Hampstead Heath . . . Oh, we also went to the pub and for a walk near my flat, which is where we lived when we first got married.'

She looks up sharply. 'I'd like to see that place.'

'You're welcome any time,' he says. 'When you go back to London after Christmas, call me and I'll show you some of the sights.'

'That'd be awesome,' Gaby says. 'But the first thing I have to do is get a job.'

'What sort of job?'

'Anything, really. Mum and Dad gave me enough money for three months without working, but I don't want to use it all. I want to get a job as soon as I can. I was going to try to be a nanny but Julia was telling me about looking after those children in Paris and it's sort of put me off.'

Richard laughs. 'She really hated it,' he says. 'Never stopped complaining. What else do you think would interest you? What do you like doing?'

Gaby shrugs. 'Finding things out, like, about the past and about how it sort of fits with the present. And I'm quite a good writer, my English teacher says I should be a journalist. I'm a bit of a feminist too, much to Mum's dismay. Although Dan always says that Mum would be if she would only stop being scared of it and listen. She's like "I'm not a feminist but . . . " and then she lists all the things she believes about women, which is just all of what feminism is about. She has all the instincts, if you know what I mean.'

'I do know exactly what you mean. What about university?'

'Oh, I suppose so,' Gaby says with a huge sigh. 'I didn't want to but now I think I might have to if I want a good job. I thought journalism probably or history, or maybe both. But I wanted to learn something in the real world first, that's why I'm here, to get life experience. Parents and teachers go on all the time about how important it is but then when the time comes, they don't really want you to go out and get it.'

'It is a bit of a wrench when your children want lives of their own,' Richard says. 'Are you going to eat that scone or just look at it?'

In silence, they pile jam and cream onto their scones.

'Bliss,' Gaby says with her mouth full. 'I am totally going to pig out. You know, I'm almost exactly the same age Mum was when she came to London.'

Richard nods. 'I realise that.'

'Am I like her?'

He leans back looking at her. 'Yes, physically very much like her, except, of course, you're quite a bit taller. You're also more confident, and more . . . aware, I suppose is the word. More in touch with what's going on in the world than Zoë was.'

'She thinks she was a disappointment to you because she wasn't interested in all the stuff that was happening in the world back then.'

'Mmmm. Well, that's true in a way. I was very caught up in it and she was so detached. It was as though she couldn't see how the revolutions that were going on around the world were relevant to her, to us generally. I found that frustrating.'

Gaby nods. 'I know what you mean.' She leans forward as though she's about to disclose a secret. 'In a way, she's still like that.'

'Yes,' Richard says. 'I realised that when she was here.'

'Want to know what I think?' Gaby asks and he nods. 'I think Gran sort of closed her in a lot when she was growing up. And when she met you, she probably didn't know how to be around someone like you. Then she had Dan and she just had to concentrate on being a single mother with a black child. It would have been really hard to think about anything else, especially when she went back to Perth and they had to live with Gran.'

'That sounds about right,' Richard says. 'I probably made it harder for her. I kept trying to change her, to make her into what I thought I wanted.'

'Did you love her?'

Richard catches his breath, taken aback by the question. 'Yes,' he says, looking into his tea. 'I did. When I met her, I thought she was the most amazing and beautiful girl I'd ever seen. I thought I'd found my soulmate.'

'But you didn't love her in the end.'

He swallows hard, still unable to look at Gaby. 'There was a short period when I hated her with a passion. But then I realised quite quickly that I could only hate her that much, that she could only *hurt* me that much, because I still loved her.' He hesitates again and looks up. 'Sadly, by then it was too late.'

'Do you think Mum wishes it had been different?'

'Gaby!' he protests, 'what *is* this? I feel like I'm being interrogated by MI5.'

'Sorry, I just wondered. It's odd, not knowing much about you but that Mum had this whole other life with you, all your plans. If it hadn't all, like, crashed, I wouldn't have been born. When Mum came back last year, she was happier. I suppose I'm just trying to understand.'

He nods. 'Okay. Yes, I see. Well, no, I don't think she wished that things were different. We talked about it, there was a lot of nostalgia, I suppose. You ask yourself all those questions about what if things had been different. But Zoë loves your dad very much, and she loves you all passionately, her family is her life. She certainly speculated on how it might have been but I don't think that ever, for one moment, she wished it were different. We may not have seen each other for decades but I think that when she was here she took a hard look and thought she was well out of it.'

'What about you, then? Did you wish it was different?'

There is a long silence as Richard struggles with whether to tell the truth or an easy lie.

'Yes,' he says eventually. 'I did, I have done for years – decades, really. When I saw Zoë last year, I wished more than ever that I . . . that we . . . that it was different. But I didn't tell her that and nor should you. I haven't told anyone.'

'Thanks,' she says. 'Thanks for telling me. I kept wondering, you see, because coming here sorted things out for Mum, I think. I needed to know.'

Richard nods. 'Of course, but cone of silence, okay?'

'Okay.'

He takes a deep breath and sips his tea; it feels good to have told the truth and he begins to relax. He likes Gaby enormously, even if she has made him a bit hot under the collar.

'Richard?'

He looks up questioningly.

'There's one more thing I need to ask.'

'Go ahead.'

'Last year, when Mum was here, did you sleep together?'

'What the –'

She holds up her hand to stop him. 'It's important, because Dad thinks so; at least, I *think* that's what it is. He was trying to get her on the phone for ages when Gran was in hospital, and he got very upset, and Julia couldn't find you either.'

'*He told* you this?'

'No, of course not. I mean, he told us he was worried about her. But even after she'd called him, he was odd, like . . . scared.

And he was weird and grumpy for ages. He still is in a way – not grumpy, but different, like he's waiting for her to tell him something but he's afraid to ask. I worry about him because once Rosie went away and with Dan gone, there was just the three of us in the house, like three points of a triangle, and things felt odd and it's never been like that before. That's why I need to know.'

FORTY-TWO

Afghanistan – Christmas Day 2001

The minute he opens his eyes, Dan is fully awake; sleeping in war zones has accustomed him to instant alertness but it's still a shock to wake inside a tent. They have been trained to sleep in the open with just a plastic sheet for shelter, being outside is safer, because it's easier to see what's happening and to react quickly; but as they push further north from Kandahar, it's just too bloody cold to be outside. The cold-weather gear they've been issued is good quality but it's not enough to cope with minus twelve degrees Celsius. Dan lies stiff and alert, desperate to shift his position but unwilling to risk losing the precious few degrees of warmth that have cocooned him. Eventually he gives in and shifts slightly to look at his watch. The luminous green figures show it's four-thirty; eight in the morning in Perth, where it is almost certainly warm and still, the sky a clear and perfect blue, and along the beach near home, the scent of the Norfolk pines will be mingling with the tang of the sea, glassy in the sunlight.

What are they all doing now, he wonders. Justine will be busy with Harry, washing or feeding him, cuddling him close to her neck, kissing the sweet scented dome of his head. Dan aches with the longing to encircle them both in his arms, to bury his face in Justine's hair, to feel her skin against his; to recapture the intense reassurance that comes from physical closeness.

'Love doesn't need proximity,' she had said the day he left. 'It's always there, always burning bright.' He'd known she meant it, and that she was making a brave effort to let him know that whatever he might have to face, anxiety about her love for him need not be a part of it.

Is Gwen with her now, and what about his parents, his sisters? Gaby should be in London but Rosie will be home. He wishes they were all together, Gaby too. Imagining them all in the same place, opening presents, eating too much, laughing, thinking and talking about him, generates a heat that's almost enough to warm him, but not quite. Moving has allowed the warmth to leak away and he now feels as though he is lying in a bath of iced water, the chill seeping through his flesh to his bones. He drags himself up, moving silently out of the tent into the devastating bite of the wind. The vast inky sky is scattered with constellations in unfamiliar positions; there is a fading moon, and the sinister silence of snow that can muffle warning sounds, and a loneliness more acute than he has ever known.

Being a parent, he realises, gives you a totally different perspective. Love makes you stronger at the same time that it makes you more vulnerable, but fatherhood is something else again. It's the intensity of it, the awesome responsibility; the fear of not being able to protect this precious creature who is so dependent on you for everything.

'I keep thinking of how it must have been for you,' he had said to Zoë, a few weeks after Harry was born. 'I never realised before how scary it would have been; no home, no money, told not to come back here, and you were so young.'

The tension had eased between them since her acceptance of Justine.

'It did seem like an enormous responsibility,' she'd said. 'I felt so alone, and very frightened that I'd let you down.'

'You never have,' he said.

'Oh, yes I have, but perhaps mostly in little ways you haven't known about. And more recently, in a big way. And I really regret that. I'm so very proud of you, Dan . . .' Zoë's voice broke and she paused, 'I know I said things . . .'

'It's okay, Mum. You were upset and I overreacted. It's over,' he'd said, stroking Harry's head and then putting his hand on her shoulder. 'One hiccup in thirty-three years is a pretty good record.'

Dan cups his gloved hands around a cigarette, lights it and draws deeply on it. Justine would have a fit if she knew he was smoking, but extreme conditions breed extreme habits. Many of them who never smoke at home do so on active duty, it's the illusion of comfort, the camaraderie. He exhales, watching the smoke drift away from him. Clandestine patrols in Taliban country, and soon, a push further north to the mountains of the Hindu Kush. What a way to spend his son's first Christmas.

❧

'Who's coming with me?' Zoë asks late in the afternoon. 'Just a stroll to South Beach, nothing strenuous.'

The turkey is cooking slowly for Christmas dinner, which they'll eat in the evening when the heat of the day has passed. The vegetables are ready and waiting, the pudding that Gwen made weeks ago wrapped in its cloth. On a rug on the grass, Justine and Rosie are trying to divert Harry's attention away from a length of silver ribbon and towards one of his Christmas presents. Archie, in his favourite chair on the verandah, is two chapters into a book Gaby has sent him about the building of the London Underground and Eileen is taking a nap on Rosie's bed before Jane and Tony arrive.

'I'll come,' Gwen says. 'If I don't do something, I'll fall asleep and wake up grumpy.'

They walk in companionable silence through the streets where the muffled sounds of celebration drift from open windows. As they cross the road near the yacht club and turn onto the beach, the sea breeze is a pleasant relief from the heat.

'I wonder what it's like in London,' Zoë says, as they kick off their shoes to stroll to the water's edge. 'Or Rye, really, that's where Gaby is. She's hoping for snow.' She sighs. 'It's strange without her; Dan's often been away at Christmas but until now, both the girls have always been at home.'

'Do you think you'll hear from Dan?' Gwen asks.

-'Maybe. But they've not been there long, and it sometimes takes a while to organise communications; I think they have to get a satellite link, so it might be too soon. People used to tell me I'd get used to this but I never have. It's the uncertainty that's so hard to cope with.'

'That's just what Justine said,' Gwen says. 'She's finding it harder than she expected.'

Zoë nods. 'It's bound to be harder now that she has Harry, and sometimes talking on the phone just adds to the fear. I was talking to Dan once and some sort of alarm went off. It was an emergency and he hung up almost immediately, but I was left there wondering what on earth was going on, and, of course, dreading the worst. Imagination is the curse of wives and mothers in these situations. Having your children leave home is hard enough without the element of danger.'

'I'm sure it is,' Gwen says. 'I felt absolutely lost when Justine went away to Europe, and she's not even my daughter.'

'But you've been *like* a mother to her.'

'In some ways, but Norah was her mother. I tried not to get in the way of that, and I still try not to, even now that she's dead. She and Justine were robbed of so much that it seemed very important to be clear about the prominence of Norah in Justine's life. I can't begin to imagine the misery that Norah endured.'

'What was she like?' Zoë asks.

'Tough,' Gwen says, without hesitation. 'Incredibly tough; there are lots of women in Justine's family, and they're all tough and wise, and such fun. You'd like them, Zoë, and you would have loved Norah. She had a wicked sense of humour and said exactly what she thought. But she was vulnerable too, especially with Justine.' She turns to Zoë as they stand there side-by-side, barefoot in the shallow water. 'I've never said this to anyone else, but I think that Norah always felt that because of what had happened, there was a part of Justine that she could never know. Seeing them together was beautiful, but it was so sad too because nothing could ever make up for what was done to them.'

Two families race into the water alongside them; the adults lifting the toddlers, squealing with delight into the air, the older children plunging noisily, joyfully, out towards the deeper water, and a large black Labrador, its wet coat glistening in the sunlight, barking excitedly and running circles around them as if trying to round them up.

The two women stroll slowly on up the beach towards the rocks.

'Justine told me what happened to her,' Zoë says and Gwen nods, saying nothing. 'It must have been hard for you too.'

'Yes, but compared to what Justine went through, it seems horribly self-indulgent to admit it.'

'How did you . . . I mean . . . what happened to him? I suppose he went to prison.'

They've reached the rocks now and, almost in unison, settle on a low flat surface that forms a natural seat.

'No,' Gwen says. 'No, he didn't go to prison.' Her heart beats faster as the old fear grips her. She should have told Zoë sooner; it's not right that both Dan and Archie know the truth, when she doesn't. She can only excuse herself because Zoë had erected the barricades that had made disclosure impossible. 'Look, Zoë, I should have told you this before now, but things weren't all that easy at the start.'

Zoë's lips tighten and she nods. 'I know. My fault. I'm really sorry, Gwen. You know that, don't you?'

'Of course.' Gwen takes a deep breath. 'I'm not proud of this but, no, I didn't go to the police.'

'But wasn't he punished? He should have gone to jail. How could you . . .' she stops suddenly, seeing the look on Gwen's face. 'Sorry,' she says. 'Sorry, Gwen; go on, tell me what happened.'

Gwen is silent, screwing up her eyes against the sun. Telling Archie had proved surprisingly easy, but she had always known that it would be harder to tell another woman. 'When I discovered what he'd done to Justine, all I felt at first was horror, and guilt that I'd been so blind, that I was the sort of person who could have that happen under my nose and not even realise it. I knew he was violent, especially when he was drunk. A few years earlier, he'd beaten up a fourteen-year-old boy who'd worked for us. He was always rough with the men, and a couple of times he'd hit Gladys and, I'm ashamed to say, I'd let him get away with that. I got used to keeping the peace, I suppose. It was tough out there, intimidating, because although the farm belonged to me, Malcolm claimed it just by being married to me. For years I felt it was him and the men against me. But that day I drove back from the hospital, I knew I wasn't going to be intimidated anymore. I was determined to get him off the farm and out of my life, and to look after Justine.'

She hesitates briefly and then continues. 'Mal had been away buying stock. I didn't even know if he'd be back, but as I drove up, there he was, out on a stretch of cleared land near his office, playing cricket with his mate Greg. It was early evening and the rest of the men had gone down to Toodyay to a dance. I felt sick with anger when I saw him there, playing this stupid two-handed game, when Justine could have died because of him. As I got out of the car, he started yelling at me and I couldn't quite hear, so he yelled louder. "I hope you've taken that boong back to the nuns." Something exploded inside me then. I walked right up to him. He was sort of crouching over his bat, waiting for the next ball, and I grabbed the collar of his shirt and shoved my face into his and screamed at him to get out, get off my land or I'd call the police.' Gwen pauses, takes a deep breath, and shakes her head.

'He laughed at me, Zoë; can you believe it? He just stood there and laughed at me, and then he grabbed my wrist and sort of thrust me out of the way, and I tripped and fell. Well, he found that hilarious. He grabbed me by the arms and dragged me onto my feet, and put his face really close to mine. He was laughing still and gripping my upper arms, and then he suddenly kicked my legs from under me and I sort of staggered. He thought that was hilarious too and he kept holding me like that. I was blind with rage by then; I'd hit my head on a rock and I could feel blood trickling down my face. I struggled to get away from him but he was much stronger than me, so I spat in his face. He went berserk at that. He threw me back against the office wall.

'"You are such a fucking tight-arsed bitch," he said. "You think you're so much better than me; your father, he was the same. But I could kill you out here and no one would know. I could put my hands round your throat like this and strangle you, and in minutes you'd be dead."

'And he did it, just started to squeeze my throat really hard. I was choking and then I heard Greg yell at him. He ran at Mal and pulled him off me, and I fell on the ground. I was dizzy and my throat was burning and he came at me and kicked me several times until Greg pulled him off again. And then he swung round at Greg, and punched him in the face, and he went down.

'I was terrified, Zoë; I was sure he was going to kill me. I was struggling to get up and I saw the cricket bat on the ground where he'd dropped it. I grabbed it in both hands and swung it at him. I was quite strong in those days and I got him across the knees. I heard the crack and he just folded up on the ground, screaming with the pain and yelling that he'd have me arrested for assault.

'"And I'll have you arrested for rape," I said.

'"And who d'you think'll believe you and that dirty little whore?" he yelled.

'And I realised he was right. The police wouldn't care about a black child being raped, and I'd just be another victim of domestic violence and they might even say I provoked it. But a white woman smashing her husband's kneecaps with a cricket bat; well, that would really get them going.

'I felt an insane sort of rage at the thought of it, and started hitting him again on his legs and then on his hip . . .' She pauses. 'And then, as he tried to roll away, the bat caught him on the head. I'd like to say that I didn't mean that to happen; but it did and I didn't care. It was terrible, *I* was terrible. I wanted to kill him. But Greg was back on his feet, and he grabbed the bat and threw it out of reach. Mal was unconscious by then, and Greg's nose was bleeding and he had a split lip. I felt as though I'd been run over by a truck; the cut on my head was still bleeding, my throat was burning, and my ribs and back and legs where he'd kicked me were in agony, but I knew I was okay.'

'God, Gwen,' Zoë says. 'He really could have killed you. Whatever did you do?'

Gwen takes a deep breath and begins again. 'Greg sent me inside for some brandy to see if we could bring him round, but it was no good and he said he'd have to take him to hospital. We got a mattress and some blankets, and put them in the back of the pick-up and then we had to lift him onto them. Greg tied the bedding somehow so that it wouldn't slide about and tied the rope around Mal too so he wouldn't roll off. Then he went in and cleaned himself up a bit. I filled some water bags and put those and the brandy in the truck. Mal looked terrible and I was scared he was going to die. But, even then, I couldn't feel any remorse, only hatred, and fear about what this meant for me and Justine.

'"Stay here," Greg said, "and don't tell anyone what's happened, especially not the police. Stick that cricket bat in the furnace, and when the men come back, just tell them Mal's sick and I took him to hospital. Trust me," he said. "I'll fix it." His father had worked for mine for years, and Greg had started his working life on one of Dad's farms. He and I had known each other as children but when Mal came on the scene, I thought Greg had switched allegiances. But there wasn't much I *could* do *except* trust him. He told me to stay at the farm until he got back, and that it might be a few days.' She pauses, recalling the fear of the days that followed; waiting, unable to sleep or eat, alert to every sound, until, finally, almost a week later, she heard the sounds of the truck rattling back along the track.

'So, did he die?' Zoë asks.

Gwen shakes her head. 'Mal had multiple broken bones and damaged kidneys, but, worst of all, brain damage that meant he would spend the rest of his life as a vegetable. Greg had told the hospital that he had found Mal beaten up by the roadside. He managed everything: the hospital, the transfer to a nursing home, the arrangements for everything Mal needed. All I had to do was pay the bills. When I asked him why he was doing it, he said it was because my family had always treated him and his father with kindness and respect, and that Mal had only got what was coming to him. "If it hadn't been you, it would've been someone else," he said. "Every one of the blokes here, myself included, has dreamed of beating the living daylights out of him." So, I owe my own and Justine's freedom to him. I ended up putting the farm in his name. It seemed a small price to pay for what he'd done.'

There was a long silence. 'So, what happened to Mal?' Zoë asked eventually.

'He stayed in the nursing home and I just kept paying the bills. He died there, ten years later, from a chest infection that turned to pneumonia. Greg married and stayed at the farm, he and his wife are still there.' She hesitated, relaxing slightly now with the relief of having told her story. 'I'm not proud of it, Zoë. All I can say in my defence is that I believed I was fighting not just for myself but for Justine. I should have been punished for what I did, but by keeping quiet about it I was able to protect her.'

The breeze had dropped now, and the sun was sinking towards the horizon.

'You did what any mother would do, or want to do,' Zoë says. 'I know it was wrong, but no good would have come from you going to prison, only harm to you and to Justine.'

Gwen nods. 'I thought so too. And my remorse was really less about Mal than about the rest of it.'

'What do you mean?'

'The poison at the heart of it, the way things were, that made it possible for me to be blind to what was happening to a vulnerable child. You know what it was like growing up here back then. Aboriginal people were nothing. When I saw Justine at the convent, I saw something in her that I thought would fill a gap in my life, so I decided I would give her a home. I'm ashamed of that now, it sounds like I was choosing a dog from the pound, but that was the way I'd been brought up. All those children were in misery but I decided to single one out and justified it by telling myself I could give her a better life. But, in my arrogance and ignorance, I ended up letting her down in the worst possible way.'

'I doubt that's how Justine sees it,' Zoë says.

'It's not. It wasn't how Norah saw it either, but, in the end, Zoë, as I'm sure you know only too well, it's not what other people think that eats away at you. It's what you think about yourself.'

Zoë looks at her for what seems like a long time.

'Yes,' she says eventually. 'Of course.'

The water is still as they wander back along the beach. There are fewer people around now; families are heading home for tea and the sunlight has softened.

'What you've told me, Gwen,' Zoë says, 'sounds so terrifying. The knowledge of what you'd done and the fear of being found out must have haunted you.'

'It changed me,' Gwen says. 'It was like an end to innocence, and I cut myself off from other people. I didn't dare to have friends in case I let slip anything that might make them ask questions. I suppose we all live with the burdens of our misdemeanours, but some are larger than others. What matters is what we do with the experience. I've had a hard time convincing myself that it's over; a hard time leaving it behind, I suppose.'

Zoë nods, wondering as they walk on how much of who she is now is still tethered to the past – to Eileen's rules and expectations, and to her own inability to consign her past to history.

When they get back Eileen is in the kitchen making a pot of tea. Rosie is feeding Harry pureed banana, while Justine is checking the state of the turkey.

'Beautiful,' she says. 'It'll be just right for seven o'clock. Perfect timing, Zoë.'

'Gabs rang, Mum,' Rosie says. 'I told her you'd ring her back. Oh, yuk! Don't spit it back at me, Harry.'

'Is she okay?' Zoë asks. 'Is she enjoying herself?'

'Oh yes,' Archie says, coming in from the verandah. 'Gaby's having a wonderful time.'

Zoë smiles. 'I'm so glad. I knew she'd love Julia and Tom. I'll ring her now.'

'Do call,' Archie says, with an uncharacteristic edge to his voice. 'And she can tell you all about it; how lovely Julia is, how funny and clever Tom is, but, most of all, Zoë, she can tell you how amazingly brilliant and totally awesome your ex-husband is. Not only is our daughter spending Christmas with him, it seems she's *also* going to *work* for him.'

'Not actually for *him*, I don't think, Dad,' Rosie cuts in nervously, one eye on Harry, the other on her father. 'I think it's some company that he owns part of, or something.'

'Yes,' Archie says, his voice rising now. 'Or something – who knows what it might be, with that bastard behind it.' And he picks up the tray of champagne glasses and walks out to the table on the verandah; there is a crash as two, or possibly more, glasses fail to survive their landing on the table. There is silence in the kitchen and the women, with the exception of Eileen, whose poor hearing has caused her to miss this, look awkwardly at each other.

Zoë raises her eyebrows and shrugs. 'Male menopause, maybe?' she says. And they all return to what they are doing.

2002

FORTY-THREE

Rye – New Year's Day 2002

While he waits for Richard to finish checking his email, Tom looks in the pantry for the ingredients for the chickpea and cauliflower curry he is planning for dinner. He has promised to make it for Gaby, who said it sounded delicious. He makes a list of the things he needs to buy for the curry and the cucumber raita, and for the lemon tart that will be the perfect dessert. He enjoys this sort of domestic pottering, always has done, as long as it's directed towards a goal. Interestingly, he thinks, he always achieves his culinary goals, unlike certain other works in progress.

Julia loves the curry too, although Tom knows that he will have a battle to stop her polluting it with some of the left-over turkey she has squirrelled away. If he has to eat another mouthful of dead bird, he's sure he'll suffer from fowl poisoning. She'd taken some out of the fridge that morning and left it to defrost on the draining board.

'You and Richard can have it in sandwiches for lunch,' she'd said. 'Nice and easy, and it'll get rid of some of it.'

She has taken Gaby to Brighton for the first of the New Year sales. It's madness, of course. Julia is not much of a shopper; she hates crowds and particularly hates clothing boutiques. But she seems to have got into some girlie thing with Gaby; there have been a lot of whispered conversations and giggling. It is, Tom thinks, Julia's curiosity about motherhood. These days, she's prone to sigh and say that she sometimes thinks it would be nice to have had a daughter to chat to.

Tom, as usual, works to his own musical accompaniment; this morning, it is a selection of hymns. He began in populist mode with 'Lord of the Dance', then ripped into the tough stuff, 'Onward Christian Soldiers' and 'The Church's One Foundation', and he's halfway through a stirring rendition of 'Jerusalem' when Richard appears in the kitchen, grimacing.

'Okay,' Tom says. 'I know you're not fond of hymns.'

'No. Nor god, actually,' Richard says. 'Although I know you still hold a warm spot in your heart for him.'

'I do, indeed,' Tom says. 'He, or possibly she, is a good bloke to have around.'

'Amazing,' Richard says, shaking his head. 'It confounds all reason.'

Tom smiles benignly and unhooks his jacket from the back of the door. 'That, my friend, is part of the attraction. It's not necessary for everything to be explained by reason, and we all have our gods.'

'I don't,' Richard says.

And Tom laughs out loud.

'Why are you laughing?'

Tom nudges the plastic crate of empty wine and whisky bottles with his toe.

'I just enjoy a drink or two,' Richard says petulantly.

'Which is why I'm surprised that you've never been drawn to a bloke who turns water into wine. Come on, let's go. I want to pop into the delicatessen in the High Street.' He picks up the plastic-wrapped frozen turkey from the draining board and they step out into the street.

'Why are we taking the turkey with us?' Richard asks. 'Are you planning a picnic?'

'I'm planning a pie and a pint at the pub for lunch,' Tom says. 'The turkey is going in the first bin we come to and we're going to tell Julia that it made delicious sandwiches.'

'It couldn't go in the bin at home?'

'Absolutely not. She'd sniff it out. You know what a fascist she is when it comes to using up leftovers.'

It is hard to walk on the cobbles because even the midday sunshine hasn't been enough to melt the ice. Everything is moving slowly this morning, and people feel their way cautiously along the walls in the mistaken hope that this proximity will lessen the impact of a fall. They totter flat-footed across the street, eyes fixed on the ground, and couples try to decide whether it's safer or more hazardous to hold hands. By the time they reach the High Street, Tom and Richard have helped an elderly woman into the bookshop, and rescued a much younger one, whose frenetic pace had been so unsuited to the conditions that, laden with bags of shopping, she had skidded off the pavement into the street and landed on her bottom in the path of a slow-moving car.

'We're heroes this morning, aren't we,' Tom says, 'rescuing women in distress and the like. Robin Hood-ish.'

'Or Batman and Robin,' Richard says. 'Who next will benefit from our courage and resourcefulness?' At which point, he slips, skids rapidly towards the wall of the bank and grasps at a passing teenager dressed in black leather and with multiple piercings.

'Gerroff, pervert,' the boy yells and shakes himself free, and Richard turns gingerly so that he is back facing in the right direction.

'I think we may have done our dash,' he says.

And Tom, grinning, leads the way into the supermarket.

Richard, still shaken from his near miss with the paving stones, watches as Tom, glasses perched on the end of his nose, browses the shelves. What must it be like, he wonders, to live your life with someone who knows exactly who you are and loves you just the same? If only, he thinks, recalling the dilemma he had struggled with at the time of his marriage to Zoë, if only he had known then what the really important things in life were. If only he had learned it in time to save his marriage to Lily.

'You're a lucky bugger, you know,' he says to Tom as they wait at the checkout. 'I know Jules is a pain in the arse sometimes, but you two have really got it together.'

'Not for want of trying,' Tom says. 'It's a cliché but you really do have to work at it, and both of us have.'

'And it's obviously been worth it. Love, companionship, a meeting of minds.'

'And lots of sex.'

'Whoa!' Richard says. 'She's my sister, remember.'

Tom pays for the food with a grin that can only be described as smug and they slither cautiously along the street to the pub.

'What about you, then?' Tom asks as they lean against the bar. 'You and Bea?'

Richard shrugs. 'Who knows? She's a terrific woman and we get along well, but you reach a point where you wonder whether you can actually handle the risk of trying to take it further; whether you have the emotional stamina.'

'You mean it takes more emotional stamina to be with someone than to be alone?'

'Yes. For me it does, anyway,' Richard says, taking a long swig of his beer. 'I've never been good at it. And Bea, lovely as she is . . . the chemistry may not be great enough to justify the risk. Same goes for her, I think.'

Tom studies his Guinness. 'Perhaps it's foolish to think you can get all your emotional and companionship needs met by one person, especially at this age.'

'Maybe,' Richard shrugs.

'Julia wants you to be madly, irresistibly in love with Bea.'

He shakes his head. 'Not going to happen.' He pauses. '"*No love beckons me save that which I've forsaken; the anguish of my solitude is sweet.*"'

'Who's that?' Tom says with a frown, 'I haven't heard it before.'

'Robert Mitchum.'

'No, seriously.'

'It is. It's Robert Mitchum, he wrote it to a girl when he was fifteen.'

'Pity he didn't keep writing. So, I suppose this is about Zoë?'

''Fraid so, last year made that very clear to me. But, clearly, it's not going to go anywhere at all.'

'Look, Rich, I didn't know you or Zoë back then, but, from what Jules has told me not a lot has changed. The things that frustrated you then are still the same. She's not like Lily, politically driven, passionately involved in causes, fiercely independent. Zoë's not interested in the things that drive you.'

'No. But just before Daniel was born, I was learning that if you love someone you have to accept them as they are.' He stops and looks into his empty glass. 'And then . . . well, Daniel was born, I lost it . . . and when I realised what I'd lost, it was too late.'

They drink in silence for a few moments, watching the flow of customers in and out, the dancing flames in the fire.

'Rich,' Tom says eventually. 'You're going to need to be careful around Gaby.'

'Gaby? Why? My intentions are entirely honourable. She's lovely, very smart. You know, Tom, she is *so* much like Zoë, and yet she's tall. I look at her and think, if Zoë and I had had a daughter, she could have been just like Gaby.'

'Well, she's *not* your daughter,' Tom says. 'Are you sure that offering her that job was wise?'

'Why not? She wants a job, and she's just what Gilbert and Linton Productions needs. It'll be a break for her; she'll go far. I can help her and keep an eye on her too.'

'She's here for less than a year, before she goes to university.'

'I doubt it, she's a London sort of girl . . .'

'Hang on. This might not be such a good idea.'

'Jules told you to talk to me, didn't she?'

Tom shakes his head. 'She hasn't even mentioned it.'

'I can't see why it should be a problem. Why don't you trust me on this?'

'Simply because of that,' Tom says. 'Simply because you can't see a potential problem and so you can't be trusted not to create chaos. Your friendships and relationships always flounder on the rocks of your own, very singular, view, Richard. You are so full of good intentions but so totally unaware of the bigger picture.'

'But that's what I do – the bigger picture, making connections, showing how things come together. That's why I've been successful.'

Tom groans. 'Professionally, but that's not what we're talking about. You crash through your personal life, bumping into people and grabbing hold of them to steady you, like you skidded into Metal Man and grabbed him this morning, then you crash off somewhere else, leaving a trail of destruction. The fact that *you* can't see a problem doesn't mean there isn't, or won't be, one. Don't stuff this up for Gaby, for Zoë, for Zoë's seemingly very nice husband, or for yourself.' Tom gets to his feet and feels in his pocket for cash.

Richard looks up at him. 'You're saying I'm emotionally selfish and arrogant.'

Tom raises his eyebrows and shrugs. 'Another pint?'

'Yes,' Richard nods. 'Please, and another chaser.'

⌘

The sales are unbelievably awful; the ferocity with which the women storm the shops, rip garments from the hands of friends and strangers, and yell at sales assistants makes Julia ashamed of her sex. She is numb with horror and they've only been in Primark for five minutes. Knowing she has only herself to blame doesn't help. In the ten days since Gaby's arrival, it's been like having an ally in the house against Tom and Richard always ganging up to tease her. In four more days, Gaby will be going back to London, so she wants to make the most of it. Making the most of it, though, has led her into this New Year sales folly.

'The sales start tomorrow, Gaby,' she'd said last night. 'I was wondering if you'd like to go.'

To which Gaby had looked up from the chess game she was playing with Tom and said, 'Yeah! That'd be cool.'

'You must be totally insane,' Tom had said later as she climbed into bed. 'You'll loathe it.'

'I know,' she said. 'I got carried away. But it's the sort of thing young women love.'

'Really? She didn't seem that keen to me; in fact, I thought she was agreeing in order to please you.'

'Rubbish. She said it'd be cool.'

'Yes, but if she'd really wanted to go, wouldn't she have

suggested it? Or at least said it would be awesome?'

'Oh Lord,' Julia said. 'I don't know. You mean, I could be doing this for no good reason? Well, too late now; I can hardly renege on it, in case you're wrong.'

She looks now at Gaby who has made a brave initial foray into the scrum beneath a sign that offers a fifty per cent reduction on hipster jeans. She emerges unscathed but with an expression that indicates she knows she's had a narrow escape.

'Find anything?' Julia asks, hoping she sounds enthusiastic.

Gaby shakes her head. 'This is totally vomit-making,' she says. 'I've never been to the sales before.'

Julia grabs her arm and pulls her out of the path of new and vigorous shoppers flooding through the doors. 'I thought you'd be an old hand at this.'

'No way, I can't do the crowd thing. I'm the only one of all my friends who never even goes to the Big Day Out.'

Julia stares at her. 'So, why did we come?'

'Oh, I thought you wanted me to keep you company,' Gaby says.

Julia is out of the exit, dragging Gaby behind her, almost before she has time to draw breath. 'I only suggested it because I thought you'd be pining to do the sales.'

They lean against the wall outside laughing. 'We could do something else, if you like. There's everything in Brighton, from high culture to sleaze.'

'Great,' Gaby says. 'Could we go to that pier we drove past? I've never been on a pier, not a huge one with stuff on it like that.'

The wind on the pier feels as though it has come straight from the Arctic Circle rather than from across the Channel, but it's wonderfully bracing with the briny scent of the sea seasoned with the aroma of fried onions from the hot dog stand. Hands buried in their pockets, Julia and Gaby stroll up one side of the pier, the wind tugging at their scarves, past the various attractions, many of which are closed. There is a clairvoyant in residence but a peek through the gap in the curtains of the booth reveals a raddled woman with bright-orange hair, wearing a pink velvet tracksuit, and an atmosphere thick with tobacco smoke. It does not inspire confidence in a connection with the spirit world. But there is a courageous lone entrepreneur running the shooting gallery and they hand over what seems to Julia to be an exorbitant number of pound coins.

'You first,' Gaby says.

Julia lines up the ducks in her sights and manages to knock off four.

'You're a really good shot,' Gaby says, positioning herself behind the rifle. 'I'll probably be hopeless, I've never done this before.' And she proceeds to fire rapidly and wipes out the whole complement of ducks. 'I can't believe I did that,' she says, as they walk away. She is clutching her prize, which is a blue plush elephant the size of a healthy toddler. 'I wonder if I could send this to Harry. I have a huge pink teddy Dan bought me for my birthday. You know, I read a book about Brighton once, it was called *Brighton Rock*, about teddy boys with flick knives; can we go and see The Lanes?'

'We certainly can, we could have lunch there,' Julia says, and they walk back down the pier. 'I used to come here years ago,' she says looking out over the beach. 'When I was engaged to Simon, and Zoë was with Richard. We'd drive down from London early in the evenings, it would have been late September. It was warm; well, not what *you'd* call warm, but a sort of Indian summer until the middle of October. See that pub over there? We'd go there for a drink first and then, as it was getting dark, we'd come down here and get our gear off and go swimming.'

'Swimming?' Gaby is horrified. 'Off that stony beach?'

'Oh, I know it's nothing compared with your beaches,' Julia says with a laugh, 'but Zoë put up with it quite well. We had such a good time.'

'Did you swim in the nude?'

'God no, wouldn't have dared, not even in the dark. We'd just swim and then lie on the beach and snog, admittedly not in the height of comfort. Then we'd go and get fish and chips, and eat them on one of those seats on the promenade.' She laughs. 'Those simple things seem so precious when you look back on them. I wish we'd had more time together, Zoë and I. We got on so well and then, of course, I got married and went to Paris. And then Zoë had Daniel and it was all over.'

'Have you got any photos?' Gaby asks. 'Of all of you then and of Mum and Richard?'

'Yes, quite a few. But you've probably seen them all, they'd be much the same as Zoë's.'

'Mum threw hers away when she moved home to Australia, dumped everything. How annoying is that? She doesn't even have a wedding photo.'

'I have one,' Julia says. 'Several, I think, and I even know where they are. When we get home, I'll find them for you. Meanwhile, maybe we should buy a postcard of Brighton and send it to Zoë. You don't think she and Archie will mind you working for Richard, do you?'

'Dad was a bit off about it,' Gaby says. 'But he's a bit off about everything at the moment. He's – well, I just need to find a way of reassuring him about something. Mum thought it was great, though. I think she thinks Richard'll look out for me.'

'I'm sure he will. We all will.'

'Yeah, thanks. But you know Mum, she was worried I'd get into trouble, be exploited, get bullied or get transported somewhere as a sex slave.'

'Strange how history repeats itself,' Julia says. 'Zoë used to say something similar about her own mother.'

Gaby laughs. 'I know, she told me, but the weird thing is, Mum actually thinks she's really different from Gran. She is in some ways; I mean, Gran's really critical and . . . bitter, I think. Mum's not like that. But she's always worried about stuff; you know, us getting into trouble, what people will think, whether she's doing the right thing, whether people disapprove of her. All the stuff she says drove her mad about Gran when she was young. Did you know that Gran never let her have friends over to visit? Mum hasn't got friends; only Aunty Jane, of course. She *knows* heaps of people but it's like she's scared of letting people in. Weird – parents are totally weird. Aren't you glad you're not one?'

'A lot of the time, I am,' Julia says, pushing open the door to a restaurant squeezed between an antique shop and a place that sells everything occult. 'But since you arrived, I've been unattractively envious.'

FORTY-FOUR

Fremantle – February 2002

Gaby's letter is among the mail in the letterbox when Zoë gets home at dusk from her art class. It's Friday and she has the house to herself for the weekend. Archie is away at some corporate team-building weekend, and Rosie is up at the winery with Rob. These days she is alone in the house far more frequently than she used to be and she's grown to enjoy these little oases of solitude that would, not so long ago, have seemed bleak and lonely. A whole weekend to herself to work at her painting now seems like a luxury. She wonders, fleetingly, how Archie is getting on. Maybe the weekend away will do him good; this strange low-spirited phase of his has been going on for too long and Zoë can't get to the bottom of it. After his dummy spit on Christmas afternoon, she'd felt guilty that she'd laughed about male menopause. He'd been so good to her when she was panicky and depressed, but now he's battling with something and won't talk about it.

The empty house makes her more acutely aware of Dan's absence. It's a few weeks since they heard from him and, while she knows that no news may only be a sign that he's now somewhere out of communications reach, it's not conducive to peace of mind. There have been stories on the news about the Australian troops being poorly equipped, and the government has been criticised for their inadequate cold-weather gear. In the mountains the temperatures apparently drop to a long way below freezing. In the searing heat of a West Australian summer, it is almost impossible to imagine what it is like to live in those temperatures. Zoë tries not to think about the awfulness of it because she knows it can overwhelm her.

She thumbs through the mail; there is a renewal notice from the insurance company, an electricity bill, and this letter from Gaby. What a treat. They mainly send emails or texts, and Zoë phones Gaby, hoping when she does that her daughter doesn't dread her calls, as she had dreaded talking to Eileen all those years ago. She makes her tea, sits down at the table and slits open Gaby's envelope.

Hi Mum

I meant to send you these photos weeks ago, like right after New Year when Julia gave them to me but I put them in the envelope and then forgot. She's got heaps so she gave me these, and I thought you'd want to see them. But you are NOT allowed to throw them away. If you don't want them I DO, so just keep them for me.

The wedding one is so dire, isn't it? You all look as though you're on your way to a funeral, and I think Julia's hat is worse than yours and so does she. You and Richard look so young! What's wrong with your face, it looks odd, as though you had a cut on your head? Had you fallen over or something? Richard got quite upset when I asked him, he walked out and went to the pub!

I LOVE working in the production company, it's cool and I've met this guy who works for the BBC. His name's Brad and I might have to lift the boyfriend ban!!!! I am having such a brilliant time, London just gets better every day. I almost don't notice the weather (lies!). Gloria sends her love,

Heaps of love to everyone and don't forget to text me the minute you hear from Dan.

Love, love, love

Gaby xxxxxxxxxxxxxxxxxxxxxxxx

Zoë picks up the envelope of photos. Does she really want to see these pictures? She could take them straight down to Gaby's room and put them in her desk drawer without looking at them. She opens the envelope.

There are five photographs, their age apparent from the yellowish tinge and faded colours. In the first, she is standing in front of one of the lions in Trafalgar Square, wearing a red coat and long black boots. Her face is screwed up with anxiety, and several pigeons are perched on her outstretched arms, one on her shoulder, close to her face. The memory of it makes her shiver; she hates birds.

'Stand there,' Richard had said, 'and I'll take your picture. Put your arms out and see if the pigeons will sit on them.'

The angry darting eyes, the vicious-looking claws and beaks made Zoë's flesh creep. The pigeon on her shoulder was so close she could feel the warmth of its body on her cheek and she was rigid with revulsion; but this was her first date with Richard and she didn't want him to think her silly. He took ages adjusting the camera, and when the picture was finally taken and she was allowed to move, the birds took off in a horrible flapping of wings that made her flinch and shudder.

In the next picture, she and Richard are in a pub somewhere – Brighton, perhaps – with Julia and Simon. Zoë is struck by how handsome Simon looks, like some Nordic film star, and how dowdy Julia looks, with that awful bob and velvet headband. Julia is no fashion plate these days but she has a certain eccentric style, and her face is thinner, which gives her features greater definition. She has definitely improved with age.

And then there it is – an exact replica of the picture she burned more than thirty years ago. It is a cold, grey day; she is standing with Richard on the steps of the registry office. Richard's suit is a little too big on the shoulders, and she is in her lavender dress and the hat she'd thought might look a little Jackie Kennedy-ish and doesn't. Her left arm is tucked into Richard's, which he holds awkwardly rigid across his body. In her other hand is the bouquet Julia made for her.

It is all there; the bruises on her face, the furrow of anxiety between her eyebrows, the tension in her shoulders, the fixed stare that Richard is giving the camera. She looks at the photo for a long time and, as she does so, her body seems to take on the tension it has in the picture. Gaby is right – they look incredibly young and very scared, which is just how she remembers it. A big lump is building in her throat and she stiffly puts the picture aside to look at the next one, also taken on the steps. In it her arm is still through Richard's, his face now a little more relaxed, and behind them are Julia and Simon, Sandy and, at the end of the line, Harry, smiling his broad smile straight into the camera. She stares into his face. It is just like looking at Dan and tears drop onto the back of her hand. She sees in Harry what she has always remembered about him; his warmth and energy, his wisdom, his capacity for love and his determination to make the best of every day.

Zoë brushes away the tears and moves on to the final photograph, in which she and Richard are cutting their cake, and there again is Harry, standing just off to one side, looking at them with the air of a benevolent uncle. And amid the turmoil of emotions that the photographs have stirred, there is a fragment of joy. Dan will, at last, be able to see what his father looked like. How selfish she had been in depriving him of that chance in order to rid herself of painful memories. She sits for a long time at the table looking at the pictures, picking them up, putting them down and picking them up again. Finally, as she groups them back together, she takes one last look at the wedding picture. And, as she looks at her face, at her anxiety, awkwardness and vulnerability, the knot of grief that has built in her chest becomes great gulping sobs. Sinking her head into her hands, she weeps, not for the loss of Richard, or of Harry, but for her young, naïve, frightened self, for the loss of innocence and opportunity, and for the length of time she allowed herself to feel like a victim. Eventually, she puts the pictures back in their envelope and, as she carries her cup back to the sink, the phone rings.

'Zoë, it's me.' Justine's voice wavers uncharacteristically.

Zoë's heart leaps into her throat. 'What's happened?'

'Nothing, it's not that . . . it's just . . . I'm so frightened, Zoë. I thought I knew how to do this and I don't. Could you . . .'

'Of course. I'll be there in twenty minutes.'

Five minutes later as she is about to leave, Zoë turns back, puts the envelope of photographs into her bag and heads for the front door.

～～

Justine slides down the wall and sits on the floor, the phone still in her hand. She folds her arms over her knees, and rests her head on them, regretting the call. What will Zoë think of her? What will they have to say to each other? But Gwen is visiting a friend in Tasmania, and it's weeks since they've had news of Dan. Justine's tension has cracked her resolve and she is compelled to reach out to the one person with whom she can share her misery in this lonely vacuum where she has no control over anything, most of all her own imagination. Frantically, she tries to drag her mind back to images of Dan safe at home, and memories of the sound of his voice calling from the garden, his laughter as he holds Harry high above his head, the way he turns to look at her when she calls his name, the scent of his skin, the feel of his body warm beside her in bed, his arms around her. Before he left, he recorded himself reading nursery rhymes and stories for her to play to Harry at bedtime. She frequently plays these herself as she tries to sleep, but recently each attempt to recapture Dan is nudged aside by images of him facing terrorist gunfire, crushed under the ruins of a bombed building, tied and blindfolded with a knife at his throat, or losing consciousness, his face encrusted with ice.

The doorbell rings and she struggles to her feet. Zoë's face is pinched and white, and her eyes are red. They face each other wordlessly across the threshold; their eyes locked in a moment of profound understanding that they have never previously shared. Justine's hand drops from the door handle and she holds it over her mouth. Zoë takes a step inside, puts her arms around her and, as the door swings shut, they stand there, locked together in their distress.

It is hard to begin with; they are not used to being alone, to talking intimately. Justine feels that Zoë must think her pathetic to crack up like this when she herself has been coping with these terrifying absences for years, and embarrassment silences her. She hopes that Harry will wake up so that they can focus on him.

'I'm sorry . . .' she begins, but Zoë stops her.

'No,' she says, 'please don't. You can't know how many times I've wanted to call you since Dan left, how many times I've picked up the phone and put it down. It is such a relief to be able to share this with you.'

'But you have Archie.'

'Yes, and he's wonderful, but for us, for the women, it's always different.'

'I feel angry that I know so little,' Justine says. 'How far they might be from anywhere, what it's like, how it all works; it's a horrible, frightening mystery.'

'I've felt that so many times,' Zoë says, 'but, you know, I'm not sure it would be any better if we knew the details. The reality is that Dan may just be out of contact for the simplest practical reasons or for the worst of reasons. All we can do is wait and hope.'

Justine nods. 'I'm letting him down. I thought I was strong enough.'

'You *are*, Justine,' Zoë says, and moves over to sit beside her on the sofa. 'You *are* strong enough. So strong that at first I was scared of you and wanted you to go away. Now I couldn't want a stronger, finer woman for my son or mother for my grandson. But being strong doesn't stop you hurting, or being driven insane by the silence. You are more than strong enough, and stronger still now that you can face the fear and share it.'

Justine thinks she may never stop crying; every time she feels it ending, it begins again. Zoë sits beside her, an arm around her shoulders, not speaking, rocking her gently. Eventually, when the crying does stop, Zoë reaches into her bag and takes out an envelope.

'Look at this,' she says, 'it's a good omen, I'm sure.'

Justine studies the faded photograph of a group of strangers standing on some steps. 'What is it . . . a wedding?'

Zoë nods. 'It's my wedding to Richard, but it's more than that – much more. Dry your eyes properly, so you can see. There, standing just behind me, it's Harry. After all these years, Dan can see what his father looked like.'

'He's exactly like him,' Justine says, peering into the picture. 'It's uncanny.'

'I know. I always told Dan that but I don't think he really believed me. But you can see it; the eyes, the smile, even the way he's standing.'

'He's beautiful,' Justine says, smiling at her.

'Yes. Harry didn't even know he had a son and now he has a grandson. He died when he was younger than Dan is now. And, you know, Justine, when I saw this photograph today, for the first time in more than thirty years, it seemed like an omen, a good one. I can't believe that Dan won't be back to see it. And, meanwhile, we can do this together, the waiting, the believing. That's all we have to do, you and I, just wait and believe.'

༺༻

When Archie gets home on Sunday afternoon, Zoë has gone to an exhibition with friends from her art class and Justine is in the kitchen icing her legendary coffee and walnut cake. The smell greets him as he pops his head around the door.

'To die for,' he says, sniffing loudly and she looks around.

'Hi, Arch; you can have some while it's still warm. How was the team-building thing?'

'Full of American pop psychology and embarrassing aphorisms,' he says. 'Nauseating. Are you okay? Zo told me about Friday.'

She looks awkward. 'I'm fine now, but I fell apart and Zoë put me back together. If it's okay with you, Harry and I are staying until Gwen gets back.'

Archie puts his briefcase on a chair and hugs her. 'Of course it's okay,' he says. 'This is where you should be. Falling apart can be a good thing. Too much being brave wears you down. I'll just go and change.' And, undoing his shirt, he pads wearily to the bedroom. He can't remember when he last felt so low on energy and his blood pressure is up. The doctor, whom he finally agreed to see after much nagging from Zoë, has told him he is suffering from stress and exhaustion, and needs to take a proper holiday.

'I made you some tea,' Justine says as he wanders back into the kitchen. 'You don't look too good.'

'Just tired,' he says. 'What are these?' He shuffles through the photographs on the table. 'Stone the crows – is this Zoë's wedding to Richard?'

Justine puts a mug of tea and an extremely large slice of cake in front of him, and joins him at the table. 'Yes. Julia gave them to Gaby, and Gaby sent them on. Look, that's Harry.'

'So it is,' Archie says quietly, studying the pictures. 'It could be Dan standing there, couldn't it? I've never seen a father and son look so alike.' He takes a sip of his tea. 'So, Dan will see his father at last; he'll be over the moon.' He spreads out the pictures, looking now not at Harry but at Zoë and Richard. Imagination does strange things, Archie thinks; he has always imagined Richard as the villain of the piece, larger, powerful – menacing, even. What he sees now is a young bloke, not yet thirty, in an ill-fitting suit, with shoulder-length hair, looking absolutely bloody terrified. Archie stares at the photograph, trying to see around and beyond this fraction of a second into the man himself, the person Richard was.

'He's scared,' he says softly, 'floundering.'

Justine puts her hand on his shoulder and leans against him. 'They both are; look at Zoë, she looks about twelve.'

Archie sighs. 'She does indeed, and they both look as though they'd rather be anywhere else than there.' He picks up the picture of the cake cutting and holds it closer. Even here the facial expressions and body language speak of two fearful, unhappy people caught in a painful trap. 'Bloody hell,' he says, looking at Justine. 'I never thought of Richard like that, I had him down as some sort of monstrous playboy.'

Justine laughs. 'I suppose you'd still like to catch him unawares and king-hit him?'

'Too right,' Archie says and it surprises him that he says it with a laugh. 'As far as I'm concerned, he remains the unforgiven.'

'That's so unlike you, Arch. And, anyway, it's not for you to forgive.'

He turns to look at her. 'What do you mean?'

'Well, it's for Zoë to forgive Richard, and vice versa. It's nothing to do with you.'

Archie feels himself bristling but is stuck for a response.

She pushes the cake closer to him. 'Eat it while it's warm,' she says. 'You love Zoë to bits, and you've been a wonderful father to Dan, but that doesn't give you ownership of what happened before you came on the scene. That's Zoë's; hers and Richard's.'

Archie looks at her for a long moment, and then takes a sip of his tea. 'I still want to king-hit him.'

Justine rolls her eyes and grins. 'Whatever. That feeling is yours, but forgiveness is Zoë's, and she's done that, hasn't she?'

'Has she?'

'Oh, I think so. I mean, when she came back from her holiday it was obvious she'd sorted something out, something big. And, anyway, she said something the other night –'

'What did she say?' Archie cuts in, his voice breaking with urgency.

Justine pulls back a little and looks at him.

'She hasn't told me anything about what happened between them,' he goes on. 'Nothing more than she told us all when she got back.'

'No,' Justine says, 'because she thinks you don't want to know, don't want her to talk about it.'

He's silent for a moment. 'I only want her to tell me what I want to hear. I'm frightened of hearing anything that . . .' he stops, unable to go on.

'There's nothing you wouldn't want to hear, Arch. Just ask her.'

'Too big a risk.'

'The risk you're taking is *not* asking and letting yourself believe that the "monster" of your imaginings still has some sort of hold on Zoë.'

'Zoë's been dragging this stuff around with her ever since I've known her,' Archie says irritably, 'you can't say it didn't have a hold on her.'

'But it's not Richard who had that hold,' Justine says. 'He was . . . well, a symbol, I suppose. The ball and chain Zoë's been wearing isn't some unrequited longing for Richard; not even any great curiosity about him, I don't think. She didn't even want to see him but she did, and she saw Julia, and that resolved it. She'd done what you're doing, really. Created them into monsters in her imagination, but they were young too. The three of them – four, if you count Harry – they all made mistakes, which had really awful consequences. Zoë's ball and chain has been her own shame. But it's over now, so why are you still stuck with it?'

Archie rests his chin on the palm of his hand, using his fingers to cover his lips, which are trembling. 'I thought . . .' he begins and then shakes his head. 'It doesn't matter.' He gives her a shaky smile and puts his arm around her shoulders. 'Thanks.'

'Eat your cake,' she says, 'or I'll be insulted. And Zoë said to tell you that when she gets back, which will actually be any time now, she wants an answer about the holiday. And "too busy" is not an option.'

∽∾∾

Richard is watchful and just a little resentful. He's fond of Brad McCarthy, whose father he worked with for a while in the seventies, and thinks he can see in Brad something of himself when young. Not that they are physically alike, no; it's the passion, the muscular mind, the feverish ambition and the streak of bloody-mindedness. But at the moment, he's mildly less fond of Brad than he has been. He and Gaby have been going out together since January, since the day Richard took her with him to a post-production party and within the first half hour, she was dancing with Brad. They've been joined at the hip ever since. Richard knows it shouldn't bother him; Brad is a young man who most fathers would welcome, and it's not even as though he's Gaby's father. It is his own feelings about the past that are bugging him, as each time he sees them together he sees himself and Zoë. But Gaby, while she looks very much like her mother, knows what she wants and she is driven by the same fierce intelligence and passion that drives Brad. Anyone else would say they are made for each other, but Richard can't quite make himself say that. He first has to cut through a skein of longing that he is still not ready to sever.

'It's not your business, Rich,' Julia says, as they sit in a Greek restaurant in Hampstead, having earlier caught up with Gaby and

Brad in a wine bar. 'You're just a friend and her employer; don't overstep the boundaries. Brad's great, they're in love. Be happy for them.'

'Yes, butt out,' says Tom. 'Not that you have butted in yet, but I can see you're itching to. Though goodness knows why; if Gaby were my daughter, I'd be delighted if she came home with someone like Brad.'

'I *am* delighted,' Richard says grudgingly. 'Sort of. Most of me is delighted, but there's just a bit that isn't. Each time I look at them, I see Zoë and me. I want to warn them of the pitfalls, manage the whole thing.'

'Christ almighty!' Julia says. 'You are so up yourself. Manage it and stuff it up for them in the process. They are not remotely like you and Zoë, except that Gaby *looks* a lot like her mother. You may find this hard to believe but not everything in the world revolves around you, Richard.'

'She's right,' Tom says. 'Not subtle, but right. Put your own emotional house in order and don't start messing around in theirs.'

'Okay, okay,' Richard says, throwing up his hands. 'Lay off me. I'll be out of the way soon, anyway. All the partners in the Indonesian project have signed on the dotted line, so I'll be off to Jakarta next month. That should keep me out of trouble.'

But even the prospect of this new documentary is not enough to distract Richard from his turbulent emotions. And, to make it worse, he has let the nursing home know that he'll be down there the following day to see his father. It's not a prospect he relishes.

When he sets out it's a cool showery morning. The traffic moving south from London is particularly slow; there seem to be endless roadworks and temporary traffic lights. Drumming his fingers impatiently on the steering wheel, he wonders why he is even bothering. Ralph, he thinks, has no idea who he is on these occasional visits on which Richard wheels him around the garden and tries to involve him in conversation. Even so, he doesn't feel he can stop going; something urges him to try to achieve a breakthrough, to get his father to communicate with him.

He arrives feeling even more grumpy than usual, the drive having taken almost twice as long as it should. He sits for a while in the car park, taking several swigs from his flask and trying to get himself in a better frame of mind.

'He's the same with me,' Julia has told him many times. 'No sign of recognition, not a flicker. Don't take it so personally.'

Ralph is in his wheelchair in the television room, parked in front of some midday quiz show. He is wearing a tweed jacket and a shirt that Julia bought for him recently in Marks & Spencer. He seems to have shrunk; the jacket droops over his shoulders and the shirt is loose around the collar. He is hunched, as though he has sunk further into his chair, as though his head is too heavy for his neck.

'Hello, Dad,' Richard says, putting his hand on his father's arm. 'Thought I'd pop in and see you. Sorry I haven't been for a while. Pretty busy; well, you know what it's like. You were always busy, weren't you?' He starts to unpack the carrier bag he's brought with him. 'I thought we'd better stock up on some of your favourites,' he says, with the superficial cheeriness that characterises most of his attempts to connect with Ralph. 'Licorice Allsorts, barley sugar, wine gums.'

There is no answer, but Ralph turns his head slightly and watches as Richard takes the packets out of the carrier bag and puts them in the canvas bag that hangs on the side of the wheel-chair. Who would have believed that some bags of sweets would end up replacing gin and tonic as his father's chief joy in life? The difference between the man he was and what he has become is depressingly hard to believe. If he were going to change, why couldn't he have become warm and loving? Richard wonders.

'Fancy a bit of air?' he asks, releasing the brake on the chair. 'It's stopped raining, so I thought we might take a turn around the garden; the roses look lovely.' There is some relief in pushing the chair; the very act of moving around, seeing different views from different angles is, he feels, good for both of them. Others have taken advantage of the dry spell too and are wheeling their elderly relatives between the flower beds, or strolling slowly alongside the zimmer frames. Many are having real two-way, even three-way, conversations. What would it be like now if Ralph could or would talk to him? What would they say to each other? Richard parks the chair facing the pond and sits on a bench, feeling the damp of the boards seep through his jeans.

'So, what do you think, Dad?' he asks, leaning forward. 'What would *you* like to talk about?'

Silence. Ralph looks out, as he always does, straight ahead. Only now he has to look up a bit from under his bushy eyebrows because his head is drooping.

'Saw Julia and Tom last week. They're off to Portugal next month,' Richard says.

The sun slips out between a gap in the clouds. In the sudden brilliance of the light, Richard looks into his father's face and, for a fraction of a second, thinks there is recognition.

'Dad?' he says. 'It's me, Richard. Do you remember?' But the moment has passed. He leans back against the seat and crosses his legs. 'Well, we never did talk much, did we, and when we did, we argued.' He knows he's making himself irritable by taking this line; he also knows that his resentment at his father's silence is totally illogical but he can't help it. 'When we were little, you talked *at* us, and when we were grown up, you couldn't tolerate us having opinions of our own. I've often wondered what your life was really like. What it was like to be you, to be married to Mum? Did you ever have fun? An affair, perhaps? I suppose you loved us, but everything had to be on your terms, didn't it? If it wasn't, you were stuffed.'

There is a long pause.

'Stuffed,' Ralph says, suddenly and loudly, and Richard nearly jumps out of his skin.

'Shit,' he says. 'Yes, stuffed. You were stuffed then, weren't you, when things didn't go your way?'

Very slowly, Ralph turns to him, and Richard waits like Moses waiting for the handing down of the Ten Commandments.

'Stuffed,' Ralph says again.

Richard, excited now, leans forward. 'Yes, you were stuffed when you lost control, weren't you? Do you remember that?'

There is a long pause. 'I was stuffed, Richard . . . I think she's dead.'

Richard's heart does a double somersault. 'Mum, yes; she is, I'm afraid, a long time ago now.'

'Diana,' Ralph says, lifting a trembling hand and rubbing it across his eyes. 'Princess Diana, dead.' As he lowers his hand, Richard grasps it.

'Look at me, Dad,' he says urgently, 'look at me. It's Richard, do you know me? You said my name. Diana's dead. She was beautiful, wasn't she, did you like her? Did you love her?'

He peers into his father's face, willing him back, but Ralph has gone, retreated once more into his solitary world, to the place where he has been living for years, perhaps, Richard now wonders, with the dead princess as his companion. Richard sinks his face in his hands, pondering the futility of these regular but essentially insubstantial efforts to connect with his father, efforts that were as unsuccessful in the past as they are today. Then, standing up, he turns the chair.

'Right then, Dad, back we go. Let's see if we can find you some lunch,' he says, defaulting once more to his persona of cheerful visiting son. He starts to push Ralph around the pond and back to the house, wondering as he does so who will come and talk to him, who will push his chair when the time comes.

FORTY-FIVE

Getting her mother from the hospital car park to the geri-atric assessment reception area reminds Zoë of taking a wilful child shopping on Christmas Eve. Not only is Eileen not particularly steady on her feet these days, she refuses to have her arm held or her hand taken, and constantly barrels off at speed in any direction except for the one they should be taking. But eventually they reach the reception desk with ten minutes to spare, thanks to Zoë's forward planning. She dreads this assessment, demanded by the director of services at the retirement village.

'I'm sorry to have to insist,' the director had explained, 'but your mother has now had two falls and twice locked herself inside her unit. Then there was the day that the cleaner went in and found the gas still on and the burnt-out saucepan. We do have to con-sider whether she can continue in independent living or whether we need to move her to the next level of care.'

Zoë knows that she should be feeling sympathy and concern, but what she actually feels is overwhelming resentment and irrita-tion. The situation has but one saving grace; she won't be required to look after her mother at home. Eileen long ago insisted that she wanted the three-stage care option – indeed, she often mentions that she is looking forward to assisted living, as though it is a level of personal service for which she has been waiting all her life. She

415

even anticipates this assessment, so disturbing to Zoë, as some sort of special honour. They settle down on two hard plastic chairs to wait, and Zoë puts on her glasses in order to fill out the forms the receptionist has given her.

'So, he's back then,' Eileen says. 'All right, is he?'

'Apparently so,' Zoë says, 'I haven't seen him yet; he only got back last night.'

'I hope he'll be over to see me soon. Today, probably.'

Zoë looks up in surprise. Eileen has never, ever expressed any desire to see Dan or to have him visit her. 'Why would you think that?' she asks, knowing she sounds curt, but decades of resentment about Dan's treatment by Eileen is hard to disguise.

'Well, I'm his grandmother, after all.'

This is also startlingly new; Zoë can't remember a time when Eileen ever referred to Dan as anything other than 'the boy'. She puts down the pen and takes off her glasses; she's preparing some sharp and accusatory response but Eileen is too quick for her.

'And I'm very proud of him.'

'Really?'

Eileen gives her trademark sniff. 'Of course, out there fighting for his country.'

'You never seemed proud of him before.'

'Rubbish,' Eileen says, shaking her shoulders irritably. 'He's a credit to us, to the family. That's what I've always said.'

'Not to me, you haven't,' Zoë says. 'Nor to Dan, as far as I'm aware.'

'I don't believe in too much fancy talk. It can turn a person's head.'

Zoë feels an overwhelming urge to slap her mother's face, but knows that this is probably not the place to do it.

'And the girl,' Eileen goes on. 'What about the girl?'

'What girl?'

'The black girl, with the baby.'

'If you mean Justine, she's not a girl. She's a woman and she's Dan's wife, and she has a name. And the baby is your great-grandson.'

'Got married, did they?'

Zoë feels a cold chill creep up her spine; something very strange is happening.

'Almost two years ago, Mum,' she says a little more gently.

'Nobody told me that.'

'You were at the wedding.'

'Rubbish,' Eileen says. 'I'd have remembered.'

Zoë opens her handbag and pulls out the slim plastic wallet in which she keeps a few favourite photographs. 'Look,' she says, 'here, a photograph of the wedding with all the family. Dan and Justine in the middle, and there's Archie and me and the girls, and there you are, between Gaby and Jane.'

Eileen peers intently at the photograph. 'That's nice. Why haven't you shown me this before?'

Zoë, recalling the enlargement that stands in a silver frame alongside others on the sideboard in Eileen's room, observes her mother more closely. It is a long time since she has looked attentively into her face; a long time since she had any face-to-face, one-on-one conversation with her. Their relationship, always strained and distant, is increasingly filtered through Archie and the girls. When they are together, they avoid anything except for minimal eye contact, their brief interactions conducted side-on or facing away from each other.

Archie had suggested some time ago that if Zoë could adopt a different attitude towards her mother, then Eileen herself might be moved to change. It's something that Zoë has tried on more than one occasion, the most recent having been soon after her return from England.

'You complain that she lacks generosity, that she never has a good word to say to you or about you, but you know, you're the same when it comes to her,' Archie had said.

He hadn't put it so bluntly before and Zoë knew he was right. After that she had tried to be more open with Eileen, to let her mother see more of the person her daughter had become. But Eileen, it seemed, was locked into her way of being and probably saw no reason to change.

Now, here in the waiting room, facing Eileen is like facing a stranger. This isn't simply because they know so little of each other but because Eileen's face has actually changed. It seems to be drooping, as though the facial muscles have slackened. The familiar beady-eyed disapproval has disappeared, and her eyes now look dull and a little vacant. The tight mouth is loose and a trail of saliva has leaked out into a trickle down to her jaw line.

'Are you ... um ... are you feeling okay, Mum?' Zoë asks, putting a hand on her mother's arm. 'You don't look too good.'

'I'm perfectly all right,' Eileen says. 'These seats aren't very comfortable, are they? I wouldn't mind an ice cream; what time does the film start?'

'They think she must have had a slight stroke during the night,' Zoë tells Archie when he gets home. 'I suppose it was a good thing we were there. I feel terrible that I didn't even notice when I picked her up.'

'Yeah, well, it's easily done, I suppose,' Archie says.

But Zoë knows he's just being kind. He, of all people, knows the depth of antagonism between her and Eileen, and the extent of her daughterly neglect. '*You* would have noticed,' she says.

He shrugs. 'Not necessarily. Anyway, what's happening now?'

'They've admitted her, and they're going to do a whole lot of tests, and do the geriatric assessment as well while she's there. She'll be there for a couple of days, apparently. And she wants to see Dan.'

'Dan? Why? Since when?'

'Since today, because she's very proud of him, always has been, it seems, and when a grandson gets back home from the field of battle, one of the first things he should do is visit his grandmother.'

'Never!'

'I kid you not. It started just after we arrived, and then she kept telling the consultant about it. Then she went on and on about it again while we were waiting for them to find her a bed on the ward.'

Archie shakes his head in disbelief. 'Extraordinary. Have you told Dan?'

'Yes, I rang him when I got back from the hospital. He says he'll go up there this evening, about seven, and he'll come in here on the way back. I said you'd call and that maybe you'd go with him. He might need moral support.'

Archie nods. 'He might, indeed. And, anyway, this is something I absolutely have to see for myself.'

'Arch,' Zoë says, hesitating. 'Speaking of moral support . . . you are okay now, aren't you? For a while there, you seemed to be, well, upset, not like yourself at all. When I got back from England I mean.'

Archie, whose fears had largely been laid to rest after his conversation with Justine, feels now as though he has been ambushed. His skin prickles with sudden heat and all the old anxiety is revived. He is a child again, desperately needing reassurance and that, in turn, makes him feel awkward and pathetic. He clears his throat and looks briefly away, hoping to hide the flush that is creeping up his neck and burning his face.

'Well,' he begins, 'since you mention it, I . . . I was afraid that something might have happened with you and Richard.'

Zoë stares at him, her puzzlement changing slowly to comprehension. 'You mean, you thought I might have *slept* with Richard?'

Archie, fixing his gaze on his work boots, nods without looking up. 'I thought it was a possibility.'

'Oh, Arch,' Zoë says, crossing the kitchen towards him. She slips her arms around him and looks up into his face. 'I'm so sorry, and there I was joking that you were having a mid-life crisis.'

'I was,' he says, 'a crisis about you and him.'

'You could have asked me.'

'I'm asking you now,' Archie says.

'Well, the answer is no,' Zoë says, stretching up to kiss him. 'No, of course not. It was odd meeting Richard again, and finding I didn't hate him. And to be honest I did wonder what it might be like, but I never once had the desire to find out. Besides,' she hesitates, 'I wouldn't do that to you. I love you, Arch, you know that, don't you? I wouldn't do anything to hurt you or to risk what we've got.'

And now Archie sees that he has always known this; the anxiety about unanswered phone calls had unleashed a primal fear that bore little or no relation to the woman he knows Zoë to be.

⌒⌒⌒⌒

Dan wonders if he should be feeling more generous about his elevation from family pariah to favourite, and heroic, grandchild, but decides that being found acceptable only when Eileen is losing her marbles is probably meaningless. When he was in his teens he had abandoned any interest in what she thought of him, so it would be pathetic to take this seriously now.

'Weird,' he says to Archie, as they leave the ward and head out to the car park. 'That was like an LSD trip.'

'Sadly, I wouldn't know,' Archie says, 'but it was certainly very strange. Makes you wonder if she's always felt like that but never found a way to say it before.'

'I doubt it,' says Dan. 'Don't they say that when people get dementia they start doing things that are totally out of character?'

'I think that's just Alzheimer's, and we don't know yet if she's got that. Maybe it's only what a slight stroke can do to addle the brain.' He presses a hand onto Dan's shoulder. 'Well, whatever, the good thing is that you're home.'

'And may not have to go back, if I can sort out the discharge,' Dan says.

'So, have you actually started the process?'

'Yep. But please don't tell Mum, because I don't know how long it's going to take and if she knows, she'll be asking for updates every day. I'll tell her when I know what's happening.'

'And Justine?'

'Oh yes, Jus knows; happy as Larry, she is.'

'And you?'

'You know how it is; you set something in motion, you know it's the right thing and it's what you want, but you have to think about the implications. Yeah, I want to get out, but, at the same time, it's been my whole adult life so far. Up until a year ago, I thought I'd be there forever. It's like rethinking not just what I'm going to do, but who I am.'

Archie nods. 'That's not a bad thing to do in your mid-thirties; work out what you want and where you're heading.'

They get into the car and Archie switches on the engine.

'How about you, Arch?' Dan asks. 'Everything okay?'

'Yes,' Archie says. 'Pretty good. Very good, really. Zo finally forced me into booking a holiday – three weeks in Vanuatu at the end of November. I resisted, of course, but now that it's booked, I'm hanging out for it.'

Dan leans back in his seat, well aware that Archie knows what he was asking, and confident that the bland response is a good sign. So that's sorted, he thinks, and feels the same relief that he'd felt as a small boy on the very few occasions that his parents had one of their fairly polite arguments. The disagreements had never lasted long but the residual tension used to scramble Dan's head until he saw that things were back to normal again. It stems, he thinks, from an anxiety from his early years with Zoë; a sense that disaster was always just around the corner. He'd been eight when Archie turned up on the jetty and baited his line, and there had not been a day since then that he had wanted to contemplate being without him.

'Zoë's got something to show you,' Archie says eventually, turning the car into the drive. 'A surprise.'

'Yeah, Jus told me but she won't say what it is.'

There are, as always, tears when he arrives home. Last night, his own and Justine's, and even tears from Harry, who looked terrified at the sight of him and had buried his face in Justine's shoulder, and then her lap, each time Dan had tried to talk to him. Now, tonight, there are Rosie's, which are joyful but brief. And then Zoë's; surprisingly, more controlled this time, but still an outpouring of love and pride. She looks different again, he thinks, lighter within herself. The biggest difference, though, is what is happening between her and Justine. As always, when on active service he was sustained by his belief in the job and thoughts of his family. If there was one thing he wished for during this latest tour of duty, it was that Justine would be able to cast off the mistrust created by Zoë's early hostility and take a step in her direction. Now, clearly, this has happened.

'I've got something to show you, Dan,' Zoë says. And Justine, Archie and Rosie suddenly find things that they have to do in other rooms, and he is left alone with his mother. 'It's a surprise and I hope you'll think it's a good one.'

'You've won Lotto?' he jokes, unnerved.

'Better, possibly.' She walks over to sit beside him on the sofa, and hands him a small envelope.

'What's this?'

'Take a look.'

There are two old photographs: battered colour prints of a group of strangers standing on some steps.

'What is it?'

'Look closer.'

He looks again and sees that the picture is of a wedding; a rather dreary-looking one with the bride and groom standing stiff and awkward at the centre. And then he realises that the bride looks exactly like Gaby, only shorter. 'It's you? You and Richard?'

She nods. 'But look again.'

And when he does, he catches his breath because he is looking at himself. Standing just behind his mother is a tall black man who looks out to the camera smiling. And it is not a smile produced for a photograph, but one that is clearly a part of who he is, of how he moves through the world. Dan swallows hard and looks up.

'My father . . .' he says. 'It's my father?'

Zoë nods. 'Yes, Dan, it's Harry.'

It is almost unbearable for him to take his gaze from the picture but slowly he slides it sideways to reveal the second photograph. Zoë and Richard are cutting awkwardly into a cake, and there's his father again, and this time Dan can see his eyes more clearly. They are full of hope and confidence; he looks like a man at peace with himself, a man you'd be glad to have on your side, a man who knows how to love. Dan drops his head and puts his hand over his eyes. He can't speak and even wonders if he might be going to pass out, and, as he struggles to draw on his training to gain control of his emotions, he realises that nothing trains you for something like this. All you can do is surrender, accept the gift and be thankful.

FORTY-SIX

'*H*igh on a hilltop above Sintra, the pseudo medieval Pena Palace stands like a fairytale castle overlooking the glorious wooded landscape beneath,' Tom reads aloud from the guidebook.

'It's amazing,' Julia says, catching her breath, which is still in short supply after the steep climb through woodland up a winding path.

'It was built in the eighteen forties by Ferdinand of Saxe-Coburg-Gotha, husband of Maria, Queen of Portugal. Apparently, the drawbridge doesn't draw.'

'Well, that's not surprising.'

'And that bloke – the statue on the top of that crag over there is . . . er . . . Baron Eschwege, dressed as a warrior knight. He organised the statue himself, for purposes of immortality. Very German.'

'He looks rather noble,' Julia says. 'But you would, wouldn't you, dressed as a warrior knight on a hilltop, hazy in the sunlight.'

'*It is a stunning fantasy of ramparts, domes and towers in shades of mustard yellow and deep rose with one section faced with azure toned ceramic tiles . . .*'

'For heaven's sake, Tom. Stop reading the book and just look at it, will you?'

Tom closes the book and looks. 'Magic,' he breathes. 'You could come up here, to your own little world, and never want to leave.'

'Just nip out each morning for *The Guardian*, I suppose.'

He shakes his head. 'No need, read it online. It's been described as a compelling riot of kitsch.'

'*The Guardian* online?'

He rolls his eyes. 'The palace.'

'Well, it's that all right! I'm dying to see inside.'

'Let's sit down for a minute,' Tom says, perching on the low wall, and Julia joins him. 'You know, Jules, I really prefer this part of Portugal to the Algarve.'

'Me too.'

'So, that flat we saw in Estoril felt . . .'

'Just right. Home from home.'

'And a flat makes sense for us; easy to manage from a distance, easy to lend to friends. Shall we do it?'

Julia smiles. 'I can see us enjoying it together, even if we only have a short time left.'

'I wish you'd stop talking as though the grim reaper is lurking just around the corner,' Tom says, standing up again, and pacing irritably back and forth. 'A couple of years ago, you were going on about me wanting to drag you into stultifying retirement, which, of course, I wasn't. Now you're planning our deaths. We could have another thirty years. I am not planning to turn my toes up yet, thank you very much.'

'Well, me neither . . .'

'Then shut up about it, and stop tagging it on to every conversation we have about the future.'

It is so unusual for him to snap at her that Julia is shaken. 'Sorry,' she says. 'Sorry.'

'Yes . . . good. I know what's behind it. You think because I'm older and I've been sick a couple of times, I'm going to die first and leave you behind.'

Julia is silent, gazing up at the tall mustard yellow tower with its black dome, vivid against the unbroken blue of the sky. 'Yes,' she says eventually. 'I suppose that's it, really.'

'Maybe I will, or maybe *I'll* be the one who's left behind. Either way, there's nothing we can do about it.'

'But it is more likely –'

'Stop,' he says, holding up his hand, and Julia thinks it makes him look like a traffic cop. 'I don't want to spend my remaining years thinking about dying. Whichever way it goes, the best thing for the one who's left standing will be to have a full life of wonderful memories to look back on.'

Julia swallows hard and looks at him. 'Yes. But I can't imagine how I'd cope without you.'

'You would,' Tom says abruptly. 'You are the most competent, self-sufficient woman I've ever met. You have plenty of friends, a list of things you want to do, and you are also ruthless and bloody-minded when it comes to getting things done.'

'I remember, years ago, having a conversation like this with Hilary,' Julia says. 'Eric was sick and she was panicking about losing him. She kept berating herself for feeling she'd be so incompetent without him.'

'Well, there you are,' Tom says. 'She wasn't in the least incompetent. I know she missed him bitterly but that's something else entirely. We have everything to look forward to, and I don't want you to spoil it with this silliness.'

Julia is close to tears. Since the night Tom had been raced away by ambulance in acute pain, she's been haunted by the fragility of life. Death was so entirely shocking. She had spent more than a year watching Hilary die; watching as she methodically went through her business and personal affairs, said her goodbyes, moved towards a physical and spiritual place of being ready to go. Devastating as it was, it had accustomed Julia to the idea that dying was about having plenty of time to put one's house in order. Tom's dramatic collapse had smashed all that. Some time after Zoë had gone home and Tom was back in circulation, she had come across an old book that she'd remembered Hilary talking about, one that spoke of death being just another stage of life, for which one should prepare. She reminds Tom of that now.

'I know the book you mean,' Tom says. 'It's a Buddhist book. I remember her reading it and talking about it, and I'm sure it doesn't say you prepare by hooking death onto everything like a codicil. It's about preparing for death by living a beautiful life in every way and accepting that death is a part of it. It must say something like that, because Buddhists don't anticipate, they accept; they are in the present, living each day, each moment, to the full and as well as they can. Something like that.'

Julia gets up and wanders closer to the parapet. 'Do you suppose Ferdinand and Queen Maria had heaps of children?'

'No idea – why?'

'They built something so beautiful and wild and quirky, it's hard to believe they didn't plan to pass it on. Do you think that this time of life is easier, less scary and complicated, if you have children?'

He sighs. 'I very much doubt it. Not if the experiences of some of our friends are anything to go by. Look at Zoë, for a start.' Tom puts his arms around her. 'It seems to me that what matters is making the most of the time we've got, whether it's three months, three years or thirty years.' He kisses her. 'I love you, Jules, and I dread being left behind too.'

'I've never really thought about the fact that I could die first,' she says.

'Think about it now,' he says with a grin, 'because right now, your chances of getting chucked off a parapet for irritating behaviour are pretty high. Come on, let's have a look around the palace and then we'll make an appointment to sign the contract for the flat.'

⌘

Richard is delighted with his room; it's more like a cottage, really. Gaby had done a great job picking this place for him, but that, of course, was before the day he doesn't even want to think about. The roof is thatched with palm leaves, the rammed earth walls are a slightly deeper shade than the pale terracotta floor tiles; it's traditional design and construction but equipped with every possible convenience. He particularly likes the bathroom; it has a shower in its own small fernery, in which you stand behind a glass screen on a bed of smooth pebbles with fronds of tree ferns brushing against you, and the roof open to the sky.

He wonders if it might be easier to live a better life in a place like this – to find peace, perhaps. Without the relentless pressure of work and the fast-paced clamorous life of a big city, would it be possible to change? To dissolve that dark side of himself, the predatory side that emerges after a few drinks? But he'd go raving mad here after a while. He knows now that he can only live in London or New York, anywhere else would bore him sick after the first month, if he even lasted that long. But, in the meantime, he's determined to enjoy everything that Bali has to offer.

When Bea had announced that she wouldn't be joining him because she'd taken a six-month fellowship with a university in Dubai, Richard's resentment had provided him with a timely insight into his lifetime dilemma regarding relationships. He wanted to be with feisty, intelligent women who had lives of their own, but resented it when they wanted to live those lives. Part of him yearned for someone to be waiting for him at home, totally focused on him and pandering to him in traditionally female ways.

'And you mean you only just worked this out?' Julia had said when he told her. They were talking on the phone; Julia had called just before he'd left Jakarta to tell him she and Tom had bought an apartment in Estoril. 'I could've told you that years ago.'

'I wish you had,' he'd said. 'It might have saved me and some very nice women a lot of heartache. Have you heard anything from Zoë recently?' he asked cautiously.

'Not for a few weeks. Why?'

'Oh, nothing,' he said too quickly. 'Nothing. I just wondered.'

'How's the doco shaping up?'

'Pretty good. We're all having the week off and then we'll meet up again back here to tie up the loose ends. Meanwhile, I'm going to be a wastrel on a glorious tropical island.'

'Is it glorious?'

'I'll tell you when I get there.' He paused. 'So, everyone's okay then? No news? Are Gaby and Brad okay?'

'You'd know more about that than I would.'

'What do you mean?' he asked, knowing he sounded defensive.

'Well, Gaby works for you, you must be in touch with her quite often.'

'Oh,' he said. 'I see what you mean. Yes, she seems okay.'

'Okay, good. Tom sends his love. You have fun in Bali and try to stay out of trouble.'

He'd laughed awkwardly then and said he didn't think there was any risk of trouble in Bali for a jaundiced old fart like him.

From the window of his cottage, Richard can see down the curving pathway to the pool, luminous turquoise and lit, at this time of the evening, with tiny pinpoints of submerged light. And beyond the boundaries of the hotel complex, there is the glittering expanse of the sea. It is a vision of paradise, and it's only when you head out in the opposite direction that you come face to face with noisy groups of drunken yobs on holiday and packed streets crammed with shops for tourists. But Richard is used to the noise and clatter of the city; he is not fazed by boisterous youths who can't hold their drink or being jostled on crowded pavements. He knows it's easy to hide in places like this, to forget your crimes and misdemeanours; here, tonight, he can be anyone he chooses, free of all the old baggage, and of other people's expectations and judgments. He's single, with time to spare, money in his pocket, and an overwhelming urge to kick up his heels.

He pulls on a clean pair of cotton trousers and a white linen shirt, and combs his hair in front of the mirror.

'I have actually seen you look worse,' he tells his reflection, 'many times, in fact. What you need, my friend, is dinner, a few drinks, and a taste of the night life.' And he lets himself out of the room.

The warm evening air is heavy with the scent of frangipani, and in the distance he can hear a gamelan band and the splashing of people taking a late swim. In the terrace restaurant, candle flames flicker, their reflections glancing off glass and silver. Richard settles at a table, savouring the prospect of relaxation, sea and sun. He thinks that tonight he'll kick things off in a club; maybe some poor deluded woman will take pity and dance with him. Perhaps, he thinks, the way for him is – has always been – being a single person with total control of what he does and with whom he does it, a life free of the need to take other people's emotional needs or practical desires into consideration. Tom, he suspects, would say that this is what he has always done anyway. He hadn't pulled any punches in the pub at New Year.

'Time to stop kidding yourself, Rich,' he'd said. 'You like the good life, you're obsessed with your work, and you're hopeless at compromise. Maybe this is the time to get to grips with enjoying life alone rather than making these serial forays into relationships that simply end up making both you and someone else bloody miserable.'

'So that's it, then?' Richard had said gloomily. 'Lone Ranger?'

'Many men of your age would be happy with a good job, enough money and no commitments.'

'But you're not one of them.'

'Of course not. But I hope that if I were like you, single and in my sixties, I'd be trying to make the most of what that offered, and not pining after something I'd proved not to be particularly good at. You know how it goes – someone else's grass always looks greener, but green may not be your colour.'

Richard had frequently revisited this conversation in the intervening months, and most of all since the disastrous incident with Gaby.

That day he'd slept through the alarm; it was almost ten-thirty when he woke with a monumental hangover that he'd acquired at a reunion of some of the old *Panorama* crowd. He'd have given his right arm to stay in bed, but there was stuff he needed to look over and sign before he flew out that evening. He got up, had a shower, two slices of toast and two double whiskies to get him going, and staggered into the office around lunchtime.

'You look terrible,' Gaby said when he arrived. 'Have you got a virus or something?'

'Yep,' he said, managing a wry smile, 'it's a particularly nasty case of *hangoveris horribilis.*'

And a few minutes later she came into his office with a plunger of coffee and a glass of some horrible fizzy, orange-coloured stuff that was supposed to be good for hangovers.

'You are a star, Gaby,' Richard said. 'I'll have the coffee but you can forget that fizzy stuff, or I'll throw up. Why is it so quiet in here today?'

'Mike and Grif are checking the new studios, Sheila's got some gastro thing, and your archive request came through, so Ed's gone over to the Television Centre to sort it out.'

'And Monica?'

'You gave her a day off for her grandfather's funeral.'

'So I did,' Richard said, pouring a couple of measures of whisky into his coffee. 'It's just you and me holding the fort then, Gabs?'

'From the look of you, I think it's just me,' she said. She pointed to a file on his desk. 'You need to sign off on those new contracts before you go away. Can you do it now, before you forget?' She went out of his office, closing the door behind her.

Richard dropped into his chair, swung his feet onto the desk and picked up his mug, watching Gaby through the glass of the partition wall. This morning she looked more like Zoë than ever; her gestures, the way she moved, the way she sat, as she was doing now, the telephone tucked between her ear and her shoulder. Richard leaned back; the brief blast of fresh air on the way in and the first mug of coffee were working. The solid dark mass that had been hovering behind his eyes and reaching back to squeeze the base of his skull was relaxing its grip, and he could actually move his face quite effectively now. He opened the file and started to read through the contracts Gaby had left for him, took a couple of calls and made a couple himself, and returned to the contracts. When he was halfway through the last one, he glanced up; Gaby was slipping papers into files and sliding the files back into the cabinet.

Richard breathed in deeply and rested his chin on his hand while watching her. Gaby was wearing a close-fitting black sweater and a short denim skirt, with opaque black tights. From this angle, she was less like Zoë. She was curvy – something Zoë had never been – and, as she twisted around to pick up the phone, there was a promising swell of generous, youthful breasts and of firmly rounded buttocks.

Richard poured himself a second mug of coffee and tipped the remains of his flask into it. Gaby closed the middle drawer and bent to open the bottom one. Richard watched her through half-closed eyes. He felt almost human again; a bit too human, judging from the size of his erection. He imagined himself lifting her skirt, pulling down the tights, feeling those juicy buttocks in his hands, sliding his fingers into the moist warmth between her legs.

Gaby straightened up, closed the drawer, walked towards his office and opened the door. 'Have you signed them yet?' she asked.

Richard hesitated, looking at her, his body caught in a frantic tussle with his head. He swallowed hard. 'Just wondering about this last one,' he said. 'Come and have a look at this section on page four.'

She walked to his desk and, seeing that he still had the page facing him, stepped around to stand beside him. 'Which section?' she asked, moving closer, bending forward to read the small typeface.

Richard could feel the warmth radiating from her body, smell her crisp perfume. As she pored over the document, her breath brushed the back of his hand. In that moment, he knew that she'd seen him watching her, that every move she had made had been for him. And now she was close beside him.

'Do you mean the part on recording rights or the one on print publications?' she asked.

'Er . . . both,' Richard said, distracted. His mouth was dry, he heard his blood pumping in his ears, his body was throbbing with something unstoppable. Without looking up from the file, he placed his hand on her bottom and stroked it down between her black-clad thighs.

'Get *off*, Richard!' Gaby cried, leaping back from him as if she'd been burned. 'What d'you think you're doing?'

'Gaby,' he said standing up and attempting to pull her towards him. 'Come on, you know I . . .'

'Stop it! Let go of me,' she said, thumping him so hard in the chest he almost lost his balance. 'You're disgusting and you're still drunk. Just because I work for you, doesn't mean you can maul me like some dirty old pervert.'

'Come on, Gaby,' Richard said. 'You know you were . . .'

'I was what?'

In that moment he knew he'd made an appalling mistake; he'd convinced himself that something was happening between them when all the time it had been happening in his imagination. Humiliation swept over him, filling him with a rage.

'Don't pretend you don't know, Gaby,' he yelled, desperate now to shift the responsibility away from himself. 'Standing out there by the filing cabinet. Oh, I could see you and you wanted me to see you, didn't you . . .' He stopped, suddenly disarmed by the way she was standing there, arms folded and glaring at him with a mixture of anger and disgust.

'Let's get one thing clear, Richard,' she said slowly. 'I was doing my job and you know it. You were once married to my mother, but I am not her, and she would not appreciate this any more than I do. I'm Zoë's daughter and I work for you. That's it! Got it?'

A red mist swirled before Richard's eyes and he swept the piles of papers, books and magazines, the stacked files and their contents, onto the floor.

'Fuck you, Gaby,' he said. 'You work for me – okay, work. Clean that lot up. Got it?' And with that, he grabbed his coat, slammed out of the office and headed blindly for the nearest pub.

He sat in the saloon bar of the Rose and Crown for some time nursing his anger, letting it swirl through him, grasping at it time and again, knowing that if he let it go, he would be left only with humiliation. Eventually, though, exhaustion overcame him; closing his eyes, he let go with a shuddering sigh and sank his head in his shaking hands.

In a few moments of madness he had destroyed something infinitely precious – Gaby's trust and her friendship. And, once again, he had betrayed Zoë. For what? A fleeting, gross and arrogant fantasy. The shame was excruciating, as was the fear of what Gaby might do. Would she tell Zoë or Archie? Julia, even, or maybe Brad? One thing was for sure, if she confided in Gloria, they'd all know. He must make himself go back and talk to her. Apologise, and, if necessary, beg her to not tell anyone and give him a chance to redeem himself. The one thing he wanted to do was to run in the opposite direction but he knew he had to go back and now.

It had just turned three o'clock when he got to the office, and the door was locked. He let himself in and walked around, wondering where Gaby was. She must have set the alarm when she left, because suddenly the brain-splitting siren reared through the silence and he had to rush back to the door, punch in the code and ring the security company and tell them what had happened. There was still no sign of Gaby and when he finally went into his office, he saw that his desk had been returned to order; far better order than it had been in for weeks. All the paperwork he needed for the trip was set out in neatly labelled files, alongside the file of documents for signature.

Gloomily, he sat down, signed everything, and then attempted to write an apology. Writing was what he did; what some people had even gone so far as to say he had a genius for. He could make words rub up against each other in ways that made readers, or listeners, stop and think. But now the words scattered and chaffed, slipped and tripped, evading his efforts to say what he really felt. There were many discarded attempts before he finally had something that came somewhere near to the apology he wanted to make. He slipped the letter into an envelope, wrote Gaby's name on it and put it with the signature file on her desk.

Then, putting the paperwork he needed in his briefcase he went home. Seven miserable hours later, he buckled his seatbelt and listened as the aircraft engines roared to full power, and he was on his way to Jakarta.

And now, here he is, four weeks later, exhausted from the filming and from the tension of wondering what Gaby is doing, whom she has or hasn't told, what she will say when he sees her again. She's still there in the office, efficiently responding to his emails, making whatever arrangements he requests, updating him on other projects. She is doing her job and that in itself is a relief;

presumably if she truly hated him, she wouldn't have gone back there. But the phone calls that would normally have come from her come from Monica or Ed. Gaby obviously, and understandably, does not want to speak to him. If she had told anyone, though, Richard thinks, he would know by now; there would have been an enraged phone call from Australia or Portugal, London or Rye. He believes she must have kept it to herself and he admires her for it.

Perhaps, he thinks, as he sits at the poolside bar with a brandy, watching the dazzlingly clear turquoise of the floodlit water, this is his epiphany; the turning point that will teach him to tread more lightly in the world.

Later that evening, Richard makes his way out of the hotel and on to the street. According to the hotel barman, the Sari Club is the place to go, and he follows his ears to the beat of the music. Squeezing through the knot of people clustered around the entrance, he edges towards the bar, his adrenaline pumping with the music, his skin prickling damply with the humidity, entranced by the hypnotic effect of lights dappling over the sinuous bodies of the dancers. He stands there, a benign observer, drink in hand, not thinking, watching, abandoning himself to the mind-numbing beat, inhaling the sheer physicality of the place. From her seat further along the bar, a woman, not young but younger than him, edges closer and leans over to speak to him. A fall of hair dyed an unnatural red brushes his face as he leans in closer to hear what she's saying.

'D'you want to dance?' she asks above the music.

'Love to,' he says, and he puts his arm around her waist and they move away from the crowd at the bar.

'I'm an old-fashioned dancer,' she says, putting one hand on his shoulder and moving in pleasantly close.

'Me too,' he says, drawing her generous curves closer still, breathing in a familiar perfume. 'I'm Richard,' he murmurs close to her ear.

'Patti,' she says, 'from Brisbane. Here alone?'

He savours the touch of skin, the mingling heat of their bodies. It is a long time since he has danced, and dance as foreplay is tantalising. 'Yep,' he says, 'the Lone Ranger, that's me.' As he tilts his head back to look into her face, there is a noise, the building seems to tremble. People are yelling in confusion and Richard grabs Patti's hand but, as they head for the door, there is another explosion – louder this time, like nothing he's heard since Vietnam – and he is hurled sideways in the air and crashes to the ground. Timber and masonry are crashing down, and Richard, still holding Patti's hand, turns to her but she has gone; her hand clasped in his is all that remains. He hears his own screams ricocheting off the unrecognisable shapes, the heaps of rubble and twisted metal. And now there is fire – fire everywhere. His other arm, the whole side of his body, is on fire, his hair is burning; it is so sudden and intense that he feels only horror. The last thing he knows is the fire.

FORTY-SEVEN

Perth – October 2002

D an arrives at the international airport and parks the car just as the flight touches down. He doesn't want to be here at all and the sooner it's over and done with, the better. Archie has an important meeting and Zoë has an appointment with Eileen's gerontologist. People crowd around the barrier at the arrivals gate, pressing closer, standing on tiptoe and straining to see. Dan stands back; he is here merely to help Zoë out. An exhausted family comes through the doors first, with a trolley piled high with cases and toys and with small, tired children hanging onto the side. A few business travellers are next and then there's a pause before the remaining passengers start to flow through.

He sees her immediately and sees that she's seen him. They are the only two black people in the crowd. She nods, gives him a half smile and negotiates her trolley through the groups of joyful relatives.

'Dan?'

'That's me, and you're Carly.'

She holds out a hand, and then drops it and hugs him. 'This is real nice of you. It's not something you should have to do.'

Her directness disarms him. 'My pleasure,' he says, taking control of her trolley. 'Mum would have come herself but . . .'

'Yes, Zoë called me. I'm sorry your grandmother's sick.'

Dan's initial ambivalence evaporates; he likes her immediately. And she's very different from what he'd expected. So, what had he been expecting? A Californian bimbo? Well, certainly someone less mature and confident; someone helpless, tearful and crushed with anxiety.

'And I'm so sorry about your father,' Dan says. 'You and your mother must be devastated.'

Carly nods. 'It sure came as a shock, we didn't even know he was in Bali. We'd been watching the reports of the bombing and then the next day, we got the call saying he was being flown to Perth. Have you seen him?'

'No, but Mum has – yesterday and again this morning.'

Carly stops walking and turns to him. 'And how . . .'

Dan shakes his head. 'Not good, I'm afraid; severe burns to the right side of his body and face, some internal bruising but it's the burns that really . . .' He stops, seeing her face crumple, and puts an arm around her shoulders. 'Look, I shouldn't be telling you this; you need to talk to the doctors. He's in the best place, they've got an amazing burns team. One of the surgeons is a world leader and this new treatment . . .'

Carly nods and attempts to smile. 'I know,' she says, 'your mom told me.'

'A friend of mine from the army was treated for burns there and they did a brilliant job.'

'Thanks, Dan,' she says. 'I guess I need to get myself a car and get out there straight away. Later on, I'll find somewhere to stay.'

'Don't be silly. I'm taking you to the hospital now, and you're staying with Mum and Archie. You just concentrate on seeing your . . . seeing Richard, you can leave the rest of it to us.' And, as a look of relief crosses her face, he realises that her initial confidence was simply a mask that she had worn to cope with meeting him. One arm still around her shoulders, he steers her and the trolley out to the car.

◈

Zoë weaves her way out of the Fremantle hospital car park through the traffic towards the city to the Royal Perth Hospital. She is edgy and impatient from having spent the last couple of hours first with Eileen, then with the specialist and then with Eileen again. It's a depressing catalogue of problems; a second small stroke, certainly some dementia, although it's hard for them to tell how much is due to the stroke or whether it is Alzheimer's. There was mention, too, of Parkinson's disease. But while Zoë is nervous, irritable and stricken with guilt at her own lack of generosity towards her mother, Eileen is having a wonderful time.

Her usual clipped sentences have been replaced by loquaciousness, and, while much of what she's saying doesn't make a lot of sense, it is also uncharacteristically lighthearted. She talks continually to the nurses, who find her amusing and, according to the sister on duty this afternoon, 'a lovely lady'. Zoë had wanted to sit the woman down and tell her a few things about the lovely lady, but managed to hold back, smile and express her appreciation of the excellent care her mother was getting. This sudden amiability is, she thinks, bizarre. Is it a part of Eileen's character that has been repressed all these years or merely a quirk of dementia? Has her mother always wanted to be 'a lovely lady' who chats easily, smiles and jokes with strangers? Zoë opts for it being a quirk; an ungenerous decision, she knows, but the leap of imagination required for the other possibilities is just too great.

The hospital car park is busy and by the time Zoë has found a space and is heading into the hospital itself, she is half an hour later than she expected. She had hoped to arrive in time to get a cup of tea and a sandwich before meeting Carly and Dan, but as she approaches the burns unit she spots them coming towards her.

'Is there any news; have you been able to see him yet?' Zoë asks when the introductions are over.

Carly shakes her head. 'We got here about ten minutes ago but they're doing something to him right now, so I have to wait.'

Zoë takes Carly by the arm and leads her over to a seat while Dan goes to get them some tea.

'Listen, Carly, I don't know how much they've told you but you do need to prepare yourself. Richard's in a pretty bad way.'

She nods. 'The nurse told me, she was real nice. Zoë, I'm

scared, I don't want to let him down. Did he talk to you at all this morning?'

'He did; he's terribly disorientated and the drugs for the pain mean he's fading in and out. But he knew he was talking to me, and he knows you're coming. There were a couple of times that he sounded really focused but mainly he was more or less out of it, thinking he was in the swimming pool. That seems to be all he remembers about what happened.'

'The swimming pool?'

'Apparently, there were so many people with burns that some were put into a hotel swimming pool to ease the pain, so that's probably what it's about.'

Carly nods. 'And he's not . . . he's going to be okay, isn't he?'

'Well, it seems they can treat the burns with this amazing new skin thing. His blood pressure was up very high and they're still giving him fluids intravenously. Nothing they've said to me suggested that Richard might not make it. It's just . . .' she pauses.

'It's what? Look, you have to tell me . . . please, Zoë.'

'It's his eyes; they're badly burned. They aren't sure if they can save his sight.'

Carly stares at her in obvious disbelief. 'You mean . . . he could be *blind*?'

'It's possible. His sight will certainly be impaired but they can't tell yet how much.'

They sit in silence for a moment.

'Did you talk to my aunt?' Carly asks.

'This morning, after I'd seen Richard. I said we'd call her again this evening. She's very upset, she and Tom are in Portugal. She was talking about flying out here, but I suggested she wait another day until we know a bit more.'

Carly leans forward, sinking her head into her hands. 'I can't believe this is happening. I mean, my dad is always okay. I just have to get my head together before I go in there.'

'You'll be fine, Carly,' Zoë says. 'It'll mean so much to him that you're here. Come on, I'll introduce you to his doctor.'

Carly looks terrified and jet-lagged, but Zoë can see that she is also strong. It shows in her eyes, in the set of her jaw, in the effort with which she draws herself up to meet the doctor and walks with her through the doors to the ward. It makes Zoë more curious about Lily – and something else makes her curious about how long Richard has known Carly's mother.

'Cup of tea,' Dan says, handing her a plastic beaker. 'Come and sit down again. You look wiped out. Was Gran okay?'

'Okay? She's become Miss Congeniality.' She brings him up to date on Eileen's condition. 'So, what do you think of Carly?'

'Nice,' Dan says. 'I like her. Not at all what I expected.'

'I like her too and she's not what I expected either.'

'I must have got it wrong,' Dan says, shaking his head, 'because I was expecting someone more Gaby's age.'

'Yes,' Zoë says, sipping the tea. 'And how old do you think she is?'

'About the same as me, except that . . .'

'Exactly,' Zoë says, looking at him. 'About the same age as you, but that doesn't make sense.'

⁂

Behind its fortress-like exterior, Lisbon's cathedral is lit within by candles and the light from the great rose window. It is still and gloomy; stripped by an earthquake of the grandeur of its original embellishments and restored by less florid decorators, the Gothic tombs behind the high altar are the only remains of the old interior. Austere is not what Tom had anticipated when he had urged Julia out of the hotel room and up the steep hill from the Baxia. For once, he would have appreciated a flamboyant rococo interior, with an abundance of gold leaf, some chubby recumbent cherubs and a few brightly clothed saints; something essentially hopeful.

'It's not what I hoped for,' he says, taking her arm and steering her to a corner, 'but we can still do what we came to do.'

They drop their coins in the collection box, take two votive candles from the box and light them.

'Is it enough?' Julia asks. 'Maybe we should light more.'

'I think one each is enough,' Tom says, putting his arm around her shoulders and knowing that her shivering is not only attributable to the gloomy chill of the cathedral. They pause in silence, thinking, praying, until he takes her hand and leads her outside to the steps from where they can see Lisbon spread beneath them. The straight, cobbled streets of the old town are busy with traffic; the mosaic sidewalks and squares with their Art Deco buildings are dazzling in the afternoon sunlight.

'It's so beautiful,' Julia says, leaning against him. 'It's so hard to see it and remember beautiful things when everything seems so terrible.'

'But it's at times like this we need beauty most,' he says, 'to help us keep perspective.'

'What should we do, Tomo?'

'Nothing at the moment,' Tom says. 'That's what Zoë said, wait another twenty-four hours and see what the situation is then. He's heavily sedated, not really aware of what's going on and is in very good hands. There is nothing useful we can do at the moment.'

'I feel I should be there.'

'I know, and maybe we will go, but at present I think we can only complicate things.'

'His *eyes*, Tom – losing his sight would kill him. His life is making television, showing what he sees.'

'We don't know yet, darling. It may not be as bad as you think.'

'And how will he manage? He won't be able to look after himself.'

'Then we'll have to sort something out for him, but we can't do any of that yet.'

'I feel so useless,' she says. 'Miles away on the other side of the world, nothing I can do.'

Tom is running out of words; the burden of supporting Julia while trying to keep his own spirits up seems too great, and the prospect that they may become carers again is daunting. But he wants to forget about Julia's brother for a while and think about his friend; his ideological and intellectual comrade, and sparring partner. He longs to be alone, to be silent and to think. He tries to imagine what it has been like for Richard; ripped from a sweaty, sensuous, scented evening in Bali, cast into fire and flown to a hospital in a strange city, sedated, bandaged, monitored, totally dependent on strangers for everything he needs.

Tom remembers Richard telling him about the time he had been close to an exploding mine in Vietnam. He talked about the sickening quality of the sound that he thought meant death, of the fierce blast of air and flying debris, of the sense of himself being hurled through space and punching down onto rocky ground, and looking up to see fire moving quickly and inexorably towards him.

'I prayed to die,' he'd said. 'I honestly prayed to die because I knew I had no capacity to withstand physical pain, no stamina for suffering, and no stomach to live with the long-term consequences.'

'Fortunately, your prayers weren't answered,' Tom had said then, 'and you did find the stamina and the stomach you needed.'

'Eventually. I was quite clear about the fact that I was capable of ending it if I had to. But there was this nurse . . .'

'I might've known it.'

'No, no it wasn't like that. She was in her sixties, a sister and a bit of a harridan, really. She said, "The trouble with you, young man, is that you think too much of yourself, so you think you're in a worse state than everyone else. But you'll be back at work in your posh job at the BBC while some of these soldiers are learning to live without limbs or eyes, so get a grip." That was it, you see; she told me I was going back to work and it was the shot in the arm I needed. I could cope with anything once I realised I'd be able to go back to work.'

Tom closes his eyes against the sunlight. He wonders if Richard is remembering this, if he is once more fighting the battle with his own darkness, and what might constitute the sort of shot in the arm that can harvest his hope and resolve this time.

⁓⁓

Justine watches Zoë from the other side of the table. It's clear that she's upset and exhausted, but there is something else that she can't quite put her finger on. She keeps looking at Carly quite intently, as though she's trying to discover something, and when Carly turns towards her, Zoë looks surprised and slightly embarrassed. Everyone is tired, of course; the tension, the emotion, the waiting. Carly, drained by the flight and the shock of seeing her father, struggles between weariness and sudden bursts of hyperactivity when she insists on doing something, clearing the table, washing things that could be put in the dishwasher. Justine thinks it might be best if she and Dan gather up Harry and leave now; perhaps then, everyone else can settle down and go to bed.

'So, how are you feeling about all this, Arch?' she'd asked as they waited for Dan, Zoë and Carly to get back from the hospital.

'Oh, a bit awkward, I suppose,' he'd said, pouring them both some wine, 'and, frankly, somewhat ungenerous. I don't feel particularly warmly towards Richard. I know he's been very good to Gaby, but, as far as I'm concerned, the less I have to do with him the better. On the other hand, what's happened to him is appalling, and we're the people who are on the spot. You can't turn your back on something like that.' He took a sip from his glass and held it up to the light. 'But, between you and me, Jus, I very much hope that we won't have to have him here while he's recovering.'

She watches him now and sees that he too is watching Zoë. Definitely time to leave.

'We should probably get moving,' she says, standing up. 'I'll go and sort Harry out.' She walks down the passage to Dan's old room, where he is sleeping soundly in the cot that Zoë keeps there for him.

Zoë, who has followed her, peeps over her shoulder. 'Still asleep?'

Justine nods and steps back so that Zoë can see him, arms flung above his head, covers kicked off, dead to the world.

'You can leave him, if you like, and I'll bring him over in the morning.'

'I think you've got enough to cope with at the moment,' Justine says. 'Are you okay, Zoë? You must be worn out.'

'Yes,' she says. 'Yes, I am, I'm very tired. Jus, what do you think of Carly?'

'Well, she seems really lovely, and she's coping amazingly well.

It's a terrible shock, a deadly journey, and now she's surrounded by strangers. It's pretty grim for her.'

'Yes, she's remarkable. I like her too. Look, I know this sounds odd but how old do you think she is?'

'How old?' Justine shrugs. 'Oh, early thirties, I suppose. Why? Oh yes, yes, I see what you mean, if she's the same age as Dan . . .'

'Exactly,' Zoë says. 'If Carly's about the same age as Dan, then I want to know exactly when Richard first met her mother.'

FORTY-EIGHT

Perth – October 2002

The darkness is peaceful, soothing, although something keeps niggling at him. He vaguely remembers a man's voice shouting out that he couldn't see; the voice sounded like his own, but he's not sure. He remembers the noise, the flames crawling up his body, the smell of burning flesh, the scorching behind his eyelids, and then the pool. He's going to be okay, though, that's what matters, he's alive after all. Sometimes he thinks he's back in the swimming pool, but then he feels the bed and remembers he's in hospital, and his hand twitches, trying to grasp another hand. He feels the pressure of the bandages on his head holding the pads firmly over his eyes. Carly is here every day, Zoë most days; doctors come and go, their voices are distinguishable now, so he knows who he's talking to. The same, too, with some of the nurses. There are more of them, so it's harder to identify them, but their touch tells him more about them than their faces ever could. Then, one afternoon when he has drifted briefly into sleep, he wakes and smells perfume in the room.

'Patti?' he says, trying to sit up. 'Patti?'

'Dorothy,' a voice tells him. 'Dorothy Connell, Mr Linton. I'm the hospital chaplain.'

'That perfume,' Richard says, 'your perfume, it made me remember. Write it down, please, in case I forget again.' He hears paper rustle, the scrape of a chair, feels a hand on his good one.

'Okay, tell me,' she says.

'Patti Brisbane, or maybe Patti *from* Brisbane. Red hair, that perfume.'

'*Trésor*,' she says and moves something closer to his face, a wrist perhaps.

'*Trésor*, that's it. We were dancing. We . . . I held her hand and . . .' he pauses, searching for the rest of it '. . . the bomb, a second bomb . . . her hand, it was there in mine.' He thinks he's crying now. The burning in his eyes is worse than ever, and his chest heaves. His good hand is twitching, grasping at the blankets, reaching for her hand.

The chaplain takes it. 'Your pain relief is here,' she says, gripping his index finger and reminding him of the clip attached to it. 'Do you need some more?'

'No,' he says. 'Not pain, the hand. Her hand in mine, that's all there was.'

There is silence and he can sense that someone else has come into the room.

'Patti?' he asks again.

'No, Dad, it's Carly.'

'Find her for me, Carly,' he asks her later when he has explained what happened. 'Perhaps she's here in this hospital.' He is obsessed with the hand, he should have kept it close to him; they can do amazing things these days, reattach fingers, toes, perhaps even a whole hand. But he had let go and it has been lost in the flames, and because of him she must live without her hand.

Her name was Patti Welmost, Carly tells him later. She has checked with the hospital and the information hotline that has been set up to deal with enquiries.

'She was a hairdresser from Brisbane,' Carly says, 'and she was on holiday with a woman friend who'd met a man earlier that evening and gone off with him to the beach. Patti stayed on alone at the club because she wanted to dance.'

'We danced,' he said. 'We just started dancing . . . her hand . . . did they find her hand? Perhaps they can . . .'

'She died, Dad,' Carly says softly, 'she died instantly at the scene.'

'Died,' he echoes, 'died, no, please not.' He feels Patti's hand cold in his own, cold and dead.

A couple of days later, things are clearer. He can remember more and, unfortunately, feel more.

'We really don't know about your eyes,' the doctor tells him, 'at this stage, it's impossible to say. One day at a time, that's how we have to progress.'

'I've brought you some talking books,' Carly says, moving his good hand towards his good ear and helping him to fit the earpiece in place, guiding his fingers over the switches that make it start and stop. She has been reading to him, every day until now; her sweet voice leading him through the newspapers, through the letters and emails, through the messages on cards. 'I won't be back today,' she says now. 'Dan and Justine are taking me out for lunch at the beach. They think I need a break.'

'Yes,' he says, 'of course you do. And Lily?'

'She calls every day,' Carly says. 'She sends you her love. I read you her email yesterday, remember?'

'Yes, I remember.'

'So, I'll see you tomorrow and Zoë will be here this afternoon. You rest now.'

Richard feels the warm swish of air as she leans forward and the brush of her lips against his cheek. How acutely aware he is of touch, how vital and tender it is when you can't see. He vows to remember that, appreciate it still, once he can see again; *if* he can see again.

'Julia and Tom will be here on Thursday,' Zoë tells him when she arrives that afternoon. 'Julia wants to stay until they can take you home.'

'God knows how long that'll be,' Richard says despondently, 'and then I'll need . . .'

'They know, Richard,' she says, putting her hand on his arm, 'they're making plans but don't worry about all that now.'

He nods slowly. 'They didn't need to come, but it'll be so good to see . . .' he hesitates, 'to have them here. I'm such a lucky bastard.'

'There's a card here for you – looks like it's from Gaby. Would you like me to open it and read it to you?'

Richard hesitates. His spine tingles with fear and every burn on his body throbs with pain. 'Er . . . yes, please,' he says, clearing his throat. He hears her tear open the envelope and take out the card.

'It's a great card,' Zoë says, 'you'll love it when you see it. It's a photograph of all different newspaper headlines, and over the top in big red letters it says "Stop Press", and when you open it, it says "Today's news is you have to get well soon".' She laughs. 'It's just the right card for you. Now, here's what Gaby says. "Dear Rich, hurry up and get well, we all miss you, even me. Love Gaby", and there's a kiss. I'll put it up with your other cards.'

He exhales with relief, relaxing into his pillows. 'Thank her for me, will you?' he says. 'And tell her . . . tell her I'm sorry for being such a tosser. She'll know what I mean.' He reaches for his beaker of water and Zoë puts it into his hand.

'Richard, there's something I need you tell me,' she says.

'I know,' he says. 'I know what it is.'

The room is silent except for the occasional bleep of monitors, the muffled rattle of a trolley in the passage, the sound of lowered voices. Somewhere in the distance, something is dropped and crashes to the ground. Richard jumps violently, almost dislodging things he's attached to, wrenching at painful parts of himself.

'I didn't know until I went back to Oakland years later,' he says. 'Even then, Lily didn't tell me straight away. Carly was away on a school camp, and her mother thought I was just passing through.'

'Like the last time,' Zoë says. 'Like you did in September sixty-eight?'

'Exactly. It took her a week to tell me that I had a twelve-year-old daughter. She didn't want me interfering unless I was going to stick around.'

He hears Zoë exhale deeply and wishes he could see her face.

'So, when Dan was born, when you and I . . . you didn't know then.'

He shakes his head. 'No idea, Zoë, honestly. Carly was twelve before I knew she existed.'

'But you did know that you and I were equally at fault, and yet, knowing that . . .'

'I couldn't tell you. I was confused when I got back . . .'

'You were vile, you behaved as though you hated me.'

'It was my guilt, that and my ambition. That trip, working with Martin, I could see what I wanted, I felt . . . you were standing in my way.'

'But you didn't end it. You could have told me you'd met someone and ended it because of that.'

'I meant to, I kept meaning to, but each time I came close to it, something held me back. I loved you and resented you at the same time. The night of the march, when you were in the hospital I was going to tell you, and then . . . well . . .'

'I told you I was pregnant. And then when Dan was born, I had to be the guilty one. I *was* guilty, of course, but you kept quiet and got to keep the moral high ground.'

There is nothing he can say to this. The silence is long, and he starts to wonder if she has actually left. He moves his hand over the blankets.

'Zoë?'

'I'm still here.'

'I should have told you when we met again. Julia made me promise I would. It's why I suggested you stay at the flat. I always intended to come home that night and tell you. I thought we needed to be somewhere together, without other people. But you were at Gloria's and still there the next morning, and up on the Heath . . .'

'Why not then?' she asks, and he hears the emotion in her voice; the hurt or anger, or both. 'Or that evening back at the flat?'

'It was such a beautiful day; and the evening, beautiful. I felt that something was healing in both of us. I felt . . .' he clears his throat. 'It was like it was the last months we were together and somehow I felt – stupidly, I suppose – that there might be a chance for us, you and me. You'd said that back then, had you known I'd wanted you back, it would have been different.'

'And you really thought that meant that it could be different now, all these years later?'

449

'You must think me stupid and selfish, but I hoped so, and I didn't want to contaminate that chance.'

'Contaminate it with the truth?'

'That's how it felt.'

'I see.'

But he doesn't think she does. And he knows that something has changed.

She guides him patiently through drinking his tea, holding the straw to his burnt lips, steering his good hand to the tiny crustless sandwiches, placing the paper napkin in his hand; she is both gentle and solicitous. Tomorrow, she says, she will be in during the afternoon, and will bring him some music, a CD she's making for him of the music he used to love. There is now no anger in her tone and the hurt so apparent in their earlier conversation seems to have lifted, but there's something else. He would know so much more if he could see her face, her gestures.

'Zoë,' he says, reaching out to find her hand. 'You and I, we . . .' he hesitates, 'well we're the products of our times and our upbringing. I'm not saying that excuses anything, but it does help to explain it. I want you to know that I loved you, I still . . . well, anyway . . . I know I've let you down again and I do understand if you feel you can't come here again.'

There is another long silence and he feels the breath of her sigh.

'What you've told me, Richard,' she says, 'it's like an acquittal. That one act of betrayal filled me with shame, and that has always been with me. I've tried to make up for it in my other relationships, with Archie, with my children, most especially with Dan. But now I know we were both culpable, we betrayed each other; I was no worse than you, but the consequences were different.' She stops and he hears her sigh again, and senses that she is moving back slightly, maybe leaning back in her chair. 'Frankly, though, I could strangle you for not telling me sooner, especially not having told me that day on the Heath. As for the rest of it, well . . . it's hard for me to understand how you thought we could be together again. I did . . . I *do* imagine that, despite everything, we are old friends. And that's why I'll be back tomorrow.'

He hears her chair move, the click of her handbag clasp, the rustle of a coat or jacket. He is hugely relieved, unbearably grateful; something has changed, but there is no hostility. He can feel her standing beside the bed, and she takes his hand again, turns it over, slips something smooth and small into it, and folds his fingers around it. Then there is just the sound of her footsteps, the creak of the door closing behind her, and the smooth curve of the enamel heart between his fingers is all that remains.

2008

FORTY-NINE

Rye – February 2008

Julia sits at the desk staring at the computer screen; there's so much she wants and needs to say but where to begin? And how can she keep some of this for Richard, for Tom and most of all, perhaps, for herself, without taking something away from Zoë?

Hi Zoë, she begins, and then stops again sighing, shaking her head. *I know Gaby called you last night with the wonderful news, so here are some pictures so you can see your gorgeous daughter and Brad in all their glory. I so wish you and Archie could have been there to see them get the award. It was a wonderful evening, and you would have been so proud of her.*

Julia stops typing and reads what she has written.

'I'm emailing Zoë about last night,' she calls to Tom through the open window. 'D'you think it's okay to mention Richard?'

Tom appears at the window, resting his arms, gardening gloves and a pair of secateurs on the sill. 'Why not?'

'You know, the past, and then the way she found out about Carly. That was all about nineteen sixty-eight and so is this.'

'But Zoë and Richard were still friends,' Tom says. 'Zoë told you that herself when we went over there to bring Richard home.'

'But I can't expect her to feel as I . . . as we do, and last night was Gaby's night – well, Gaby's and Brad's.'

'But not to the exclusion of Richard. Zoë knows that without Richard, this wouldn't have happened . . .'

'It wouldn't have happened without you either,' Julia cuts in.

'Probably not, but that's not the point; we're talking about Richard.'

'Maybe,' Julia says. 'Maybe you're right.'

'Of course I'm right,' Tom says with a grin, pulling on his gardening gloves. 'I'm a man.'

'Oh, bugger off and prune things,' Julia says, and starts to type again.

I wished so much that Richard could have been there. It was the one award he always coveted and never managed to win. He and Martin thought they would win it for that first civil rights documentary in sixty-nine but someone else just beat them to it. But he would have been thrilled for them both, you know how fond he was of Gaby.

They put a dedication at the start of the film and they mentioned him in their acceptance speech. 'Our dear friend and mentor who died before this project came to fruition, but without whose inspiration and guidance it would not have been made'. It's on the DVD too, right at the start and on the cover. I wept of course; even Tom had a tear in his eye. The BBC is packaging Tom's book and the DVD together as a special 1968 memorial pack, and I'm going to post a couple to you today.

She stops again and looks at one of the packages beside her on the desk. Tom's book; she is embarrassingly proud, and so very thankful that she has trained herself out of teasing him about not finishing things. There are even photographs in there of some of those crumpled fliers and torn posters from Paris, and on the back his own photograph, smiling, thoughtful. If only Hilary and Richard could have seen it. And the companion DVD; Gaby and Brad's name on the reverse, with their photographs and a little box at the side with a picture of the book cover and explaining the tie-in.

'Sometimes I just want to shake you,' she says, looking up at Richard's photograph above the fireplace. 'Couldn't you have waited a little longer to see them finish it? Couldn't you have waited to celebrate this with us, especially with Tom?'

But she knows he couldn't; the blindness had beaten him. He had fought the depression and carried on for as long as he could, he and Tom talking endlessly with Gaby and Brad about the research, the various narratives, the angles to take, and then he had described the way he had imagined it, the way it would come together. That done, he had stepped back and begun the slow downward spiral until he was ready to go. Julia's eyes fill with tears, as they always do when she remembers the day she came home to find Tom waiting for her in the doorway.

'It's Richard,' he'd said, his voice faltering. 'It's over, Jules, he's ended it.'

She was supposed to believe that Richard died alone, that he chose a time when she was going to be away overnight at the London flat and Tom was also supposed to be out all day; that he waited until he had plenty of time alone and then took the tablets he had been storing for months. It was a couple of days later, in that distressing and awkward period before the funeral, that she discovered what had really happened.

'It's so sad that he felt he couldn't go on,' she had said, 'but the worst part of it is thinking of him dying alone. Imagine it, Tom, taking the tablets and then sitting there alone, waiting to die. It's so . . . so desolate . . . thinking about it is unbearable.'

There was a longish silence before Tom, looking at her steadily, said quite slowly, 'yes . . . *if* that was what had happened, it *would* have been terrible.'

It had taken several minutes before Julia registered what he had actually said.

'Would have? You mean . . .'

He nodded, still watching her. 'Yes.'

It seemed a lifetime before she could speak and in that moment she hated them both for excluding her, hated Tom for agreeing to it and herself for not realising it sooner, for not understanding that it was something that was likely to happen.

'How *could* you, Tom? He was my brother.'

'He was also my best friend,' Tom said, 'and nothing was going to stop him. He asked me. I couldn't let him die alone.'

She'd stormed out of the house then, got into the car, and roared off at top speed to the beach. She struggled up through the dunes to the flat sand, where half a dozen riders were galloping their horses through the shallow water. Despite the sun and the almost cloudless sky, the wind was freezing. Tears pouring down her face, Julia started walking, thrusting on against the wind and thankful for its wintry chill on her burning face.

Tom was in his study when she got back but came out to the kitchen when he heard her. 'I was worried about you,' he said. And she walked over to him and he put his arms around her. 'Your face is freezing and you taste of salt.'

'You were right,' she said, burying her face in his neck. 'You did what I would have done if . . . if he'd asked me. Only you . . . I'm sure you did it better than I could.'

'He was very peaceful,' Tom said, holding her closer, 'more peaceful than he had seemed at any time since Bali, or a long time before that.'

Julia reaches across the desk now for some tissues and dries her eyes. 'You had to have it your own way right to the end, didn't you?' she says to the photograph. 'It really pisses me off because I didn't ever thank you for saving me from the stinging nettles, or tell you how much I loved you. I hope you bloody well know it now.'

And she turns back to the keyboard to finish her message to Zoë.

⌁

'Are we nearly there yet?' Harry asks from the back seat.

Justine, driving, catches Zoë's eye in the rear-view mirror and grins. 'It's still quite a long way,' she says.

Harry sighs, the weight of the world on his shoulders. 'But how much *longer*?'

'An hour, maybe a bit less.'

'We could play a game, if you like,' Gwen says, swivelling around in the front seat. 'I Spy, or vegetable alphabet.'

'Or a quiz,' Zoë suggests, remembering back to long drives south with Archie and Dan, just a little older than Harry is now, and looking and sounding just the same.

Harry shakes his head. 'We did that on the plane. Can I play the games on your phone, Mum?'

Justine takes her mobile phone from the bracket on the dashboard and hands it to him. He settles back in the seat, his fingers moving like lightning over the phone keys. From her seat in the back, Zoë watches Justine's profile as she drives. There is a different sort of confidence about her here, when she is back in her own country. Until she came here for the first time, Zoë had given little thought to what that link to land and family might mean to Justine. She seemed, by then, so much a part of Zoë's own family, but in this place, Zoë can feel its power. Justine, she thinks, is an extraordinary woman, strong, wise and loving. Zoë has gained another daughter; a very different woman, who has stitched another seam of love into her life.

'Can I phone Dad?' Harry asks now, brandishing the phone in the air.

'Darling, you know there's no signal out here,' Justine says. 'You can ring him when we get to town.'

Harry gives another of his enormous sighs. 'I wish he and Granddad came with us.'

Zoë smiles, watching Harry as he goes back to the phone for another game. Back home, Archie is running the nursery while Dan is managing the subcontractors who are building a second nursery further up the coast.

I know you must miss Gaby, Julia had said in her email. *But you'll soon have your second grandchild – I hope Rosie's keeping well. And hopefully Gaby putting down roots in London is not as hard to bear as it was to have Dan racing off to war zones. Your loss is, of course, our gain. It may have started off with us keeping an eye on her, but these days I get the feeling she and Brad think they are keeping an eye on Tom and me.*

'It's so sad that Richard couldn't have been there to see them get the award,' Zoë had said to Archie a few days earlier as she looked again at the photographs. 'He wanted it so much, and should have won it in sixty-nine.'

'And if he had, and if you'd been there with him, as he'd hoped you would be, we would never have met,' Archie had said. 'And I would have been a worthless, directionless beach bum without a good woman to keep me on the straight and narrow.'

'I doubt it,' she'd said, laughing and kissing him. 'Some other woman would have been a pushover for your fatal charm and boyish good looks.'

'Maybe. But I'm very glad it was you.'

'Me too,' she says, 'very glad.'

Zoë rests her head against the window now, watching the clouds of fine red earth billowing up from the tyres of the four-wheel drive. Ahead of them, the unsealed road stretches into the distance, red dust and gravel bordered by low scrub, and beyond that the haunting red and rocky plains of the Pilbara that she once feared and now has a longing to photograph and paint. A few years ago she wouldn't have dreamed of coming here, bouncing over unsealed roads to a remote settlement, and sitting under a tree in the late afternoon, talking to Justine's numerous aunties and cousins, losing herself in their storytelling. She still doesn't feel completely at ease in this strange and eerie landscape, but she's learned that a certain level of dissonance doesn't have to be frightening. It's like the gypsy with the lavender had told her; it's what you do with it that matters.

'You okay, Zoë?' Justine asks now, catching her eye in the mirror once again.

'Fine,' she says, 'just thinking, wondering why I spent so much of my life reacting to the past instead of thinking about the future.'

'We spend far too much time on it, Zoë,' Gwen says. 'You and I, constantly mulling over, whether we behaved nicely, or could have done better, the things we should have done and didn't. I think it might be pure self-indulgence. We're older and wiser, and we don't need to apologise for being who we are.'

'*I* know who you are,' Harry says, looking up from his game. 'You're Grandma and Nanny Gwen. I could of had three grandmas, you know, if I'd got born quicker. I would of got Granny Norah too, that would've been cool.'

'Cool?' Justine says, laughing and looking across at Gwen, and then back again at Zoë. 'Terrifying, more like. You three would have been a formidable trio.'

The class starts at ten and it's just a few minutes to the hour when Zoë parks her car and hurries through the entrance to the courtyard. Ahead of her, a woman carrying a canvas bag with brush handles and a shiny new palette sticking out of it, pauses and looks around.

'Excuse me,' she calls out to a young girl who is wiping the café verandah tables. 'Where do I go for the beginners' watercolour class?'

The girl directs her and returns to the tables, and Zoë slowly follows the woman into the building, remembering her own first day; the anticipation of discovery, the fear of looking stupid and of being the only one in the class unable to learn. Madness, she thinks now, the madness of her self-inflicted isolation. She is still surprised that all she'd felt was relief at Richard's confession. Anger and reproach would have been logical but it seemed that the time for that had passed. As she put the pendant, that lifelong reminder of guilt and shame, into his hand, she'd known she was releasing herself to fly out of the cage she had built from the past.

And now Richard is gone, by his own choice, and, she hopes, in some sort of peace. And Eileen is also gone, seeing out her last years as the life and soul of the nursing home, boasting about her grandchildren, particularly her grandson, leading the singing and playing Scrabble with words of her own making. Was this the girl she had once been, the woman she might have become had she not caught the eye of that unknown sailor? Zoë hopes that dementia banished her mother's own guilt and shame, and let the real Eileen shine through. Sometimes Zoë feels she should have tried harder, that if she had been more forgiving and worked harder at her relationship with her mother, things might have been different. But she has lived too long with regret to let it rule her life again.

A soft murmur of voices drifts out through the open door of the studio as she makes her way up the stairs. The studio where she sat at an easel for the first time is filled with another group of cautious beginners, each one assessing the others, fearing their own lack of creativity and confidence, wondering if they alone will fail to make the leap of imagination required to do something meaningful, possibly even beautiful, with paint and paper.

Zoë pauses in the doorway, looks around for Gwen and edges towards her between the easels.

'Were you able to pick up the photos?' she asks. 'Are they any good?'

'They're great,' Gwen says, handing her a packet of prints.

Zoë opens the packet, shuffles through the pictures and lets out a low, soft whistle. 'They really are brilliant, aren't they? Thanks so much, Gwen.' She hesitates. 'Are you sure you want to do this class again, it'll be the third time.'

'I'm sure,' Gwen says. 'This is where I want to be.'

Zoë shrugs. 'Up to you. Time for a coffee later?'

'You bet.'

Zoë makes her way to her own easel and turns to face the class.

'Hello, everyone,' she says, 'welcome to the beginners' watercolour class. My name's Zoë. When I came to this class a few years ago, I hadn't done any painting since junior school. I think I was having a bit of a mid-life crisis, because I turned up with some tubes of paint, a little curiosity and a rather heavy heart, convinced that I hadn't a creative bone in my body. Well, painting introduced me to my creativity, and showed me different ways of using it. I had a lot of fun, learned a bit about painting, and a lot more about myself.'

There is an appreciative rumbling and rustling among the women in the group. They look around again, the smiles a little more confident now; they are settling in.

Zoë takes the photographs from the pack, hands them to a woman at the end of the front row and asks her to take one and pass them along.

'It's something of a tradition in this class that we start with a Western Australian landscape,' she says. 'Last month when I was in the Pilbara with my friend Gwen over there, we took some photographs and I thought it might be fun to work with these as a guide. It can be an eerie place, but the horizons, the colours and the contrasts are magnificent. This is my daughter-in-law's country and through her, I'm learning to see it in a different way. And that's part of what I learned in that first watercolour class, that it's always possible to see things in a different way. That's been hugely important for me, as a woman, as a mother and as an artist. So, I hope that together we can make this work for you too.'

She pauses, watching the women examining the photographs. This is the moment she loves in every new class; the one in which they begin, and in which she can measure how far she has come.

'Right,' Zoë says. 'If you're all ready we'll get going, and the first thing to remember is that with watercolour, the way you use the water is just as important as the way you use the paint.' And she dips her brush in the jar and confidently strokes the water across the paper.

ACKNOWLEDGMENTS

Special thanks are due to my publisher, Cate Paterson, for her patience, advice and faith which never failed through some very rocky patches in the writing of this book.

Thanks too to Emma Rafferty and Sarina Rowell for their creative involvement and thoughtful, meticulous editing; to Roxarne Burns for reading an early draft and being honest about it; to James Fraser, Jeannine Fowler, Jane Novak and the terrific Pan Macmillan sales and marketing team for the huge effort and commitment that gets books onto shelves and into the hands of readers.

Special thanks to Doreen and Freda who generously shared their experiences of being taken from their families.

Love and thanks to Graham Murdock, for sharing his memories and interpretations of 1968, and to my wonderful family, Neil, Mark, Sarah and Bill, for their support and encouragement.

And finally, thanks to the many people who have written or emailed to tell me to hurry up because they are waiting for the next book.

The following books were very helpful to me in writing *Bad Behaviour*:

Duchen C, *Women's Rights and Women's Lives in France 1944 – 1968*, Routledge, London, 1994.
Halloran J D, Elliot P and Murdock G, *Demonstrations and Communication: A Case Study*, Penguin, London, 1970.

Kurlansky M, *1968: The Year That Rocked the World*, Vintage, London, 2004.

Human Rights and Equal Opportunity Commission, *Bringing Them Home: Report of the National Inquiry into the Separation of Aboriginal and Torres Strait Islander Children from Their Families*, Human Rights and Equal Opportunity Commission, Sydney, 1997.

McPhedran, I, *The Amazing SAS*, HarperCollins, Sydney, 2005.

ALSO BY LIZ BYRSKI IN PAN MACMILLAN

Gang of Four

She had a husband, children and grandchildren who loved her; a beautiful home, enough money. What sort of person was she to feel so overwhelmed with gloom and resentment on Christmas morning?

They have been close friends for almost two decades, supporting each other through personal and professional crises – parents dying, children leaving home, house moves, job changes, political activism, diets and really bad haircuts.

Now the 'gang of four', Isabel, Sally, Robin and Grace, are all fifty-something, successful . . . and restless.

Praise for *Gang of Four*:

'A wonderfully written story about women who dare to move away from their everyday way of living.'
HERALD SUN

'Finally. A coming of age novel for the rest of us.'
SUSAN MAUSHART, AUTHOR OF *WIFEWORK*

'This is not a book about mid-life crisis so much as mid-life opportunity. The characters are like people you know – and there will be people you know who could learn something from them.'
SYDNEY MORNING HERALD

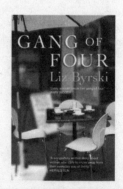

Food, Sex & Money

It's almost forty years since the three ex-convent girls left school and went their separate ways, but finally they meet again.

Bonnie, rocked by the death of her husband, is back in Australia after decades in Europe, and is discovering that financial security doesn't guarantee a fulfilling life. Fran, long divorced, is a freelance food writer, battling with her diet, her bank balance and her relationship with her adult children. And Sylvia, marooned in a passionless marriage, is facing a crisis that will crack her world wide open.

Together again, Bonnie, Fran and Sylvia embark on a venture that will challenge everything they thought they knew about themselves – and give them more second chances than they could ever have imagined.

Praise for *Food, Sex & Money*:

'In a word: inspiring.'
HERALD SUN

'*Food, Sex & Money* is an entertaining, ultimately optimistic, novel.'
WEST AUSTRALIAN

'The issues of financial security, emotional independence, career, diet, motherhood and sexuality transcend age, making this a relevant, enjoyable read for all women, and for men who seek to understand them.'
GOOD READING

Liz Byrski
FOOD, SEX
& MONEY

Belly Dancing for Beginners

Gayle and Sonya are complete opposites: one reserved and cautious, the other confident and outspoken. But their lives will be turned upside down when they impulsively join a belly dancing class.

Marissa, their teacher, is sixty, sexy, and very much her own person, and as Gayle and Sonya learn about the origins and meaning of the dance, much more than their muscle tone begins to change.

Belly Dancing for Beginners is a warm-hearted, moving and often outright funny story of what can happen when women, and the men in their lives, are brave enough to reveal who they really are.

Praise for *Belly Dancing for Beginners*:

'Byrski's forte is getting inside women's heads and hearts.'
AUSTRALIAN WOMEN'S WEEKLY

'A very funny book yet one with a serious point – women in their 50s and beyond can still have challenging, rewarding and hugely enjoyable lives.'
SUNDAY TASMANIAN

'Byrski's women have something of the wisdom of age but still grapple with the complexities of relationships with husbands, children, parents and friends. They are also still intrigued by romantic possibilities and the search for love.'
WEST AUSTRALIAN

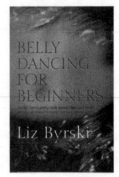